María

BOOK 2

FRANK W. LEWIS

MARÍA

Santa Fé to California · 1835-36

THE WILD WILD WEST

©Western Tales Publishing, Inc.
1155 West Fourth Street, Suite 210
Reno, Nevada 89503

ISBN 0-9653923-8-4

María

Disclaimer:
Fra Vincente Francisco Sarría, Thomas Larkin, Captain James Grant, Peter Skene
Ogden, Joseph Walker, were historical characters of the time of this story. These
names were included in order to give the story historical perspective. All other
persons and the events surrounding them in this story are fictional, and any
resemblance to any person living or dead is purely accidental.

Frank W. Lewis
Western Tales Publishing,Inc.,
1155 West Fourth Street # 210
Reno, NV 89503
All rights reserved.
ISBN: 0-9653923-8-4
ISBN-13: 978-0965392389

Visit www.booksurge.com to order additional copies.

CONTENTS

Chapter 1 - Shoot Out...................................1

Chapter 2 - Rancho de Vargas...........................9

Chapter 3 - María Takes Her Blouse Off...............21

Chapter 4 - La Capilleja de La María.
  (The Chapel of the María).........................41

Chapter 5 - Love Leads to Passion....................45

Chapter 6 - María....................................53

Chapter 7 - Looking for the Devil in Her.............83

Chapter 8 - San Fernando de Taos....................105

Chapter 9 - Rendezvous at Green River...............139

Chapter 10 - The Slave. The Valley of the Yellow Stone.....151

Chapter 11 - Beaver-Catcher.........................159

Chapter 12 - Rescue.................................177

Chapter 13 - Heading West...........................187

Chapter 14 - To Fort Hall...........................197

Chapter 15 - Paiute.................................215

Chapter 16 - The Sierras at Last....................225

Chapter 17 - Time for Baby..........................233

Chapter 18 - Mission Nuestra Señora de la Soledad.....241

Chapter 19 - Monterey Bay...........................251

Chapter 20 - Renegades..............................271

Chapter 21 - Los Angeles............................281

Chapter 22 - Priest from the Past...................293

Chapter 23 - Two of a Kind..........................307

Chapter 24 - Sex With The Master....................325

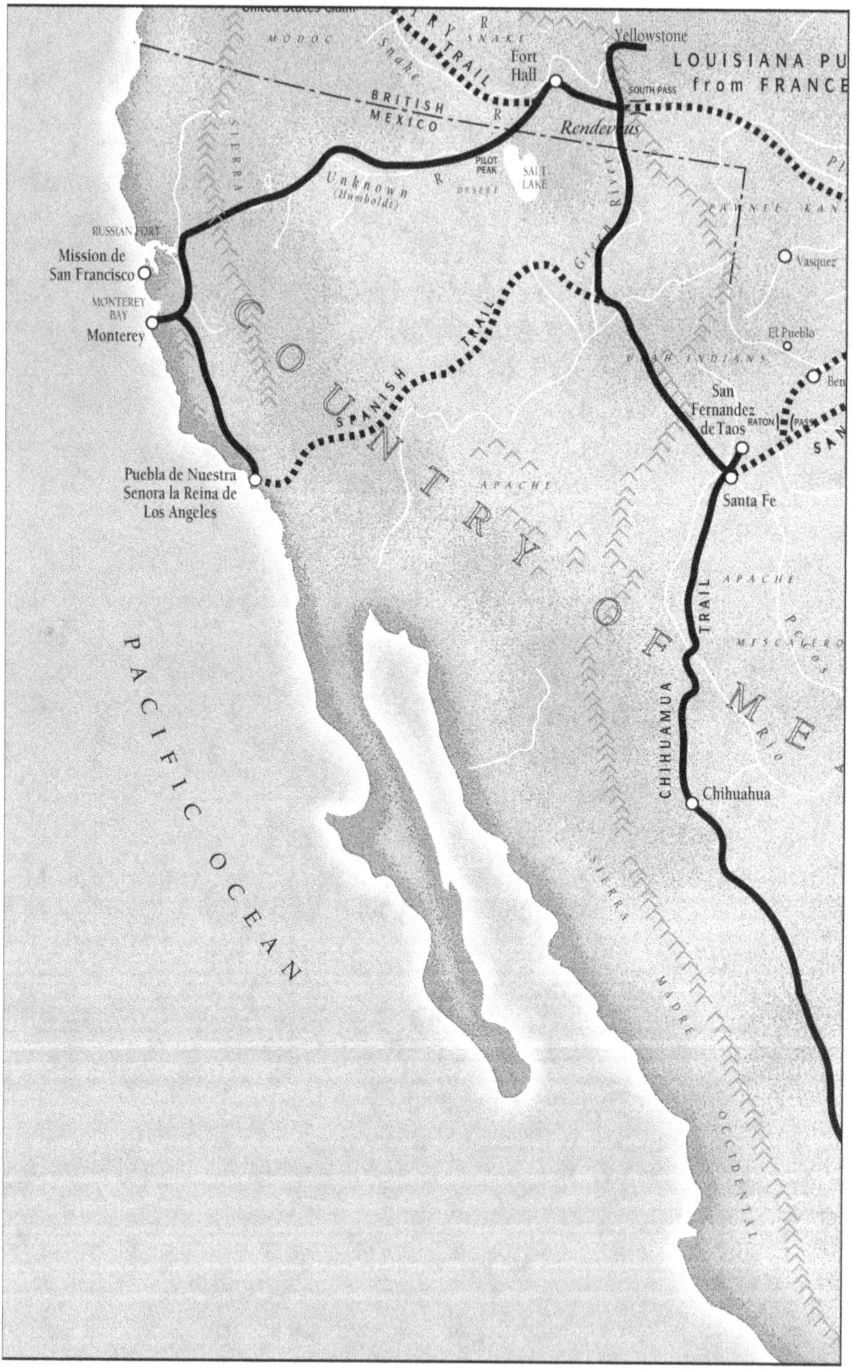

MODOC
SNAKE
Snake
TRAIL
Fort Hall
Yellowstone
LOUISIANA PU
from FRANCE
SOUTH PASS
BRITISH
MEXICO
Rendevous
SIERRA
PILOT PEAK
SALT LAKE
Unknown
(Humboldt)
DESERT
Green River
PAWNEE
RUSSIAN FORT
Mission de San Francisco
MONTEREY BAY
Monterey
Vasquez
El Pueblo
UTAH INDIANS
COUNTRY OF ME
SPANISH TRAIL
San Fernandez de Taos
RATON PASS
Santa Fe
Puebla de Nuestra Senora la Reina de Los Angeles
APACHE
CHIHUAHUA TRAIL
MESCALEROS
PECOS
RIO
Chihuahua
PACIFIC OCEAN
SIERRA MADRE OCCIDENTAL

RCHASE
1803

DAKOTAS

SAC

IOXE

and CLARK

ALGONQUIN

OTTAWA

HURON

LAKE ERIE

INDIANA ERIE

MIAMI

TO OREGON

Platte and OTOES

River

River

Fort
Leavenworth

ILLINOIS

KICKAPOO

Independence

MISSOURI

KENTUCKY

s Fort

SANTA FE TRAIL

Cimarron R

Canadian

R

Pecos

Arkansas

R.

R.

R

CHEROKEE

IROQUOIS

TENNESSEE

CHICKASAWS

MOBILIAN

Mississippi

GULF ROAD

CHOCTAW

ARKANSAS
TERRITORY

MISSISSIPPI

GEORGIA

CREEK

CHOCTAW

TEHUACANA

LOUISIANA

ALABAMA

KIOWA

1810–1812

R.

San Antonio

New Orleans

MEXICO

Grande

R

GULF OF MEXICO

SIERRA MADRE ORIENTAL

Mexico City

VeraCruz

OTHER BOOKS BY FRANK W. LEWIS

RUMPAH. ISBN 0-9653923-0-9.
An adventure story situated in a small Nevada town during the 1990's. The story is about a struggle between Bill Aaron and an old prospector, Whiterock, with a large mining corporation over mineral rights. Intrigue, murder, love.

FRONTIER JUSTICE – 1835. ISBN 0-9653923-1-7. Book one of a series.

MARÍA –1835, 1836. ISBN 0-9653923-8-4. Book two of a series.

THE 3 SISTERS, 1837. ISBN 0-9653923-3-3. Book Three of a series.

INTRODUCTION:

In the previous book, *Frontier Justice*, we saw Caleb work his way across the great Prairie Ocean from Independence, Missouri to Santa Fé. Santa Fé was then a part of Mexico. The full name of what we now know as *Santa Fé was Villa Real de Santa Fé de San Francisco*, or The Royal Town of the Holy Faith of Saint Francis.

Here, Caleb travels into the Stony Rocky Mountains and then to California. The violence of this period of time is commonplace as he and María fight Indians and renegade whites on the frontier, as well as the elements.

Mexico gained its independence from Spain in 1821. The boundary along the 42nd parallel that now separates Oregon and Idaho from Nevada separated the Oregon Territory from Mexico. Both the United States and Great Britain claimed the Oregon Territory.

The lands from Texas to California belonged to Mexico and then to Texas, considering the revolt of the Texans and their claim. The territory of this vast area from Taos and Santa Fé to the 42nd parallel to the Sierra Nevada mountains, including Arizona, Utah, Wyoming and Colorado, was a vast wasteland occupied only by savage Indians and an occasional American or French-Canadian trapper who were frequently wilder than the savages.

The plight of women in those early days was much different than it is for today's liberated women. Still, their needs, intelligence and ambitions were the same. Their complexities, and their strengths and weaknesses were no less present. As María matures and becomes involved with Caleb and other lovers, her confusion is compounded by her sexuality as well as the circumstances surrounding women of that period.

CHAPTER 1
Shoot Out.

Caleb watched helplessly that day in 1835 from his hiding place on a ridge overlooking the Arkansas River. He saw Blackie Parsin and his gang of renegade mountain men attack the freight train owned by the Bartholomew Brothers and shoot down the wagon drivers and bull whackers who controlled the oxen and mules. The only survivor of the wagon train massacre was Polly, a young woman who had been away from the wagon train chasing a loose thoroughbred stallion that smelled one of the mares in Caleb's herd of horses, which was in heat. The wagon train was about half way on its journey from Independence, Missouri, to Santa Fé when the ambush occurred.

Several months afterward, Caleb saw the same gang of thieves cold-bloodedly gun down the grandfather of Juan, his 12-year-old friend, while rustling a herd of *Miguel de Vargas's* cattle. *Miguel de Vargas* was the *patrón* of the *de Vargas* Rancho, which made him all-powerful, a virtual lord, controlling the lives of the five hundred souls within the boundary of his rancho. He even supported the priest who was in residence there. He was the *patrón* of this huge rancho 70 miles from Santa Fé in what was known as the New Mexico Territory. At that time, Mexico owned what is now the southwestern United States.

A month later, the *alcalde*, or mayor-sheriff of Santa Fé, ordered the Captain of the Guard and two soldiers to go over to the El Burro Cantina and bring Blackie Parsin in for questioning. The captain and his men did not know that Blackie was going to be ready for them, thanks to a clerk in the *alcalde's* office who had sped over to warn Blackie they were coming for him.

Caleb thought that walking headlong into the cantina and confronting Blackie was foolhardy. He had warned Phillip Bartholomew, owner of the freight wagons, not to enter the cantina with the soldiers because they had no idea what they were walking into. But Bartholomew and the others ignored him.

"Juan, you stay right there on that bench and don't go inside!" Caleb told his young friend. "I'm going around in back to take a look at the horses and see if I can tell how many mountain men might be inside."

The small horse shed and stalls behind the cantina smelled of hay, saddles, and manure. There were three horses in the corral and saddles stored inside the shed.

Caleb paused in the shadowy doorway of the corral shed, which faced the rear of the cantina, and peered nervously at the back door. He'd seen these men in action, and knew what skilled fighters they were. Except for the captain, who was carrying a single-shot flintlock pistol, they were poorly armed. The two Mexican soldiers' guns were old and rusty, and the soldiers were poorly trained.

The cantina looked quiet enough from the outside. But inside, Blackie and his two fellow mountain men were ready. Their guns were loaded and fresh primed with powder in the pans of their weapons. When the soldiers, accompanied by Miguel de Vargas, his son Don Pedro, and Phillip Bartholomew (who wasn't even armed) entered the dark cantina from the sun-washed street they were temporarily blinded by the dark interior. Blackie could hardly believe how easy they were making it for him.

Caleb heard at least three shots fired from inside the cantina. *I'll bet those shots are from the mountain men. I can tell from the sounds of the rifles,* he thought. Caleb was tempted to rush inside to see if his friends were all right but decided he could be more helpful where he was, if he waited. *If the mountain men win, they will have to come for their horses and saddles,* he told himself as he hid inside the horse stalls. *If I can catch them when they're not expecting it, I might be able to stop them.* He pulled both of his cap-and-ball six-shot revolvers out of their holsters and looked them over to make sure they were ready to shoot. Few people on the frontier had ever seen multi-shot revolvers like he had, let alone used one. Most were still using single-shot flintlock weapons. (The first Colts were experimental.) They were six-shot weapons and used the new percussion caps. The caps were a leap forward over flintlocks, and provided multi-shot capability and firing dependability.

Blackie peeked out the rear door. "Looks clear in the back," he said to his companions. "Slim, fetch yonder young'un pup Don Pedro, an' we'll mosey over to the corral an' skedaddle out o'hyar a-fore the whole

Mexican army comes to-callin'. This'n hyar pup Don Pedro ought to make a good hostage to make sure we gits out o' hyar without any fool takin' no shots at us'ns. We kin sell 'im back later for a pretty peso-dollar, too!"

The trio of gunslingers, dragging the tied and gagged Don Pedro, hurried across the alley to the corral. While Blackie stood guard, the other two leaned their rifles against the corral so they could squeeze through the corral railings. As soon as the other mountain men put their legs between the poles and started through, Blackie rested his gun against the fence to follow them. For a brief moment, all three rifles were leaning against the corral fence, out of the gunmens' reach.

Now's my best chance, and the only one I'm likely to get, Caleb thought as he stepped quietly out of the barn and leveled his pistols. Blackie's comrades, who had reached the inside of the corral fence, were straightening up and reaching for their rifles. Saying nothing, Caleb took careful aim and shot Slip Fields with the revolver in his right hand.

When Juan heard the second round of shooting, he could tell it was coming from in back by the corrals where Caleb had gone. Juan jumped to his feet and darted for the corner of the building. The second shot was fired before Juan could see what was happening. He reached the corner and peeked around the edge. He saw Caleb inside the corral with two smoking pistols in his hands. Two of the mountain men were lying on the ground.

Juan saw Caleb fire a pistol again, this time at Blackie, who was just starting to aim his flintlock rifle at Caleb. The ball from Caleb's pistol glanced off part of Blackie's bullet pouch and then struck his solar plexus, knocking the wind out of him. He dropped his rifle, holding his hands to his stomach and trying to catch his breath as he reeled backward against the corral railing. He looked at the young stranger standing in front of him.

Blackie, a large beefy man, stared at the smaller, skinny Caleb. A mere young boy. He didn't look like a threat to anyone. And he was obviously nervous. Blackie couldn't believe that such a whippersnapper could have shot both of his partners and him too. *How kin this be? This must be a accident or some kind of fluke. We mountain men be the best fightin' men in the world!* Blackie was not about to let this young stranger take him to the *alcalde*, Mayor. He had always been able to shoot his way out of tight spots before, and he was going to show this kid a thing or two now.

Caleb was not afraid. He was nervous, even excited yes, but not afraid. He had traveled all the way across the prairie from Independence, Missouri, to Santa Fé—alone, except for the last part of the journey when Polly was with him for part of the way. He had survived an 800-mile trek through primitive and violent areas. He survived because of his determination and inner strength of character—and because he had to, or die.

The horses in the corral milled nervously, creating a lot of dust, frightened by the pistol shots and the smell of gunpowder. The aroma of human blood in the air excited them further. They raised a cloud of dust as they did their best to stay away from the shooting and avoid the men lying on the ground.

Juan squinted, trying to see what was happening through the dust and black-powder smoke. Then, he saw the wounded big man suddenly jump sideways, pulling his pistol out of his belt as he moved in a clean, swift, practiced motion. As he did so, both of Caleb's pistols spoke as one. *Bang!* More black-powder smoke added to the cloud of confusion.

The force of two lead balls penetrating his chest forced Blackie back against the lower corral pole as he fell onto the ground, blood spurting from the bullet-holes in his chest. His unfired flintlock pistol dropped to the ground. The big mountain man had gambled on his dexterity, and the swift move sideways, to outmaneuver his youthful antagonist and the fact he thought the boy's pistols must be empty. But he had failed.

Blackie's last thought was astonishment that this skinny boy could have gotten the best of him. It shouldn't have happened. *Musta been a' accident. Pure luck.* He laughed wryly to himself as he thought, *Ha! Ha! Out-gunned by this youn'ng whippersnapper! The mountain men back in Taos would die-plumb to laughin'. They'd never believe hit!*

When Caleb was sure Blackie was dead, he turned his attention to Don Pedro. He had a nasty bump on his head but was otherwise not hurt. Caleb holstered his pistols and began untying him. It was a slow process because the rawhide thongs used to tie his hands behind his back were tight and wet with blood where they had cut into his skin, making them slippery and hard to undo.

Slip, the first man Caleb had shot had laid quietly, playing possum. Although he was bleeding, he hadn't been badly hurt. His mind was working furiously, *As soon as yonder pistol-shooter turns his back, I kin skinny under these hyar corral poles an' skedaddle out o' hyar.*

4

When Caleb turned to help Don Pedro, Slip quietly rolled under the lowest rung of the corral. In the alley outside of the corral, he sprang to his feet like a cat. His moccasins made no sound as he quietly began running down the alley, away from Caleb and the violent scene where his companions lay dead.

Juan was still watching the action from his vantage point by the edge of the building. "*Señor* Caleb! Look out!" Juan hollered in Spanish when he saw Slip roll under the corral bars and get up running. "That man is running away!"

Caleb whirled, pulling his right-hand pistol, but Slip was already behind the corral rails and running full tilt down the alley. He instinctively kept the rails of the corral between himself and Caleb. By the time Caleb ran over to the fence and squeezed through the rails so he could get a clean shot, Slip had disappeared around the far side of the building.

Caleb did not really care. He was not there to apprehend anyone. All he had wanted to do was rescue Don Pedro, and he had done that. The authorities could take care of Slip. The rest of it was none of his business.

As he resumed untying Don Pedro, Juan ran up to help him, jabbering excitedly in Spanish. "*Señor* Caleb! You have shot all three of them, but that one was able to run away! I recognized him. He was the one who shot my grandfather when these men rustled the cattle! I wish you had killed him, too!"

"Thank you, Caleb, for saving me," mumbled Don Pedro in broken English, dazed and hurt, as Caleb and Juan helped him to his feet. "My father and the others are tied up inside the cantina. We must go untie them."

Juan and Caleb followed Don Pedro through the back door into the cantina. For the first time, Caleb was able to piece together what had happened inside when the soldiers and his friends entered the cantina's darkened interior. Blackie and his two companions had shot the captain of the guard and the two soldiers and tied up Don Miguel, Don Pedro, Phillip Bartholomew, and the captain. The two soldiers were dead, lying where they had fallen. The captain, Don Miguel, and Phillip Bartholomew were lying on the floor, hog-tied and gagged. The captain had been shot in the right shoulder. Phillip Bartholomew and Don Miguel were unhurt, except for their pride. Juan, Caleb, and Don Pedro untied them and helped them to their feet.

The captain could not move his right arm because of his gunshot wound, but he was angry at having been bested so easily by the mountain men and he wanted to go after them immediately. Don Pedro put his hand on the captain's unhurt shoulder to restrain him and calm him down.

"But, Captain," said Don Pedro, "two of the men, including Blackie Parsin, the one you came after, were shot dead by *Señor* Caleb, here. They now are face down in the corral awaiting your pleasure. The other man is wounded; he's making fast tracks by now. And you are hurt. You should see a doctor first."

"Are you all right, Phillip?" asked Caleb.

"Yes, I am all right. My dignity is bruised, but physically I guess I'm OK." He was looking at Caleb with a new respect. "You were right, Caleb. I should have listened to you and not come in here without better preparation. I apologize for ignoring your good sense. Now the Captain is wounded, and these other two poor men are dead. We must report this to the *alcalde* at once."

After hearing the story from Don Pedro about how Caleb had shot the three men and rescued him, the captain said, "You have done Mexico and the world a great favor, *Señor* Caleb. And I for one feel that I owe you a debt of honor. I am sure that the *alcalde* will agree. We will immediately put out an order to arrest the mountain man called Slip Fields. He is a slippery one and will head for the Rocky Mountains I assume, but perhaps carrying your bullet will slow him down enough so that we can apprehend him. Next time, I will shoot him on sight and be done with it. I will leave now. Perhaps your young friend, Juan, can help me get back to the *alcalde's* office; and we can send out an alarm for this Slip Fields. I am a little unsteady on my feet."

Juan was very proud of the fact that his friend Caleb was the one who had saved the life of Don Pedro. "*Caramba!* My saint and friend has saved Don Pedro from these bad mountain men, as he did me when the rustlers were going to kill me. I prayed to the Virgin Mother of Christ and asked her to save me. *Señor* Caleb was sent by her just a moment before one of those rustlers was going to shoot me. Only because *Señor* Caleb shot him was my life spared even as that rustler pulled the hammer back on his gun and pointed it right at my head. It was when those cattle rustlers were stealing Don Miguel's cows—Glory be to God and our Mother, the

Mother of Christ!" Juan was grinning as though he himself had saved the day.

"This man Caleb saved me," said Don Pedro to his father. "He killed two of the murderers. The one called Slip Fields ran away with one of Caleb's bullets in him, too. If Caleb had not intervened, I would still be their captive. And I doubt I would have lived through it."

Don Miguel suddenly embraced Caleb. "Thank you! Thank you for rescuing my son. I am forever in your debt. You saved his life! I can never thank you enough, *Señor*." Don Miguel kissed him on his cheek and hugged him profusely. The old man was crying with joy, as tears coursed down his cheeks.

Caleb was dumbfounded. He had never seen one man embrace another man in such a fashion before. The Spanish custom of one man hugging and kissing another was foreign to him. He was embarrassed, and did not know what to do.

"It was nothing," Caleb said awkwardly, blushing over the attention he was receiving. He was trying to move away from Don Miguel's enthusiastic hugs and kisses.

Phillip Bartholomew laughed at his young friend's plight. He knew what the problem was because, as an Englishman once new to the Spanish society in Santa Fé, he had experienced the same embarrassment. He came forward then and shook Caleb's hand, pumping his hand and arm up and down again, smiling, and letting him know his embarrassment was all right.

"Nothing? Nothing? Ha!" Don Miguel cried, waving his arms. "You are too modest. We are going to have a great fiesta at my hacienda. It will last for three days, maybe even a week. We are going to have a *baile*, a dance, and *you*, *Señor* Caleb, are going to be the guest of honor. Everyone in this area of Santa Fé will be invited to see you, meet you, and greet you. You are a great hero! You have saved my son, who is the greatest good in my life, as you tried to save my cattle when this gang was rustling them. You have twice served me, and I will not let this pass again without thanking you properly. You have shown us that you possess more courage and good sense than all the rest of us put together." Don Miguel embraced him again as he heaped praise on him!

"You will come home with me, and your servant, Juan, too. You will be our guest of honor. I will present you to all the members of the *de*

Vargas family there. My home shall henceforth always be your home. You will see that I am honored by your presence forever! You will see that I can be the most gracious host in all of this New Mexico Territory."

"May we come downstairs? Is it safe? Are those bad mountain men gone?" A female voice called hesitatingly, from the top of the stairs. It was *Doña Salcedo*, the proprietress of the cantina.

"Yes. Come down immediately, and get us some wine. We need a drink to settle our nerves," Don Miguel ordered.

CHAPTER 2
Rancho de Vargas.

Don Miguel's rancho was actually one of the smaller ranches in the Mexican Territory of New Mexico, but it was the whole world to the five hundred *peóns* and others who lived there. Although not considered large compared to some others, it took two full days on horseback to cross the rancho. Santa Fé was a three-day ride away.

At the rancho, Don Miguel saw that Caleb, who was dressed in crude animal skins, was given new clothing of the Spanish gentry style, like *the patrón* and his son Don Pedro wore. The whole household took it upon themselves to dress him appropriately. They made a great game of it.

Caleb tried on a hand-crafted leather and cloth jacket, or *chaqueta* as they called it, over a colorful blue silk shirt. The pants, which were made to be tight-fitting, tended to make his legs appear even skinnier than they were, except where they flared out at the bottom. The Mexican men wore their pants open at the seam part way up the sides of the legs, showing a one-inch-wide band of flesh. Caleb, who was self-conscious at having the opening up the side, asked that his be sewn up. He told them he was afraid he would get sunburned by exposing his light skin to the elements. They laughed at him good-naturedly but let him have his way. So the braid and buttons down the side were sewn in place; and he was given a beautiful, fine wide, dark-blue silken sash to wear around his waist.

Finally, to complete the outfit, Don Miguel gave Caleb a sombrero. The sombrero, with its wide brim and low crown, sat on his head with comfort after a few days. But at first Caleb thought it seemed top-heavy and cumbersome.

"Here, Caleb, is a *serape*, or blanket, with a slit through the middle for your head when it is cold or rainy. You can drape it over the front or back of your saddle when it is too hot to wear it, or draw it up around your shoulders or even pull it over your head when you need warmth and protection from rain or snow."

His host was disconcerted when Caleb insisted that he would not be without his pistols and knife, and that they had to hang on his belt. He put them on over the other clothing. The weapons looked out of place, but Don Miguel and his family tolerated this as graciously as they could. The weapons had become so much a part of Caleb that he was uncomfortable without them.

It was fun for the family to dress him up like a Mexican *caballero*. And Caleb certainly enjoyed the friendly attention, even though it embarrassed him. They were good to him and made him feel welcome. But, he was unsure about the behavior associated with the new stature he had assumed. He decided the best way to learn how to behave like a Spanish gentleman was by watching Don Miguel and his son Don Pedro. And when no one else was around, he practiced the manners he learned from watching them. He was practicing the courtly bow when María caught him.

She laughed, "Not like that you silly boy," and she showed him and gave him lessons.

Miguel's daughter, *Señorita* María, was near Caleb's age only being just a little older than he. María was the product of the Spanish-Mexican aristocracy. Raised on her father's rancho, she was idolized by her mother, her father, the servants, and all of the rancho hands as she had grown up. She had been spoiled and became rebellious until she had been sent away to school, and was trained by the Nuns.

With her father's and her brother's encouragement, she had begun to tease Caleb about his clothes and skinny frame. Perhaps that would bring her out of the dark mood she seemed to have fallen into since she returned from the school. At least they hoped it would. She had seemed depressed and withdrawn since returning from the school in Mexico City.

Don Miguel had sent María away to school for two years when she was thirteen because she rebelled and refused to obey him. Now sixteen, she had been home for several months. Don Miguel thought the school had done her a world of good. She was much more respectful, obedient, and pious now—but she was no longer happy. Before she went to school, rebellious as she was, she was laughing, and smiling and happy most of the time, laughing perhaps too much, he had thought.

Since her return, the rebellious nature that dominated her character before she left had been replaced by a morose moodiness and a disinterest in her surroundings. She was quiet and rarely smiled.

Don Miguel began to wonder whether her constant praying in the private family chapel might be unhealthy. She spent hours there every day, on her knees, alone, praying and saying her rosary over and over again. When she was not praying, she spent her time in his library reading from the two trunks full of books she had brought back with her.

She had laughed when they told her that Caleb, of all the men, had saved the day for the family honor and that he had single-handedly killed two, and wounded one of the bandits who had raided their cattle herd. She concluded that it must have been a fluke. Moreover, she thought that having a fiesta in his honor was the funniest part of all and laughed at the very idea of it.

It irritated Don Miguel that she did not show proper respect for his attempt to honor Caleb for saving his son. Her family was pleased when she began to make fun of Caleb. He took her humor without offense; it was only the truth. He was, in fact, very skinny, and he liked the jesting that María directed in his direction.

María was tall and thin, with black eyes and curly black hair that once again was growing below her shoulders. Her head had been shaved at the school. The fact that her beautiful hair was beginning to attract male attention had not been lost on her. In the house, she wore a short, full, brightly-colored skirt and a loose, low-cut blouse like all the other non-servant women in the household as all the *ricas,* wore. Caleb thought she was the most beautiful girl he had ever seen.

She found the young man humorous and entertaining, a novelty in the day-to-day happenings on the remote rancho. When they were alone together, they could relax and become friends. As contemporaries, they shared a number of interests. She began to help him with Spanish language lessons, and he coached her with her English pronunciation. She loaned him books to read from her own and her father's libraries.

But after a while, she began to lose interest and retreated once again into her gloomy silence. She was barely civil should they pass in the hall. She was haughty and aloof, and her mind seemed far away. Her strained expression made her look much older than she actually was. And she had begun her prayer vigils again.

The *de Vargas* family were all extremely proud of their rancho. It was not the biggest in the territory, but it was certainly one of the best managed. The managers, all men born on the rancho, were selected for their efficiency and loyalty to Don Miguel, as they had been to his father who founded the ranch. The *peóns* who did the physical labor on the rancho were worth less than a cow or even a sheep to the rancho owners; not only on this rancho but on all the others as well. They had little value and could easily be replaced by those waiting for their jobs. Some of the managers had grown cruel to the *peóns*, treating them as if they did not matter to anyone.

The lord, or *patrón*, was Don Miguel. He had as much authority within the confines of the rancho over the lives of the persons living there as any king ever had. He could have anyone on the rancho whipped, or even killed, for anything or nothing, and no one could deny him the right to do so. Don Miguel was no better and no worse than any of the other rancho owners. This was the system that had been put in place by the Spanish kings and adopted by the new Mexican government when Mexico became a nation in its own right with the 1821 revolution from Spain.

Today, Don Pedro, the son, was to take Caleb on a ride around Don Miguel's property to familiarize him with the extensive rancho. They planned to ride all day, so the cook packed them a large lunch.

Caleb was surprised when he found María on her horse ready to ride with them. She had invited herself to go along for the ride. The one outside interest she seemed to have was to go riding. She was an expert horsewoman.

Her clothing for the ride was actually much more practical, Caleb thought, than the men's. She wore a flat-topped leather hat, which had a leather-thong chin strap fastened with a small bead, with a hole in it for the thong, under her chin. This chinstrap would keep her hat on no matter how hard the wind might blow. Her leather jacket fit tight over a calico shirt, and she wore tight leather pants that would protect her legs from brush or tree limbs.

It infuriated her father that she rode astride a horse like a man, but she maintained that she was soon going a thousand miles to California, to marry the man he had promised her to, and it would not be possible to ride all the way there side-saddle, no matter what anyone else thought about it. She carried a long quirt, or riding whip, that was attached by a leather thong-loop to her wrist.

The beautiful black-and-white pinto mare she was riding would not stand still even for a second, dancing and prancing, even rearing a little now and then, wanting to be off on a run. With María on the mare's back, the two of them seemed beautiful, wild, and uncontrollable. Riding her horse was the only time María seemed completely happy.

Caleb was riding Steven Johns's Horse, as he called his palomino gelding. Before he mounted his horse he loaded on his bullet pouches, powder horns, hand ax tomahawk, and the other travel equipment he always carried on the trail. He also loaded two scabbards, each containing a Kentucky flintlock rifle that he and his father had made. Both of the rifles had a name, which was a custom among the frontiersman. One he called "Meat-Getter," and the other was one his father called "Hair-Saver."

They were only going for a few hours' ride. But Caleb did not feel comfortable without his equipment and his weapons, which had almost become a part of him on his long journey from Independence. Just a few steps away from the rancho, Caleb and the *de Vargas* were back in country where an Indian raider might be found at any time. It did no harm to be prepared.

Don Pedro led them easterly, showing Caleb the villages of the *peóns*, the farms, adobe brick manufacturing site, cattle and sheep herds, and the springs and creeks that were part of the irrigation canals, which were the life's-blood of the rancho. Wheat and corn, as well as other crops, were growing around the villages. The houses were clustered together in groups to help protect the families from marauding Comanche and Apaches.

They had ridden 5 miles away from the *hacienda*, and Don Pedro was getting ready to turn back on the return journey when they heard a rifle shot.

"We should investigate, I think," said Don Pedro, "but we should remain hidden in these *piñon* pine trees until we see what is happening. Caleb, you and I can go forward on foot through these trees and look over the rocky ridge ahead there to see what is happening."

"*You* stay here out of sight with the horses while Caleb and I take a look," Don Pedro ordered María, pointing his index finger with authority at her.

Caleb got both of his rifles out of their scabbards too, as he fresh primed both of them with powder just in case it should be necessary. The two young men moved cautiously forward the 20 yards to the top of the ridge so they could see what was happening.

They could see four of the rancho guardsmen in a small clearing below. There were four of the guards that Don Miguel had on constant patrol against Indians. The four men were well mounted and well armed. They had captured two Mexican-Indian women and a young girl.

"The men are our rancho guards. We should not interfere," Don Pedro told Caleb as they peered through the *piñon* pine trees. "Let us go back to the horses and be gone from this place, and let them alone. My sister should not witness this. She is but a girl."

The women and the girl, who were on foot, had been caught red-handed with a sack full of stolen chickens. The women lived on the lands of Don Pedro, but had no jobs on the rancho. They had come down from the mountains to steal chickens because they were starving. It was not an uncommon event on the rancho. Thievery was a constant problem.

One of the women was tied to a dead tree, facing Don Pedro and Caleb. Her clothing had been stripped off her, and she had been whipped with a bullwhip. They could see the reddened lash marks even from this distance across her breast and stomach. Strips of flesh hung in pieces across her breasts and abdomen. The other woman was dead. The shot they had heard was no doubt the one that had felled her when she tried to run away. She had also been stripped naked and whipped before she tried to run.

The guards below were laughing, enjoying their work. They were protecting Don Miguel's property, and administering his justice, as they were paid to do.

The young woman tied to the tree was watching in anguish as the men repeatedly raped her eight-year old daughter. Laughing, they would occasionally let the girl escape in order to enjoy chasing and bringing her back in front of her mother. Two of the men were raping the young girl as Caleb and Don Pedro watched from the cover of the *piñon* trees and rocks on top of the hill. The guards' britches had been hastily piled up beside them where they were sexually administering their brand of justice to the youngest chicken thief.

Caleb was sickened by the sight of the beatings and the rape of the young girl. But he was only a guest here. It was none of his business, so he turned away to go back to the horses. He had only taken a few steps away when he heard a gasp from Don Pedro, *"Dios mío!* Oh, my God! Look there, it is María!"

Caleb rushed back to see what was happening.

"She must be crazy!" Don Pedro said excitedly. "She is attacking my father's men!"

María was racing her horse wildly, swinging her quirt like a whip. Both of the men who had been raping the girl were trying to run away from her on foot—without their pants—as she chased after them. She rode one of the men down and knocked him to the ground with her horse. Then she wheeled her horse around and chased the other rapist, beating him with her quirt whenever she caught up to him.

The other two men, both of whom were armed, had taken refuge behind the tree that held the woman captive. They knew the identity of Don Miguel's daughter, who had ridden into their midst like a crazy woman. They had seen her at the rancho. They were dumbfounded at the sight of her here, and couldn't figure out what they should do. How could they repel an attack by the daughter of Don Miguel, their *patrón* and their master? If they even so much as looked with disfavor on her they would lose their jobs or have their backs whipped raw, and they knew it. Therefore, they did the only thing they could think of to do: they ran their horses and took off in the opposite direction. In no way would they want to be caught in opposition to one of Don Miguel's children. That was out of the question.

"You dogs! You rapists! You murderers! Lecherous dogs!" María was screaming and crying at the two men who were on foot as she chased and whipped them. She pursued first one and then the other until the men reached a stand of trees, where they could dodge and hide from her, still running away, on foot, without their guns or britches.

By the time Don Pedro and Caleb got back to their horses and rode at full gallop down the hill, María had returned to the woman who was tied to the tree. María, sobbing uncontrollably, struggled to untie the leather thongs that bound the Indian woman's hands behind the tree. But she could not untie them because the knots were so tight and slick wet with blood. María ran over to the britches left behind by the two rapists and found a large butchering knife in the sheath-knife scabbard of one of the men. She was in the process of cutting the leather thongs when Don Pedro and Caleb rode up to her.

Don Pedro was agitated. He got off his horse and ran over to her shouting, "You must not do this! We cannot interfere with the rancho men's work! This is wrong! This is our father's business!" He grabbed her shoulder to spin her around, away from the woman she was trying to help.

María turned toward her brother furiously, her eyes blinded by tears and rage. She swept the knife blade sideways towards her brother, slashing the cloth sash around his waist. Had it not been for the thick layered sash, she would have laid open his stomach, and he knew it.

Astonished by her action. Don Pedro jumped back and stayed away from her. He had never seen his sister in such a state of irrational excitement. He had almost become used to her moody, quiet, distracted, even overly-religious behavior since she had returned from the school of the nuns; but this outburst was beyond his comprehension.

"Are we murderers and rapists of women and children? Is that our business?" she screamed at him. "How dare you condone such conduct? What kind of people are we to treat these poor wretched human beings in this fashion! Look around you. Are you so blind and so stupid you cannot see what has happened here?"

Caleb knelt by the young Indian girl. All four men had abused her repeatedly, and she was badly hurt. She was in shock and barely conscious. Blood was flowing profusely out of her vagina, and her arm was broken and hung at an odd angle at her side.

Caleb tried to give her some water from his canteen. She could not drink, so he wetted her lips with his fingers. Having moistened her lips, he tried to wash some of the dirt off her wounds by using his sash as a rag. Uncertain what to do next, he tried to make her more comfortable. He took off the beautiful new jacket that had been a gift from Don Miguel and fashioned a cover for her with it.

Tears were rolling down his cheeks as he tried to minister to her wounds. He couldn't help himself. He had begun to confuse his grief for this mistreated girl with his tormented feelings for another woman, Polly, whose life he had been unable to save so long ago to him, so very far from here back on the prairie. He temporarily strapped the girl's arm against her chest with strips of cloth he cut from his sash to immobilize the limb.

María had freed the other woman and lay her down on the ground. The woman was slowly bleeding to death from her cuts and lash strokes.

María ran over to see what Caleb was doing to the little girl. She watched him as he tried to bind her wounds. She saw his tears. "Can she live?" María whispered in anguish.

"I don't know." Caleb shook his head negatively as he stood up to talk to María. "Maybe, if we could get her help. A doctor. Her arm is broken. I have tried to bind it to her body to hold it steady. I feel so helpless in not knowing how to treat her broken bones and wounds."

From the cover of the trees and bushes, another pair of eyes was watching what Caleb and María were doing. The twelve year-old son of the woman who had been shot watched as María, her brother, and the stranger seemed to be trying to help his little friend and her mother. He knew his own mother, who had been shot, was beyond help.

He was too afraid for his own safety to come forward, but he would survive to tell the story that would soon be on the lips of everyone on the rancho and the territory: how the lady, María, had galloped up and whipped the murderers and rapists, as she herself had called them, and how Caleb and María's brother also seemed to be trying to help.

Caleb got his *serape* off his saddle and covered the woman with it. Then he tried to bind some of her wounds and stem the flow of blood. Again, he used pieces of his silken sash that he cut up with his knife. María, too, tried to help him bind the wounds. Still sobbing, she was trying to control herself so she could help. She kept wiping the tears from her eyes and face with her now blood-covered hands, staining her own face grotesquely with dirt and blood.

Don Pedro could not understand what the two of them were doing, trying to help these chicken thieves. He had found the sack full of chickens that they had stolen. He loved his sister, and he was obligated. And, yes, he even loved Caleb, whom he publicly declared had saved his life. But Don Pedro most definitely did not understand their behavior toward these *peón* chicken thieves.

Then a feasible rationalization occurred to Don Pedro. *An act of charity. Yes. That is what this must be. This is an act of charity. This is a religious act of charity for the poor. I understand the foolish sympathy an unknowing, teenage María might have for one of the Indian women or her children. She simply does not understand the rules of the rancho. It is unimportant. We can afford to humor her. We can dispose of the Indian women and girl later.* He felt better, now that he had been able to give it a name. "What can I do to help?" he heard himself ask.

"We can make a travois or get a wagon, or we can set up a camp here," Caleb said. "These two need a doctor badly. I honestly think a travois would give them a better, quicker, more gentle ride back to the rancho where we can nurse them, since there are no nearby roads. If that is what you want me to do, I will build one."

"If you think that is best, then that is what we must do," María said. But she did not even know what a travois was. "You will have to tell us what to do. How do we go about building one?"

"Don Pedro, round up the horses of the two *caballeros* María chased off and bring their lariats and *serapes*, I can start cutting two poles for the travois," Caleb said as he took his tomahawk from his belt. "You know, I almost didn't bring this hatchet. Without it we couldn't cut the trees."

Caleb set to work. The travois would be crude. It would consist of two poles placed across his horse's saddle and lashed together with ropes. The two poles would stick out behind the horse and drag on the ground. One cross-member would be lashed onto the poles near the ground and a second one nearer the horse. Then ropes to form a platform or bed would be woven back and forth across the framework of the side and cross poles. Finally, the *serapes* from his horse and the horses of the two men who had run away would be placed on the woven ropes to make a crude hammock.

He used his own horse to pull the travois because he knew it had a steady temperament. The other horses seemed too spirited. They would not tolerate dragging the strange contrivance behind them as well as his horse might.

When the travois was finished, Caleb and Don Pedro placed the mother and the little girl onto the hammock. Then he lashed the girl and young woman on with more ropes. He walked, leading his horse for the first mile in order to make sure it was not going to spook and bolt. It was 5 miles back to the rancho house, and they made their way slowly so as to make the ride over the rough ground as gentle as possible.

Caleb asked Don Pedro, "Could you ride ahead and get a place ready for these people and send for a doctor?" There was, of course, no doctor at the rancho. It was a long two-day's ride to Santa Fé, and there was no certainty one could be found there.

CHAPTER 3
María Takes Her Blouse Off.

It took many hours to travel slowly by the smoothest paths they could find to get back to the rancho yard.

When they got to the rancho they were met in front of the *peón's* chapel by Father *de Silva*. Father *de Silva*, the resident priest on *Don Miguel's* rancho, ministered to the *patrón's* family and the other residents both as to their souls and as to what first aid he could supply. "Come, come," he told them. "Bring the wounded into the infirmary. I have set up two beds for them. We can take care of them here and make them as comfortable as possible."

"María stopped at the entrance way and gasped at the sight of the infirmary and the chapel. "This is a terrible place! Not only is this room small and pitiful—it is decaying, and the walls are tumbling down. It is only an old run-down log barn." Father *de Silva* had set up the infirmary next to the barn-like building that was used as the chapel for the poor péons. María had never been inside this chapel or the infirmary before. "My horse is kept in a better building than this! Both the chapel and this room have open windows with no shutters. Sick people in the infirmary, or even worshippers in the chapel, can look up at the ceiling and see blue sky and clouds, or feel the rain and wind in bad weather."

"Yes, my child, what you say is true." Father *de Silva* was sadly shaking his head. He brought his hands together in front of him as if praying. "Both the infirmary building and the chapel were used as chicken coops at one time. I have tried again and again to get permission from our *patrón* Don Miguel to build a new chapel and a new infirmary, but so far I have not been successful, despite my prayers."

The *ricos*, or rich members of Don Miguel's family, had their own small but well-constructed and well-appointed chapel attached to the rancho residence. It was clean and neat with a good roof and shutters. It had a dirt floor as all the rooms did, but there were thick carpets on the floors, with cushioned knee rests for those praying. Of course, only members of Don Miguel's family used it. The log walls were plastered over with white plaster, as were all the rooms in the *de Vargas's* residence.

"Has the doctor been sent for?" María asked Don Pedro.

"No," Her brother answered. "Father would not send for anyone," he answered reluctantly. "He said it would be too expensive, and the lives of one *peón* woman and one small girl are not worth the cost. These are not even workers. They are just living on the rancho in the outlying area stealing from us at that. They have no value, and they are thieves too. He is mad that we interfered with the men in their duties."

Caleb carried the wounded girl inside, and Father *de Silva* and two female assistants brought the mother in. They lay them on the two board-beds Father *de Silva* had prepared, which were just two old wooden benches covered by a tattered cloth. Father *de Silva* had asked the women from his parish to help care for the wounded woman and her daughter, and they immediately began to wash and clean the wounds with soap and water. They had no medicine of any kind.

María was distraught. She was crying almost hysterically again. Caleb and her brother helped her to the hacienda main house, and her mother and the women servants tried to lead her to her room. She broke away from them and ran to her father sobbing uncontrollably and praying irrationally. She threw herself to her knees in front of her father and begged him to help the injured woman and the little girl. In the name of God, send for a doctor father!" She begged him.

Don Miguel could not understand her bizarre behavior. It was not sensible or proper for her to be carrying on about such a trivial matter. He reacted furiously when he heard that María had interfered with the rancho guards' duties in punishing the chicken thieves. He would have to punish her now. His wife tried to calm him as he began shouting abusively at his family, but everyone knew that his fury was directed at María.

Later that evening, Don Miguel grew even more infuriated when his son reported that María had left her room, against his orders for her to stay there, and was in the *peón's* chapel. She had cast off her beautiful riding habit and donned the clothes of one of the servant girls. She had given confession to Father *de Silva* and taken the sacrament in the *peón's* chapel. Not only that, she was still praying, kneeling upon the filthy dirt floor."

"Her behavior is shameful," Don Miguel said. "It is beneath the dignity of a member of this family to visit or pray in the *peón's* chapel, much less grovel on the *peón's* dirt floor in such a shameful fashion."

"Well, that spoiled child will not stay on her knees very long." Don Miguel was extremely irritated at the trouble and embarrassment that María was bringing upon him. "Let her stay there in the dirt on her knees! That will bring her to her senses. She will tire of kneeling on a dirt floor soon enough. She needs punishment. She is acting without proper respect for me, her father, the *patrón*." He pounded his fist on his chest. "Let her punish herself! No one can stay on their knees more than an hour or two. I will ignore her! That shall be her part of her punishment!"

"I hope so, Father," Don Pedro said shaking his head sadly, "I am sure you are right. I can hardly stay on my knees for the length of a Mass, even in our own chapel where we have soft cushions for our knees. But I don't know María any more since she returned from the school with the nuns. She hardly speaks to me or anyone, and she hardly ever smiles any more. Her eyes are sunken, and she has dark circles under them. Can she be ill, do you think?"

"I thought I saw a change for the better in her when she went riding with us. She seems to be friendly toward Caleb, at least sometimes. She was even teasing him again and making fun of how skinny he is. It was the first time I saw her smiling in weeks. Now this irrational behavior! I simply do not know my own sister any more."

"Spoiled, is what she is!" Don Miguel was pacing back and forth, trying to calm his nerves. Throwing his arms out in a gesture of frustration, he yelled, "Willful! Spoiled and disobedient! I thought the school had taken that out of her. It cost me a fortune to send her there! I thought she would learn how to be a lady and to be more obedient. I prayed to God that they could make her more docile and happy. I even lit a candle in our private chapel and asked Father *de Silva* to pray for her. After all, I am honor-bound to fulfill the agreement with my cousin in California that María will become his wife. If she behaves this way with him, she will dishonor me, and our family."

"We have this fiesta coming next week, and your trip to California next spring to prepare for, and this rancho to run. And here is María causing problems by worrying about some valueless *peón* Indian woman."

"And," he said, turning around and facing his son, "she also interfered with our workers' duties to protect our property. We cannot permit *peóns* to steal our chickens and other livestock, and go unpunished."

"María will tire of being on her knees quickly enough. Of that I am sure. And this idea that my own daughter would don the cloths of a *peón*, I cannot understand this defiance. I will have to punish her now! I will not permit her to attend the fiesta. That will teach her a lesson. I will lock her in her room. I may even have to horse-whip her!"

The next morning Father *de Silva* requested an audience with Don Miguel. Don Miguel, who was studying his account books, did not like the interruption. He was deeply troubled because for the third year in a row he was losing money. His accounts were out of balance, and his guards had reported more losses of sheep to Indian raiders. The Indians were harvesting more of his cattle and sheep than he was able to gather and sell.

"*Señor*, Sir, *Patrón*, I am worried about María," said the old priest, clasping his hands as if praying to Don Miguel. He was obviously disturbed, and very much afraid. "She is still on her knees on the dirt floor of the workers' chapel. It was very cold last night, and she did not move. She will not eat anything or drink water. I have been giving her Holy Communion and hearing her confessions, but she refuses to leave the chapel."

"She told me that she has made a promise to Christ and the Mother of Christ not to move until the men who killed the one woman, bull-whipped the mother, and raped the little girl have been punished. She is also asking for a doctor to be sent for to fix the broken arm of the little girl. I do not know what to do! What are your orders, *Patrón*? I fear she is serious about not moving!"

"What? What are you saying? Are you telling me that she was there all night on her knees? Has she gone mad? That is impossible!" Don Miguel rose up out of his chair, his face turning red with rage. He smashed his fist into the middle of the books he had been working on.

Father *de Silva* sank onto his knees in front of his master, and clasped his hands again and bowed his head. "I swear it is the truth, *Señor*. I have not left the chapel for a moment all night myself. The *peón* women are coming in from the hills. They come into the church and kiss the hem of her skirt. Then they ask for me to hear their confession and take the sacrament. I have been up all night hearing confessions. Women whom I have never seen before are praying and asking for Holy Communion. Two dozen women have taken up a vigil in the back of the chapel. They have resolved not to leave until she does. Some husbands are complaining that there is no one to take care of their children or cook their suppers. They are blaming me for the absence of their women from the kitchens because they are in the church. They think I am holding them there, but I have not done any such a thing."

"Please tell me what I should do? This is beyond my experience. Could the devil have possessed her? Or has Christ taken her over? Or is it the Mother of God? I simply do not know what to do. You must tell me what it is you want me to do. What are my orders, *Señor?*"

Don Miguel bellowed for his son. "Don Pedro! Don Pedro! Come in here!" he raged, screaming out the doorway and down the hall toward his son's room. Don Pedro came running into the room with a panic-stricken expression on his face. His father had never screamed like that before in this household. The servants had all hidden themselves to get out of the way of his rage.

"Now hear this!" he said, pointing his finger at his son and speaking very clearly and trying to control his temper. "You are to go to your sister. She is in the *peón's* chapel still on her knees, defying me. You tell her she is to come back here immediately, come back here and go to her room, or I will personally come down there and whip her into submission. She has disrupted the entire rancho. I cannot let her defy me like this. Give her this one last opportunity to come to her senses."

"Yes, Father, I will go immediately." Don Pedro turned and hurried out of the room.

A crowd of women talking in front of the church saw Don Pedro coming. They curtsied as he walked by, but no one smiled at him. He had always gotten along well with the women. Many of them had served him when he was a child. They had given him food, love, and affection. But they were uncertain why he had come here, so they regarded him suspiciously. Their eyes were filled with mistrust and anger. But why? He had done nothing to them.

The back of the chapel was full of women on their knees, but no men were there. María was kneeling before the makeshift altar, with her back to the door and the *peón* women were well back and behind her. Her posture was as straight as if she had just knelt down. She was still moving her fingers energetically through her rosary beads in silent prayer, her lips were moving through the ritual words. Don Pedro could hardly believe that María had spent so many hours in such a position. *Perhaps father de Silva had exaggerated how long she had been there,* he thought.

Don Pedro marched up beside his sister and waited courteously for her to finish her rosary. He knew that she must have seen him waiting to talk to her, but she did not pay any attention to him. When he saw her start her beads over again, he interrupted her. "María!" he said sternly. "I have come at the command of Father. He is furious that you would defy him so. He is deadly serious about this. He has ordered you to come back to your room and stop this foolishness immediately. He has instructed me to tell you that he will personally come here and use a whip on you and drag you back to your room if you do not come. You must obey him! You must come with me this instant!" Then he pleaded almost in a whisper, "Please come home with me I beg you."

The women in the back of the church were hanging on to every word Don Pedro said. They all expected María to obey, for this was a direct order from the *patrón*. Several made the sign of the cross, and one began crying.

"Thank you, brother." María looked up at Don Pedro with a slight smile. "I have heard his message. I know it is a sin against God for me to disobey my father, but I have given my oath to Christ and the Mother of Christ that I will not leave my vigil here until the murderers and rapists are punished and the sick have a doctor. I am deeply sorry for my act of disobedience, but there is nothing that I can do now because I have made my vow to the Lord God and the Virgin Mother of Christ. Tell my father to whip me all I deserve. Tell father that I am prepared for my punishment, and I accept it. I expect it. I know I deserve it because I am a sinner. Please also tell him I love him. Tell him that I will do my best to receive his punishment as both a servant of God and as a dutiful daughter should. I am taking my shirt off so his whip will not tear the cloth of this shirt."

Still on her knees, she took the peasant shirt off right in front of her brother and in full view of the other women in the chapel and even the priest. A gasp went up from the crowd in the rear. No one there had ever seen such a thing done before in a church or chapel or anywhere else, in public, for that matter. Several of the women began to moan and cry loudly, and rock back and forth as if in agony. Some were rocking back and forth, and saying prayers. Some lay their heads down on their hands in front of themselves so they could not see what was to happen next.

Don Pedro was aghast at her lack of modesty and decorum. He knew then for sure that his sister had lost her mind. He picked up her shirt, intending to forcibly put it back on her—but then he saw the scars on her back. They were long, ugly gashes and raised lines of tortured healed flesh.

He could not believe his eyes. The scars were like a magnet drawing his attention. *Those grotesque whip marks! I had no idea María had ever been beaten like that,* he thought. He had not known she had ever been beaten at all. His father must have ordered it. He must have permitted it. Perhaps he had even done it himself. He had just heard his father say he was coming here to horse whip her. He dropped her shirt back onto the floor. *How could this be?* In confusion, he made the sign of the cross and left the church with her message.

María turned back toward the altar and resumed saying her rosary. Her bare back was visible to all the women sitting at the back of the church. Some of them were crying openly, their tears falling on the dirt floor in front of them as they looked at the scars on her. Many of the women in the church had known the whip. They all knew what those scars meant in pain and degradation.

Don Pedro returned to his father's ashen colored face. His voice was peculiar, withdrawn, and unsteady. Was it even without respect? "I delivered your message, Father. She is prepared for you to whip her *again*. She has removed her shirt for you to begin *another* beating! She told me to tell you that she loves you and is prepared for her punishment, but that she cannot break her vow she has made to God and the Mother of Christ."

"What? What did you say?" Don Miguel stammered as he rose out of his chair in a fury. "How dare you talk to me and in that tone of voice? Has everyone in this household gone crazy? What do you mean *again*? I have never beaten María in my life. I have never even spanked her. That's what is wrong with her. She needs a good beating!"

Don Pedro did not think that he believed his father. "I have seen her back, father," he said accusingly, "she has the scars there. Everyone in the church has seen them now. I wanted to cover up her nakedness, but something stopped me."

Father *de Silva* was still on his knees in the room, praying. He was listening to the exchanges of conversation between father and son. He made the sign of the cross and said, "It is a miracle! It is a miracle! Don Miguel wished her beaten, and the scars came upon her back as a miracle. Father in heaven . . .," He began to pray again in Latin, frightened by the meaning of it all.

Suddenly Father *de Silva* asked, "Don Miguel, do I have your permission to return to the chapel? I have been giving Holy Communion to María three times a day. I have insisted that she also drink from the cup, and I have been getting her to take a little moisture in this fashion. I feel she will be dead in a few days. But maybe another miracle will occur, and she will be saved in some way. In the meantime, I think I should give her the Last Sacrament of Extreme Unction. It would be better if I do it now in case God takes her from us suddenly."

His shoulders were sloping now as Don Miguel waived him away without saying anything. He could not believe that his 16-year old daughter, who had never been farther off the rancho than Santa Fé except when she had been sent away to school with the nuns, could be causing him so much trouble. And over what? Two absolutely worthless *peón* female chicken thieves! He muttered in disbelief as he sat down again. "Nothing! All of this over nothing! I can't believe it!" He poured himself a large glass of wine and drank it down without pausing.

Don Pedro looked out the window and saw Caleb sitting on the verandah reading a black, leather-covered book. Don Pedro walked out to him. "I am sorry to be such a bad host. I have neglected you. But my father has been having a domestic crisis of sorts, and he cannot seem to resolve it. He does not appear to know just what to do. My sister is defying him. She refuses to come out of the *peón's* chapel. She refuses to listen to me. But she likes you and respects you for helping her with the woman and little girl yesterday. Perhaps if you talked to her it might calm her some, and she would come home before she gets into more trouble with Father. Would it be possible for you to talk to her?"

"Of course, Don Pedro. I will do anything I can to help you and your father." Caleb closed the Bible that he had been reading. "What can I do?"

Don Pedro said quietly, "María is very upset because father's men killed the one woman, and beat and raped the other woman and the little girl. The men went too far, I admit; but it is our way here. Those people were caught stealing Father's property and had to be punished as an example to the others. They are only *péons* and of no value."

"Now, María has gone into the chapel of the *péons*. She has made a vow to God that she will not leave her vigil, nor eat nor drink, until the men who were following father's orders are punished. But he cannot punish them for doing their duty as he has always instructed them. This would, of course, dishonor him. Now, to make matters worse, other *péon* women of the rancho have gone into the church, and they all refuse to work or cook for their families."

"In all our family's years of experience on this ranch, we have never had such a problem. Would you be willing to talk to María? I am embarrassed to ask this of you, but I do not know what else to do."

"Of course I will go to her immediately and see if I can help. I will be glad to talk to her."

Don Pedro and Caleb went inside the house and got Don Miguel's permission for Caleb to talk to María. The old man was glad that Caleb was going and hoped that he would convince her to come home.

Juan, who had been watching from across the road, came running up to Caleb as he left the house. "*Señor* Caleb, all the people are talking about how you brought the little girl and her mother here on a travois!" he chattered in Spanish. "I have been telling them how you came in answer to my prayers when the rustlers were going to shoot me. The people are asking for you to go and save *La María*. Please, try to save her. Will you?"

"You place a mighty heavy burden on a friend, Juan. But I am going to talk to María if she will hear me. This is the craziest place I have ever been to. Show me where she is." Caleb was still carrying his Bible in his hand. He had forgotten to set it down.

All of the *péons* were standing in groups of two and three along the street leading down into the peasants' area of the rancho, where the chapel was. They seemed to be waiting for something, but no one knew what that might be. What was going to happen next remained a mystery.

The women who looked at Caleb as he walked past all made the sign of the cross. Some of the men took their hats off for him. They were all looking at him. He felt very uncomfortable. The *péons* acted as if they were expecting him to do something miraculous. He knew he was not a miracle worker, even if they did not.

When he entered the chapel, he was surprised at how small and dilapidated a building it was. It had been a chicken coop. It still had droppings on the floor. It had gaping holes in the walls, just like the infirmary next door. There were no benches, and the floor was nothing but uneven dirt. The thirty or so women at the rear of the chapel were all on their knees. No men were there except Father *de Silva*, who was doing something on a small table at the front. He was pouring some mixtures back and forth among cups and decanters while chanting unintelligibly in a language that to Caleb was strange. He had never heard Latin spoken before or seen a Mass prepared, like this.

Some of the women Caleb passed as he walked toward María had taken their blouses off. Their nakedness seemed appallingly out of place in a church. Caleb could see horrible scars on one woman's back.

María was still in the front of the chapel on her knees. Caleb knew she had been there since yesterday. He saw a large wet spot behind her where she had evidently urinated. She had not even gotten up to go to the outhouse.

He approached her, trying to come up with something to say. He could not think of anything that made sense. He stood there beside her, with his hat off, awkwardly, feeling foolish.

María saw him and smiled. "Thank you for coming. I have heard that you can do miracles. I hope so. Please kneel down next to me." He saw her kiss the black onyx cross with the fourteen small bands of gold she always wore around her neck. It was as if she were thanking it for something.

He clumsily got down on his knees as she had requested.

"No, come closer." she directed him. "Come right up here next to me so that I can close my eyes and lean my head on your shoulder just for a moment. I am growing weaker."

He did as she asked.

"I have been wondering. " María had her eyes closed and was talking to him with her head resting on his shoulder. "Why did you shed tears for the little girl when we found the women that the guards were punishing? Tell me, why did you shed tears for *a peón* you did not even know?"

"I don't know for sure." Caleb was confused by her question. "The little girl reminded me of something, someone, I loved very much. This happened months ago. Her name was Polly. She was on her way to Santa Fé. I found her in the middle of the prairie after everyone else in her wagon train had been killed. She was killed later while we were traveling together, before we could reach Santa Fé. She had been shot and clubbed, and I could not save her. I felt so helpless. I felt the same way about the little girl. She was so small and helpless. I just couldn't help myself. She reminded me of Polly, I guess."

"That explains it then," María sighed audibly. "In Spanish we would say you are *simpático*. With sympathy. You have a heart! In this country of yours to the east, the United States, do they rape and kill children there only for the sake of a chicken? Or is it better than here?"

"I don't know if it is any better. I think maybe it is a little better, but there are bad people everywhere. My own father was murdered. The American men kill and rape the Indians, and take their land. In return, the Indians kill and rape and torture the whites as well as each other. It seems to be the way of things. The Bible says, 'Thou Shalt Love Thy Neighbor As Thyself.' But no one seems to pay any attention to it."

"Please tell me if there is anything I can do to help you," he continued. "Is there any way that I can speak to your father to bring peace between him and you? He is upset, very troubled and hurt. I know he loves you, but he is very confused as to what he should do."

She ignored his question and asked one of her own, "This woman that you loved. Had she been whipped and raped, do you know?"

"She had been whipped," Caleb acknowledged. "I saw the scars on her body. I don't know about the other, but I think maybe it was so. Her man, who was named Jeremy, was killed earlier on the way out here. She liked me, but it was Jeremy she loved with all her heart and soul. I am sure they are together now in heaven, at least I hope so. I pray that it is so."

"That explains why you of all people have been sent here," María said to him almost as a sigh. "I, too, have lost my greatest love other than my love for our Lord Jesus Christ and the Madonna, of course. But you are *simpático*. I understand that now. That book in your hand. What is it?"

"It is the Bible. It is the story of Christ, and before."

"Do you read it often?"

"Almost every day. Perhaps not every day, but I try to study it. My father told me that there are many answers in it for our troubles. I was in the patio reading it when your brother asked me to come and speak with you. Your brother is deeply troubled, as your father is. Your father wants to make peace with you, and gave me permission to come and talk to you. But you have to help him."

María straightened up. She had regained a little strength from resting her head on his shoulder. Once again she kissed the black onyx cross on the gold chain around her neck.

Although Caleb had only been on his knees for fifteen minutes, they were already hurting him. He squirmed, trying to find a more comfortable position. María noticed him squirming and smiled at his discomfort.

"Is there a trick to it? It hurts like the dickens. I am not used to it," he asked, changing position again.

"Yes, there is a trick to it, as you say. I learned it from the nuns. The trick is to enjoy the pain. If you do it because of a true love of God and you believe it is important and useful, you no longer mind it. You even enjoy it. Read to me from your Bible."

Father *de Silva* had heard the rumor that Caleb had either performed a miracle or been a part of one, but he didn't know which. *It is logical and right that Caleb is here. He was sent here, no doubt,* concluded the priest. Father *de Silva* saw with his own eyes, as María rested her head on Caleb's shoulder, that the young man could calm her more than anyone else had been able to. She smiled at Caleb and continued talking to him. *A good omen, undoubtedly.*

Father *de Silva* approached Caleb and made the sign of the cross in front of him. The priest wore a large brown-stained wooden cross on a leather thong around his neck. He placed the cross on top of Caleb's head and kissed its wooden surface. Then he went down on his knees in front of Caleb to embrace him, and then kissed him on each cheek.

Caleb, who was not really a Catholic, so he could not receive the sacrament; but he could receive the priest's blessing. *Who could say where a miracle might come from?* Wondered Father *de Silva*. *Look at La María's back. The scars had appeared by our Father in heaven's intervention so Don Miguel would not beat her and disgrace himself in the doing.* Father *de Silva* had heard Don Miguel swear that he had not put them there, so there was no other explanation. *Only God could have done it. Surely this was a miracle!* But the miracle was not over yet. Whatever was to happen, this young man was somehow part of it. He felt it, though he did not know why.

Father *de Silva* told her that he had been instructed during the Mass to include her in partaking of the blood of Christ. The thought that he should do so had suddenly materialized in his head. He did not put the thought in his head himself, so surely the message was from God. How else could such a message have entered his consciousness? María must receive the bread and wine because he had been commanded to include her as a full participant in the Mass. She could not disobey God's message, nor could he.

The old priest gave María a piece of bread as the Sacrament of Communion, the literal body of Christ. It was much larger than the wafer he usually used. This was a quarter slice of bread, as much as he thought he could place in her mouth at one time. He gave her a few moments to chew it and then poured a full glass of wine-and-water mixture down her throat. He would try to keep her alive, at least for a while, by giving her some liquid nourishment, nourishment both for her soul and for her body. It was permitted, he was sure of it.

Afterward, he walked behind María and kissed the scars on her back. The women in the back of the room murmured and gasped, and then resumed their crying and wailing.

Caleb began to read his Bible aloud. He droned on long into the afternoon, until his voice became hoarse. And after many futile attempts to find some comfortable way to kneel, he finally had to sit back on his haunches and give his knees a rest. He noticed that María never seemed to move at all. He did not know how she could stand it. *Perhaps women do not feel pain as men do,* he thought.

While he was reading the Bible, the women in the chapel came down, most not understanding one word of what he said reading the English Bible. They knelt in front of him and embraced him though no one knew what he was saying, just as they did not understand one Latin word Father *de Silva* said in their masses.

Caleb's voice was beginning to fail him, and he finally read, "Submit yourselves to every ordinance of man for the Lord's sake: whether it be to the king, as supreme; or unto governors, as unto them that sent by him for punishment of evil doers, and for the praise of them that do well."

"If your father would punish these men, what kind of punishment would you think is just? Must he kill them, too?" Caleb asked María, as he tried to figure out just what it would take to end this madness.

María was quiet for a long time as she thought about his question. Then she said, "My father is the *patrón* here. He is the master of us all. He owns us just the same as he owns the cattle and the sheep. Justice and punishment are his to determine. But surely stealing a chicken is not so great a crime as to warrant murder and rape. Can starving persons be blamed for putting food into their mouths? There should be some mercy with justice."

"There are fourteen stations to the cross. Even if you make all crimes equal and whipped a person fourteen times with a whip, it would be something to consider as just punishment for a crime. And, the punishment should be given out or at least observed by my father. He would never permit murder of a woman or rape of the children in his care, in his presence."

"My father is a good man. He is an honest man, and he has a good heart. Should not punishment and justice be dispensed by him? Some of our people here are starving. That is the real problem. Father *de Silva* has begged my father for food to give to the starving people on this rancho. Father *de Silva* should have an allowance of some kind to help the poor. People should not have to steal chickens to keep from starving to death."

"I am not here to embarrass my father, nor am I here to try to run his rancho or interfere in his justice. My only purpose here is to plead for his mercy for this one woman and the child. Ask my father if, in his wisdom, this is an honorable thing to do. I will listen to him in all humility, if he will only consider it. And that little girl needs a doctor to set her arm, unless someone here can do it."

Two of the women in the church understood English, and could hear everything that was said.

Caleb nodded. It sounded reasonable to him. "I will try." He had been on his knees for most of the past four hours now. His knees were unbearably sore, and his legs had gone to sleep. But worse even than that, was the pain in his back. When he tried to get up, he fell over onto the ground. Juan, who had been standing outside the door, watching, and ran to help him. Using Juan's shoulder to steady himself, Caleb limped out the door. Then he rubbed his numb legs to restore circulation.

There were now about forty women in the church, all praying. Those who had scars on their backs had taken their shirts off. The men were standing across the street, generally irritated, sullen, or excited. Some of them were drinking liquor, and swearing and talking about what to do. They all took their hats off respectfully as Caleb walked by this time; some even made the sign of the cross. They knew he was trying to help, and they knew he had helped the *peón* mother and the child. Some had also heard that he had saved Juan's life as part of the answer to a prayer for help to our Mother of God.

Caleb walked, limping, back to the hacienda to report. Six men were standing in front of Don Miguel's doorway. They all had bullwhips in their hands, and they were grim-faced, waiting.

Don Pedro came out to meet Caleb. "This is getting worse all the time. My father is beside himself. He has already drunk a whole bottle of wine and is starting on a second one. These men out here have all come to confess to having stolen chickens at one time or another; and they are asking my father to beat them so María can complete her penance. They have heard she has taken the Last Sacrament and is going to die. It is terrible!"

"People keep coming to the back door with chickens for the poor. My father is ashamed. We have received over fifty chickens so far. We have no place to keep them. People from faraway ranchos are beginning to come to see the miracle written on my sister's back. They believe it might cure their sicknesses if they can view it. Some have heard the scars show a picture of the Madonna, but only at times. If you can see it, you are blessed and may be cured."

Caleb talked to Don Miguel for several hours. Their conversation rambled over many subjects as Don Miguel continued to drink wine. Caleb was given a glass too, but he only took a first sip for politeness.

"The problem is that I cannot go back on my word." Don Miguel was sad but determined. "These men were acting under my instructions. I cannot whip them for doing what they thought I had told them to do, that is, punish thievery. I will have lost everything if I lose the honor of my name, and the authority and the respect of my men."

"There are doctors in Santa Fé. And another one in the Army. One of them will come here for a price. I will send for one of these men. I will give the orders immediately."

"I will give an allowance to Father *de Silva* to feed the starving as he has been asking me to do ever since he has been at my rancho. I will even allow him to build a better chapel for the poor people. But I cannot punish men for doing what I have told them to do. That would dishonor my name. I cannot do that even if I die myself. I will not do it. Even if María must die, then it must be so. That is too much! That is the one thing I cannot and will not do! I will not dishonor my name!"

"Can I talk to the men who whipped and raped the women. Would that be all right?" Caleb asked.

"Of course! Of course! Talk in my name. You have my complete authority. Anything to try to get this straightened out and ended. I will do anything reasonable, anything that preserves my honor."

Don Pedro sent out a call for the men who were present at the massacre, as it was now being called. Caleb met them in front of the rancho, where the men awaiting their punishment for stealing the chickens were also standing. Juan and Don Pedro were there to help him with the language problem.

Caleb stood before them but could not think of anything to say. The men went down on their knees when they understood he would be speaking for the master of them all, Don Miguel. They wanted Caleb to make a miracle.

But he had no miracles to offer. He couldn't think of even one word of wisdom that might help him deal with the problem. What an awkward feeling it was. All the *peón* men were on their knees waiting for him to give them wisdom, waiting for him to wave his arm and make all their problems go away. He resented their unrealistic expectations. He could not make a miracle. They stared at him, and he turned red in the face. In desperation, he got down on his knees so he would at least be on the same level with them.

He opened his Bible and began to read in English. He knew they could not understand what he said, but then they did not understand what the priests were saying either when they intoned Latin phrases in their Mass.

They knew what he was doing, and all made the sign of the cross and bowed their heads. "Happy is the man that findeth wisdom, and the man that getteth understanding," he read. He continued reading until his voice failed. Caleb closed his eyes in silent prayer then and asked God to give him wisdom to know what to do. But no thoughts of wisdom entered his mind.

When he opened his eyes, one of the men called to him. *"Señor!* I was one of the men who had been at the scene of the killing and rape. I was the one who had shot the young mother. *Señor*! I understand that God has asked through *La María* that I be whipped fourteen times for what I did to the women. Will you please do this for me, so that *La María* does not have to die for what I did? I know that she has taken the Last Sacrament and will soon be at death's door. I cannot bear this burden. Please help me. Will you do it for me and for her? I beg you to please release me in this way!"

Then the other three men who had been at the massacre asked that they too be whipped so they could be absolved of the responsibility of the death of *La María*. They begged Caleb to use the bullwhip on them, having heard that this was what María had asked to be done as punishment for the shooting of the women, and rape of the women and the little girl.

Caleb thought these people were all crazy. He was not about to flog the four guilty men with a bullwhip. And it looked to him as if the rest of them would demand punishment, too, if he whipped the guilty ones. He had never whipped anyone and had never even seen anyone whipped in his entire life. He would get up and simply walk away. Let them solve their own problems. Leave them to their own misery. *These people deserved to be miserable,* he thought.

His mind got up and walked away, but his legs had gone to sleep again from kneeling in front of the men. He struggled to get up but could not stand. He certainly could not walk. Juan helped him as he struggled to his feet unsteadily.

He could have walked away from the troubles and problems of these men, who were all strangers to him. But he could not abandon Juan and walk away from him. Juan had saved his life and was his friend. He simply could not walk out on Juan, who was also pleading for him to help *La María*.

Then Caleb spoke. "You four men may, if you want to, whip each other on the church steps fourteen times each, and not more than fourteen times. You other men who stole chickens are ordered by me in the name of Don Miguel to throw one bull-whip into the river. To lose your whips is your punishment. You will also watch what these other men do at the steps of the Church as a lesson to you."

"Furthermore, and most important of all, every one of you will then go to Father *de Silva* for confession and seek his help in finding forgiveness in the eyes of the Lord, our God. From this day forward, there will be no whipping or shooting of anyone for stealing chickens. Stealing chickens is no longer a serious crime. In fact, it is a small crime because the chickens are small. This I tell you in the name of *Don Miguel de Vargas*, your *patrón* and master of us all on this great rancho."

"If the whipping takes place on the steps by the hands of you men, then María will come out of the church," Caleb continued. "I promise it! The whippings are not ordered by our master, *Señor Miguel de Vargas*, but they are permitted in voluntary admission of your sins. They will be administered by the men themselves to save María. You men are not being punished. You are honorable. This is self-sacrifice to atone for sins against God."

Don Pedro was swiftly interpreting for him as he spoke.

Caleb had spoken without even realizing that he was going to do it. He had to somehow put an end to this foolishness. Could these strange ideas that popped into his head possibly help?

The men were all getting up. They embraced him and smiled at him, slapping his back. They were thanking him for finding the solution to their problem. They were not afraid of the whip any longer. They wanted it and looked forward to it.

They swaggered pridefully as they walked up the street behind him to the church steps, promising each other not to spare the whip blows. They were saving the honor of the rancho. They were the *bravo*, brave. The chicken thieves were sorry that they had only been directed to throw a whip in the river. They would have preferred to be *macho hombres*, big men, men like the four honored ones, to do something to save *La María*. But only the four men who had been at the massacre would be so honored. It hardly seemed fair to the others.

Caleb went inside the chapel and kneeled down with María as he had before. She did not say anything. She was swaying a little and nearly in a coma. She noticed him, lay her head upon his shoulder, and closed her eyes. There was a breathlessness to the atmosphere. Everyone felt that something momentous was about to happen. But those inside the chapel had no knowledge of what.

"SLAP!" Suddenly, they heard the sound of the whip coming from the chapel's front steps. María was immediately alert. Her head raised upright as the sound of the whip blow filled the room. "SLAP!" it resounded again. She straightened her back, and held her head high as two twin tears rolled down her cheeks.

"SLAP!" It was repeated four times with fourteen blows. The men themselves were whipping each other willingly, voluntarily, for the sake of *La María*. They loved *La María*, who had interceded for one of the least of them.

The whipping was finally finished. *Don Miguel de Vargas* would retain his honor and the honor of his family. The men who had punished and tortured the women chicken thieves were regarded as heroes. They were the brave saviors of *La María*.

"Now, María, your father has sent to Santa Fé for the doctor to set the little girl's arm. Also, he has agreed to give an allowance to Father *de Silva* to feed the poor. He even has agreed to build a new chapel. The men have been whipped, as you thought would be just. You heard it happen on the steps behind us."

"I have given my word of honor that if these things were done, as you said they should be, that you would come home with me. It is now time for you to come home." Caleb knew from experience that he could probably not stand up until he got some circulation going in his legs and feet. He knew too that she could not possibly walk after her long vigil. He turned his head and motioned with his arm for Juan to help him. With Juan's support, he rose and rubbed his legs to restore circulation.

Caleb then picked María up in his arms while Juan retrieved her blouse and laid it over her to hide her nakedness from all the eyes outside. Caleb began carrying her out of the church. Juan helped by supporting some of the weight of her legs. Together, they carried her back to the hacienda.

The women in the church were putting their blouses on and going back home, and the crowd of men that had gathered across the street was breaking up.

Caleb thought María was delirious, or barely conscious; but when he picked her up, she put her arms around his neck. He felt her embracing him, holding herself tightly against him with her face pressed in against the side of his neck. She kissed his neck over and over again. She was mumbling incoherently, or so he thought.

"Now I want to go to my sanctuary," she muttered. "You may come too; but you must always ask my permission. And, I will never say no to you!" It meant nothing to him, but it was strange. Puzzlingly strange. He felt that she was talking to him and that she knew exactly what she was saying. But he did not understand what she was talking about.

Caleb did not say anything. *Sanctuary, my foot. Now I'm going to take you back home and put you to bed! We've had enough trouble with you to last us all a lifetime,* he thought.

Don Pedro and Don Miguel, along with María's mother, met Caleb and María at the door. "Here, Caleb, bring her this way. Put her in her room on her bed." Don Miguel was crying, as were the rest of the household. He kept saying, "Thank God! Thank God!"

When Caleb put María down on her bed, she clasped his hand and whispered, "You see, Juan was right. You can perform miracles." She kissed his hand. Only Juan, beside Caleb, heard her say it. But then, Juan already believed in the miracles that Caleb could bring about, so he was not surprised. He just grinned his understanding. His friend Caleb had saved *La María*, as he had saved him.

Caleb knew he hadn't performed any miracles and felt he had really done very little to help the situation. The *de Vargas* family, the managers, and *peóns* had resolved everything on their own. *Oh, well, maybe I helped just a little bit by reading the Bible.*

CHAPTER 4
La Capilleja de La María. (The Chapel of the María).

Work began on the new chapel two months later. Don Miguel sent to Santa Fé for an old priest, Father Hidalgo, who had experience in building churches in the territory. Father Hidalgo came with drawings and a man with whom he had built other churches, who would supervise the work. The new chapel would quickly become a central part of the activity on the rancho.

"What shall we call this new chapel?" Father Hidalgo asked.

Don Miguel was surprised; he had not given any thought to a name for it. Father *de Silva*, the rancho priest, beamed the answer. "The people already call it The Chapel of *La María*! The *La Capilleja de la María*! It is an honor to the *de Vargas* family itself. It is being built because of the miracle and because of María."

"So be it, then," Don Miguel decreed. "But what shall be its theme? We must have a theme. Let us ask María what she thinks would be a good theme. Where is that girl?"

The activity of building the new chapel made a dramatic change in María. It brought her out of her depression. She seemed to have a purpose to her life again.

"Right there, Father, on the patio," Don Pedro said. "She is talking to the American, Caleb. He is reading the Bible to her and teaching her English, I think. I will call them in here, and let's ask her opinion. They are too serious, always reading the Bible or praying. Excuse me *padre*, I did not mean that the way it sounded." Don Pedro apologized to Father *de Silva* and Father Hidalgo for his ill-considered remark.

"You two!" Don Miguel hollered out the door. "María! Caleb! Come in here! I want you to meet someone. I want you to meet Father Hidalgo. He has come all the way from Santa Fé to help us with the planning and building of the new chapel. We will now have only one chapel for everyone on the rancho instead of two separate ones. We will build a section for our family members near the front, and the rest of it will be dedicated to the workers. We want to ask María what she thought the theme could be."

Caleb and María came into the office. Everyone looked at María although they did not expect her to have a comment to make or even understand what they meant, at least without spending a great deal of time thinking about it. The fact that Don Miguel was even asking her, a girl, for her opinion was in itself unusual.

She answered when they looked at her. "Give me a piece of paper, pen and ink, and I will make you a sketch. Then we will find the best artist on the rancho to paint this for us. Everything we can do must be done by the people living on this rancho to protect Father's purse and to make this a project of all of Father's people. We will all enjoy working on it for the sake of our souls—and in God's honor and in Father's honor, too, of course."

"See, here in the center," she began to sketch as she talked. "There will be a large painting in a beautiful frame made of the finest hard wood from Father's mountains. In the center there is to be a picture of the Madonna. The Madonna will be clad in a loose, flowing robe. The portrait itself will have a drapery-like border along the sides painted to look like curtains. This will give it the appearance and feeling of depth. In the center of the picture, the Madonna will hold the small Christ Child against her shoulder, turned towards those who pray here. The Madonna will be standing on clouds swirling at her feet, partially covering them. A bright light will seem to be pouring out from clouds behind the Madonna and the Christ Child."

"Along the walls of the chapel, going back to the front door will be the fourteen stations of the cross. They will be set into indentations in the walls. The statues and scenes will all be hand-carved by our people. Father *de Silva* can help us write the message for each station. The women of our villages will make clothing for the statues out of cloth they weave, so the statues will look real, and be a part of all of us. We will be able to walk along the fourteen stations and experience with our minds the pain of Christ, who suffered so for our sins."

"Next to the picture in the front of the chapel we will have a large wooden cross. It shall be painted black and have fourteen tiny gold bands on it, like this one around my neck."

She looked questioning at Don Miguel. "Do you approve of this, Father? I am not being too bold in making such suggestions, am I?" They all laughed at her afterthought about being modest and temperate.

"Oh, and one other thing. On top of the building will be a metal wind-vane. It will have a hen-chicken on it to turn into the wind when it blows! *Una polla.* It will be fun for the children to watch. Is that all right, Father *de Silva?*"

Father *de Silva* frowned, "Well, we want it to have dignity. A rooster might be more appropriate, but give me an opportunity to pray about that. I will need to think of this hen-chicken. To tell the truth, I wanted it to be more serious; but perhaps if it would encourage the children to come to church . . . .," He held his chin in thought. "I will discuss this further with Father Hidalgo. He has had more experience in such matters." He looked up suddenly, smiling. "Come to think of it, I would stand on the roof myself if it would make the children want to come to Mass and confession!" Everyone, including Father Hidalgo, laughed at his sudden humor.

"María, I like your suggestions and ideas," Don Miguel said smiling. "We will try to fit them in somehow so it will please you, and all of us." He was beaming with pride at the suggestions his daughter had made, and with the prospect of a new building on the rancho. "It has been too long since anything new has been added to our rancho here, and maybe by building a new chapel, God will smile upon us and let us have a profitable year. The rancho has a run-down, worn-out look about it, and this new chapel would add to its dignity. This would give a whole new appearance to our property."

"It is too bad we will not have this finished before our fiesta, which by the way is only two days off now." Don Miguel was beaming and happy with all of the activity. "Everyone is coming from all over the area. We will have three days of festivities. The steers and goats have already been slaughtered so the meat can be hung and aged to make it tender. We have dug the roasting pits, and the fires are being started so as to reduce the wood to coals. We will then cover and bury the meat, and let the coals cook the meats for twenty-four hours. We will have food and wine and music and dancing. Everyone on the rancho is to come. All our neighbors are to come. I've even invited some of the people of Santa Fé." Don Miguel took a deep breath and continued.

"This fiesta is in honor of Caleb, although I think it honors us all. And surely everyone will have a good time. I have just learned that this very week he will be sixteen years old. And I thought he was at least one hundred because of his wisdom and courage in rescuing Don Pedro."

They all laughed good-naturedly as Caleb turned red at the praise being heaped upon him by Don Miguel. He lowered his head in embarrassment.

María was sixteen also, although in some ways she was much older. María was looking at Caleb intently. She was seeing more in him all the time. *Has he grown taller since I first saw him?* It was puzzling how she missed him and how he kept coming into her thoughts when they were apart. Even in the night when she was in her bed, she would see him in her thoughts, and miss him, and wish he was there so he could talk to her. It was a strange feeling. A peculiar shortness of breath seemed to overcome her when she thought about him. *What a strange feeling this is,* she thought. *He is too thin, that is true, but he is also handsome in a rugged sort of way, for an American.*

CHAPTER 5
Love Leads to Passion.

The fiesta music had started and the guests had been arriving all day. Children were running everywhere, excited by the sight of all the strangers and the music.

Father *de Silva* gave a long blessing and talked of the new chapel of *La María*. He explained how much of a blessing this would bring to the rancho and its *patrón*, *Don Miguel de Vargas*, their master. He did not mention that the Indian woman and the girl, who were much improved, were now helping him prepare food for the poor. No one who came to the back door of the church in trouble was ever to be turned down for a bowl of soup and package of tortillas, and some food to take away with them. The *patrón* had ordered it so.

It was time for the formal beginning of the fiesta. *Don Miguel de Vargas* was to dance the first dance with his wife, the *Señora*. Just before beginning the dance, Don Miguel looked around but could not find Caleb. "Stop! Wait!" Don Miguel stopped the musicians who had started to play already. "Our guest of honor is not here! He should help me start the dancing. Where has Caleb gone?"

Caleb was in the shadows behind the crowd watching the festivities with some *peóns*. When Don Miguel called out for the music to stop and inquired where Caleb was, the *peóns* standing beside him all called out, "He is here! Here he is!" They all pointed at him, grinning at his discomfiture at having everyone looking at him. Most of the guests had not met or even seen him yet.

Don Miguel heard the *peóns* and saw them pointing at Caleb at the back of the crowd. "María, you go fetch that bashful boy out there and make him dance with you," Don Miguel told his daughter, pointing his finger toward Caleb. "I order you to bring him up here now. Go and do it!" With a big smile, she ran to Caleb, grabbed his hand, and pulled him out of the shadows. At the same time, the crowd around him was pushing him forward and laughing at him in a friendly way.

"But, María," he argued, "be reasonable. I have never danced before. I don't know how to dance!"

"Then pray for another miracle for your skinny legs because you are going to dance every dance with me. My father has ordered it, and I obey my father's orders—and so must you when you are on this rancho! He is the master here!"

Don Miguel, Don Pedro, and María were all laughing. Of all the people on the rancho, only Caleb was frowning and embarrassed. But he tried to follow María through the dance steps as best as he could. After the third dance he was doing fairly well, passably well, or at least he thought so. It was good enough, although dancing was not to be his strong point, it was obvious to everyone.

María teased, "Don't be sad that you have difficulty dancing. Almost everyone here can dance. Even the smallest children can dance, but you are the only one here who can perform miracles!"

"That's it!" María said approvingly. "Now stand there a few moments and let me look at you. Turn around slowly. Not with your head down! You are not a dog. You are a beautiful young man. Stand up straight and put your shoulders back. Suck in your stomach. Hold your chest out. That's it! That's it! Stand up tall, and be proud! Smile! You have a beautiful body, be proud of yourself. You are truly beautiful! Remember that!"

She laughed at his confusion over what she was saying. It was as if she were not talking to him but rather some ghost in her own mind. "Come, we will go into the shadows and practice some more." She led him to a place she knew, out of sight of the others, behind the buildings and down a dark passageway under an old arbor covered with vines that had to be parted to let them in. This place was dark and cool. A forgotten place of sanctuary where she sometimes came to think, dream and remember. It was a quiet, secluded small patio, located next to a low wall. There was a massive flat-timber bench where she sat sometimes and contemplated and prayed and thought of her previous lover. It was dark here, very dark. No one could see them. They could hardly see each other. But they could still hear the far off music and feel each other. She should not have led him here.

"María, we should not be here alone. Your father will worry about us. Let's go back," Caleb told her.

"No! There is no going back now!" she said, as she maneuvered him in front of the low wall and backed him up against it. She leaned against him, still pushing him back with her own body, toward the bench holding him to her, pressing her body against him and kissing him. She kissed him as Polly had kissed him on their ill-fated trip to Santa Fé.

María kissed him as a lover would kiss, with passion and promise. She could feel her passion grow more intense every time she thought about Caleb. She could feel him responding. She knew now that in the secret places of her mind she had been consumed with desire for him ever since he had come to the ranch. She had waited a long time for this moment. No, there was to be no going back.

She kissed him again and again, inviting more, pressing her tongue into his not unwilling mouth. He tried to stop her. He knew the surge of Polly's passion, the woman he had traveled across part of Mexico from Independence with. He had truly come to love her. But Polly was dead. Slowly he succumbed to her, knowing he should stop and wanting to stop; but he couldn't help himself as she forced her tongue into his mouth. He drank in her sweet juices, unable to resist. She tasted too good to be denied. He could tell that her breathing was becoming more labored. She pressed her bosom against him even harder. He could feel her deep breathing coming faster and faster. She pressed her vagina, her sheath that would engulf him, toward his now responding organ. He was reacting too. He couldn't help himself.

"No, María, don't!" he told her, but without much conviction. He tried to stop, but only half-heartedly.

Wildly, she pressed him back down onto the bench. She raised her skirt—she was wearing nothing underneath. She had not worn underwear, for in the back of her mind she had already planned this encounter. She had fantasized last night and all day about how to manipulate him to just this spot. She wanted to be ready. And because she had helped make his clothes, she already knew where every button was on his trousers. In her mind she had already undone them dozens of times. She eagerly pulled open the front of his trousers.

Her vagina had been wet almost continuously throughout the day as she planned what she would do with him. María had made up her mind. She knew what she wanted, and she was not about to let him put her off. The more he tried to stop her, the greater her determination became.

And he was human, too. His body was responding even while he tried to ward her off. She had him lying down on his back on the bench.

Caleb decided that he had resisted enough. He would not try to stop her any more. In fact, he would not have let her stop now even if she had wanted to. He was her's now; and she was his in their uncontrolled passion of youth. If his passion was not as forceful as hers, it was now at least fully turned on.

She pulled her blouse up, baring her bosom to him. "Touch them! Hold them!" she ordered brusquely. Her voice broke, as she demanded that he grasp her breasts and caress her nipples. She did not have to ask twice. His lips found her lips, and his hands kept hold of her breasts, knurling the nipples between his fingers and pulling them, just as she wanted. She had lighted his fire, and now it would have to be quenched.

She roughly grabbed his hot-tipped penis, already dripping wet. His mind said no, but his body and passion did not agree. She forced him into her hot, wet vagina, holding him there in a vice of passion that gripped them both.

She felt the change in him as he gave in to her. She felt his arms embrace her, and she relaxed. She knew there would be no turning back now. He was no longer resisting. He was thrusting now. How could he have stopped it at that point? He couldn't, of course; and he definitely didn't want to. A few minutes earlier she had treated him resentfully because he was resisting her advances or seemed to be, and she could not tolerate being on the verge of rejection. But now she knew he was not going to reject her.

What else could he do except enter wholeheartedly into the wanton lovemaking orchestrated by this willful teenager who would not stop at anything once her mind was made up? Once he succumbed, his own passion grew to match hers. She was only doing what he subconsciously wanted to do. After all, this was merely a release of his own desire. But never had he experienced such wild and wanton passion.

It had started out as a sort of game to María. She was stalking him. He was so awkward and bashful that she was sure she had superior knowledge in these matters. She would make him do what he did not want to do. She would not take no for an answer. However, his ignorance in these matters did not quite work out the way she expected. His response was more experienced than she thought it might have been, but so much the better for the pleasure of it.

She felt the strange and wonderful hardening of his penis just as he came inside of her. Somehow it thrilled her to know she had captured his moment of maximum pleasure, and had presented it to him. But she was disappointed at his dwindling effort and drive after he had his orgasm. She was not finished. She wanted more! She could tell she would have to wait and be patient, at least for a while.

She would not let him withdraw. She would not let him get up yet. But he didn't want to anyhow. Her vaginal contractions on his softening penis were just too pleasant a feeling. Yes, his penis was soft now; but the internal contact still felt good to both of them. She would wait for him to gather strength, and she would not be denied. She continued to lie squarely on top of him.

She was still kissing him. Playing tongue games with him. Purring sweet Spanish words into his ears that his brain did not quite understand but his heart understood full well. After fifteen minutes she began to rock back and forth on him, testing him. And she began to taunt him. She was now daring him to try again. It did not take long. They both felt him begin to react. Once again he was stirring, slowly he was responding to her once again.

His response was slower this time. They both wanted to fulfill her hunger. He kissed her lips, her neck, her eyelids. Her heart was beating rapidly again. He told her sweet things in English that she could not understand, but her body understood. She felt the meanings of his words; and she reveled in them. He tried to tell her sweet things in Spanish as he pushed up inside her with his penis. She heard what she wanted to hear. She felt him reaching into her, and she felt what she wanted to feel.

He finally convinced her to let him get up, once he assured her he would not stop. He wanted to get on top. She wanted him on top too. He took her blouse off and laid it on the board under her. He kissed her breasts and suckled at each one. He lifted her skirt, his nostrils reveling in the fragrant expression from her excited vagina, taunting him, inviting him. He stepped out of his pants and took his moccasin shoes off. It was too dark for her to see him prepare himself, but she was secretly laughing at the impracticality of men's clothing. So unhandy. Why didn't they wear a skirt like a woman? It could be lifted at any time for immediate access.

He moved his thumb onto her clitoris, his finger slipping down inside of her. She moaned as he stroked her, in and out for several minutes. Even if he did not quite have the experience and sensitivity of her former lover, it was still good and satisfying. She pulled him over on top of her, and was glad when his penis entered her exactly on cue. He slowly increased his tempo but was doing it too slowly for her. She wanted fast now. She wanted climax. She knew it was out there somewhere.

The second climax was even better for Caleb. He enjoyed it greatly. It was everything it could be for a man. He was still holding her right nipple in his hand as she worked up and down under him.

It never occurred to María that the foreplay, which had been so slow and so maddening to her, would prepare her for a response beyond anything she could have dreamed of.

She was rising to meet his every thrust. She turned and twisted under him, trying every way she could to get the greatest possible satisfaction. She manipulated his penis wildly to bring more depth and pleasure to her senses. She was panting. Her nostrils were flared and swollen. She was pulling his buttocks down with her hands, molding them, almost hurting them. The two lovers were lifting and plunging in unison, over and over, rapidly, as they settled into a natural rhythm.

It was like an explosion between her legs, in her mind, in her heart, in her breasts. She had never imagined that another lover could bring her as much pleasure as her first and only other lover had done. Her thoughts were in a tumult. *Was Caleb just as good as her other lover had been? Or was he even better? Could that be possible? No, it could not be. Or could it?*

Finally. "There it is! That's it! That's it!" she moaned. "Don't stop! Oh! Ooooh! Oh!" She had reached the top, her apex, and her zenith. Her moment was achieved!

This time she moaned and groaned so noisily that he feared she would call the whole rancho down upon them. He began to kiss her again more to quiet her than for any other reason, but she answered his kisses by sucking his tongue down into her mouth and moving her whole head back and forth in ecstasy. He was a bit relieved that she was on the way down now, her spasms slowly receding, tightening, then letting go of him.

She was still holding him down on her, kissing him, sucking his tongue. She was smiling now, her wild passion and abandon slaking.

She was enjoying the completion, relaxing but still feeling the joy of her fulfillment. She was holding him tightly to her. "I will never let you go!" she whispered into his ear.

The day after the fiesta, Caleb told Don Miguel that he was going to Santa Fé to pick up his supplies and pack horses, which were still at the Bartholomew store. The time had come for him to move on. He planned on taking his trading goods to the valley near Taos to trade for furs. He would start there and then work his way to the rendezvous he had heard about in the Stony Rocky Mountains to the north. A rendezvous was a summer meeting, or marketplace, of trappers, traders, and Indians in the Rocky Mountains. Large profits could be made there. He had heard that as many as 200 trappers and hundreds of Indians met there for several weeks to trade furs and peltry for guns, powder, lead, whiskey and other goods.

But first he had to get away from María. During the three days of the fiesta she had stalked him relentlessly, demanding that he take her back into the arbor. Once she would get hold of his hand or arm she would not let him go until he promised to meet her there. There was no denying her.

Not that he wanted to refuse her. She excited him, and he wanted her as much or more than she wanted him. He was being drawn closer to her, and could not take his eyes off her when she was around him. Worse yet, she used every possible opportunity to brush up against him and press her breasts against his arms. She laughed at him. She teased him. She would blow kisses at him in the hallway, in the patio, whenever their eyes met.

Caleb knew they were bound to get in trouble with her father if he stayed there. It was just a matter of time. He did not want to get her in trouble, nor let his friends down. She was already promised to another. He had to flee, and quickly too, for both of their sakes.

Don Miguel was a worldly man. He knew the signs. He was relieved when Caleb told him that he was leaving and he knew why, although he did not say so. Teenage girls, he was learning, were difficult to manage. And they could be quite strange. One moment they were on a religious crusade, and the next moment they were chasing a boy shamelessly down the hall. She was beyond his understanding. She was beyond his control. The quicker he could get her married, the better off they would all be.

Caleb's horse was saddled and waiting for him, and Juan was already on his horse. Caleb said good-bye to Don Miguel, and then to Don Pedro and the *Señora*. Only María was missing. He hesitated awkwardly because he wanted to say good-bye to her. Finally, as he was getting ready to mount his horse, the crying, sobbing María came running out of the house and threw her arms around his neck, to the dismay and consternation of her father and everyone else who was there.

"I know you have to go. It is right that you go!" She sobbed. Then, in front of everyone she kissed him on the mouth and told him, "My heart goes with you, my miracle man. Go with my blessing and God's. Take my heart and go now! I love you, and I always will!"

Don Miguel started forward to stop her, but his wife the *Señora* held his arm and whispered to him, "Wait! She is saying good-bye, and that is the most you can hope for or expect. Let it go."

María then ran back into the house sobbing hysterically. Even though Caleb was not María's first love, parting from him tore at her teenage heart, her soul, her being. She knew that it must be done so in her father's world, but that only made it hurt more deeply, because there was no hope at all for her love to be fulfilled.

She would retreat to God, Christ, and his Mother, and wallow in self-pity and anguish for her lovers' sake. What else could she do? She would miss him so. She would take her rosary, and get on her knees and pray and pray for his well-being. But although prayer helps a little, time is the only true cure for this kind of pain: a broken heart. Already it had been broken twice, and she was still so young.

CHAPTER 6
María.

To know María better we will have to go back three years. María was less frightened than the other six girls waiting with her. She had traveled 1,500 miles from her father's ranch, to get here. And she was certainly not afraid of a bunch of nuns cloistered away for life in a tiny school 15 miles north of Mexico City.

On the long journey from New Mexico to Mexico City she had turned 13 years old and bled for the first time. Her aunt, her chaperon, helped her and showed her how to take care of herself. He monthly event after that was quite regular and bothered her less all the time as they continued their journey.

The four-month trip to Mexico City was the greatest adventure of her life, although it had been full of danger, and excitement. She loved the opportunities to learn new things and thoroughly enjoyed the physically demanding trip. She traveled with a large caravan of cargo wagons sent to Mexico City to deliver freight and bring back supplies. A retinue of servants pampered María and her aunt, who had come along as her chaperon. They treated María and her aunt with every courtesy and care every step of the way, washing their clothes, cooking their meals and setting up their tent every night.

Even though María was only thirteen years old, her father had decided to send her off to the school because he could no longer tolerate her rebellious behavior. He had lost his patience with his beautiful, headstrong, spoiled daughter.

When Don Miguel told María that he was sending her to school in Mexico City, she refused to go. She ran to her room and refused to come out. But in the end, when he lost his temper and threatened to knock her door down and beat her, she finally gave in—but only because she could not think of an alternative. She considered running away to the mountains, but rejected the idea after realizing that being captured by wild Indians did not seem a better alternative than going to a far away school, after all.

María was further upset when she overheard her father telling her mother that when she returned after two years, she was to be sent to California to marry her father's distant cousin, *Don Alfonso de Vargas*. The purpose of this marriage was to unify two great ranching families. She had never seen her uncle, but she knew that he was over 50 years old; and his wife had died in childbirth with their eighth baby girl. Don Alfonso had tried everything to have a son but had failed, at least so far. Don Alfonso's oldest daughter was fifteen years older than María, and his youngest was just a little older than María.

María was already almost older than she should have been for marriage. Twelve, was thought to be the most desirable age. It was thought wise to marry a girl when they were young because then the husband could train his wife to do as he wished. María was definitely not ready for marriage. She was a long way from being an obedient child-bearer who would help Don Miguel protect his family interests and cement his relationship with his far off cousin.

After all, a wife needed first of all to be obedient. María was not even respectful. Willful better described her frame of mind. She would not willingly help in cementing his interests with her betrothed. In fact, just the opposite might prove to be the case unless Don Miguel could somehow bring discipline and obedience into her life.

He had heard that The School of the Nuns of the Stations of the Cross specialized in transforming wayward and disobedient female children into dutiful wives and mothers. The school served the best families in Mexico. The girls sent there would be kept cloistered for two years to learn their lessons of obedience, humility, and love of God. Self-discipline was the major attribute they would be taught. They would learn obedience to their fathers and husbands, and how to take solace in prayer. This sounded good to Don Miguel, the perfect formula for training María and preparing her for the husband to whom she had been promised.

There was something wrong with all of these girls, or at the least their fathers thought something was wrong with them. Why else would they be here? If they had all been dutiful and obedient, they would be promised in marriages arranged by their fathers, or already married and bearing children for their husbands and for the Church. But instead, they had all been uprooted from their familiar surroundings and sent off to this school to be educated in what was important for women to learn.

Their wealthy, upper-class families had reared the other girls waiting with María, whose ages ranged from 11 to 15, in the traditional Spanish-Mexican ways. Accordingly, most of them could neither read nor write, and their experiences beyond the walls of their *haciendas* were very limited. They would learn to read and write, a very little, at the school, yes, but only a little.

In contrast, María could read and write, and was in fact quite well read. An aunt had taught her reading, writing, arithmetic as well as some history and geography. Once she learned how to read, María hungered for knowledge. She read every book on their New Mexico rancho, mainly the ones her father had on the shelf in his office. He had not read all of the leather-bound volumes himself, but María had read them all at least once and the classical literature twice or more. Her imagination was stirred by the stories of kings, knights, Spanish soldiers, and priests of the Old World in Spain.

The library also held a small group of books written in English, mostly classical novels and textbooks that her father had used in school. María taught herself a fair amount of English from these books, and was somewhat proficient at reading it, though she could not pronounce the words, as her father would not teach her or help her.

Don Miguel had not sent her to this school to be further educated in either a worldly or classical sense. It was thought that women did not need to read or write, and it was probably better if she was not well educated at all. Don Miguel realized too late that it had been a mistake to teach María to read. This lay partly at least at the root of her problem. She already knew too much, and thought too much, as well as having too much imagination and ideas of her own about what she wanted and liked.

The other girls were all from near Mexico City, while María was from the frontier territory—from the wilderness. The others immediately regarded her as an outsider. In addition, her haughty, know-it-all manner conveyed what she thought about them and how deeply she resented being there.

The girls were picked up from a central plaza in Mexico City and driven to the school in a large carriage drawn by six horses. Two men sat in the driver's seat on top of the carriage. Two nuns dressed in black robes and white hats, or in habit, as it was called, were inside, one on either side by the doors. Once they were all loaded and the carriage was on its way, the nuns took up stations by the windows, closing the curtains so the girls were sitting in semi-darkness. The girls could not see the city or the countryside, and it was stuffy and hot in the closed cramped carriage. The trip could have been enjoyable if they had been able to look out the windows, and feel the breeze. But, as it was, it was unpleasant.

María complained to the nuns about the closed windows. "Open the curtains so we can get fresh air and look out!" she demanded. "We want to see where we are going and look at the countryside. It is stuffy in here, and we can hardly breathe. Open the curtains!"

"Do not talk! Remain silent, you insolent girl!" The older of the two nuns barked at María. "The windows are ordered by the Mother Superior to be closed. They must remain closed until we arrive at the school." Then the nun scolded her rudely, "You should remain quiet and pray for your soul!"

They traveled all day and into the evening hours in the miserable stuffy, semi-darkness. They stopped only three times for a brief rest and to go to the toilet. It was evening when they finally arrived in front of the tall wooden gates in the adobe wall that surrounded the school. The wall was 3-feet thick and 15-feet high, and was topped with pointed ironwork bars that rose up another 4 feet. The wooden gates were opened after the hallooing of the driver continued for several minutes.

The girls did not even see the outside of the school wall, because the curtains were not drawn open until the carriage was inside the courtyard in front of the doorway to the waiting room. They had seen nothing on the entire 15-mile trip. They did not even know which direction they had been traveling.

María had made up her mind to complain to the Mother Superior about the lack of courtesy of the two escorting nuns, who made everyone sit in semi-darkness and prohibited them from talking or looking out the carriage windows. Such rude rules did not make any sense.

An unsmiling nun dressed in habit, a black robe, black shoes, black stockings, and white hat, led them into the waiting room, which also served as a prayer room. The nun did not speak to them until they were inside of the building, and then it was to tell them to be quiet and wait.

When their guide left the room, she closed the thick wooden doors that led outside. The girls heard the wooden timbers drop noisily into place on the other side. A pair of timbers, or bars, on the outside of the door could be dropped into a U-shaped holder, and opened only from the outside, thus keeping everyone in. And the timbers on the inside could be dropped into place only by someone inside, keeping everyone out. The girls were locked in now, and everyone outside was locked out.

At María's father's hacienda they had similar wooden bars to hold the shutters and doors closed against Indian attacks, and to keep wind and rain out of the house. They had one servant whose duty it was to close and latch the storm doors from the inside every night, but she could not imagine why they were also locked on the outside.

The girls did not know it yet, but they would be inside the walls of the school for two years. Here they were cloistered completely away from all outside influences. The school servants and workers lived in cottages outside of the walls. Inside the walls there were five teaching nuns plus the Mother Superior and, of course, the 35 students. The girls would not see any members of their families again for two years, nor would they ever set foot outside of the walled compound during their stay. They could not even write letters.

Sister Seraphena was in charge of the small wing of the building that was to house the seven new girls. For this group of girls waiting inside the reception room, Sister Seraphena was to be their only contact with anyone except for each other and an occasional priest at Mass. There were, however, the other students with whom they would study and attend classes.

It was Sister Seraphena's responsibility to mold and plan the future of these young ladies, while in this school, and afterward. They would each become obedient to their father's will and God's will. Sister threatened that if they did not behave well when they got out, they would be sent back to school for two more years. None ever actually returned, but this threat always got them going in the right direction during the first few weeks.

The girls stood awkwardly in the entrance room. Beside each one was a small satchel, which held the few possessions they would be allowed to keep. The short list of permitted personal items was limited to essentials. They were allowed only a few items of clothing: five pair of under-drawers, two nightgowns, three handkerchiefs, seven pair of knee-length black woolen socks, one comb and one hairbrush, and two pair of plain lace-up black shoes without fancy stitch-work, embroidery or buckles. And every girl was to have a rosary and prayer book, of course. Everything not on the list was to be furnished by the school. The girls would all wear identical uniforms. They would all have their hair cropped, which the nuns would tell them was to minimize the risk of head lice. (Although María's father had been told that his daughter's hair would be shorn, he had not passed that information on to her because he knew it would only trigger more tantrums.)

Neither the girls nor their parents knew the primary reason for requiring the girls to wear uniforms, and have their hair cut short, was to transform them in every way possible into identical clones. The purpose was to stifle their individuality and high spirits, and thus make them more receptive to the lessons they were to be taught here.

The windows of the waiting room, high up just under the ceiling, contained beautiful religious scenes made of stained glass. The evening sunlight streaming in through the glass set off patterns of beautiful colors. Each stained-glass window illustrated one of the Fourteen Stations of the Cross, with seven scenes on either side of the room. The windows were some 10 feet from the floor, much too high for anyone to look out, even if one could see through the stained glass. And there were iron bars on the inside of the windows. The bars were ornate and artistic; but they were, nevertheless, bars.

Along the long side walls of the room at the floor level were indentations containing beautiful religious scenes representing the Stations of the Cross. There was a different scene in each of the 14 alcoves. Each niche contained a statue dressed in beautiful cloth and displayed in front of painted scenery. Latin inscriptions, explaining what each station was celebrating, were also indented into the wall.

The Fourteen Stations of the Cross arose as a devotion sometime prior to the fifteenth century. The Franciscan Fathers developed this devotion to venerate those special places that were sanctified by the sufferings of Christ as he made his way to the cross. By visiting the Stations of the Cross and meditating at them, one could gain special indulgences, thinking of the passion and death of their Lord Jesus Christ.

María admired the pictorial representations in the stained glass and noted the wrought-iron bars in front of the widows. *Perhaps the bars are to offer protection from anyone outside trying to get in, but they are just as able to keep anyone inside from getting out. What kind of school is this, anyhow? This is almost like a prison!* María frowned, irritated at the thought that they were locked up inside this place.

The floor under their feet was made of a beautiful warm-hued brown quartz-sandstone that sparkled and glittered with very fine particles of mica schist embedded in it. The hand-chiseled and polished stones fit so tightly together that there was no room between each irregular shaped tile.

At the end of the long room was a small dark-stained wooden platform with a low railing in front of it. This was the whole focus of the room. On a stand on the platform was one larger-than-life-sized painting encased in an ornate golden-colored-frame. On the platform was a small stool-like stand holding a large golden candelabrum. Five candles were burning in this stately candelabrum, lighted to enhance the beauty of the painting, and focus attention on it.

A black polished-marble cross, 4 feet high, stood besides the painting. On the crosspiece of the crucifix were six narrow bands of gold, three on each side. Eight narrow bands of gold encircled the vertical portion of the cross, three above the cross-arm and five below it. There were, then, a total of fourteen bands of gold on the beautifully polished cross.

The number fourteen had great significance to this order of nuns. The name of the school was The School Of The Nuns Of The Stations Of The Cross. And the order's theme, the Fourteen Stations of the Cross, was repeated in various ways throughout the school.

The room was dominated by the large painting of the Madonna, in a long flowing robe, holding the baby Christ child. She was holding him lovingly against her shoulder, and he was facing forward so his circumcised nakedness could be seen. The Madonna was standing on swirling clouds that partially covered her feet, creating the sensation that she was suspended above the earth. A bright heavenly light seemed to be pouring in from behind her. On either side of the Madonna were the pictures of two people kneeling before her. At the lower front of the picture were two winged, dimpled cherubs looking out from the picture. From some angles the cherubs seemed to be looking up at the

Christ Child. The painting of a drapery along the top and sides of the picture created a depth of field and tied all of the elements of the painting together as if it were a play, instead of a picture.

María thought that the painting was the most beautiful thing she had ever seen. She made the sign of the cross and stood in awe of its perfection. Then she noticed that the Madonna's eyes seemed to follow her wherever she stood in the room.

Mother Superior was 80-years old now, and she devoted herself mostly to prayer and work in the small flower garden outside her private quarters. She walked dutifully through the school several times a day to make sure all was in good order, smiling and nodding to the other nuns. She frowned at, or ignored, the students and almost never spoke to any of them. It was not her place. The students were to look only to the sister who was in charge of their group for directions and instruction.

Sister Seraphena had arrived here when she was 20-years old, straight out of the nunnery in Mexico City. She had been here 12 years now and had never once set foot outside of the convent-like school. She had no desire whatsoever to leave these premises. These walls held her entire world. She had taken vows to stay cloistered with the children within the school.

Her behavior was so exemplary that Mother Superior had taken notice of her. She had seen to it that Sister Seraphena was being considered to replace her as director of the school when she died, or was too old to function. This time was drawing very close now, and she knew and accepted it. Soon she could see God who she had devoted here entire adult life toward, and now she was looking forward to it.

Sister Seraphena did not know she was being considered to replace Mother Superior, an idea she would have rejected anyway because she knew herself to be too unworthy. Sometimes she felt she had sinned so much that she did not deserve to be a nun at all. She loved the life here too much to be worthy. Surely no one should be as happy and satisfied as she was.

Sister Seraphena herself had become a full-fledged nun to avoid marrying the man her father had selected for her. Her reasons for rejecting him were complex, and she herself did not even fully understand them. In the first place, she had only met him twice. He was a lecherous old man of 45 years whose wife had died in childbirth. His teeth were rotten, and he smelled bad because he did not bathe. These were reasons enough to resist him, although not the paramount one.

There were urges within Sister Seraphena to avoid the loving arms of a man, any man at all, and especially this man. She hated him on sight. She got sick at her stomach in front of her father when they discussed her betrothed. This behavior brought her another whipping from her father with the thick leather strop that he used to put the fine edge on his straight razor blade. He used the same 3-foot long 4-inch wide, thick leather strop to beat his children when they needed it. And in his view they needed it often.

The truth was that Sister Seraphena despised all men, particularly her father, who so little understood her. He was mean to her mother, whom Seraphena deeply loved and respected. He spent most of his nights away in a villa he kept for his many lovers, while she and her mother spent their evenings secretly ranting against him. Because of Seraphena's refusal to marry, her father had sent her to be a novice in a nuns' school in order to learn discipline and obedience. While in the school she learned that she could not possibly contemplate marrying any man. It was while she was there that she realized she hated men, all of them.

When Seraphena first went to the school to study to be a nun, she was assigned the room adjoining that of her prefect. Her prefect was a senior novice with the right of discipline, though not yet exactly a nun yet herself. Seraphena considered her a nun already. There, Seraphena spent two heavenly years, where her own dormant natural instincts had been allowed to mature and flower. She learned the lessons of humility, obedience, and love of God. But at the same time, she fell deeply in love with her prefect, teacher, and eventual secret lover.

Sister Seraphena loved being a nun, but she was not proud of her secret sexuality. Nevertheless, she had come to grips with it. She hid it every way she could. But she now freely admitted to herself that she was what God had made her, so it must be that was what he meant for her to be. She had joined the cloistered nuns to avoid having to marry the man whom her father had selected for her and had found love of a very different kind.

Six of the seven new students were standing ready to meet Sister Seraphena. The haughty, insolent-looking one had sat down in the only chair in the room. Sister had already looked upon them from the walkway that led into her dormitory wing. She held a list of names on a piece of paper but could not yet connect the names to the faces. However, she had memorized the list of names, as well as the letters of introduction, each father had sent to her. The fathers had described the habits, faults, attitudes, and special problems that needed her attention in each of the young ladies.

All of the sisters wore a smaller replica of the black marble cross that stood beside the picture in the prayer room. Identical black ebony crosses with fourteen tiny bands of gold were suspended from a chain of fine gold that hung around their necks. The cross was the badge of their devotion. It hung in front of them when they walked. It was held in their hand when they were at prayers. It was the symbol of their holy order. As Sister Seraphena observed the new group of students from outside the room, she absent-mindedly kissed her cross, something she did at least a hundred times every day.

Sister Seraphena straightened her shoulders, stood up straight, and walked swiftly and stiffly into the room. It was important to establish absolute authority immediately, and no other nun was more authoritarian than Sister Seraphena. Her stiffly starched black robe grated on the floor noisily as she walked. Her white hat had a rounded crown and a large brim that curved up all around. Sister Seraphena was an intimidating presence.

She slowly passed in front of each of the awkwardly standing girls, asking their names. She looked piercingly into their eyes until they lowered their heads in submission. She scowled at each one. They thought her eyes were the meanest they had ever seen. After she identified each face in front of her, she knew that the one girl she had not yet spoken to must be the one called by her father, María.

María was still sitting in the room's single chair, watching the menacing nun as she confronted the other girls. She was already determined that she would begin her list of complaints as soon as the officious nun came over to ask her name.

Sister Seraphena stood in front of María and looked at her with contempt. "Get out of that chair!" she barked. "That chair belongs to Mother Superior, and no one else sits in it! Who are you, and what do you think you are?" Sister immediately attacked her verbally. "But then we know about you, don't we? You must be María. We already know that you think you are better than everyone else here. You think you should sit while the other girls and I stand. That's it, isn't it?" Sister turned away from the confused María and walked back to the other girls before María could say anything. María stood up in confusion beside the chair. But she could feel her temper rising.

"Line up!" Sister barked again, this time at all the girls. "Line up and quit smiling. No talking!" she admonished one of the girls, who had attempted to greet her. "You may talk in your rooms. You may answer questions when I or one of the other nuns speak to you. You may talk in the courtyard when you have rest time in the afternoons. Except for that, you will always be silent, and you will listen. Place your bags open in front of you and line up along the wall there. Hurry up!" She clapped her hands smartly three times for emphasis. The girls laid open their bags and stood awkwardly behind them.

Dolores, the oldest, was fifteen and fat. She already had a double chin. In her bag, on top of everything else, was more than 10 pounds of chocolate. Sister looked sternly at her. "Hand me that chocolate, you fat pig of a girl, Dolores! Do you know why you are here? You are here because you are too fat for your father to find any man who will have you as a wife! You are a disgrace to your own family as well as to yourself and God! You are guilty of the sin of gluttony. You are obese. Hurry now, move quickly! You will eat no candy here, Dolores, and you will lose weight and become slim, so you can fulfill your father's wishes for you. Do you understand me?"

"Yes, Sister." Dolores was on the verge of tears.

"There will no crying, either. You are a woman full grown, past your prime already. You are too old to cry, for no good reason. Stop it, or I will give you something to cry about!"

Sister stopped next in front of María, who was now standing behind her satchel, which was much larger than the other girl's satchels, frowning her defiance. She was looking Sister in the eye and refused to lower her gaze.

"Your name is María!"

"Yes, Sister. María, Sister." She curtsied. "I am sorry I sat in the. . . ."

"Silence! Do not talk unless I ask you a question. Then only answer the question."

"Yes, I know you, María! You are the worst girl of the lot. You are disobedient to your father, and you have been spoiled. You will do penance here. But in the end, if you survive here, you will be the better for it so that you can marry the man your father has chosen for you and bear him children, as you are supposed to do, in God's order of things."

Sister Seraphena frowned her disapproval at María. But inwardly she liked what she saw. María was tall, slim, and beautiful. Sister admired the shining black eyes, waist length long hair, and the jeweled crown-like pearl-adorned comb in her hair. She held her head high. She was haughty and proud. Her thirteen-year-old tiny breasts were just budding out in front. She was not afraid, like the other girls. She was angry and ready to rebel at whatever she did not like. Sister was happy with what she saw. Very happy. But she gave no sign of it. She scowled at her, instead.

"Give me that comb setting on your head like a crown! You were told to bring only one comb for combing your hair. That jeweled comb in your hair is a mark of your sinfulness and disobedience. You are trying to defy me in front of the rest of these young ladies even now, aren't you? You think you are better than everyone else here, don't you?" She held out her hand for the comb.

María resentfully handed the comb to the frowning nun. She had forgotten it was even there on top of her head. It was insignificant. She always wore a curved comb in her hair to keep the mass of hair in place. Her hair would fall all the way down her back below her waist if it were not supported in some way. She was very proud of her long beautiful hair. She showed her displeasure by plopping the comb down disrespectfully and smartly in Sister's hand, almost hurtfully.

Scowling at María, Sister scolded her further. "Go back to the doors there where you came in. Lower the bars and lock the doors here on the inside. Kneel down beside the doors and pray. That is always to be your station here. At prayers you will always kneel there by yourself, so you can remember not to sit in the chair. Do not move off your knees until I tell you to move. Take your satchel with you. Be silent and pray." María did not know it, but she had been selected from all the girls for special treatment. She was the one to be tested.

Whirling around to Dolores, Sister said, "Dolores, you are in charge of these other young ladies as you seem to be the oldest. They will look to you for their care and comfort. You will learn not to be lazy, and you will lose that fat! Yes, you will lose all of the fat, and you will take care of these other young ladies as if you were their mother, and you will learn responsibility."

"If they get sick due to your neglect and if you fail in your duties, or if you talk to María, you will then take the place of María, who is the worst of the lot of you. If you take her place, you will scrub floors every day in penance. If your young ladies are not happy, and if they do not do their lessons well, you will take María's place. And believe me, you will not like it! None of you are to speak to María. Only I may speak to her. Do you understand me? Answer me when I speak to you!" She reached up and pulled a strand of Dolores's hair as hard as she could, pulling out several hairs.

"Can't you see that these young ladies who are in your charge are frightened? Hold the hand of the youngest there and pull her in close to you. Hug her! Protect her! How can you expect to comfort your ladies if you do not show them affection? What sort of mother will you turn out to be? You are to love these young ladies as you love life. That is the lesson you are to learn here. Do you understand me? Love these ladies and protect them!"

"Yes, Sister." Dolores was crying, huge tears rolling down her fat cheeks. She pulled the youngest girl in next to her, holding her close to her side as she had been told to do. She was hoping, too, that doing so would protect her from Sister Seraphena. She placed the youngest between herself and the Sister as a sort of shield.

Sister noticed what she was doing and started to say something, but then she decided she had already said enough. It was not perfection coming from Dolores, but it was a start toward obedience. "Now you other young ladies, you are to look to Dolores here. She is to take care of you. If she fails you, you tell me; and we will punish her. Pick up your satchels and follow me down this hallway to our wing of the school. This is your new home."

"Now, Dolores, you are in charge under me. All of you follow Dolores, and Dolores will follow me. And remember this! You are not to speak to María!"

She walked back to María, who was still on her knees by the door. She crooked her finger calling María, "Come, everyone, follow right behind me," she ordered and then strode off without looking back. She led them into the wing of the building that was to be their home for the next two years.

"Dolores, you will put your satchel into this third room, in the middle of your girls. You will assign the rooms on either side of you to the two youngest ladies. You have connecting doors into their rooms. If they or the other girls knock on your door, you let them in. Dolores, you will assign each girl her room and help her get settled. You are to help these young ladies get into bed."

"No one will have supper this evening because you are too fat," Sister announced to Dolores. "Everyone will go to bed without supper to help you in your sinful obesity. I will, of course, also go without supper. We will all do penance for your sin. You will show your ladies how to pray on their knees. You will personally take each one of them through their rosary and prayers, one at a time, and ask their forgiveness for your obesity."

Turning then to all of the girls, Sister said, "In the closet across the hall from your rooms are your skirts and blouses. You will put the clothes you have on now and your other things away in the drawers in your rooms, and you will not wear those clothes again until you leave. In the meantime, you will all dress in the uniforms that we provide you."

Then Sister turned again to Dolores. "Dolores, you will fit each of the young ladies in your care with clothing of the right size. If necessary, there are needles and thread in this closet in the sewing basket. You will help them and teach them how to repair their clothes should they need mending or altering. You are to help each girl select two outfits and put the spare one in the drawers in their rooms. Do you understand me?"

"Yes, Sister," the hapless Dolores answered. She made an attempt at a curtsy.

After handing Dolores a lighted candle, Sister picked up two blouses and two skirts that she thought would fit María. "You follow me to the end of the hall." She pointed at María and gestured that she was to follow. "This last room will be yours, next to mine so I can keep my eye on you." There were three empty rooms between Sister's and the last of Dolores's young ladies. She and María would be isolated from the other girls at the far end of the hall.

The walls and ceiling of María's tiny room had been whitewashed stark white. The room measured 10 feet by 12 feet. It was immaculately clean. The floor was made of the same material as those in the prayer room, although not as smoothly sanded and polished. There were no windows in any of the rooms. Instead, a slit about 4-inches wide by 18-inches long near the ceiling provided some air and light. There was no glass covering the slit. A little light was still coming in the opening, along with the evening's chill.

María looked around her room. There was a wood-bottomed, narrow bench-like bed with three blankets folded at the foot, but no mattress or pad. A small desk and a tiny narrow chair stood beside the bed. A set of three drawers were fitted into the wall. A small table held a pitcher of water and a bowl-shaped washbasin. Beside the table was a night-vase, or chamber pot, with a lid. A hand-painted picture of Christ hung on the wall above a small shelf containing a candleholder; however, there was no candle in the holder and nothing with which to light it.

"Now, I am in the room next to you," Sister told María. "Should you want me, you may knock three times very lightly on the connecting door; and if I want to see you, I will tell you that you may enter. But not tonight, I am too tired tonight. You are to go to sleep, and I will speak to you again in the morning. Do not forget to say your prayers this evening and do your rosary at least three times. Now go to bed."

"Do not leave this room. You are never to leave this room once you return here after supper." Sister disappeared through the connecting door between the two rooms and shut the door before María could say anything. María was alone in this strange room, which by now was barely lighted by the high slit in the ceiling. The room was so cold that she did not take her clothes off. She decided to lay one blanket on the raw wooden boards of the bed and cover herself up with the other two. She was afraid now, and miserable.

She decided that if she could see Mother Superior tomorrow, she would complain about the unfair treatment she was receiving. She had done nothing wrong, other than sitting in a chair by mistake. Of course, there was the comb. But having a comb in one's hair was not a sin. She had always worn such a comb, even at Mass.

At sun-up, Sister Seraphena came into María's room carrying a large brass bell by its wooden handle in one hand and a candle-holder containing three lighted candles in the other hand. *Clang! Clang! Clang!* Sister vigorously rang the bell, and María awoke in a fright. Never had she been so rudely awakened. "Get up, you lazy, sinful girl! Get those clothes off and get into your uniform. Sit on your bed until I come for you!" She slammed the door as she left.

María was freezing as she dressed in the mandatory black skirt and black blouse. It was still early in the morning, just daylight. Only a trickle of light was coming in through the slit in the wall. She opened the door and looked down the unlighted hall, watching Sister with her candleholder and bell. Sister went to Dolores's room and rang the bell, instructing her to get the other girls up, and quickly.

"Get up and get dressed, you fat, ugly girl! And get your young ladies dressed! It is time for prayers and then breakfast. If you do not hurry, you will skip breakfast. But we will never skip prayers."

María's group marched toward the prayer room, where they and their belongings had been the previous afternoon. They were the last to enter the room. Now there were thirty-five young ladies together in the prayer room. Each group of seven was accompanied by one of the nuns, and the room was filled to capacity. The other young ladies were already on their knees in front of the picture, praying silently. Each one held a rosary. Except for the noise the new entrants were making, the room was perfectly silent. No one even looked up at the new group.

Mother Superior was sitting in the chair by the door in the back of the room, holding her rosary in one hand and a prayer book in the other. The fact that she was sitting on the chair was the one compromise she had allowed herself, because of the cancer that was growing in her, including the bones of her right knee. She hated to give in to it, but she was no longer able to pray on her knees. If she did so, she could not walk for several hours. She did not mind the pain, but it disrupted the other nuns, who would then have to help her walk.

Three-quarters of an hour was devoted to prayer every morning, seven days a week, before breakfast. Mother Superior determined the length of time they were all to remain here by counting the number of rosaries she went through on her beads. Ten Hail Mary's preceded by one Our Father and followed by a Glory Be to the Father was a set. She estimated the elapsed time by counting the sets. No one had a clock or watch. Time was measured by the Mother Superior and her prayers.

María was directed to take her position near the doorway, across from the Mother Superior, away from the other girls. This suited María, since she intended on talking to Mother Superior about how she and her group had been treated. But Mother Superior did not look at her, not even in her direction. She was moving through her rosary beads in prayer, whispering silently with her lips moving. No one said anything. Everyone was quiet. Everyone was going through their rosary beads. Everyone, that is, except María, who was looking for the opportunity to make her complaints known. She was looking for a way to escape this hellhole, as she was now calling the school, or at least get transferred away from Sister Seraphena, whom she already despised.

The new group of young ladies squirmed. They were uncomfortable on their knees on the rough stone floor for such a long period of time. The nuns stayed in position on their knees, uncomplaining, setting an example of devotion for the young ladies in their charge. The older students moved very little, if at all. They had become used to it.

Sister Seraphena never seemed to move, although the pain on her knees must have been as severe for her as anyone else by then. Sister's back was always straight as a board, never moving during prayer. A very faint smile seemed to be upon Sister's lips as she went through her rosary. It was obvious that she was happy in her prayers.

As María looked around the room, she could see that a sort of rapture shone on the faces of all of the nuns. *How anyone could be happy kneeling on this rough stone floor in such a miserable place is beyond me. I can't understand it!* She thought, almost out loud, irreverently sitting back on her heels to alleviate her own discomfort.

When Mother Superior stood up, it was the signal that prayers were over. No one said anything. They filed silently out of the prayer room, each group silently following their own nun to the breakfast room.

They went into the dining room, where they were greeted by a warm, friendly fire in the fireplace. One of the servants from outside the school was fixing plates of steaming wheat cereal, a large mug of milk, and a huge piece of brown bread for each of the girls. For breakfast once a week, each girl got one fried egg, and twice a week they got two large pieces of bacon. Small slices of melon accompanied breakfast in season.

"Dolores, you take your young ladies to the table in front," Sister whispered so she would not disturb the silence of the room. You are not to eat any bread, just the milk and cereal. Give your bread to the other young ladies this morning in equal portions because your sins cost them their supper last night. Every morning you will do the same. You are not to eat any bread until and unless I tell you differently."

Dolores started to say something.

"No talking in the dining room!" Sister admonished her, pointing a stern finger in her direction. "María, you will eat at the other end of the table with me."

There were four other tables full of girls, in exactly the same uniforms. Each table had a silent nun in identical habit in charge. The Mother Superior was also here. She was sitting at a small table by herself, smiling and nodding to the five sisters and the thirty-five children as she peered around the room. She was happy that her school was prospering because of its fame at making disobedient girls into obedient young ladies. There was a long waiting list to get into this school. The school was considered progressive, meeting the high standards she had set and it had a reputation for successfully molding wayward young ladies into ideal Catholic mothers, and obedient wives.

This group was the quietest Mother Superior had ever had in the dining room. It was quiet and pleasant. She sighed her approval. She was eating the identical breakfast the girls were having, but in much smaller portions. Mother Superior did not eat very much at all anymore, a few spoonfuls seemed to be as much as she could get down and that almost forced.

After breakfast the girls were off to their schoolwork rooms. They had classes in religion, sewing, weaving, candle making, soap making, and weaving rugs and cloth. In addition, they were taught how to organize a houseful of servants. For two hours each day, they studied Latin, English, literature, and geography, as well as enough about mathematics and money so they could purchase groceries and household items for a home. The curriculum was designed to bend their wills and educate them to be ideal wives, mothers, and housekeepers.

The classes were kept together in the same groups as in the dormitories. Nuns rotated from room to room, each specializing in one subject or another. The nuns themselves had been taught very little in the way of scholastic subjects. Generally, the order of The School Of The Nuns Of The Stations Of The Cross thought that too much education would be counterproductive to their mission of shaping subservient, obedient young wives and mothers from spoiled, headstrong girls.

After breakfast the next morning, the girls in María's group were told that their class schedule would begin later than usual because there was something else that had to be done first. They were not told where they were going, as they were marched single file down a hallway. Today was the day they would get their haircuts.

"No talking!" barked Sister Seraphena. "Stand there along the wall and pray. I will show you into this room one at a time." Another nun was inside the room with scissors and comb. As each girl was finished, she was directed out the other side of the room into the other hallway, out of sight of the girls still waiting, where another nun was waiting.

María was the last one to enter the dim room. As she entered she saw the pile of long hair that had just been swept toward the wall. She would have screamed and run away, but she already knew there was no place to run to. From the amount and length of the hair on the floor, she knew the nuns did not intend to give her a normal haircut. This was going to be much, much more. Sister Seraphena and the other nun ordered her to sit on a low stool in the middle of the room. One of them wrapped a piece of cloth around her neck and shoulders, and the second nun started to cut away at María's hair without saying a word.

María jumped up out of the chair, "I do not want my hair cut!" she screamed.

"It is not for you to decide. Sit down, and remain silent. Who do you think you are that you would be the only girl with ugly, dirty long hair?" Sister Seraphena admonished as she grabbed María's arm and pushed her forcibly back on the stool. "Remain silent and pray for forgiveness, you naughty disobedient girl!"

The nun only left about a half-inch of hair on the top, and cut her hair shorter still down the sides. María felt violated. She was sickened at losing her beautiful hair. She sobbed at the indignity. *How could they do this to me?* She asked herself, sobbing. *I am being punished, but have done nothing to deserve this.* Some of the tresses of long hair were at least three feet long. These cuttings would be given to the servants on the outside of the enclave to be woven into rope or used for other practical purposes. It was not to be wasted.

That night at dinner, María took a closer look at the other girls. Now, everyone had the same closely cropped haircut. Then she realized that the older girls had looked like that before. It was nothing new to them. It was just that María's senses had been so disturbed by all the new things at school that the haircuts had not registered in her mind. She wondered how she could have overlooked something that obvious. She now knew that protesting would get her absolutely nowhere.

María was the most advanced student, scholastically, in the entire school. In fact, she was better educated than any of the nuns. No one had read as much as María had. The other students in her wing resented her ability to answer the questions first and most completely. The other nuns quit calling on her to answer questions. She was a know-it-all. Her superior knowledge set her further apart from the others.

At half-past three in the afternoon, every day, the girls were turned out into the courtyard. They could talk and play and do what they wanted to do for an hour and half, before evening prayer and supper.

But María was not to play with the other girls. There would be no playtime for her. Instead, she was told to report to Sister Seraphena in their dormitory wing. She went to the hallway of their dormitory and was surprised to find Sister already on her hands and knees. She had a large hand brush, and a bucket of water with a bar of lye-soap floating in the middle of it. Her sleeves were rolled up above her elbows. She was vigorously scrubbing the already perfectly clean hallway.

"You see, María, I am doing penance because of you. We are both sinners, you and I; and perhaps it is I most of all. You will find your scrub bucket and brush at the other end of the hall. You begin there. We will scrub the floors of the hallway and the prayer room because of our sins. We will do this every day for one hour before suppertime. You will then be allowed one half-hour in your room alone for prayers. I hope this will help you and me to gain humility and grace, and to be obedient to our Lord's will."

María started to protest, "but Sister I have not done anything . . ."

"No talking! Get to work at the other end of the hall, or you will get no supper this evening!" Sister did not even look up at her, as she continued her own vigorous scrubbing.

After dinner, María was sitting on the bed in her room. Her knees were raw and sore from kneeling to pray and scrub, and her hands were inflamed from the strong lye soap used on the floors.

She was trying to think what it was that had gotten her off to such a bad start here. Sister was mean to her, spitefully so. None of the other girls would talk to her. And this was supposed to be a school, a place of learning. *Perhaps if I apologize and ask for forgiveness I can start over again*, she thought. She was perplexed and angry as she thought her way through these strange events. *I cannot understand what is happening to me. I do not even know what I did that was so wrong. Surely it could not have been the wearing of a comb. That is such a small thing. I will apologize to Sister and ask her what I did wrong so that I can ask her for forgiveness.*

She knocked three times on the connecting door to Sister's room.

"Take all your clothes off and hang them up, and put on your nightgown. Then you may come in and pray with me," Sister responded through the closed door.

When María entered the room, Sister Seraphena was in her nightgown, kneeling beside her bed, leaning her elbows on the bed and holding her rosary as she intoned through the liturgy. The single lighted candle in the room was on a small stand by the bed. The room was only a little larger than María's.

Sister's uncovered head was shaved almost bald. Her hair was less than a half an inch long on top. Her hair was shorter even than María's. This was the first time María had seen under the flat white hats that always covered the Sisters' heads.

María started to say, "Sister, I want to apolo. . . ."

"Silence! Do not talk. Get on your knees beside me, and we will silently go through the rosary together. Because you are late, I will have to stay on my knees longer so you can catch up. Sit closer. Give me your hands. Hold my hands in your hands as I go through the beads. Lean your head on my shoulder, close your eyes, and pray to God for forgiveness. Ask God for his forgiveness. It is His will that you are here, not mine. I did not ask that you be sent here, remember that."

When they finished the rosary, Sister said, "now you listen to me very carefully. Everyone needs a sanctuary. My sanctuary is here in my room in my bed. Whenever you wish, whenever you are sad or afraid, you can come into my bed; and this will be your sanctuary also. You will always ask my permission before getting into my bed, and I will always give you permission. We will be just two people, alone and afraid. You can say or do anything in your sanctuary. I can say or do anything in my sanctuary. Those are the rules. In that way, we can help each other. Do you understand me?"

"I think so, Sister, but I wanted to to apolig . . ."

"Good!" Sister interrupted her. "You understand the rules. Now, I am going to get into bed and my sanctuary. Blow the candle out so we do not waste it."

María blew out the candle. It was pitch dark. She could see the high slit in the ceiling in Sister's room by the faint light that outlined it, but almost no light reached down to the floor level. She could hear Sister getting into bed but could only see vague movement.

María had a choice. She could go back into her unlighted room and go to bed on her cold board bed, alone, or she could ask permission to remain here with Sister. It was entirely up to her. "May I please join you, Sister?" she asked hesitatingly.

"Yes, but take your nightgown off, as I have done. You have soiled your knees on the dirty floor, and I do not want my bed made dirty! Hang your nightgown up on the hook beside mine. Then come get under the covers and get warm." Sisters voice sounded lighter and friendly, even eager.

María could remember where the bed was, but she had to feel around in the dark to find the hook on which she was supposed to hang her nightgown. Naked, she cautiously approached the bed. She had never slept naked before.

She found the covers and got under them, trying to stay as near the front of the bed and as far away from Sister as she possibly could. There were three blankets on the bed, one underneath them and two on top. The only difference between this bed and hers in the next room was the thin straw mattress underneath, and this bed was a few inches wider and longer.

"Come, child, move against me so we can warm each other." Sister reached out and put her arms around María, pulling her close so they lay face to face, their chests touching. Sister giggled like a young girl. "Well now, relax. Come on, warm me up. This is sanctuary, and we are to make each other happy and warm here."

Sister pulled one of María's legs under her and pressed her crotch against María's thigh. "Remember, this is sanctuary. This is for both of us, and not just for you. Everything goes! We can do or say anything." She laughed happily and quietly.

María started to say something, but Sister interrupted her by kissing her lips very gently and tenderly, and hugging her so tightly and warmly that María had to gasp for air. Then Sister began to rub María's aching muscles and joints. It felt good, and she relaxed under the rubbing. Again she started to say something. "Sister . . . ."

"Shush! We will be warm in a few minutes. Shush! Don't say anything just now. Shush! Just hold onto me. Learn to speak with your body. You may kiss my lips anytime you wish. Do that instead of talking. I will understand your meaning."

"Shush! This is warm and nice, now isn't it? You can return to your own bed anytime you want to. Remember that. You are here only because you want to be here." This would be all of the intimacy for tonight. Sister did not want to frighten her neophyte student by moving ahead too far too fast. But she was happy, very happy, and warm.

María did not answer. But she did not want to go back into her own freezing-cold cell either, so she lay quietly, still confused. She could feel the warmth coming from the strange and unpredictable Sister. Sister was cuddling ever closer to her, intimately pressing herself even harder onto María's leg and then moving occasionally as if she were itching herself. It was not unpleasant. Just the opposite was true. Since her arrival at this school of misery, this was the first warm, friendly, and comfortable moment María had experienced. Exhausted she fell almost immediately asleep in the warm arms of Sister.

It had been eight nights that María had been coming into Sister's bed, and Sister was getting more and more excited. She had moved slowly so she wouldn't frighten María, but now she was impatient to escalate the intimacy of their lovemaking.

María knocked three times. "May I come in?"

"Yes, enter. You may come in and pray with me."

María knelt closely, so that she and Sister were touching, as she had been guided before to do. She could feel the warmth from the nun's body through their identical nightgowns.

Sister put her arm around María's shoulders and pulled her even closer and slightly in front of her. She let María put her hands on the rosary. Then Sister's arm circled María's back with her right arm, pulling her ever more tightly. She kissed her ear softly. When Sister placed her cupped hand on María's tiny breast and gently squeezed it every now and then, the squeezes were so tender as to be barely discernible. But María knew she was doing it, and it was not unpleasant.

At the same time, Sister pushed her very small breast solidly against María's arm, using Sister's breast to rub María's arm. This was not the first time she had done it, but María was somewhat disconcerted by it. She knew by now that Sister would enjoy it if she pushed her arm slightly against the proffered breast. María did that as she decided to dutifully keep on with her prayers. What else could she do, except go back into the cold darkness of her own room? She had learned that she could tease Sister and disconcert her.

After completing the rosary Sister said, "I am going to bed." She took her nightgown off and hung it on the wall. This was the first time she had not told María to put out the candle before taking off her own nightgown. Sister was quite tall and very slim, skinny even, with cord-like muscles that gave her a masculine boy's look. Her face was handsome as that of a young boy, very fine-featured; and her short haircut made her look even more boyish.

Sister stood closely in front of María and turned around slowly. She obviously wanted María to look at her nakedness. She was posing impishly. Her pubic hair stood out in bold relief as she turned. María was spellbound by the surprisingly lush mat of pubic hair that was curly and dark red, not to mention the stark white nakedness of her body. Her tiny breasts were tight and small, with nipples pointing sharply out and up.

Then Sister sat down on the middle of the bed with her legs crisscrossed under her. Her vulva, or pubic area, was fully exposed as she spread her legs. The lips of foreskin, or labia, under the hair were drawn back so that María could see the most pleasure-sensitive external part of her body; María knew where the clitoris was, as well as the entrance to her vagina. Sister drew her hand through this center of her body slowly and provocatively.

María had long ago found the pleasurable part of her own anatomy. When she was alone in bed. She had experimented by touching it herself, more and more frequently, as she got older. She knew it felt good. But never before had she looked at another one so boldly exposed as this. It fascinated her; she could hardly take her eyes off the area. Her cheeks got red with embarrassment over such intimacy. Her imagination took off and bizarrely, she thought for a moment that the area between Sister's legs might speak to her. After all, it had lips. She had felt her own, both the outer pair and the inner lips. She forced the thought out of her mind in confusion. María was quite flustered by Sister's nudity. This was entirely different from sleeping or laying with someone, cuddling and petting a little in the darkness, as they had been doing.

Sister was still sitting there completely naked, almost grimly smiling at María and almost taunting her. She was happy and extremely excited, but still uncertain. She was obviously challenging María. María thought, *Is Sister trying to make me run into the cold darkness of my own room so she can laugh at me?*

Then too, it seemed Sister was obviously laughing at the embarrassed María. She was waiting to see what she would choose to do. The next move was María's. She had a choice: she could go back into her dark, cold room and sleep on her boards or join Sister in the warmth of her bed. María knew, too, that she would be kissed and rubbed, and hugged in Sister's bed, as she had been every night. That certainly wasn't an unpleasant prospect. She had liked the intimate touches and the massage even at the beginning, and looked forward to them with greater anticipation every night.

Somewhat grimly she set her jaw and said, "May I join you, Sister?" María asked nervously.

"Yes! Of course you may! But only if you want to. Leave the candle lighted. Take your dirty gown off and hang it on the hook there. I want to see you."

María now knew it was not the dirt on her gown that made Sister order her to take it off. Still embarrassed, María took her gown off in the dim candlelight, as Sister had already done. She could do no less if she wanted to get into the warm intimate bed and share Sister's touches.

"That's it!" Sister said approvingly and excitedly. "Now stand there a few moments and let me look at you. Turn around slowly. Not with your head down! You are not a dog. You are a beautiful young woman. Stand up straight and put your shoulders back. Suck in your stomach. Hold your chest out. That's it! That's it! Stand up tall, and be proud! Smile for me! You have a beautiful body, María. Be proud of yourself. You are truly beautiful! Remember that."

"Come, get in the bed facing me. Sit up as I am doing." Sister's lips were quivering a little as she worked herself up to a nervous state. "Now kiss me!"

As María came onto the bed, Sister placed her so they were sitting up facing each other. They both had their legs open in a cross legged sitting position which meant they were spread open as wide as they could to make it easier to view each other. It was quite exciting to María, although still embarrassing. Sister had a half smile on her lips while she was looking at María's private parts, and María was looking at hers. They stared at each other for a few moments.

"Kiss my mouth, María, as we have been doing in the darkness at night!"

María leaned forward, kissing her lightly, with her mouth tightly shut.

"No! No! Not like that!" Sister frowned in disgust at the timidity of the kiss. "That's terrible! Have you learned nothing from me? You do not know how to kiss, and you cannot please your husband or me by kissing in that way. You must be a willing pupil if you are to learn anything from me."

"Like this!" Sister gave her an open-mouthed kiss. She squeezed María's jaws to open her mouth, pulling her forward in a tight passionate embrace. She forced her tongue in María's mouth for several moments, tasting her like a piece of chocolate, then placing the tip of her tongue into the soft tissue under María's tongue, probing there. Sister laughed. "That's better now, isn't it? That is the proper way to kiss, and don't you forget it again. Now you do it to me exactly as I did it to you, you naughty disobedient girl!" It was not said in a mean way, but playfully.

María kissed Sister, holding her cheeks and squeezing them open, even roughly, just as it had been done to her, although that was unnecessary, but she was taking charge. Sister was already hungrily sucking on María's tongue, tasting her once again and drinking her juices.

Sister was very agitated by now. She lay down on her back with her legs spread and said to María, "Give me your hand! Lay your head down next to mine and watch your hand as I move it, and remember what you do." Sister was getting more and more excited now. "Pay close attention," she said. She guided María's hand over her breasts, first tickling them until goose bumps formed. Then she cupped her whole breast with María's hand, squeezing, lifting them up, and pulling the breast forward, and sliding her fingers and palm around it several times. Then she placed the nipples between María's fingers, massaging and rolling them, pulling them and then letting them go so they snapped back, to begin it all over again. She used María's hands to massage each nipple, holding each one and then sqeezing them.

"Watch them! Watch them!" Sister made sure María was watching what she was doing because it was how she wanted María to do it to her. "Watch! Watch!" Sister whispered again, excitedly. "See how you are making them swell up and grow? Look at them! *You* are doing that. Your hands, your touches are making them grow, making it happen! They are swelling up and growing for you, asking for your touching. Isn't that amazing?" The skin had become drum-tight over the tiny breasts as they became larger with response to María's stimulation.

María could see they were truly growing, swelling up, getting larger in front of her eyes. This surprised her. She sat up and worked the breasts as Sister wanted her to do it. This was interesting. The wonder of Sister's breasts rising up in response to her touch awakened a new feeling in her own breasts. She felt her own tightening up. She could feel it in her own nipples, as if they existed as separate entities, separated from her consciousness. She felt something else much lower, a new sensation that she liked.

Sister let María continue manipulating her breasts for a long while. Then she caught María's hand again and moved it down onto the mound of pubic hair on her mons veneris ("the mountain of Venus").

"Watch your hand, María, watch your hand!" Sister's voice was strangely hoarse and pitched lower than it usually was. Her speech was slurred with her excitement. Sister guided María's hand as it moved and titillated, anticipating their next move, holding off. She scratched and tickled the mons. Sister found her clitoris and massaged it with María's fingers and then her thumb.

María was breathless with excitement and wonder, she was excited, wondering if Sister was going to press her hand down further. She could hardly believe what was happening or that she was causing these strange reactions to Sister and herself doing this.

Now she could smell Sister's musk-like scent coming from the area of her vagina. She had smelled it before, but it was more pronounced now, it was a different, an unusual odor. Again María had a fleetingly bizarre thought that the odor or something was calling her, inviting her to find its source and investigate its meaning. She wondered just exactly where it was coming from, although she thought she knew. The thought occurred to her that she would like to dip her finger in the well she knew was there, and see if that was the well source of the odor.

Sister worked and worried the area of the mons, moving María's hand and the back of her fingernails back and forth, teasing, tarrying here and then there for a few moments, scratching and rubbing. Earlier, María had almost decided that she would not go down any further. But now she was disappointed! She wanted to investigate further. Was it just curiosity? Or, was it something else?

Then she could feel her hand once again being guided and pushed, continuing its journey down further, going now to the area she wanted to explore. The strange, haunting odor was even stronger now. She wanted to discover its source, to feel the liquid-warmth between her fingers, to see what was down there that was exciting Sister so. Sister guided both of their hands down to the wet lips between her legs. "Look! Look! Pay attention!" Sister croaked, her voice breaking. "See what is happening down here?"

More and more blood was being pumped into the pelvic region in response to María's caresses, enlarging the lips of Sister's vagina as had happened to her breasts and nipples earlier. María could see the labia becoming larger and opening up. The inner lips of Sister's pubic area were also swelling under the pleasant stimulation. They had begun pushing aside the outer lips and opening up to offer entry into the vagina within. They had become warm, wet, and slippery slides for her fingers into the inner sanctum of Sister's body.

Sister was already wet and immediately began to move María's finger along and over her clitoris. She guided María's fingers and hand, leading them completely around the oval of the now swollen, opening. María felt her middle finger pressed in here, pushed there, the warm, slick milky fluid over everything. Then her hand and fingers were moved back to the upper area.

Sister used María's finger as if it were a stick, pushing and pulling it across her clitoris, then pushing her finger along and down the wet-warm-slippery slide until her finger was in as deeply as it could reach. Sister groaned, in pleasurable response, as she moved up and down in rhythm. María's finger was all the way into the hot vaginal cavity now, always moving back and forth, in and out. Sister held it in there for a moment of ecstasy as she pumped it up and down.

Exquisite joy was overtaking Sister. "That's it! That's it! Keep doing that!" she softly hissed. Then she moved her hand away to let María caress her by herself. "Keep doing it! Keep doing it! Don't stop until I tell you to stop! And pay attention to what you are doing! Look at your hands. Look at my hands." She moved her own hands up to her tightened breasts, and in full view of María in the dim candlelight she began to pull and twist the nipples, increasing her own joy. "Keep going! Don't stop!" She was breathing rapidly and loudly.

María could see the exciting changes coming over Sister. Her cheeks were reddened. The cords were standing out on her neck. Her lips were pursed tightly together in concentration. Her eyes were now closed as her breathing moved faster through flared nostrils. Her heart was pounding; María could see it pumping against her chest. Sister moved convulsively, thrusting forward on each of María's finger movements.

María suddenly realized that she had power over Sister, to change her from a stern, forbidding nun to a woman utterly responsive to her touch. She knew that she was being taught to make Sister excited, to transform her breasts and make her vaginal area grow and become wet and smell so. She knew that she was gaining control over Sister in this way. She could make her crazy with desire. And she could feel her own excitement build as she caressed and explored Sister. She knew her own vagina was wet and excited too, that it exuded that special odor and that it was good. This was fun!

María could see that she was bringing Sister Seraphena to some sort of climax. She began to work her finger faster and faster, probing deeper and deeper into Sister, as Sister laid her hand on María's vagina. Suddenly Sister moaned, "Oh! Oh! Oh!" In a spasm, she brought her legs together tightly on María's finger, then lifted her legs sideways and pulled her knees up to stop the finger motion, finally satisfied.

"Thank you! Thank you! Bring your lips to mine, you angel, you!" She kissed María again and again, making little noises with her mouth and in her throat. "Now you know I need you and must have you." She pulled María's face up to hers and looked into her eyes, smiling with happiness and satisfaction. "Thank you! Thank you! Now you kiss me properly, like I showed you."

"I need to rest a few minutes and hold you close to me. Then I will show you some things that I like; and in time you will like them, too. In our sanctuary here we will find pleasures and happiness, you and I. We have a long way to go yet, but our journey is now truly started!"

Finally, María kissed Sister tenderly. It was fun and so exciting. Tentatively, she pressed her tongue inside Sister's mouth, as Sister had shown her. María felt the suction draw her tongue inside Sister's mouth to dance there in unison, tongue with tongue. It felt like it belonged there. She sighed with her own delight. María was content, and felt wonderful.

CHAPTER 7
Looking for the Devil in Her.

Catholicism came to Mexico and the rest of Central and South America when Spain conquered and proselytized the area. The "witch-hunt" mind-set of the Inquisition led to the early murder and rape of the native Indians by their "saviors," all in the name of Christianity, to save their souls. Violence, murder by torture, especially being burned alive, and yes, even rape, were some of the abuses practiced by individuals within the Church during the Inquisition.

By 1835 the main power of the Inquisition had been partially weakened. However, fear of the Inquisition and of the Dominicans who administered it still haunted Church members. A number of the attitudes and much of the politics that had brought about the Inquisition were still operative, if somewhat less violent and much less public.

This change had been brought about by the persistent pressure of non-violent, more religious priests in the Church. Public torture had been tempered somewhat to avoid criticism. However, thousands of Indians were still being killed every year to save their souls and make good Christians of them; but fewer Spaniards in the old world and new world were being burned alive or torn limb-from-limb by their own Church.

Progress was being made toward extinguishing the freedom of the Indians because those who resisted were systematically exterminated. Had it not been for the fact that the Spanish-Mexican governments and their sophisticated populations wanted the natives to do their labor, the Indians could have all been killed or driven from their homes as they were say in Colorado when it came into American control. Whole nations of Indians were all driven from their lands or killed.

Throughout the Americas, there were instances of Indians revolting, raiding, murdering, and raping. They too coveted the lands, property, women, and food of those who were trying to subjugate them.

The Indians were not as well organized, as well armed, or as persistent as the Spaniards and now the Mexicans. But they could be just as ruthless. Had the Indians not depleted so much of their energies fighting each other, they might have defeated their invaders. But their own greed and hatred toward one another kept them from defending themselves effectively. In addition, the Spaniards-Mexicans, and also the Americans, were experts at setting one group of natives against another. The general population of Native Americans or Indians was never able to understand the larger picture of what was happening to them.

Half the land and property in Mexico belonged to the Catholic Church. The Catholic Church was a religious institution, yes; but it was also a political one. It was the place where adventurers as well as pious men came to pray, and prey. At least half if not more of the priests were good, pious men who would still kill Indians or torture them, but only as a last resort to save their souls.

Once the Indians gave up their freedom to worship and live according to their own customs and beliefs as the padres of the Church wanted them to do, then the padres frequently became benevolent dictators. They shepherded those who accepted the faith and worked the Church's fields. These more benevolent priests treated the natives as slaves on the missions, but at least they were kind masters after the transformation to Christianity took place.

But to the other half of the priests, that was an entirely different matter. These priests ran the whole gamut of human frailties and ambitions. Many kept women for their own pleasures of the flesh. Some were pedophiles, who ravished the bodies of little boys. In addition, many were alcoholics. And some were torturers, who enjoyed killing and maiming and whipping the flesh off a man or a woman for the pleasure of hearing them shriek and beg for mercy or even death. These men-torturers used every conceivable means of rendering pain. Their music was the scream of pain and agony, rendered in the name of religion, and to drive the devil out of the hapless victims once they were chained.

Father Ignacio had come to The School Of The Nuns Of The Stations Of The Cross to hear confessions, say Mass, and give the Sacrament of Holy Communion to the worthy. This was his regular route. He was supposed to come here often, but he found many excuses for not doing so; in fact, he had not been to the school for many months. The staff and students of the school would, of course, all be worthy of the Sacrament with boring regularity. What else could one expect of students and nuns in a cloistered school such as this? He did not like coming here. It was boring. Furthermore, it took him days on foot to get here from Mexico City. But the population at the school, especially the nuns, eagerly awaited his visits so they could gain the grace of the Mass and confessional.

At morning prayers, Mother Superior informed the other nuns that as soon as their prayer time was over they should march with their students to the chapel for confession and Mass. The priest had arrived and was prepared to hear confessions before celebrating Mass and Communion. Mother Superior herded her flock along, watching to make sure they all took this opportunity. She also wanted to give her own confession and partake of Communion to raise her own level of grace. It had to be done before breakfast so they could take the Sacrament on an empty stomach. You could not mix common food with the flesh of Christ before Communion.

Sister Seraphena was distraught at the thought of what María might say in confession. Had she had time, she would have warned María, and counseled her to be discrete. But there had been no opportunity to speak to María under the watchful eye of Mother Superior. No talking was permitted for anyone on the way to Confession or in Church once they were there, and that included the nuns.

One by one, the young ladies and the nuns went into the confessional box, and one by one they came out to say their Hail Marys and Our Fathers the assigned number of times as penance for their sins. A Rosary consists of 15 *Pater Nosters*, and *Glorias*, and 150 *Ave Marias*, to be recited on Indulgence beads. All of the nuns and students were absolved of their sins by Father Ignacio because they had given their confessions and were forgiven by him. That was his duty. Everyone could take Holy Communion and attend the Sacrament of the Mass, receiving the literal body of Christ. There was one that he took special notice of however, one who needed special attention for her sins.

"I have observed a great evil in that girl who is the last one in the row there," Father Ignacio told Mother Superior, pointing at María. "I will keep her for further counseling and questioning. I will pray for her and minister to her and examine her. I may have to keep her here for a long time, depending on the scope of the problem with her soul."

"Yes, I too have observed problems in this girl," replied Mother Superior sorrowfully. "She has brought down much penance on herself. She spends every day doing penance on her knees, scrubbing the floors as punishment for her sins. The other girls do not even speak to her. Try your best, Father Ignacio, to get her back on the right course of righteousness and grace in her life. Her father will, I am sure, appreciate it." Mother Superior was very sad that one of her charges was so thoroughly sinful as to even call attention unto herself by the priest on his first visit here in a long time. But that was his job, to ferret out evil and displace evil if he could. She would pray for him and for the girl.

Everyone else had left the church. María was still there doing her beads. Father Ignacio had taken off the ritual garments he had worn for the Mass and was now wearing his priestly robe. He came out to the waiting girl, who was still on her knees, still doing penance, still rotating her rosary beads through her fingers in prayer. She was basking in the wonders of the Sacrament that she had just received. In her own eyes, as that of the Church, she had literally eaten of the flesh of Christ in Holy Communion. Christ was at that very moment inside of her. She was determined in her mind to be better, to be more of an obedient person, and to be more prayerful. According to the Catholic Church's teachings, she was at that moment in the highest state of grace that it was possible for her to achieve. Her resolutions were going through her mind, as they should have been in her state of grace. She had given a full confession, told the priest everything, and had been forgiven of her sins so she could partake of the Sacrament of Communion. She was as free of sin as it was possible to be and full of the Spirit of Holy Communion. She was euphoric with resolve to be a better, more religious, person.

María had really known only one priest before, Father *de Silva*. Her father supported Father *de Silva* so he could take care of the family members, *peóns,* and Indians on her father's rancho. He was a kindly old man who would give his last piece of bread to the least valuable person on the *Miguel de Vargas Rancho*. She had given him her confession as long as she could remember. Father *de Silva* was everything a priest should be. He was religious, kind, selfless, humble and celibate now that he was old, at least. He was always asking her father for things for the poor and homeless on the rancho. This was as it should have been, and what María expected of all priests.

"Follow me," Father Ignacio told the girl who was still praying on her knees. He led her back into the vestibule, a room behind the altar. The room was furnished with a table, a chair, a small closet in which to store his garments when he was there, and a cot with a straw mattress so he could stay overnight from time to time. There was also supplied a quantity of wine for the comfort of the priest, to which the priest had already liberally imbibed.

"Get on your knees, girl! What is your name?" he demanded loudly. He was gruff and rude, and he frightened her.

"María, Father," she whispered. She lowered her head in subjugation and knelt in front of him with her hands clasped in prayer. She was hoping for, even expecting, his blessing. That's what Father *de Silva* would have done back on her father's rancho.

"Our purpose here is to find the evil in you through examination," the priest told her matter-of-factly. "If you cooperate, we may be able to cast out this evil, this devil, from your soul. It will not be easy, but we will try."

"Tell me again and show me exactly what you have been doing, as you told me in the confessional," he commanded. "I want to know every detail of what has transpired between you and Sister Seraphena. Details! I want to see and hear the details so I can understand this devil in you!"

María started to speak, but he interrupted her.

"But you are not doing it. You're not telling it to me, and showing me, exactly as you told me in the confessional!" His tone was agitated now. "You said you had no clothes on when you performed these sinful acts. You are not cooperating with me! The devil in you is fighting me!" He was building up a rage, his face already red from wine, was turning redder still, and he was screaming at the frightened, confused girl. "How can I help you if I cannot see this devil? Take your clothes off and start over again. When you have your clothes off, get up on this couch exactly as you told me you had been doing with Sister."

María moved over to his bed-couch as he had ordered her, but she stood by it not knowing what to do. She could not think of undressing before the priest, this stranger—this man. He was standing behind her holding his walking staff now, which was a solid piece of hardwood an inch and one-half thick and six feet long that he used not only for walking but for other purposes as well.

María was hesitating, not removing her clothing as he had ordered her to do. She was resisting his orders. She was not being obedient. The devil in her was defying his priestly orders. With no warning, he hit her as hard as he could swing the staff, striking her across her back and shoulders and knocking her forward onto the couch. She lay there stunned as he went over and latched the door so no intruders could interrupt his priestly work.

"You are being disobedient again." His tone was now conversational, matter-of-fact. He knew he had her now where he wanted her, stunned and unable to move. "Mother Superior said you were disobedient. We will try to get this devil out of you. I will take off your clothes as I told you to do, and then we will begin again!"

María was stunned by the heavy blow, as he knew from experience that she would be. She was conscious but unable to move or resist him. This was exactly the proper state for her to be in, to get the most good out of his interrogation and ministrations. Father Ignacio was an expert at such things; he had been trained in Spain by the Dominicans.

Father Ignacio held his staff in front of him, looking at it admiringly, almost lovingly as he worked his hands up and down the smooth polished surface. The wood grain was perfectly straight without even the slightest knot or imperfection. It was so smooth that he could work his hands up and down it, and never get a splinter from it. He had brought it all the way from Spain. It was made of a special hard wood, carved in an octagonal shape, with leather coverings at either end so the leather would wear instead of the wood when the staff would hit the ground as Father walked.

The staff could also be used for protection against dogs, wild animals, or even against humans who might attack him. It was, in fact, a long club; and in this case it made an ideal whipping-club that was heavy enough so that when it was swung even with moderate speed it would raise a huge welt on the unlucky victim. Repeated blows would break the skin, leaving meaningful scars. It was not as good as a real whip like he had used in the dungeons in Spain, interrogating heretics and sinners, before coming to New Spain (now Mexico). But under these primitive conditions it was a good, solid, and practical substitute, and could inflict scars admirably well, so the sinners could remember the ministrations he would give them. By leaving them well marked they could remember it and resist sin in the future.

María had seen the *peóns* and servants on her rancho punished by whipping, sometimes with many lashes from a long bullwhip. Like the other members of her family, she had grown up with it. It did not bother her. María had never considered the *peóns* to be human beings on the same plane as her family. She was brought up with the concept that the *peóns* were more on a level with sheep or goats, or even unruly dogs. Whipping was a part of life on her father's rancho. It had never even occurred to her that someday she might be subjected to similar punishment. She was the daughter of the *patrón,* and not subject to any discipline other than his. And it was not conceivable in her mind that her father would ever whip her or have her whipped.

María had never experienced punishment like that which Father Ignacio was meting. She fell forward, stunned, unable to move because of the pain and shock of the blow across her back. This clearly was not the first examination that Father Ignacio had performed. He was an expert at it. He knew exactly what to do with sinners. He pulled her clothes off and threw them on the floor. She lay on her stomach on the bed, completely naked now, gasping, writhing in pain, trying to get breath into her lungs, pleading with her mind silently asking the priest to stop. She was whining, literally, like a dog, the only sound she was able to make.

Father Ignacio had his own form of penance for a sinner such as María. She was now ready for the first part of the treatment. This was actually the part Father liked the best. He called it "The Stations of the Cross," punishment, and it encompassed all fourteen Stations of the Cross.

Slap! Father hit María across the back with his staff again with the full force of his strength. The sound of the blow reverberated in the small room. A huge long red welt appeared. The blow also drew a little blood. *This was for the first Station of the Cross,* he thought. The very first blow he had administered when he knocked her down, did not count because it was intended only to get her attention and get her ready for the real treatment. He began counting out loud, slowly, for María's benefit. He knew that anticipating each blow was a necessary and a good part of this treatment. By anticipating the blows, the Devil could then leave the sinner's body in order to avoid the excruciating punishment.

"First Station. Jesus is condemned to death," he spoke slowly and distinctly. Each time he applied the rod he piously announced the summation of each Station of the Cross, first in Latin and then he repeated in Spanish.

Slap! He struck her again. "Two! Jesus is made to bear his cross."

Slap! "Three! Jesus falls the first time under his cross."

Slap! "Fourth! Jesus meets his afflicted mother."

Each Station of the Cross, was just as important as the others, and in Father Ignacio's mind all fourteen blows had to be delivered with equal determination. He continued the treatment.

Slap! Fourteenth! Jesus is placed in the sepulcher."

Father Ignacio was puffing from the exertion now. Driving the Devil out of a sinner was hard work. It was work he enjoyed doing, of course; but no one could say it was not physically demanding of him. He circled her purposely so that the welts crossed and crisscrossed each other. At the end her back was a mass of bloody elongated welts that crisscrossed each other.

María would carry the fourteen Stations of the Cross in scars on her back for the rest of her life. Her back was bleeding profusely now along the lines of the multitude of blows. The welts were already rising up along the lines of the broken and bruised skin. Yet she was lucky. No bones had been broken. Father avoided breaking bones because fractures reflected negatively on the quality of his administration of the treatment.

He rolled her over. "Devil, depart this woman's bosom!" This part of the treatment was to drive the Devil out of the front side of her body. *Slap! Slap!* He struck María twice across the breasts as hard as he could, one blow for each breast. One blow was for her and one for him, to drive the Devil away.

María had been only semi-conscious as the priest took off her clothes. Undressing the subject always excited him. Now, he took his own clothes off. Beating her had excited him even more. He was becoming euphoric as he anticipated the part of the examination that he enjoyed almost as much as the beating. This was such a good part of the treatment. It brought him into direct contact with the soul of the woman. This was the part that made him sleep well at night. It was the part he could savor until the next time he came here.

He spread María's legs roughly. She left them as he placed them, because she could not move. He smiled happily when he noted that she was no longer insolent or fighting him. She did not move. She was not being disobedient. This proved his ministrations were doing her good.

Then he mounted her, forcing his penis into her vagina. María's mind screamed as he raped her, but no sound came from her paralyzed vocal cords. He took his time and enjoyed it immensely. It was greatly satisfying to him. He was exhilarated by the whole episode. She had been subdued and was obedient now.

To María, drifting in and out of consciousness, it was almost as if all of this were happening to someone else. But it was not happening to someone else—it was happening to her, and she was totally aware of it.

Father Ignacio smiled with satisfaction when he completed his task. Sometimes, like now, he enjoyed being a priest more than most other times. For example, he dreaded the long walk to this school, so far from the comfort of his apartment in the abbey in Mexico City; but now he was glad he had come. This trip had been well worth it, despite the long walk.

He smiled at her now. "You tell Sister Seraphena that she should be more careful in her confession. She should make sure she gives a complete account of her sins if she wants to take Mass again." He helped María get her clothing back on. She was hysterical and barely able to walk. He unlocked the door and pushed her through it with his foot, to make her way back to her room on her own.

When she staggered out of the chapel, Sister Seraphena was waiting for her. Sister was white-faced with rage and shame, but she could take no action against the Church or the male population who ruled it, and everything else on earth. The men had total control. Priests could not be judged in regard to a crime, except by the other male members of the clergy. All priests were exempt from civil laws and civil authority, and she knew that well.

Sister draped one of María's arms over her shoulder and placed her own arm around her waist, thus supporting most of her weight. She led her back to their sanctuary. Sister was crying as she undressed her. She washed her bruised and battered body, kissing each injury tenderly as she ministered to the hurt and abuse. She talked to her soothingly, explaining to her about men.

"Priests are men first. Men are like that. The confessional is no place to be too open if you do not know the priest well enough to anticipate what he might do. Only half the priests are good," she told María through her own tears. "That means that the other half of them are bad. Remember that. You are old enough now to know you must use your head and keep your mouth shut when necessary. Keeping quiet about your most intimate practices, is a necessity." She held María lovingly in her arms, giving her sips of wine until the exhausted girl fell asleep, or unconscious.

Sister did not sleep at all that night. She held María and prayed for guidance. The next morning, she ordered María to stay in bed all day and told Mother Superior that María was sick. Sister took food and wine to her, and salve to keep the scabs from hurting as much as they otherwise would have. María stayed in Sister's bed because it was the more comfortable.

That night Sister made her stay in bed while she alone knelt and said their prayers.

"I will join you, Sister. I feel better." María started to get up.

"No. You stay in bed and rest," Sister ordered. "You can follow me in my prayers from there. Tonight is to be special for you. I am so ashamed of what has happened to you. It is my fault, and we both know it. I failed you! My duty is to take care of you, and through no fault of your own, I failed you!"

At the end of the prayers, Sister began sobbing again. "I failed you."

"What is wrong, Sister? I am feeling much better now," said María, trying to comfort the nun. "Do not cry for me."

"I am sad for what has happened to you," Sister said. "It is my fault. I should have counseled you better, at least, or protected you better. It is my fault. I am to blame for this. You were punished for my sins. I am so sorry—so ashamed."

"Stand up. I want to examine your wounds and wash them again." Sister slipped María's nightgown off gently and carefully, and examined the black-and-blue, scabbed over welts, and the torn places of flesh. She kissed each one.

In the evening three days latter sister said, "I will take all the pain from you that I can in this fashion. Lay down on the bed. Tonight is your night. I have been selfish with you, thinking only of my pleasure and happiness. I realize that now. I am sorry that I did not prepare you better; but I did not know he was coming, or I would have warned you. I will do my penance unto you now as best I can," Sister said. She gently kissed María's breasts where they had been struck with the wooden staff, and suckled on the nipples. She licked every inch of María's breasts and her stomach, too.

Sister went down on María then, flicking her tongue persistently in and out, worrying her clitoris and rubbing the most sensitive regions of her pubic area. She took the salty-sweet moisture into her mouth, occasionally leaving the taste on María's lips when she kissed her. Sister suckled the outer lips and then the inner lips of the vagina, and every place that had been violated and injured by Father Ignacio. She didn't miss anything that her tongue or her lips could touch and reach.

Despite the pain of her wounds, María felt herself on the verge of a powerful new feeling of ecstasy. And Sister did not stop for more than a brief moment. She licked the edges of María's vagina all around, slowly and deliberately coming back to the center of pleasure, the clitoris. After every journey she suckled the vaginal opening again and again.

Slowly María felt herself being swept up along the same pleasure-path that Sister seemed to have been on when she worked her finger in and out of Sister's vagina. María could feel her own breasts swelling up, craving to be touched and fondled. And she did so even as Sister had done to her. Pulling them. Letting them snap back. Rolling the nipples gently in her fingers, pulling them again. She searched for and found the most sensitive areas of her breasts and concentrated her self-stimulation there.

Sister smiled when she saw that. She was herself excited by watching María and felt a response in her own breasts and groin. Sister began to use her fingers in conjunction with her tongue, tickling, rubbing, and suckling. She, too, was experiencing the sensuality that was building in María as it was in herself. She knew the passion that was working on her young novice. The exercise was exciting Sister as much or more than María. She, too, was being swept along the path of ecstasy.

Blood poured into María's breasts and pubic area on cue, swelling her breasts and clitoris until they were large and tight with pressure.

FRANK W. LEWIS

The same thing was, of course, happening to Sister. Her own excitement was building even faster than María's. Now, María began undulating forward and backward in a rhythmic response to the touch of Sister's tongue and fingers. She began to pant and make noises like the ones Sister had made.

And then: "That's it! That's it! There it is! That is where I want it. This is what you had, and now I have it, too!" María knew suddenly the beating was worth it. Her mind said *I am whole! I am in ecstasy, too!* Her pain was forgotten as she held Sister's face between her hands and looked deeply into her eyes and kissed her. They both laughed then.

María teased her, "Now kiss me as you taught me to do, and we will rest a few moments here in sanctuary!" They both hugged and laughed quietly in each other's arm.

They were now mated as lovers. The cruel priest had completed the bridge and brought them together. At that moment at least, María also hated men, all men. Men were mean and brought pain, not love. What she and Sister now shared was true love and true pleasure. From then on, María's love for Sister and their lovemaking were almost all that she thought about during the day. At night she gave expression and passion to the daydreams. Never had two lovers been more grateful for the darkness of evening, and, the time to go to bed in sanctuary.

It was two months before the priest; Father Ignacio came to the school again. Under Mother Superior's watchful eyes, again, all of the nuns and all of the girls went to confession. María's confession was of menial, small sins only. There was no mention of Sister or the bedtime games of love or sex.

At the end of the confession the priest told María, "You are to wait for me after the Mass. I will want to talk to you and interrogate you. You are better, as indicated by your confession—but we must be sure!"

Father Ignacio forgave everyone for their sins and gave them penance to do, and everyone later participated in the partaking of the Sacrament of Communion.

When Sister Seraphena learned that the priest had told María once again to wait until after everyone else left, she ordered her: "María, you go up to my room and wait there for me. You are not to go near this priest, Father Ignacio, alone ever again! I will talk to this priest instead of you."

94

When Father Ignacio came out of the vestibule to greet his waiting sinner, he was surprised to find the nun there instead of the girl he had ordered to wait for him. Sister was on her knees praying, her rosary was in her hand as well as her cross with the fourteen tiny bands of gold was draped openly across her chest.

"Why are you here?" thundered the priest. "I ordered the young student sinner to come here for instruction and interrogation!" He was agitated at the audacity of the nun, countermanding his orders, especially this sinner-nun because he knew her intimate secret. She was the one who had lied to him in the confessional. She had no right and no authority to countermand his orders to the young student that he intended on interrogating further to see if she had cast off the evil that was in her.

"I came in her stead, Father. Bless me, for I have sinned, and let this be my penance. She is too ill to come anyway. I am prepared to receive thy interrogation for María. Her sins are greater in me than in her, and I need thy instructions and the gift of penance worse than she does. You may interrogate me in her stead." Still on her knees, Sister's hands were clasped in prayer in front of her, and she was whispering Hail Mary's and Our Fathers, through the use of the rosary that was wrapped tightly around her wrist. She was praying over and over again as rapidly as she could. A line of sweat was beaded across her upper lip. She was very nervous, and frightened too. The priest smelled of tobacco, wine, and sweat. He gave off a strong, unwashed, male smell not unlike that of the man her father had intended for her to marry. She found him revolting and she was on the verge of being physically ill at his presence.

"Follow me then, Sister!" He nodded his head and pursed his lips in disgust at her. He led her with him into the vestibule. "Get on your knees, sinner." He pointed to the stone floor near the middle of the room. Then he shut and latched the door. He was greatly agitated by her defiance of his orders. It was obvious to him that the Devil was in total control of this false-nun. Never before had he had such an immense challenge.

The blow on her head and the back of her neck by his staff knocked her forward. She had not anticipated it. She fell onto her stomach on the floor, sprawling in the direction that his blow had sent her tumbling. Without removing her clothing, he hit her fourteen more times, loudly intoning the Stations of the Cross as he did so. The blows were given slowly and purposefully. He waited between each one, making sure she knew another one was coming before he struck. He gave her time to recover, sometimes taking a gulp of wine, watching her, between blows so that she was fully conscious as he delivered each one. He had a peculiar smile on his face; only one side seemed to warp up. Such blows did no good if administered to an unconscious victim. They would be wasted. All of his considerable skill, training and practice had taught him to make sure the penitent sinner was aware and awake at every step of the treatment. Otherwise, how could it do her any good and be considered a sacrament? He was well schooled that a person undergoing the sacrament of penance was actually receiving the Grace of God.

After the fourteenth blow, he turned her over. Her sins were so great that he gave her seven extra strokes across her breast and stomach. Then he opened her legs and administered one blow in the vaginal area. He did not strike that area as hard as the other parts of her body. He did not want to destroy it, just awaken the Devil he knew was there.

Again and again he had beaten her with his long wooden staff until he was tired of the physical exertion. But the whipping had excited him, as it always did. He dragged her limp body over to the couch. He took his clothing and laid them neatly on the table. Then he stripped off the tattered remains of her habit. He looked disdainfully down upon her thin frame. Blood from her wounds had begun pooling underneath her. He laid her flat on her back, spread her legs apart, and mounted her.

She was conscious, but hurt and unable to move. She watched him disdainfully as he emptied his groin into her. This was the first man she had ever received. She hated him. She hated all men. But she had saved María from further violation at the hands of this man, this false priest; and she had done penance for her own part of the sin. Sister was satisfied. She had done her best to take unto herself that which was meant for the girl who was her responsibility.

When he was satisfied, he dressed himself and demanded, "Get out of here, you She-Devil." He unlocked and opened the door but did not attempt to help her. He sat down in his chair and poured himself another glass of wine, watching her slowly recover enough to move.

After what seemed forever to her, she summoned the strength to roll over, grabbed her tattered garments, her rosary, and her black cross, and crawled painfully toward the vestibule door and up the aisle of the chapel. She could not stand up, and she was slowly crawling in first one direction and then another. She was unable to coordinate her movements as the result of the beating. As she crawled on her hands and knees her buttocks swayed back and forth peculiarly, sideways, as a drunk person would walk or crawl.

Father Ignacio watched her go. He smiled again, promising himself that he would come back soon to this school. There was more work for him here at The School Of The Nuns Of The Stations Of The Cross than he had ever imagined. It was worth the long walk. It really did not matter which one of them he interrogated. They were both liars and sinners of the worst kind. They had even lied to him, the priest, in the confessional. He had enjoyed administering Sister Seraphena's penance even more than that of the young girl. He would sleep well tonight; he chuckled to himself, as he poured himself another glass of wine.

María was hiding in the bushes just outside the door to the chapel. Her mind raced as she wondered what to do. It was such a helpless feeling. She wished she had a knife so she could sneak up behind the priest and plunge it into his back. He deserved to die. In her mind she stabbed him again and again. She gasped when she saw Sister slowly crawling towards her, trailing her garments. Her back was raw and bloody, and already swelling from the priest's beating. María ran to her, crying hysterically, "Oh, Sister, it was meant for me! You should not have gone in my place!"

"You are still being disobedient, María," she slurred. "It is my place to decide these things. Now you will have to do penance for disobeying me." Sister talked as if she were drunk, her speech slurred, words not forming correctly. She was struggling to get to her feet, but her legs would not hold her up. She fell down as she tried. María helped her put the rags of her clothing on and stand up.

"That priest certainly does have a way of driving the Devil out of a person," Sister said. She tried to smile but was unable to do so. With María's help, she somehow found the strength to make her way back to sanctuary.

With tears rolling down her cheeks, María washed her wounds, kissing each place where the rod had broken the skin. Sister lay exhausted but somehow happy in the knowledge that she had saved this lovely, innocent girl from the hands of an evil man. In her own mind, she was now a martyr—in a way. Isn't that what every good religious person, especially a priest or nun, should aspire to be? The priest had brought her grace, at least in her own mind.

"You must understand, María, that a good nun takes upon herself the burdens of her children. I am only doing what is expected of a nun. But I appreciate your helping me. I love you, María!"

It took several days for Sister to partially recover. María had gone to the Mother superior and told her that Sister Seraphena had a bad cold and that she was going to take care of her. Sister said, "It is odd, but every time you kiss me the pain is driven away from that area. Please do not stop. I will just lay here and enjoy your ministrations. Do not think I am not appreciative. It is just that I am too tired and sore to move to you."

"*I know! I know!*" María was still crying over the beating her Sister had taken in her stead. "And I have known for some time what you wanted of me, though you have never asked me to do anything that I did not want to do. But I was not ready. I did not love you enough. But I am ready now! I will not hold anything back in my love for you any longer."

In the shadows of the one candlelight, María began to tenderly suckle and kiss the bruised and wounded breasts before her. She licked every inch of them as Sister had done to her. She was ever so gentle because she knew how she had been hurt. It was only a matter of a few minutes before she was suckling at the wounded vagina.

Tears were still rolling down her cheeks because she knew the indignity that her Sister's vagina had been through for her sake: to save María from the filthy torture of the priest-rapist-man. The least she could do was take into her mouth the juices that she knew Sister wanted her to bring to her lips. And because she wanted now to do it, it was all the more pleasurable for the both of them.

Weeks and months went by. Every time María made love to Sister, she enjoyed it more. She reveled in the variety of experiences that they discovered as they experimented with more and more positions. They worked to bring joy to each other, which of course brought more joy unto themselves. The more Sister enjoyed it, the more María would enjoy it. It might have been teenage love on her part, but it was the more intense because of that.

For the next year, while in sanctuary, María focused on making the most ardent love to Sister that she could. She gave Sister everything she had to offer, and received everything possible in return. Sister was having difficulty keeping up with her now that the floodgates of love and affection were wide open in the candle-lit sanctuary. No love statement was unsaid and no loving act withheld. They made love almost every night, with few exceptions. It was as near to heaven as they could possibly get on earth, and they knew it. They cherished their time together.

Scrubbing the floor was no longer penance for María or Sister either, for that matter. They laughed as they scrubbed the hallway and the chapel while the other young ladies were outside in the sunshine playing in the courtyard. These two could look down the hall at each other over their scrub buckets. Sister would look stern and scowl, and María would laugh and blow kisses. She was no longer afraid. The veil had been lifted. When their scrubbing brought them together in the middle of the hallway, María would steal a kiss, touch a breast, or place a hand up under Sister's gown. When Sister would scold her, María would grab her hand and pull her into the closet. There, in the darkness, she would kiss Sister passionately, ardently pressing her young body against her and forcing her against the wall, telling her she loved her with all her heart. Holding Sister tightly, she would refuse to let her go until they kissed again.

The priest ordered María to appear before him the next time he came to the school, but during confession, Sister told him, "NO! I have ordered her not to come. None of the girls will ever come to you again to be tortured and abused. If you want to see anyone alone, it will have to be after I have confessed the whole set of circumstances to Mother Superior. I will renounce my vows, and go to your superiors and tell them everything that you did. They can then do with me as they will, but they will know what you have done, and what you are. You have whipped and abused the last person here at this school. You will never touch another person within these walls!"

When another priest came to take confessions and say Mass, Sister and María heard that Father Ignacio had been sent to Alta California to work with the Indians. Strangely, Sister was glad he had helped her achieve a greater grace and world of pleasures both for herself and María.

Because of him, they had managed to accomplish everything in love that two people could achieve on this earth. It was he that proved to be the catalyst that brought them so close together.

Then there was the awful day when María realized that her two years were coming to an end. Saying good-bye to Sister Seraphena would be the most painful thing she ever had to do. It was far worse than the beating the priest had given her, and far worse than the penance of the school. María never would have gone away had not Sister herself insisted that the time had come for her to go home to her father. She did not want to go home. She had learned to love the life here. "I want to become a nun!" she told Sister, sobbing. "I want to stay here with you and serve here with you forever!"

"No!" Sister said sternly, "Even if you become a nun, you will have to go away to school; and they would never send you back here. You would be sent elsewhere. Most important of all, you do not have a calling to be a nun. You must return home, you must be obedient to your father's will. Our time here is over. It has to be. It must be! By the grace of God you were sent here to me, and we found a miracle of love. But we must now be prepared to give it up, for our love of God must always be greater than our love for each other!"

"All right, Sister, I will go if you say I must! But remember this in your mind and in your heart: I truly love you. I will never love another as I love you. I will do as my father orders me, but my heart will always remain here with you. I love you!" Tears rolled down her cheeks as she embraced Sister's nude body for the last time in sanctuary. Their last night together brought neither of them any pleasure. It was not sexually or emotionally satisfying because they were overwhelmed by their misery over parting. Neither slept all night; and in the morning they were exhausted, dark circles under their eyes making them look even sadder.

All of the girls in the group that had accompanied María to the school were packed and ready to go. Their satchels were on the floor beside them as they knelt facing the painting of the Madonna holding the Christ Child, with the candles burning beside the large marble black cross with its 14 bands of gold. As they had all outgrown the clothes they came in with, they were allowed to keep one of the dresses and blouses from the school. This would be their last prayer in front side of the picture and the cross of The School Of The Nuns Of The Stations Of

The Cross. All of the girls were sad to be leaving. Sister Seraphena went to each one and placed a smaller version of the cross with the fourteen bands of gold on each girl's neck, suspended with a fine gold chain, to show they had graduated with honor and would remember the lessons they had learned here. Sister kissed the small black onyx cross and placed its chain around each girl's neck. Then she kissed each girl on the cheek. By the time they parted, every girl was crying.

Sister stopped in front of Dolores, whose cheeks were wet with tears. Sister said, "Of all the girls here, you are the most beautiful, Dolores. Your family will be so happy to see how slender and elegant you have become. Always remember how beautiful you are. You will make us, and God—happy with the children you will bear. You will find the husband your father wants for you, and you will make him happy and be the best mother possible. God bless you! You have blossomed like the most beautiful of flowers in God's garden!"

Lastly, she went back to the door and kneeled in front of the sobbing María. She put the gold chain and cross around María's neck, kissed the cross, and then touched it to María's lips. She kissed her on both cheeks, embraced her, and then deliberately kissed her mouth passionately. No one could see it. All the other girls were facing forward, as they had been trained to do. Sister was crying. "Take my heart and go, my love!" she whispered, her voice breaking up, as she hugged her.

Sister stood up then and said loudly, trying to control her voice as best she could, "María, I release you now. Lift the bars and open the doors you last closed, and lead the other children out to the carriage! God bless you, one and all!"

Both Sister Seraphena and María were crying as the young ladies began to get into the carriage for the ride to Mexico City. María sat with the six other girls with whom she had come. Dolores helped the younger girls into the carriage, clucking like a mother hen over her charges and shooing them inside to their proper seats. They sat in the same places where they sat when they arrived. The two older nuns accompanying them pulled the curtains, but said nothing. María looked at the closed and shuttered windows and smiled, shaking her head at how far she had come.

Neither Dolores nor any of the other young ladies spoke to María. They were not in the habit of talking to her, and she was not in the habit of talking to them. There was no reason to begin now. It was as if she were not even there. They had learned different lessons at the school, and they did not seem to have anything to say to each other. The two Sisters who had come out with the coach from Mexico City checked to make sure the heavy curtains were tightly closed as the horses went out the gate. No one thought to ask the silent nuns to open the blinds—they had learned their lessons well.

This was the first time in two years that any of the girls had been outside the protection of the gates. It was frightening to them to be in the outside world, away from the protection of the sisters and the walls. They had thought they would be glad to leave, but they definitely were not. Given the chance, most of them would have preferred to stay there, or thought so now.

Standing beside the doorway of the school, watching the girls board the coach, stood a new nun with a small valise in her hand. She had been brought out with the carriage to replace Sister Seraphena, who had not yet been told that she was to be the new Mother Superior and supervise the entire school. The retiring Mother Superior was to stay on and help her learn her new duties for six months. As of today, Sister Seraphena was the new Prefect.

In this religious order, all directives and decisions were made at a high level and passed downward. The old Mother Superior had recommended that Sister Seraphena should replace her because of her own fading health. Her recommendation was accepted by the higher authorities. And of course, their decision would have to be accepted by Sister Seraphena. Seraphena's direct contact with young ladies was at an end. Henceforth, she would not even be in a wing of the school with them. She would be in the part of the complex where the administrator stayed, completely isolated from direct contact with the students or any one else, except the other nuns. After the old Mother Superior left in six months, Sister Seraphena would be alone. Her affair with María had worn her out. She wanted and needed a rest, but not a whole lifetime of it. Her new penance would be a hard one to endure, but she would endure it for the love of God. Sister Seraphena would be celibate henceforth, and seldom smile, except when alone at night in her sanctuary when her thoughts and dreams would wander to her last love—María.

María was a thoughtful, better educated, and, surprisingly, more religious young woman when she returned to her father's rancho. She would obey her father. She would be the wife of her father's choice, as he wanted her to be. She would go to Mass and pray often. She would kiss her black onyx cross of The Fourteen Stations Of The Cross frequently during the day as well as every night at her prayers. She would never take it off. All of these things she promised God and the Mother of Christ.

María's heart, mind, and dreams recreated the vision of Sister Seraphena when she was alone at night. Her love of Sister was so great, so personal, that it would be enough to have her in her heart and in her mind. What else could she do but dream and pine for her lost lover? She would never need or want another love for the rest of her life.

Or so she thought.

CHAPTER 8
San Fernando de Taos.

B ack now in Santa Fé, Caleb was trying as hard as he could to get María off his mind. He was very much in love with her, he discovered; but he could not see any future in a relationship with her. However, forgetting her was no easy task. He had been on the edge of doing something foolish that he knew would be disastrous for both of them. After all, María had been promised by her father to another, and there was nothing she or Caleb could do about that.

His friend Phillip Bartholomew, owner of the Santa Fé portion of the trading firm of The Bartholomew Brothers, had counseled him about his future. "Do you intend on returning to the United States? If so, you will of course want to keep your United States citizenship. But if you plan on staying here in Mexico, you must become a citizen of Mexico and join the Catholic Church in order to own land and do business here. With the political troubles the Americans are causing in Texas—the revolution, I mean—I am not even sure the Mexicans would allow you to become a citizen of Mexico. However, because of the service you performed in helping the *alcalde* and the captain of the guard, I am sure they would smooth the way for you. Now would be the time to take advantage of their help, if you are interested. I can talk to them for you if you want me to, and smooth your way with the priest. The priest is a good friend of mine, and a good and kindly old man too."

Caleb mulled over the matter of becoming a Mexican citizen. He knew he was not going back to the United States. He simply could not return because he had killed the man who had murdered his father. For all he knew, there were arrest warrants posted for him in the United States.

His only alternative was to go forward here in Mexico as best he could. The main stumbling block for him was joining the Catholic Church. "I am having a problem joining the Catholic Church," he told Phillip. "My father never spoke highly of it, and in fact he didn't like any organized church too well. He felt that a man with a Bible, if he read it every day, was more religious than most preachers or priests."

"Don't worry about that," Phillip replied. "What you do on your own after you go through the formalities is your own business. They don't force you to worship; they only force you to join. The minute you are baptized, that is the end of it as far as I can see. I have never let it bother me, nor do any of the other Americans who join. But in any event, joining the Church and being a citizen is the only way you can own land and trade freely in Mexico. Otherwise, you simply cannot function here. It's the law. Consider striking while the fire is hot and take advantage of your opportunity. You will, of course, have to follow your own conscience on what you should do."

And so it was that Caleb became baptized in the Catholic Church. He took out Mexican citizenship under the sponsorship of the Captain of the guard and the *alcalde* himself. Phillip gave a party and dance at his house in celebration, which was even attended by the priest who did the honors. Caleb was given documents to prove his citizenship and a personal letter from the *alcalde* calling attention to his assistance in apprehending the notorious criminal Blackie Parsin and saving the life of Don Pedro, son of Don Miguel, a member of one of Mexico's noted families. The goods Caleb had brought with him from Independence up the Santa Fé trail were more than enough to get him started in the trading business. He now had six horses loaded full.

After these supplies ran out, he would purchase more from Phillip. Phillip would sell Caleb all of his supplies at wholesale prices as long as he sold them away from Santa Fé. Phillip was losing most of the Taos Valley fur trade and all of the trade that was being done at the various rendezvous in the Rocky Mountains. Fur trading at the rendezvous was lucrative, although it was also difficult and dangerous. Phillip agreed to pay Caleb top dollar for any furs he delivered. They sealed the arrangement with a handshake.

It would take a year for goods ordered by Caleb to reach Santa Fé. He placed his large order with Phillip and gave him a deposit. The furs he had already given were included in the deposit. Delivery of all goods was guaranteed to Santa Fé.

Caleb ordered 100 rifle blanks so he could continue making rifles, as his father had taught him. The rifles Caleb ordered were not the older flintlocks. He wanted the new style that could be ignited using caps, like the ones his revolving pistols used. Even single-shot rifles using caps were an improvement over the flintlocks. He would still always have plenty of the older types of flintlocks taken in to trade for those who could not afford the better guns.

He gave Phillip several samples of the caps along with one of the small tins marked with the name of the manufacturer, "Eley Bros., London, England." He ordered 5,000 caps. It was obvious to Caleb that the day of the flintlock would soon be over. The percussion system, using caps, would soon replace the flintlock rifles, because it was more efficient. The caps were more dependable and, best of all, waterproof. Caps could become a necessity for every person who obtained one of the rifles that used them, which from the trader's point of view was another reason for encouraging their use. The people owning those rifles would need a continuous supply of caps.

He also wanted a quantity of revolving pistols and rifles like his. They were expensive, but Caleb was convinced that the mountain men would buy them once they knew how good they were. The five and six shot revolving cap-and-ball pistols and rifles would soon become the standard. The earliest ones mostly carried cylinders of five shots. Soon though, models carrying six, seven, or even eight cylinders would be made.

This order of guns and ammunition, along with trade whisky, powder, lead, metal arrow points, and the usual goods for trading with the Indians were ordered from Phillip to replace the stock he had brought with him from Independence. He also wanted a couple of mandrels for making rifles, and some tools. It was a very large order for The Bartholomew Brothers. Much of it would come from Phillip's brother in England, but some would also be bought from his other brother in Independence.

A special item Caleb wanted was an order of laudanum plus other medical powders and dressings, and a set of medical books and tools for repairing wounds. Laudanum was a mixture of opium and alcohol taken to minimize pain. Having seen injured people writhe with pain because no one had any means of alleviating their suffering, Caleb wanted to acquire medicines for sale.

Santa Fé had been a novelty for the first few days after he said good-bye to Don Miguel, Don Pedro, and María at their hacienda. Caleb had enjoyed learning about the rancho life of the *ricos*, or rich, landed Spanish gentry while staying at the hacienda of Don Miguel de Vargas. It was a new experience, and they had treated him very well, even giving him fine clothes.

He had enjoyed staying with Juan's parents, too. They were amongst the poorest of *peóns*, earning a meager salary to tend the cattle of their *patrón* Don Miguel. Their life was in stark contrast to the affluent lifestyle of Don Miguel and his family. He had found their sincerity, in nursing him back to life—as well as Juan's loyal friendship—a rewarding experience.

When Caleb had intervened to save Juan's life, he had been wounded by one of Blackie Parson's rustlers who were stealing Don Miguel's cattle. Juan and his father had saved his life and protected his goods while they nursed him back to health.

Caleb had been used to being with Polly on the trail, and his memories of their time together were becoming more and more idyllic. He now found that thinking of Polly helped drive thoughts of María out of his mind. He realized that putting his relationship with María behind him would not be easy, but nothing on the frontier was particularly easy he knew well.

Although Phillip did everything he could to make him comfortable, Caleb did not want to stay in Santa Fé much longer because he could not realize his ambition to set up his own trading center. And, he could not trade his goods here because of his non-competition pledge with Phillip. The cockfights on Sundays were entertaining the first few times he saw them, but his interest waned after a time or two. The entreaties of the dark-eyed *señoritas* and even *señoras* trying to entice him into their gambling dens to play Monte or into their bedrooms, where for a price they would lay down with anyone, tempted him. But he decided he did not want any more women in his life just now. And besides, there were too many people in Santa Fé to suit Caleb, now that he had been out on his own.

He wanted to leave town as soon as he could. He preferred the quiet challenge of being on his own, alone. He looked forward to getting back on the trail to continue trading for the skins of beaver and other animals. He liked trading, and he was finding that he could do it as well as any man.

The war in Texas between the Mexicans and Texians made him determined to stay away from there, even if you could buy over 4,000 thousand acres of land for $200, as some people told him your could. He remembered what his father had told him: "Stay away from wars and that kind of trouble. Wars make the generals famous but leave the common soldier hurt, broke, lame, or dead."

Caleb was ready to leave Santa Fé after a week's preparation. Juan, his 12-year-old companion, would go with him. Juan was much more than an employee; and he certainly was not a servant. Juan was his trusted friend and companion. There was a bond of trust between them that had already been tested. They had saved each other's lives once already.

Juan and Caleb were going to travel the 80 miles from Santa Fé to *San Fernando de Taos* as fast as they could move their pack animals. The journey would take five days. Towards evening of the first day, they came upon a small mission. A priest there had numerous Indians plowing and planting his fields. Caleb and Juan obtained the priest's permission to camp nearby. The hospitable priest prepared food for them and told them of local news over glasses of his homemade red wine.

The next night, they stopped beyond the village called *Elgidonis at St. Thomas.* This was a long name for such a small village. They camped beside the *Rio Grande del Norte River,* which was a wide, not very deep, muddy stream. On either side of the river for 5 miles the stream gave life to the valley, and much of the valley along the river was cultivated, or being used as irrigated pasture for cattle or forage for sheep. The adobe houses and small huts of the shepherds and ranchers were spotted here and there without any apparent plan or organization, except they followed the river.

On the following day, Caleb and Juan reached a more rugged area and stayed outside of a small group of adobe houses. In this country, the well traveled trail wound around areas of sparse *piñon* pine, rough, multi-colored rock mesas, and countless *arroyos*. The *arroyos* were devoid of water at this time of year, although they became rushing muddy torrents in the infrequent storms.

There was actually no town named Taos. The town's name was *San Fernando de Taos,* or *San Fernando In The Valley Of Taos.* But the American trappers who were wintering there called the area Taos, and soon the local Mexican population was doing the same.

The village of Taos was nestled at the foot of the mountains in a beautiful high-desert valley. There were also several smaller communities in the valley. One, 5 miles away from Taos, was named *Los Ranchos*. The valley's elevation was just below 7 thousand feet. The *Sangre de Cristo* Mountains to the east rose to 13,000 feet, partially surrounding Taos. The *Sangre de Cristo*, or Blood of Christ, mountains were so named because they turn a pink-red blood-like hue in the evening's waning light. The tiny town, with only five hundred souls, was much smaller than Santa Fé. It was beautiful, with a hodgepodge of whitewashed walls and rambling adobe buildings, with no seeming reason why one ended where it did, and the next began.

Taos was widely known as the headquarters of many of the beaver trappers. It was here that many of the pelts, (called plews) or beaver skins of prime quality, ended up. Even many of those traded for at the mountain rendezvous were brought through Taos on the way to Santa Fé and the United States. Many of the trappers lived and headquartered at Taos when they could not trap because of the cold weather and loneliness in the mountains. It was not possible to trap the streams when frozen solid and the animals hibernated. Bartering the furs sustained the trappers until the spring thaw, when they could begin trapping again.

It was here that Caleb could learn more about the peltry business, and perhaps make and repair rifles as his father had taught him. He had whiskey to sell, gunpowder, rifles, pistols, lead, beaver traps, and the other items necessary to start trading. All he needed was a handy headquarters and some customers.

Caleb wanted to scout around to learn about Taos and the countryside that surrounded it. By talking to some of the people he could learn what was going on. This was necessary before he decided on a business site. So he and Juan set up a temporary camp west of the main part of town, where Juan would stand guard over their horses and packs. Caleb rode through town and looked into a few of the businesses. He also spoke to a few of the residents but did not stay long. He could see that there was a lively competition amongst the traders already established in the town. The fact appeared that they did not need another trader in town. They might even have too many already.

An idea came to his mind: *If I could establish the first trading station in the path of the trappers and Indians coming down out of the mountains, I should be able to get some of their trade. If I try to start up here in town where the other traders are already established, I will starve to death. A site on the trail to the beaver country a long day's journey north of town should give me first crack at the mountain men and Indians as they move south when loaded down with furs.*

Caleb spent several days scouting, riding completely around the town and talking with the few people he encountered. Then he went 20 miles north along the main trail. He was crisscrossing the country close to the trail when he found land that looked promising for his purposes.

Here three trails forked, going north, west, and northwest. This was obviously a junction for the main artery out of Taos to beaver country. The site was on the edge of the *Arroyo Seco River.* Caleb found a small, run-down adobe house nearby, off the main trail. He almost missed seeing it because it was so well hidden behind a small hill.

The house looked so rundown that he thought at first it was abandoned. Everything on the premises was in a state of collapse. The first hint that anyone was there was one old horse in a small fenced pasture. Then as he moved closer he saw two goats, one kid, a few pigs, and half a dozen chickens in a small well fenced yard. A wisp of smoke was coming from the fireplace chimney.

Caleb walked his horse toward the house in plain sight. He stopped in front of the door but did not dismount. "Hello, the house!" he hollered in English first and then in Spanish. "Anybody to-home?" He kept both hands in plain sight on the pommel of his saddle so anyone watching him could see his intentions were peaceful.

"I gots ye covered, so don't git offen yer horse 'til I tell ye to! Whats ye wants hyar?" The sharp voice was coming from a rifle slit in a boarded-up window by the front door, directly in front of Caleb.

"I am a stranger in these parts," Caleb answered. "I am just looking around to see what sort of places might be for rent or for sale for me and my pack horses. I mean no harm, and I will leave if you want me to."

"No! Ye kin git down. Leave your rifles in the scabbards an' leave yer pistols tied up with yer dust covers, jist like you gots 'em. Ye kin come in and have a cup o' coffee an' a smoke. But that's all ye'll git without payin' fer it. I have a lot o' drifters com' by hyar out o' the mountains. The ones that gots their peltry skins keeps a-goin' til they hits town and the fancy women thar. The ones that is broken down on their luck without a peltry to their names comes in hyar lookin' fer free grub and to rob me. I have to be keerful. I been poorly for a right-smart spell, an' I am jist about out o' most victuals."

"I got me a woman here, too. Half the wild mountain men in this area been a-comin' out hyar a-sniffin' at her skirt, all wall-eyed, pantin' like a pack o'houn' dogs, to see iffen I be dead yit. Well, I ain't dead yit, mores a miracle o' the Lord; but it myan't be long, I fear. They all pine an' pant fer the woman, but I ain't a-given her away fer nothin', ya hyar! I got to gits paid, an' a-plenty, too. Then I be a-headin' down to Santee Fee. I've had it with this hyar country. So's iffen ye be a-wantin' a place this'n hyar be it, bein' ye gots hard gold or silver coin to trade fer hit."

"I'll throw the woman in as I don't want to be a-toting her with me nohow. I got her a couple a months ago. She be a Mex that were captured by the Apaches. She been handled pretty rough, but she still got her teeth and is a good-looker betwixt her legs. Not that it would do me no good. I ain't got nary a kick in my barrel no more since I lost my health an' got so stove up. I bought her to take keer o' me, but she can't cook nothin' I likes to eat no-how."

"Well, to tell the truth, I don't want a woman. That's for sure," Caleb answered him in disgust. "What I'm looking for is a small piece of land that I can set up a trading post on and keep my horses on. If it had some pasture I might be able to board some of the livestock for the trappers while they're down to Taos town. I learned rifle-smithing from my father, and I am a fair rifle-smith. I could set up my tools and fix a few rifles between now and spring. And if there are Indians about, I could trade with them a little for furs. That's why I'm looking here to the north of town. I was hoping there might be some trade coming down out of the mountains, and I could get first crack at them as they come by out of the mountains. I don't want to put you out none. If you don't know of any land that I might get, I will mosey on."

The front door swung open on its leather hinges. A skinny old man dressed in ancient, soiled almost black deerskin came out the door. "My name's Thomas Lyon. Come in then, an' sit a spell. I'll git the woman out hyar and make her take her clothes offen iffen you'll pay cash fer her."

"No, I don't want a woman, any women, and that's final!" Caleb was getting more and more agitated at the old man's insistence on selling him the woman.

"Git down offen yer horse and come in hyar or I'll blow a hole in your back when ye rides offen iffan ye don't. This whole set-up's for sale cheap, an' yer the fust live prospect I seen this year hyar. Ye ain't a-gittin' away that easy. Ye said ye was a-looking fer a place. Now I'm a-sellin' this hyar place to ye, and that's the final agreement. It's cheaper as anythin' else ye might be a-findin'.

"I got nigh onta six hundred acres hyar. I bought it from the Mexicans. It's got two springs on hit, an' yonder trail over thar goes right through the center of hit. So's it's jist what ye be a-lookin fer. I'll give ye th' whole kit-an'-caboodle fer a hundred pesos cash money, gold or silver, English or Spanish coin. No worthless paper money neither. That's jist what I paid fer it mor'n ten years ago. Kin ye read? I got's the papers in me box hyar showing I got a receipt fer hit. Hit's in Spanish, but official 'cause I showed it to the *alcalde* in Taos an' he signed offen the bottom o' it an' entered it in his'n book o' land titles.

"I've gotten so stove up with the rheumatiz I kain't do no trappin', farmin', nor work of no count no more so's it's no good to me. That cold water walkin' after beaver peltry in those mountain streams plum got me stove up with the rheumatiz, ye know, crawling around in the ice water cotchin' beaver pelts. I gots two goats, one kid, some pigs, a few chickens—an' the woman—but they don't bring no cash. They goes with the place."

Caleb was worried about the old man's threat to shoot him in the back if he rode away. But when he could see that the man could barely walk and one eye showing an empty socket was closed where it had been poked out, Caleb decided he wasn't so dangerous after all.

The old man wasn't holding the gun in a threatening position. He was using it as a cane. He was so stiffened up with rheumatism that he could only hobble. The one good black piercing eye, under a large bushy gray eyebrow, peered at Caleb. His gaunt face had a stubble of whiskers. But despite his obvious physical infirmities, something about the old man told Caleb he was still completely capable of using his flintlock rifle if he wanted or needed to. There was a heavy old-fashioned pistol in a holster at his side too.

As Caleb walked through the door he saw the inside of the cabin was a shambles. The back part of the roof had fallen in from the weight of the snow, and the old mountaineer and the Mexican girl were living in a small area under the roof that was still standing, near the front of the building. The woman looked to be about 35 five years old to Caleb, but she was actually only 23.

"Get us some coffee, Isabella! And mak-er snappy, or I'll whip yer bottom!" the old man barked at her. He was showing off, giving orders; but his tone was not as unfriendly as the words implied. She did not seem to take offense and put a coffee pot over the fire.

Isabella was tall and attractive, with broad, strong shoulders and arms that were unusually muscular for a woman. The Spanish and Moorish blood mixed with Indian made her beautiful. Her complexion was brown. Her nose was well developed, not huge; but not small, either. Her ample breasts protruded forward and upward under the one-piece animal-skin Indian-style dress. She was clearly a proud woman. She ignored the ranting of the old mountain man and flashed a bright, toothy smile at Caleb although she did not say anything.

When she brought the two of them coffee, she told Caleb in Spanish, "don't pay any attention to Thomas. He didn't buy me from anyone. I was captured by the Apaches and had been a slave to one of them for three years. I was doing all right, but the Indian that owned me was killed by White Mountain men set on stealing his furs. They killed both our children, too. I escaped and crawled up here like a dog, hurt and starving, about two months ago. He took me in and shared what little he has with me. He figures that anyone who takes me on and doesn't pay a good price for me wouldn't value me enough and might sell me back to the Injins. He's truly a very good man. He's just been sick so long that he hides behind that rifle."

"Be quiet, woman, or I'll beat ye within a inch o' yer worthless hide! Git out o' hyar an' git out to the barn an' do some chores. We be a dickerin' fer this place, an' I don't want ye to go a-spoiling my dicker by yer woman-talk gibber-jabber. I got a live'un hyar, and I don't mean to let him get away! Now, whar was I before she stuck her big sha-dup-trap into it?" Thomas paused a moment to gather his thoughts.

"Oh, yeah! Hyar's the map written right on the back o' tha deed," He pulled the deed and its drawing and some papers out of the table drawer. "See, hyar is th' trail marked with the dotted line, an' this be the foothills to the north. See how the line goes along the crest o' 'em. Hyar's the one creek called *Arroyo Seco* a-comin' across. They's fish in' 'er, too. Hyar's the smaller crick to the east, and hyar's the big pile of rocks down below towards Taos town. Them's the boundaries. Ye kin go look fer yourself, iffen ye wants to. Well, what ye say? Is it a deal, er no?"

"I want to go look at the springs and creeks and things," responded Caleb. "I also want to go talk to the *alcalde* in Taos and make sure it is legal for me to buy it. If it's all as you say it is and if they will let me buy it, I will buy it for just the 100 pesos you said you wanted! But you will have to find a place for the woman. I don't want the responsibility. I can't take care of her because I will be gone much of the time. I definitely do not want a woman in the deal. She's your problem to deal with."

The old man's face lighted up with a huge grin. "I knew it! I knew it! I knew it the minute I set my eyes on ye. I said to meself, 'Thar yonder young'n is the bright cub that's a'goin' to cash me out o' this hyar flea-trip-trap.' Dag-nab-it, ye musta been sent from the One above. I knew it the minute I lay eyes on ye. Shake, pard! She's a deal." Caleb took the man's hand in his own. His grip was surprisingly strong. With good food and perhaps a little medicine, he might improve.

Legalities in the Spanish Territory of New Mexico were very complicated. There were three authorities that had to be dealt with. First was the military. They and they alone could discipline soldiers of any rank, no matter what crime they might be accused of. Then there was the ecclesiastical authority of the only church that was allowed to exist, the Catholic Church. No priest could be disciplined in any way except by a church authority. Finally, there was the civil authority that ruled the rest of the population.

The general population in this area was ruled by the *alcalde* of Taos, who was every bit as powerful as the *alcalde* in Santa Fé. The *alcalde* was judge, jury, sheriff, and executioner for the other residents. He did not actually govern from a set of written laws for the most part. He himself *was* the law. He would listen to an accuser's story; and if he believed it, he would call the accused in and listen to the other side of the story. He would make a decision on the spot, and justice would be carried out immediately. If a person did not like a decision, it was theoretically possible to lodge an appeal in Mexico City, 1,500 miles away. However, as a practical matter appeals were rarely made, and then only by the rich.

Caleb rode to Taos and visited the *alcalde* to make sure he did not do anything wrong. He wanted the authorities to know exactly what his plans were so he would not get off on the wrong foot and have difficulty with the law. The *alcalde* listened to him and found nothing wrong with what he planned to do. Caleb was a citizen, and his papers were in good order, but the *alcalde* wanted to study the matter for a while. He was friends with many of the Taos traders and he wondered if the competition might hurt his friends.

Caleb was impatient to get started on his project before winter came. He offered the *alcalde* two silver dollars, as Thomas Lyon had told him to do, if he could approve his deed assignment and sign the document the following day. The *alcalde* smiled and agreed to Caleb's request, extending his hand for the coin.

Caleb was to ride back out to Thomas Lyon's shack, and get him to sign on the bottom of the deed and receipt that he had been paid. Then the *alcalde* would record it in the official book of his office. As soon as the *alcalde* endorsed the deed, the transaction would be complete. The *alcalde* told Caleb, laughing at him, "You're paying the old man just exactly twice as much for the property as he paid for it ten years ago; and the house, although old then, was in better shape."

When Caleb returned to get the deed, he told Thomas good-naturedly, "You overcharged me, you old skinflint. In Texas I can get over four thousand acres for two hundred dollars. This six hundred acres or so that used to belong to you looks a bit dear, wouldn't you say?"

Thomas Lyon did not look perturbed, "I don't know 'bout that. Down thar in Texas, I'm-a-told, ye gots to fight a war for it with ten thousand Mexican regulars. So's how cheap's cheap? I'm told the landowners down thar is a-mostly runn'n skeert with their tails twinxt their legs. How many lead balls go with the ballast might make a difference, an' I ain't a-given ye back one red-cent nohow even if ye is a Injin-giver!"

Caleb laughed. "You can stay in this old place here as long as you want. You won't hurt anything here." He was catching on to the ways of Thomas Lyon.

"I'm going to set up a camp over by the road and start building my station there. I want to start on it right away. I'm not familiar with using adobe bricks. Could you recommend someone to put up my adobe walls for me? I would like to build them like the other places I've seen around here. Adobe looks warm in winter and cool in summer. And since we're going to be a long way out of town and I will have a store full of goods, the adobe has to be strong enough to withstand any Indian attacks.

"What I need is a good-sized room, maybe twenty-five feet by thirty-five feet. One large, long room with thick adobe walls and a strong roof to start with should be good for my purposes. There will be only one door, at the front. It has to be a large door because we will bring the livestock inside in case of attack. I want to have a parapet or a couple of rooms in two corners, high up off the ground, so we could crawl up there and defend ourselves with rifles in case we are attacked!"

Thomas thought a moment. "Yes, in Taos thar be a man name o' Santoza who makes adobe bricks. He has thousands o' them, more than enough to do what ye wants to do. They's good'uns, too, better ones than ye kin make on yer own, an' that would take ye a year. Iffen ye have him put up your walls an' sich an' put on yer roof ye kin do it in a month or so. He has lots of men to help him. An' winters a-comin. He would build it with his crew o' men an' could do it fer ye faster an' cheaper 'cause the bricks are already made, and aged in the sun. An' he knows what he's a-doin', which ye'uns don't. A good adobe brick is made o' the best clay that used to be rock. So when ye pours it and tamps it into the mold what ye is actually a-doin is making the stone dust back into stone. You mix it with straw or grass, to act as a binder, wet the clay, and compact it. Fer good bricks, they are best made by the Mexican women. Men don't do it as well as the women does it. A good brick is heavy and his is 10 by 18 by 5 inches thick. You want's yer walls at least six feet thick up off the ground to keep the Injins from chopping through the walls easy with an ax.

"He has the timber poles fer the roof, too. All ye have to do is put poles solidly across the top, with poles under 'em near the middle to hold the roof up, an lay four or five layers of adobe brick on top o' it. Then ye puts mud clay on top, betwixt each layer an' it will make the roof waterproof as solid rock. Ye slant your roof so the water runs off. Iffen ye cotches the water in a cistern or barrels ye can keep fresh water all the time. She be fireproof, too, in case the Injins attack. I'm not 'xactly sure what it would cost ye, but ye might get 'er done fer two hundred pesos. Kin yer pocketbook stand the strain, or did I git it all?"

"Wages fer Mexicans is two or three dollars a month. They's good solid hard workers an' they work from dawn to dark. Iffen ye gets four or six o' them ye kin finish th' job quick an' git inside it—quick-like. Before the snow she-flies. I agree ye should make one large room. Then once't yer inside ye kin make some partitions iffen ye wants mor'n one room. One's always been enough fer me. I likes yer idear about them corner rooms above the roof at two corners. Make them plenty strong. Ye kin use them as a couple o' bedrooms, and ye can lock yerself inside them an' hold off a whole passel o'Injins plinkin' off out yer rifle slits 'til they gits the idea they hain't welcome. The walls of the upper rooms should have rifle slits so's ye kin rake th' walls below with rifle fire. Ye kin fix it so's ye kin even lift up the ladder, inside, to them rooms so's no one kin git at ye even iffen they should get inside."

"Yessiree, I like's yer idea right smart! Them upper rooms will have to be made o'timbers to stay up thar an' hang over, but ye kin have Santoza put a couple o' layers o' adobe bricks an' clay mud on th' outside fer fire protection, inside too, iffen yer a mind to." The old man was stroking his chin and nodding his head affirmatively, obviously approving of Caleb's plans.

"Iffen ye don't want th' woman, we'll throw her out to the wolves or sell 'er back to the' Apaches. Or she kin go down to Taos town an' sell her pussy-cat fer a meal or two a week, I s'pose. We'll kick 'er broad beam out'n yonder door when I takes off an' that will be the end o' it and her too."

"You kin slop yer own pigs, milk yer own goats, an' chop yer own fence posts and fire wood. An' ye kin jack yer own pecker, too, I guess, iffen your'n even works. Ye is prob'ly too mean an' small a yung'un ter git a good hard-on, nohow, see'ins how ye don't take no truck o' womenfolk. It'd be waste o' good woman-flesh ter waste 'er on sich as ye be, not havin' even normal wants in yer bones." Thomas was looking off out the window pretending to be minding his own business.

Caleb should have known better than to accept the goats, pigs, and chickens. He knew he was being suckered in, but he hadn't decided yet how he could get rid of the woman. He certainly did not want to see her sold back to the Apaches. But a woman was the last thing on earth he wanted at his new station. He didn't want her around, but someone would have to help him and Juan build fences if he was to pasture horses for the trade he hoped would be coming down from the hills with their peltry. *Maybe she can stay just for a little while,* Caleb conceded to himself.

"We'll see what happens when you get ready to leave. I can go to Taos with her and try to help her get settled. This old place here under your roof won't be fit through another winter. It's getting ready to collapse on top of you. One more good snow on your roof, and we will have to dig you out of your blankets with a shovel and ax."

"By the way, do you have any axes and shovels and saws? An anvil, maybe? I'll need some tools to start work. I forgot to ask you if they went with the place when I bought it."

"Talk to the woman." Thomas said looking out of the corner of his one good eye. "I give all thet thar to her'n, when I sold out. I didn't need 'em no more. Mayn't she'll let ye borray 'em. Whyn't ye ask 'er? Your the muckety-muck landlord big-stick around hyar now. I is jist a trespasser. Ye ought to do it a-fore ye throws her outn't the wolves though, don'cha thinks?"

Caleb was angry at being manipulated by the worn-out old mountain man, who obviously was holding in his laughter. Talking to the old man was like playing a chess game. He was always two or three moves ahead.

"All right! All right!" Caleb knew he had to do something to get the tools he needed. "Perhaps the woman can help with the fencing. She can stay until we find a better place for her. Now, are you satisfied? You've poured it on thick enough. But only for a little while. I don't want a woman around, and that's final!"

"Yessir! Yessir! I'll send her an' her tools over in the mornin'. I had the anvil buried. She'll dig it up fer ye with her shovel an' pick ax see'ins as how ye ain't got nary tools o' yer own. She kin push it over in her wheelbarrow. She got a old two-wheeled *carreta*-cart I give her, too. She kin bring a couple o' yer horses to drag some o'her fixin's and your livestock. She can cut grass an' hay if you plant some, and haul it fer ye in her *carreta*!"

"Ha! You'll never make it with these hyar mount'in men," Thomas lectured Caleb, turning his thumb down in derision. "They be too intelligent fer ye, most of them's as still got their hair, that is. Ye ain't good quick-witted 'nough. Ye jist ain't got it 'twixt the ears, nor dried behind the ears! They'll skin ye right out o' yer britches an' moccasins, an' take yer pipe with 'em jist fer the fun o' hit."

"I might even come yonder an' watch ye fail. It'll be funs watchin' ye slowly go under an' starve to death. I might could stick around an' hep ye a mite iffen ye want. I kaint do no work to amount ter nothin', but I kin shoot a rifle a fair smidgen when the Injins be a comin'. They will be a-comin' too, they always does when there's loot."

"And I know peltry bett'r'n anyone you-all knows. I know every mountain man goes up this hyar trail, alive'uns—the dead 'uns too, fer that matter. Not that they all like's me. I wouldn't go that fer, but some o' them don' mind me. An' I've slept under a single blanket with some o' the best, as well as the worst. What say ye? I might like ter stick around an' watch ye go broke like I almost done jist fer laughs iffen you'd throw a little grub into me pot. Yer sich a pilgrim it's a-goin ter be fun watchin' ye go under."

Caleb did not answer. He would have to think that one over first.

Caleb and Juan brought the packhorses to the trail junction in two days. They arrived in the late afternoon. Isabella had already arrived with saws, axes, the anvil, bellows, a large lead ladle, cooking pot, Dutch oven, frying pan, and other assorted tools and equipment. "Juan, you and Isabella unload the horses," Caleb directed. "Make a temporary rope corral. Hobble them and stake them out down by the river where we can keep our eyes on them until we get a corral built."

"I also want you to make a temporary *jacal,* shelter, for us to live in out of brush and saplings. When the new building is finished, the shelter can be used to keep the chickens and livestock in, and for storage, so plan it that way. You can sharpen the tools and then start cutting poles and limbs along the river for the shelter. When you get the roof on, get our packs stored inside so as to protect them and keep them dry for now."

Caleb's first job of the morning was to select the site for his new station house. He wanted it to sit just off the road with enough room in the front to make a place for potential customers to tie up their horses at the hitching rack he would build out front. He remembered that he and his father had discussed a passage that they had read in the Bible to try to understand its meaning, it read: "Therefore whosoever heareth these sayings of mine and doeth them, I will liken him unto a wise man, which built his house upon a rock."

The site he selected for his new building was a large level area that overlooked the creek at the back and was raised up slightly above the surrounding countryside. The floor would be laid out upon a solid piece of hard granite rock. No Indian could dig under it if Caleb's station were under siege. It would have a solid rock floor and footing, like the Bible said. This would be his station. "Lander's Station!" he said to Juan. "I like the sound of it. It will be solid as a rock, too! And we will have a cistern to catch rain and snow water. "

With the site laid out, by mid-morning Caleb was riding into Taos to find Santoza, the contractor with the adobe bricks. The round trip would take three days.

He made his arrangements with Santoza, who promised that he would start out with the first load of bricks in the morning. Caleb had already marked the four corners, and the contractor would do the rest. They agreed on a price of $350, which included strong doors and shuttered rifle slits capable of standing up to an Indian attack. The building was taking on the appearance of a small fort in Caleb's mind. He wanted to be able to defend himself.

The building plan was simple. It was almost identical to the building Caleb had planned with Thomas Lyon. It was to be 25 feet wide and 35 feet long on the inside. There would be only one large double-wide door, at the front, large enough to bring the animals inside during an attack. The tower-like second-floor rooms would be 6 1/2 six feet high on the inside and 10 by 12 feet wide. They formed the basis of Caleb's protective plan. The rooms, which could also be used as bedrooms or storage, were located diagonally across from each other and built into the roof and walls. They would be too high for anyone standing on the ground on the outside to see into. From the inside, ladders, which would lead up into the rooms, could be drawn up into the rooms for extra protection.

A defender would always be able to fight from them with a clear view of fire along the walls. In case of an attack, a person could climb up into one of the rooms and shoot from firing slits in the walls, floor, even the roof. And the two rooms would protrude out far enough so a person inside with a rifle or pistol could shoot downward at anyone trying to break in the door, or cut through the walls.

It would also be possible for defenders in the rooms to shoot anyone who might get onto the roof. Sharpshooters in the rooms could see and shoot in all directions. Caleb planned to keep several rifles and shotguns always loaded and stashed in the towers. They could be primed and fired immediately. One thing he had plenty of was rifles and pistols for trading, or for his own use.

Isabella went with Juan to Thomas's old house to bring down the livestock, so she could take care of them at the site of the new camp they were moving to. She used an old two-wheeled *carreta* that was at the house. The massive wheels of the *carreta* had been cut out of a large tree. Around the perimeter of the floor of the cart bed were upright posts and railings except at the rear, which opened with a gate. A six-inch pine pole, six-feet long, inserted through the center of the wheels served as an axle. Because the bed of the cart was small, the payload they were able to move on the *carreta* was small too. A longer pine pole, a single tree, was affixed under the axle, under the bed of the box. It protruded out the front and served to hitch the horses to, by make-shift harness they lashed up.

Isabella and Juan harnessed one horse on each side of the pole. At least four or, better yet, six horses would have not been too many to pull the peculiar-looking contrivance if they were going any distance. But because the distance was short and down hill, they hoped the two horses could pull it alone. Isabella used wetted soap to grease the axle, as Thomas had told her to do, but it still squeaked and protested loudly when it moved.

The creaking and squealing of the axle on the un-greased wheels made the horses, which had never pulled any kind of wagon, wild and nervous. They kept trying to bolt. Only when Juan and Isabella each led a horse were they able to control them and move the contrivance at all. The fact that the wheels were not well rounded further contributed to the problems, causing the *carreta* to sway and bump up and down as it moved down the trail over uneven ground. In addition, the two goats tied at the rear of the *carreta* were pulling in the other direction, trying to get away from the awful racket. And the chickens with legs tied together were inside their cages, which had been put inside the cart. The chickens were squawking and clucking, and occasionally flapping their wings trying to get up, as the conveyance bumped over the uneven ground.

Thomas Lyon was in a fit of laughter as he watched Juan and Isabella walk the horses down the path. The unlikely looking couple trying to keep the horses from bolting looked so out of place in the wilderness. The mere sight of them left him weak with laughter. He had to turn away because it hurt him too much to laugh so. He was talking to the open window through which he was watching: "This air a-gettin' curiouser an' curiouser: Caleb, who is after all only-est a y'ung'un boy, not even dry behindst the ears; Juan, who is just a baby-child; Isabella, who is jist a Mexican slave girl; an' a one-eyed old cripple too stiff to tie his'n own shoe. Now iffen that don't make a comedy o' errors I'd like ter know what does an' put in with ye! This are jist too good! I kain't leave it." He laughed and laughed.

For the first time in her life, Isabella was in a place she wanted to be. Until now, she had been someone or another's slave and could not escape. She was nervous and uncertain about this new arrangement, but she was determined to make herself wanted and useful to the thin, strange-looking youth who had suddenly become the owner of this property. She could be useful here if only he would let her stay, but he already had said he did not want her. She set to work plotting the best way to change his idea about that. He was strange and elusive, but she would do her best to make him want her. She worked hard for the three days Caleb was gone to make arrangements with the building contractor. All day long she and Juan worked to build the shelter and move the materials from Thomas Lyon's old rancho building, she was also thinking about her plan to make Caleb let her stay. She had some ideas about how to achieve that.

Isabella placed the goats and pigs inside the partially constructed shelter and the chickens at one end of the structure. During the final trip from Thomas's cabin, she and Juan brought the balance of the livestock and tools, some small pens for the chickens, and even some building materials from the barn and corral to make the *jacal* more weatherproof.

A temporary fireplace of stones stood in the center of the almost-roofless *jacal*. Only the first few branches that would form the roof had been put in place, but even in this unfinished state, it would protect against some of the wind and hold in some heat from the fire because it now had brush walls. As soon as she and Juan could cut more saplings and brush, they would add more branches to the roof so it would shed most of the rain and snow and break the force of the wind. Smoke from the fireplace would drift upward through a hole in the middle of the roof.

Juan had laid out his blankets in the middle of the shelter, and Caleb's bedding had been spread by Isabella, at one end. She put a mattress of dried grass, which she had cut with a butchering knife and pulled up by hand, under his blankets to make him more comfortable.

A cooking pot full of stew was warming on the fire. Isabella had gathered a few roots, wild onions and added dried meat from Caleb's pack to make the stew. She had the coffee pot filled with water, and she planned to put coffee on to boil as soon as she saw his horse coming. It would be hot and fresh by the time he came into camp. A little cold water sprinkled on top of the boiling grounds would settle them so he could have a fresh cup. As evening approached, Isabella was getting more and more concerned whether Caleb would return before dark, or if ever. She peered anxiously up the trail to the south as the shadows lengthened. Finally, she was relieved to see him coming, although he was still a long way from their temporary camp.

Caleb returned tired from dickering with the contractor and the forty-mile round-trip to Taos. He was surprised and pleased at the progress Isabella and Juan had made toward a temporary camp. The whole place had a warm, welcoming feeling to it.

Isabella ran out to meet him, taking the reins and leading his horse. "Welcome, *Señor*! Welcome to thy *hacienda*. Let me take thy horse, *Señor*. I will place the saddle by thy bed. There is fresh coffee boiling in the pot, and I have placed your plate and cup by the fire for thee." She was careful to address him in the formal Spanish that servants used when they addressed people they served. It certainly didn't hurt for her to appeal to his ego in this way, and show respect for the new owner of the property.

Caleb served himself out of the stew pot simmering on the fire. As he ate he was pleased by the goodness of the simple hot meal. He watched her smooth, strong movements, which were accented by the flat layer of deerskin she wore. He wasn't sure but guessed she had no underclothes on.

"Let me show you how I want you to hobble the legs of the horses, Isabella," said Caleb when he had finished eating. "I want you always to put hobbles on one side. The horses are used to it, and it is a better way to keep them from running off than hobbling the two front legs. Always do it the way I show shown you. Once we get corrals up, it might be safe to take the hobbles off. I wish we had someone who could act as guard for us, especially at night."

"Thee might consider asking Thomas to come down here," Isabella told him. "He doesn't sleep much; he sits up most of the time. Thee could have him be thy night guard to alert thee in case of attack. The Indians never bothered him up at his place because he didn't have much to steal, and he was always alert. The mountain men do not bother him, either."

"Do you really think he could be a guard?" Caleb was interested in her idea but doubtful about the old man. "He is not well, and he has only one eye."

"He is truly like a cat," she said, "always prowling with that one good eye of his. He is brave and not afraid of anything. The Indians fear him. I think they think him a little crazy. He has survived out here for more than thirty years, which is proof enough of his ability to stay alive."

"But I thought he wanted to move to Santa Fé." Caleb was not at all sure he liked the cantankerous old schemer who had outdone him in their land deal. "Doesn't he plan on going down there?"

"He really doesn't want to go to Santa Fé, *Señor*," Isabella told him earnestly. "It's only a dream of his. And now that he is face to face with leaving here, he does not want to go. He has nothing down there. I think he would rather be here and help thee. He would be a lot of use to thee."

But can he do any work? Caleb questioned himself silently. He was beginning to realize he was already saddled with a young boy and a woman. What he needed now was a strong man to do hard physical labor and protect the place. Caleb was curious about just what Thomas Lyon could contribute to his enterprise.

"He can't do any physical work, 'tis true," she said. "That's because of the stiffness in his bones. But he is smart and has experience, and he could supervise and give you advice. I think if thee told him what thee wanted him to do, he could get some of his friends from the old days to do some business with thee."

"When the trappers come down out of the mountains, they don't like to have to sell their horses and mules. The men get attached to them and don't want to have to buy new ones every year. If thee wouldst keep their animals for them during the winter and not charge them too much, they would have to come out here to get their animals when they head back into the mountains. And because the trappers would already be here anyway, they might buy some of their supplies from thee. The two could work together." Isabella had sat down very close to him by the fire. She was touching him, helping him plan.

"That's a very good idea, Isabella." He turned his head towards her. He could feel the warmth of her body, and it was pleasant in the cool evening. "If Thomas wants to join us, I will let him, if he can help us sell some of our goods."

"And I want to talk to you about your pay, and Thomas, too, if he is going to help us. As I told you before, I am not going to keep you here; but you can stay until we find a good place for you that is also where you want to go. In the meantime, I would like you to work for me; and I want to treat you fairly. Everyone has to be paid an honest wage. I won't be able to pay much, and if I don't make some money along the way I won't be able to keep it up. But I want to start out right with you."

"Money for me! Ha! Ha!" Isabella laughed in surprise, and her teeth flashed in the firelight. She placed her hand on his leg. "I have worked since I was old enough to walk. I was a slave for the Church, tilling their fields and serving the priests for their pleasure. Then I was a slave after I was captured by the Indians."

"I have never in my life been paid anything, not even a *claco* copper coin, a measly half cent. The nearest I came to it is when the Franciscans gave me to one of the older priests at the mission farm. He whipped me with a bullwhip to make me more attentive to him and my prayers. He told me at the time that that was my payment for my sins. I do not expect to be paid anything more than my food and a place to stay. If you will give me food, it will be enough for me. That's all I could get somewhere else, if I was lucky enough to find a place that would have me."

"But there should be plenty of people who could use a good strong woman such as you," Caleb responded. "You did a good job here. I am surprised at how much you and Juan have accomplished. Couldn't you get a job in Taos?"

She took his hand and held it to her cheek. "There are hundreds of *peóns* with no *patrón* to take care of them who would come here to work for thee if thee would take them in. Thy problem, thee will see, will be to keep them out. On the ranchos even though they say they pay men two dollars a month, they first deduct what they feed or give them. So when thee dies, thee owes them money. Women are usually paid fifty cents a month, not in coin but in credit on their books. It is the Mexican way of treating the *peóns* here."

Caleb shook his head stubbornly. "No, I want to set a fair wage. I am told that they pay workers around here two dollars a month. Juan's father was paid five dollars a month, but he had to buy his necessities out of that for the whole family. We will start with two dollars a month. I will pay you, Juan, and Thomas the same for helping me get started. That's over and above your food and necessities. You can't read can you? I know that Thomas can read a little bit, and that will work to our advantage."

"Well, it might surprise thee that I, too, can read a little and write a little, also." She replied. "Not much, thee understands, but some. My father was a priest, and he taught me. They are not supposed to teach women how to read or write, but he and I used to play games when I was a child. He would show me the letters and words, and then I would try and remember them. He liked it because I could usually remember the meanings from one day to the next. It is, of course, Spanish. I learned to speak a little English from Thomas. And if reading will serve thee, I will learn more if it pleases thee, and if thee will give me the chance."

"My father, the priest, was the master of my mother. She was one of his mission Indians. She and I were the property of the Church. They owned us body and soul. I guess thee could say she was a slave although my father, was very good to her. And he acknowledged that I was his daughter, which was more than most of the priests would do with a bastard child."

"My father was from Spain. He was from Castile, so the Spanish I have learned is not just like that spoken by most Mexicans. Castilian Spanish is more formal, so I have been told. I learned to speak Spanish from him while learning the Apache tongue from my mother." Isabella lay her head upon Caleb's shoulder and looked at the darkness overhead as the fire burned. She reminisced about her pleasant memories of her father. "My father was a very good man and mingled with the Indians walking bare foot, as they did, in humility."

"When my father died the new priests came. I became their slave and have been a slave ever since. I was handed down from one priest to the next until the Apaches took me. When the Apaches came, they killed all the priests and all the Spanish-speaking men. They kept us women and the children to serve them. I became a slave. The Indian that fathered my two children was actually better to me than the priests had been after my father was gone. My Indian master hardly ever beat me, except when he got too much of the white man's whiskey. When he got drunk he always beat me, of course. Indian women believe that men do not care enough about them if they do not beat them. They expect it, actually demand it. I never understood that."

"In addition to Apache, I can speak some pueblo Indian dialects, which might prove to be useful to thee in thy trade." she continued. "Thomas speaks the sign-language that is used by many Plains Indians. It is wonderful to watch them talk for a long time with complete understanding while not saying a single word beyond a occasional grunt." She got up and pulled on Caleb's hand to help him up.

"If thee has had enough to eat, come and I will show thee where thy blankets are. I have thy bed ready. Thee must be tired. Here, let me help thee get thy clothes off and get into bed. I have laid clean grass under thy blankets so thee will be comfortable, until I can make thee a better, thicker, mattress. I took a bath in the river today to please thee and be clean for thy pleasure. I have been thinking about thee all day. I know that thou dost not want me to be here with thee, but I hope to change thy opinion if thee will but let me try, *Señor*".

"I want thee to know that I want to be with thee either paid or as a slave. It doesn't really matter to me. I can't imagine any place that would be any better than here, and I like being with thee. That is the truth. I swear it before God as my witness."

"Isabella, you don't have to sleep with me. I will give you half my blankets."

"Don't be foolish," she interrupted. "I am a strong, healthy, passionate woman who has been dreaming of being with thee all day. I will be good for thee. If we do as thee suggests, we will both be cold and unhappy all the time. The Indians believe that for a man to sleep alone makes his arms weak. I have been thinking of thee all day, and I am already warm-wet between my legs hoping you would return to me and relieve me. Come, give me a chance to warm thee. I will do my best to make thee happy under the covers. *I want to!*" She took his coat off, smiling and then removed his pistols and belt. He was embarrassed. She knew she had already had an affect on him as they sat by the fire. The anticipation and attraction did not belong to either one of them alone.

"I keep my pistols and rifle next to me under the covers," he protested.

"Of course. And on the other side I will lay with thee, and try to watch out for thee and protect thee. We all depend upon thee now, so we have to keep thee healthy and happy, and most important of all, alive. You are the *patrón* here now."

Isabella pulled her Indian animal-skin dress up over her head and stood before him naked. Then she untied the leather thong string that held her hair out of the way during the day and shook her head, shaking her curly black mane loose. It flowed over her shoulders, part in front and part in back. She was proud, and she knew she looked good to men. Her Moorish and Spanish ancestries, mixed with the Indian were apparent in the different shades of her dark skin where her clothes protected her from the sun. She was not pasty-white like Caleb.

Caleb thought she was beautiful, standing there in the half-light made by the fire, which reflected off her brown skin. He could not help but look at her admiringly. The whip strokes across her shoulders stood out as dark lines in the twilight. He turned her around and looked at her back, which was covered with more scars from the lash. He could tell, she had been whipped many times. He shook his head. Why anyone would want to beat such a pleasant woman was beyond his understanding.

"Look at me, Caleb. Am I so ugly that thou wouldst make me stay alone and cold in a single blanket at thy feet?" She slowly raised her arms up so her breasts were held up in front of him in full view. The pose also drew in her stomach and showed off her perfect round navel. Sparkles of light reflecting off the fire highlighted her black pubic hair as she moved. She turned slowly sideways so he could see her from the side, her head held high and looking upwards. Proud. Then she flashed him a smile. She drew her hands, which were still up in the air, slowly down across her breasts, across her stomach, and down her thighs provocatively.

Isabella knew that Caleb did not want her on the property. But she was determined to stay. She would change his mind if she possibly could. She would use the one 'weapon' she had that no man had.

"Am I the worst woman thou hast ever seen?" she almost sang. "The most ugly? The least desirable?" She was teasing him, showing herself off to him. She began to dance suggestively, moving her body forward and back, and her hips from side to side, licking her lips, smiling coquettishly, holding her hands up under her breasts as if she were presenting them to him, then letting them go so they could swing to the music of the movement of her body. "Wouldst thou throw me out into the cold darkness to sleep amongst the owls, coyotes and wolves?" Her teeth flashed again in the darkness, as she chanted unintelligibly to him in one of the Indian chants she knew, in cadence with her dance.

He knew her lips would taste sweet.

Isabella was almost as tall as Caleb. Her body was shapely and strong. The bottom of her stomach protruded like a small pillow because of the two children she had borne. Her large breasts, at which two children had already suckled, were still firm. She smiled as she saw him watch them swaying. They bounced tantalizingly as she moved her lower stomach forward and back, teasing him. She kept up her slow dancing as she began again undoing his shirt front, smiling at him. Her cheeks were turning a slight red under her brown skin as her own temperature was rising. She knew exactly where she was going.

She understood his look. Her dance and song was having the desired effect that she had hoped for. She began to move a little faster and slightly more expressively to the increasing tempo of her song. Isabella loved to dance and sing. She especially loved to dance and sing for Caleb because it was working, as she had hoped it might.

He could not take his eyes off her bouncing bosoms. They were exciting him. The nipples and the surrounding skin were dark red-brown. She took his hands in her's and placed them upon each bosom, holding his hands there until she felt him grasp her breasts of his own volition. "Hold them! Hold on! Hold them tight for me," she whispered, "until I get thy shirt off. It will warm me." Of course it was warming him, too.

She knew she had warmed him enough now, and that he would not turn back. Then she took his pants down, stroking his already awakened penis, holding it in her hand. His hardened penis, warm and pleasant to her touch, was by this time slightly wet in her hand, as his lubrication began to spill out its tip. She kissed it and tasted it.

She brushed against him, still holding onto his penis all the while, titillating him, her breasts still firmly in his hands. He had no intention of letting go as his fingers found the large nipples and tightened on them, knurling them playfully, giving himself as much pleasure as it gave her.

The feint odor of her vagina wafted up to his nostrils, calling to him. She continued to hold his now fully hardened penis. "We will have to be careful so as not to waste thee too soon," she whispered. She laughed again, a throaty laugh, as her own passion was beginning to deepen and take hold of her.

Putting his hands behind her back now and encouraging him to hold her, she moved firmly against him, pressing his body to hers. Her hands went up around his neck, holding him and lightly pulling his head down towards her lips. She pressed against his hard-on with her stomach, as she had tilted it upward.

"You are a lovely devil, Isabella. I can see that you would make me the slave. I confess that you are in charge." The fire was reflecting off the back of the partially built *jacal* hut, but it was getting cold at this high elevation, especially the side of them that was away from the fire.

"That is as it should be under the covers when we are alone at night," she whispered, kissing his lips lightly. "When the nights are dark and cold most of our time will be spent under the covers, so we must be prepared to enjoy our time together. The nights are long, and there is nothing else to do." She pressed herself tighter against him, kissing him again. "Come. Get under the covers. Let me earn thy pleasure and bring thee what contentment I can. I want to serve thee. I have something for thee." She laughed again as she pulled him, naked, down beside her into the bedroll and blankets. She grasped his penis again.

"Yes, I can see that you do," he acknowledged. "I am sure you do. But I have something for you, too." It was Caleb's turn to laugh. "And if you will but let go of it, I would like to give it to you now." He rolled over on top of her, looking down on her exquisitely happy face.

She knew she was bringing him pleasure. She wrapped her strong arms around him; smiling happily at the attention she was getting from him, now spreading her legs and moving herself so as to get into position to receive him. Her scent was stronger now, and it excited them both. Her vagina lips were open, swelling, and wet in anticipation of that which it was soon to receive and engulf.

"Yes! Yes! I have been looking forward to receiving thee all day. I could hardly wait, not knowing when thee wouldst return or if thee might reject me. Preparing your bed and blankets, and hoping you would let me share them with thee excited me. It is strange, isn't it that I would look forward to such a thing under the covers? I am grateful that thou wouldst take me in, even if only for a little while. I promise thee to serve thee well. I wouldst hope I do not disappoint thee."

"But remember, Isabella, you are only here because you want to be. You can leave with my blessings any time you want. You are nobody's slave any longer. I will help you find a better place in Taos if you want me to."

"Why is it that I always have this strange feeling that thee will always be trying to send me away?" she asked with a laugh. "There really is no place I would rather be than right here in thy arms under you."

She raised her knees up, to either side of him, legs spread wide, encouraging him to come into her and moving her body slightly towards him, seeking out the tip of his penis. Her feet were flat on the blanket under them. Her vagina was open to him, wet-hot, swollen, now inviting him in. She was as ready and willing as any woman could be.

There was hardly a moment's hesitation as he moved forward and slipped inside of her. She tightened down her welcome on him, sighing her pleasure at receiving him. He was delighted with her tightness and warm, wet welcome. "Mmmm!" he groaned happily. His fit between her legs was natural for both of them. She was perfectly positioned so she could time herself to meet his thrusts by lifting up under him. She moved her hands down his back in a hurried caress and placed both of her hands on his buttocks, bringing him to her as deep as he could thrust.

She kissed his lips, reaching for the sound with her tongue, making a happy, welcoming sound with her throat. "Mmmm!" The sounds of pleasure coming from him made her redouble her effort to bring him his few seconds of extreme happiness. She did not want to talk any more. She did not want him to talk any more. The time for talking was over.

She kissed him hard, opening her mouth to receive his tongue, sucking him and his saliva, as she felt him to press further into her. He stopped several times to enjoy a moment, only to have her tighten down on him and encourage him to continue. *Keep moving*, her vagina seemed to be saying. *Don't stop. Cum into me.* She would maneuver under him to keep him moving in her, encouraging him to the cuming, the dispensing of the seed was what she was after. She knew exactly what she wanted and she was now getting it.

He would lie still a moment, kissing her, enjoying her pillow-like breasts pressed against his chest, savoring the pleasure. Then she would undulate more strongly under him making happy, throaty noises while pushing on the lower center of his back and directing him a little this way and that way to best feel him in her and meet his thrusts into her. It was not to be very long this first time.

Later, after a rest, they would take much longer in their coitus, and she would experience ecstasy beyond her expectations. Her snare was set, and his rabbit was nibbling at her bait; gobbling might be the better term. She wanted his sperm. She would take all of it she could get. If she could father his child, it would help her position with him. If she could give him a son, her status would be perfected.

Isabella had become an expert in the use of her body for the pleasures of men. Who but men had demanded it of her and trained her to it? Could anyone blame her for using this talent to further her own objectives, to find a place for herself and try to keep from starving to death? What other prospect did the female child of a priest have in a world where women were worth less than fifty cents a month and could be sold or traded for a rifle or two horses or even loaned to a friend at will? So if he got caught in her womanly trap, what else could he expect?

Juan was not asleep in his bedroll at the other end of the roofless shelter they were all sharing—Caleb, Isabella, Juan, and the animals. He was listening to their muted voices. He heard them talking, making plans, making love, as children used to do when people lived in one-room cabins on the frontier.

Before Caleb got up the next morning, Isabella had a fire going and was warming the stew from the previous evening. She had two eggs ready to drop onto the frying pan the moment she would see him move. She had already poured half a cup of goat's milk in his cup. It was warm and sweet because she had just pulled it down out of the goat, and she would mix it half-and-half with his coffee with which to greet him when he stirred.

Caleb was irritated that she had gotten up ahead of him, although the sun was now just barely beginning to lighten up the sky. He would find out it was going to be very difficult for him to get up earlier, or stay up later, than Isabella.

She saw him rise and brought him the cup of coffee and warm goat's milk. She kissed him good-morning and helped him get his shirt on. She wrapped the belt holding his pistols, knife, and other equipment around him. Almost accidentally, her hand fell upon his private parts and held him for just a moment, so he would think of her during the day and not forget to come back at night.

"I hope that once I get this building finished, you and Thomas will be able to manage the store for me when I am gone." He had all but conceded her place at his fire. Where could he possibly get better help than he already had, or better companions?

"My *Lord*, you will see that I am a very strong woman. I might even be as strong as thee in the long run. Thou art too skinny. I will make it a part of my responsibility to fatten thee up," she said as she prepared his food. "We have to prepare your camp first. Then I want to bake bread for thee and prepare better meals. But for the time being, I feel thee wants me to help with the preparation of thy camp."

"Look, our chickens are doing their part already. I got two eggs this morning. If I can make you happy at night, which I will try with all my body and heart to do, it might help thee gain some weight. During the day I will trap and cook rabbits, birds, and fish, and dig roots for thee along the river. You will find us a deer, maybe even a bear or other animals, and bring them home to me; and I will clean them and cook them and dry the meats for wintertime. I can also pick *piñon* pine nuts, roast them and store them for the long winter. In the spring, I will plant and tend thy garden. We can have a good life here. I know nothing about thy trading business, but I will try to learn all thee wants me to learn. Here, have some more coffee. It is hot and good for thee, and the goat's milk is sweet-tasting."

Plans and ideas flowed out of their minds as the sun came up, bringing the new day. "We will keep our accounts in Spanish and English," he told her. "It is important to keep a record of everything. We have many plans to make. Can you shoot a rifle?"

She laughed. "That is one thing none of my masters ever wanted any of us slaves to learn how to do. Guns were forbidden to us."

"I have this flintlock rifle here, I want to give to you. It is yours to keep. My father and I made this a long time ago. It is light and shoots true. I have been teaching Juan how to shoot, and he is already practically as good a shot as I am. It will help him with his confidence if you let him teach you. I call this rifle "Meat-Getter"."

"I will also give you this belt and holster for pistols, and this great long butchering knife. It is very sharp. It used to belong to a very good friend of mine, a woman named Polly. I loved her."

"Good," Isabella said, accepting the rifle. "I can learn to shoot and help protect thy property here as well as protect my own self."

Pleased with her willingness to learn, he continued giving her assignments. "You and Juan go out along the river there and get us a deer. You are to run away from the bears unless Thomas or I am with you. They are dangerous to shoot. Never shoot a bear if you can get away from it."

"I also have two pistols that my father and I made together. One is for Juan. The other is for you. Keep these weapons on your side of the bed, and be prepared to use them at all times. Keep them within arm's reach. We have to be prepared to protect ourselves both from the Indians and the white men too."

"Yes, of course I can do it," Isabella assured him. "I have seen men shoot and load their weapons, and I will be able to do it in no time." She put the pistol in the belt he had given her, and hung the ball bag and powder horn over her head on a leather strap as he was wearing his.

"You and Juan, take the cart and bring Thomas down here. Bring everything he wants with him. I would like him to set up a guard station right out there by the road. He will watch for trouble. And if any mountain men or friendly Indians with furs come down the road, we will set up a table and a place for them to sit right here in front of this *jacal*. Thomas is to give every man that comes down that road going to or coming from the mountains one free drink, a 'drink for the road' we will call it. I hope they will buy a few more drinks and perhaps make some purchases. I want to get our items for sale and trade unpacked and laid out so they can be seen by any customers that might come by. We are in business, as of today. We will cover them with canvas at night to keep any moisture off."

"I have started a list of the values for our goods in both what we will pay in trade and what we will sell for," Caleb continued. "It is not exact. It will only be a guide that we can all work from. Juan cannot read, but he can learn, you can teach him as much Spanish as you know. Most of the trade will be done in terms of trading for the peltry of animals. Thomas can help us with the values, and help you learn how to read English. This is only a start toward getting the values correct, a sort of guide until we become more familiar with the values from other traders in Taos. We will adopt their prices so no one will feel we are taking advantage of them, and still earn a profit for ourselves. Right now I am very confused as to values and measurements. Most people do not seem to have gold or silver, so we will list everything in the customary terms the people use for bartering." Caleb had already stared the trading list

LIST FOR TRADING WITH TRAPPERS AND INDIANS

Item	Beaver Skins (Plews)	Coin
Medium calicos		31 cents yard
1 rifle with bullet mold	30	pay $10. Sell for $25
1 pistol with bullet mold	30	pay $5. sell for $15
4 pounds of powder	2	sell for $4 lb.
1 pound of lead	2	sell for $2 lb.
Wine-barrel	10	pay $7.50, sell for $15
Aguardiente - Barrel of brandy	10	$8.00 sell for $16
Sheep	8	50 centavos, sell for 1 peso
Wool per fleece	1	pay 3 centavos each, sell for 6
Iron knife	1	pay $1.00 sell for $3
Flour - 100 lb	5	pay $1, sell for 8 pesos
Salt per mule load	5	pay $2.50, sell for $5
Beeves (beef)	5	pay $2.50, sell for $5
1 horse	5	pay $5, sell for $15
Mule	20	pay $10, sell for $30
1 saddle	15	sell for $30
1 coat	1	sell for $8
3 feet twist tobacco	1	sell for $2
1 beaver trap	4	pay $4, sell for $8

TRADE VALUES WITH INDIANS HERE AT THE STATION

Plews (beaver skins) are the returns expected from trappers who are loaned the goods in advance of the season's hunt. These are deducted before purchasing the balance of their peltry. They are obligated to bring us their pelts and sell them to us if we make them an advance like this.

A trapper will turn in his skins and can catch about 120 in a season, on average. 120 skins are worth about $1,000 in New York ($8.33 each). Most of the companies or traders issue the trappers' goods at about 600% of their cost in Missouri.

A beaver trap is valued at from 12 to 16 dollars. It has a five-foot chain with a swivel at the end to keep it from twisting. 6 of these are considered an outfit for one man.

At rendezvous, sugar is worth $2 a pint, tobacco $2 a pound. (At Philadelphia, tobacco is bought for 10 cents a pound)

Black powder $2 per pint, coffee $2 pint, blankets are worth $25 each. At California ports, cowhides are worth $.50 each. Tallow is 6 cents a pound.

Cowhides are worth 50 cents to us in trade goods only.

Alcohol $3 a pint, or one pelt, on sale here at the store.

A 50-pound ingot of silver is worth about $1,000.

Mexican Money: 12 Granos = 1 real. 8 real = 1 peso or dollar. Claco (tlaco) a copper coin worth about one-eighth of a real or one-and-one-half cents. Copper coins claco or jola = one eighth real. Cuartilla = one quarter real. Avoid the copper coins and refuse any form of paper money is the rule.

Silver coins. Medio six and one-quarter cents. Real is twelve and one-half cents. Peseta = 2 reals. Tston or half-dollar. Peso is one dollar.

The gold coins. Doblon or a (doubloon) with the same subdivisions as the silver dollar, which are also of the same weight. The dobloon is worth sixteen dollars. One customary method of enterprise is to advance the trapper his necessaries for the trapping season. He is given $400 advance in goods. Camp tenders earn about $200 in goods and can be advanced the same amount of goods if they have at least two trappers they are working for.

Flour sells for $20 or 5 cows per 100 lbs. At Fort Hall in the Rocky Stony Mountains. Cattle at Fort Hall are worth from $5 to $10 per head. A horse $15 to $20. A horse in Santa Fe is worth $5.

The Indians trade beaver skins worth between $2 and $3 apiece, buffalo robes worth $1 to $2 apiece, for one pint of water-cut whiskey. A 20-gallon cask of whiskey is mixed six-to-one with water over 100 gallons of trade whisky. 4 quarts in a gallon x 100 = 400 quarts x 2 pints = 800 pints from one 20-gallon barrel of alcohol = 800 pelts worth about $8 each, or $6,400, all from a 20-gallon barrel of alcohol.

A riding horse is equivalent to about 8 buffalo robes, or a used gun and 100 loads of ammunition; or 3 pounds of tobacco, or 10 weasel skins, or 1 skin-shirt and leggings.

1 buffalo robe is equivalent to: 3 metal knives, or 25 loads of ammunition, or a 1 gallon metal kettle, or 3 dozen iron arrow points, or 1 yard of calico decorated with human hair and quills.

Flints cost one-third of a cent in Missouri. We charge 50 cents per dozen or ten cents each. A dozen is paid by us at the station for one beaver plew.

Two grizzly-bear skins are worth one beaver, and four small bear. Must not be mangy, but prime.

In general, the cost of goods at Santa Fe is three to five times those at Independence, Missouri. Wholesale is half what I pay at Santa Fe to Bartholomew.

Spanish, French, and other foreign coin are good specie. Some United States gold bullion by weight may be seen, but Spanish pieces of eight are most likely to be offered. It is valued at eight "reales" or a Spanish dollar.

Pounds, shillings, and pence are the English values.

French gold coins. Louis VIII 20 Francs = one fifth ounce of gold.

Be sure to note if gold coins are shaved. If so, devalue the price allowed for them.

Landers Station, New Mexico Territory, Mexico

CHAPTER 9
Rendezvous at Green River.

There were two seasons for trapping beaver in the mountains, spring and fall. Beaver pelts are at their prime when the weather is cold, when the animals are not shedding. Beaver cannot be trapped in midwinter when the water in the ponds is frozen and they are hibernating. So optimal beaver-trapping weather was the fall and spring when there was ice on the ponds, but rivers were not frozen solid.

The rendezvous was more than a meeting of the trappers and traders. It was an annual event where the trappers, traders, and Indians held their get-togethers. The mountain men, and some Indians came to trade their furs for the supplies they needed, especially those they could not make themselves, like whiskey and gun powder. These gatherings were held in several of the more accessible places throughout the Rocky Mountain region: Pierre's Hole, Green River, and Powder River to name a few of the more prominent locations. The trappers and Indians were the only year-round residents of the mountains.

On the advice of Thomas Lyon, Caleb and Juan made their way to Green River Valley in the summer of 1836 to trade with the mountain men. They trailed four packhorses loaded with goods to trade, plus two extra packhorses to bring back the heavy peltry they anticipated to receive in return.

The valley along the Green River, which was located in the Oregon Territory, was an idyllic setting for the mountain men's rendezvous. Every summer some two hundred trappers would make their way down out of the Rocky Mountains and from other trapping areas as far away as the northern part of the Oregon Territory. In addition, two thousand Indians would visit the rendezvous if you counted the squaws and slave-women the bucks brought with them.

The Green River Valley was an oasis within the rough mountain country surrounding it. There was water and feed for the horses, and wood for fires. The river contained large trout that were easy to catch with hook or spear. Sometimes, the trappers would bet a pile of pelts or other items on who could catch the largest fish with his hands. It was also an opportunity to get fresh meat because buffalo, antelope, and elk could be taken within walking distance.

Every rendezvous would be one long trading and party frenzy, and Green River was no exception. After months of isolation, the men partied constantly at their rendezvous. Trade whiskey flowed like water every night as long as the trapper was solvent and held furs to trade. The more prudent men purchased their supplies first and would simply leave camp when their excess peltry was gone. What furs they had left over after they had stored up on powder, lead, traps, coffee, tobacco, whiskey, and sugar were only good for one thing—a frolicking good time.

There were no laws, no inhibitions, and no limitations to the imagination of the trappers. These wild men were among the most unfettered humans ever to exist. They could do whatever they wanted by way of quenching thirst or feeding hungers so long as their supply of pelts, which they used as money, held out.

The rendezvous was an annual summer-long event. It was continual bedlam. Dogs barked, snarled, fought with each other, and occasionally snapped at strangers. There was constant rifle-fire from muskets being tested before purchase or from hunting, target-shooting, or just plain cavorting and firing up into the air.

Every manner of man could be found here: the French Canadians, who were as wild or wilder than the wildest Indian; the Indians running their horses through the camps; the mountain men, some roaring drunk; Indian girls being traded, loaned, and sold. The traders, trading their goods for pelts before the customer gambled them away and gamblers, always looking for an easy score, were all in evidence.

There was dancing with the Indian women and perhaps most important to the mountain men, a fresh new crop of young, eager Indian girls for sale. What wild mountain man, who had been holed up in a cabin or cave for several months alone or with other men, could resist such inducements? Even the trappers who had left their own squaws back in their camps would at least want to sample the new merchandise.

The Indian girls would often ride their horses through the crowds of men while dressed in their finest tanned and decorated deer skins, tiny bells around their necks, in their hair, and around their ankles. The girls wanted to be purchased. They did everything they could to entice the mountain men to bid the highest prices for them. The girls desired to get a new start with the white-man trappers and a life they thought would be an improvement over the Indian camps, where they were often poorly treated. The girls themselves did not see any of the merchandise and peltry that the men paid for them. Their father's received all such payment. Not all the Indian girls or all of the fathers did this, but there were far more than enough to fill the demand. Indian girls were forms of merchandise or trading goods.

Although it may have seemed otherwise, the traders, mountain men, and Indians were not all there at once. Some left when their supply of peltry ran out. Occasionally, a trapper would lose pelts worth a thousand dollars to the gambling men who also found their way to these gatherings. "Thar goes his beaver an' his hoss," their contemporaries would laugh as the inept card player, went slinking off with hurt pride and empty pockets and tried to borrow enough to start up again in the mountains.

The early comers to the rendezvous had already come and gone by the time Caleb and Juan reached the valley. They set up their camp at the edge of the crowd but did not unpack their goods the first day. Caleb was here to learn and observe and make judicious trades, and he was in no hurry about it. He made a determined effort to take things slowly until he understood the ways the other traders did things. Caleb also had to learn the proper prices of furs here relative to the prices paid at Landers Station. He had a big order pending with Bartholomew, and it was here he hoped to earn enough to pay for all of it.

So far, Landers Station, his fledgling enterprise, had been a financial disappointment. They had broken even, barely covering expenses; but there was little profit so far. On the positive side, they had not been robbed, and they were earning the cautious respect of the few trappers and Indians who had favored them with some business.

Caleb laid out some of his goods on the second day. He was determined to match his prices to those of the lower-priced traders he had observed without undercutting his competitors. He did not want to bring the ire of his competitors down upon himself. There was simply no need to do that.

Caleb sat on his blankets with his wares displayed in front of him, drinking coffee and repairing one of his flintlock rifles. He hoped the trappers and Indians would notice him making the repairs and would then know he did that kind of work, as well as trading.

He was concentrating on fixing a broken rifle when an Indian sat quietly down in front of him on the edge of the blanket. Caleb was surprised when he recognized the Nez Percé he had traded with a year ago on the plains during his trip across the prairies from Independence. The Indian was smiling broadly at Caleb, having recognized him as the trader who had given him good value for his pelts.

Caleb got up and shook his hand warmly. Not only had this Indian returned a lost horse to Caleb, he had also warned Caleb that he was approaching a large band of hostile Indians and should change his direction immediately to avoid them. He probably had saved Caleb's life. Caleb gave him a large cup of coffee well laced with sugar. This was one Indian who had turned down hard liquor. Caleb noted that he was trailing two packhorses bearing over two hundred beaver pelts.

Caleb had been learning some of the Plains Indian sign-language from Thomas Lyon before he left Landers Station. Eagle-Man had also learned a little Spanish. This was the first chance Caleb had to use the sign-language he had learned to use. He signed hello to his Indian friend and clasped the Indian's arm warmly in an Indian arm-hand shake. The Indian broke out in a huge grin, understanding right away that since the last time they had met, this white man had learned something of the sign-language of the Plains Indian. They could talk now.

Caleb introduced Juan to his Indian friend, whom he now knew was called "Shakantai-Hama," or "Eagle-Man" in English. Caleb instructed Juan to bring them both a plate of stew from their kettle on the fire. The two men sat, making signs. Eagle-Man was still carrying the rifle that Caleb had traded him last year for his outdated one with a broken stock. Caleb got the Indian's old rifle out of his store of goods to show him. He had completely rebuilt it. The workmanship was so good. Eagle-Man could barely recognize it as his old rifle. Caleb had upgraded the rifle by substituting a flintlock system for the one using a wick as a firing mechanism. It was one of the trading articles that Caleb had brought with him. They sat all afternoon visiting, smoking and drinking coffee.

Eagle-Man got up towards evening and brought his two horses forward. He offered Caleb the furs. Caleb found out what supplies he needed and laid out a fair trade for the skins. The Indian was beaming with satisfaction at the fairness of the payment. It was a liberal payment, but not overly so. It was fair to both parties.

Two Nez Percé Indians, no older than fifteen, had been watching them for an hour before they completed their transaction. They looked at each other and nodded when they witnessed the large payment Eagle-Man got for his furs.

By signing, Caleb made each man understand that he had a trading post near Taos, or Fernando in the valley of Taos; and they would be welcome to come there and trade furs for supplies. He tried to make them understand they could get better prices for their furs by delivering them to the station.

In four more days of trading, Caleb expended more than half of his supply of trading goods and amassed over a thousand pelts of prime quality. Most of his trades were with Indians because the word went out that he treated the Indians fairly and with courtesy. There were more of the heavy pelts than the six horses he had brought along could carry back to Landers Station. He had to find someone to purchase additional horses from.

Caleb had noticed a group of Apache Indians here at rendezvous. They were here to sell a large herd of horses they had stolen from the Spanish. He approached them and began to dicker for two of the horses.

An old chief, known as "Two-Dogs," was called upon to assist the young warriors in the discussion because he could speak Spanish. When Caleb looked at the man, his heart sank. He was barely able to hide his emotion. Two-Dogs had hanging around his neck, suspended by a leather thong, a black onyx cross with fourteen small bands of gold. It was identical to the one Caleb had last seen on a gold chain around María's neck, on the rancho of *Don Miguel de Vargas* out of Santa Fé. He felt a sinking feeling in the bottom of his stomach.

Caleb tried not to look at the crucifix. His mind raced as he wondered how this could be. It could be a duplicate. It could be that María had lost it, and it had been found by Two-Dogs. *Perhaps another Indian had found it and traded it to Two-Dogs.* Thoughts as well as a sort of panic worried his mind. He was determined to find out where the old man had gotten it, and how. Almost ill from concern and worry, Caleb had to hide his feelings. He was no longer a self-confident trader. He was a worried-sick lover who feared for the well being of someone he cared for.

He invited the Apache chief to come to his camp and drink whiskey while they completed the trade for the horses. They could converse there in Spanish. The Chief spoke good Spanish, and Caleb's Spanish was now quite conversational. Caleb poured generously large and potent drinks of whiskey for the Indian, trying to get the old man drunk to loosen his tongue. They talked of many things.

Caleb was slowly able to draw the story out of Two-Dogs: "Some of the young Indians from my tribe were recruited by the white man, Slip, to help him on a raid. He was going after a large party of Mexican men driving a large flock of sheep to California. Several women were with the party, including a young woman who was wearing this cross. Our raiding party caught the drovers and the guards by surprise one night during a rainstorm. The young braves killed all the Mexican men, except a few shepherds who were kept alive to mind the flocks of sheep for us."

Two-Dogs laughed and in slurred speech said, "Of course, we kept the women to sell and trade. The youngest of the women, who seemed to be favored by the rest, was wearing this cross." Two-Dogs was drunk now, and pulled the black cross forward on the leather thong to show Caleb. It was no longer on the gold chain as it was when María had worn it. "When the raiding party returned to our camp, I received all the women, including the young one who had been wearing this."

"She was sullen and not good in my blankets, so I sold her to a solitary member of our tribe called 'Beaver-Catcher.' He lives alone in these mountains much of the time, trapping beaver like the white men. He has gone with her north into the valley of the Yellow-Stone, as the white men call it, where he spends his winters trapping for the beaver."

"Ha! Ha!" Two-Dogs chortled. "Beaver-Catcher tried to cheat me by trading a horse with two hurt forelegs for the woman. The horse is now well and a good animal, and he has the most worthless woman who was ever created! Perhaps he has killed her by now, I don't know." He held out his cup for more whiskey, which Caleb poured full.

Two-Dogs asked, getting back to business, "Do you want to buy the two horses?"

"Yes," Caleb agreed. "I will purchase the two horses and pay you two butcher knives and a twist of tobacco, two pints of sugar, and a skin full of whisky, like this one. I would also like you to trade me the black trinket you wear around your neck. I want to see this woman you describe. If you will lead me to her and this man Beaver-Catcher so I can talk to him, I will give you a flintlock pistol. Here it is. You can look at it yourself to see how fine it is." Caleb handed the Indian a pistol from his trade goods. It was a beautiful slim dueling pistol with a little silver inlay decoration of a horse, a buffalo, and a dog worked into a brass plate on the side of the white bone handle.

"I would like to look at such a woman," said Caleb, pretending to be a little drunk. "If I like her and the other Indian whom you call Beaver-Catcher will sell her to me, I will buy her. If possible, I want to leave tomorrow afternoon because I have to make arrangements to get my packs sent back to Taos. I will only pay you if we go alone."

Caleb did not want a lot of other Apaches around because he knew they would rob and kill him. "I will bring one helper with me to help with my pack horses, but only one." He looked toward Juan, who was standing with the horses and working around his camp.

The old Indian had already observed Juan tending Caleb's camp and nodded his approval. "Yes, you and your young boy can go with me. I will go alone. But you must pay me now a pint of whiskey to seal the bargain, and one gallon more when we find the camp of Beaver-Catcher. I must get paid even if she is dead. I must get the whiskey and the pistol even if she is not still alive. That is the bargain. It will not be my fault if she is dead. She was sullen and troublesome and not pleasurable, as well as weak and worthless. I had to beat her every time I took her into my blankets. It was fun the first time or two, but became a lot of work and trouble after that."

The two shook hands on the arrangement, and Caleb tucked the pistol back in his belt so the Indian could see it, with the silver inlay showing and sparkling in the sunlight.

Caleb went to his friend Eagle-Man and explained the problem. "Will you accompany us? I do not know this country, and I don't trust this Apache chief, Two-Dogs. He will get me lost, and then kill me and take my horses and guns. I am not afraid for myself; but if something were to happen to me, then I could not rescue this girl who means a great deal to me and to her father. I am not good enough in these mountains to outwit a man like him. Even if I could kill him, I could never find the girl by myself. We will have to trick him into keeping his part of the bargain."

Eagle-Man smiled, "Yes. I will be glad to go with you and assist you. I know these Apaches well, and you are wise to mistrust them. They would enjoy robbing and killing you. If he comes alone, we can handle him. If he sets up a trap for you using many of his braves, you will have to kill him if he does not kill you first."

"I know the country of the Yellow-Stone," Eagle-Man continued. "It is a huge country. Without knowing at least the general vicinity of the man and the woman, it would be impossible to find them there. I agree that we must keep Two-Dogs alive until we sight the place where the woman and the Beaver-Catcher are, or at least get close."

Caleb was relieved that his friend who knew this country well would go with him. "Here is a pistol, the shot-mold, the lead shots for it, and a full powder-horn," Caleb said. "This will be your payment for helping me, and it will also help give us more protection on the way. It's too bad that we can't trust Two-Dogs, but he is our only hope of finding the girl. We will just have to keep our eyes on him at all times. You take the two packhorses with my goods and start north up the Green River. The Apache Two-Dogs and I will catch up with you by tomorrow evening. I don't want him to know that you are with me until it is too late for him to turn back. He will think that Juan is going to be going ahead with the packs."

"I will have Juan return to my station at *San Fernando de Taos* with the pack- horses. Do you think the two young Nez Percé boys from your tribe would be dependable and willing to accompany him? I need someone to help him with the packhorses and deliver the peltry. I will give each one of them a rifle, powder, and lead balls if they will assist him."

"Yes. That is a good plan, and you are offering fair payment," Eagle-Man said. "They are good and dependable young men. I have known them since they were small children. They will do their best for you, and I think they can deliver your pelts safely. In that way they will come to know your station and bring you more pelts in the future."

Caleb made the arrangements with the two young Nez Percé Indians, who were delighted with their good fortune to be earning rifles and ammunition of their own. Prior to receiving these weapons, they only had bows and arrows, and knives made of stone. Caleb gave each young man a rifle, balls, powder, hatchet, and a butchering knife as payment in advance for delivery of the goods to Landers Station. By receiving these weapons now, the young men would also be better able to protect his goods. They were instructed to start immediately, sneaking away quietly, in the darkness, and were not to tell anyone they were leaving or where they were going.

"I will take the balance of our trade goods, two loaded horses, with me," Caleb told Juan. I may need some of them to trade for María. If I can rescue her, I will return here to rendezvous and continue trading for pelts. You will have your hands full with the four horses loaded with pelts."

"I am pleased that you trust me with your goods, and I will be glad of the help from the two young Indians," Juan responded. "We will deliver your goods to the station. You can depend upon me." Juan knew that he was being given a great responsibility, and his smile indicated his pleasure with so much trust.

"When you once get there," instructed Caleb, "send this message to Bartholomew. I made two copies of it. One is for Bartholomew, and one is for Thomas Lyon."

The letter read:

Phillip Bartholomew, Santa Fé, New Mexico
Dear Phillip:

I have a valuable load of furs for delivery to you at the station. You can pick them up, or Thomas Lyon will make arrangements for delivery to you. He is in charge of my affairs, with the able assistance of Juan Castro and Isabella. I am sending this letter back to the station in care of Juan. It is a heavy burden for a young man, but I have found two young Nez Percé Indians to assist him. I have confidence in his ability to accomplish this. There is no other way I can see to do it.

There are one thousand prime pelts in good condition. You should process them as we agreed and apply the proceeds to the outstanding order I have with you. All surplus should be applied to the next order, which you should double.

I am deeply troubled. I have seen a very distinctive cross, which I have every reason to believe was worn around the neck of Don Miguel's daughter, María. I know she was to be sent to California; and from the story the Indian Two-Dogs told me, I am certain she has been taken captive and sold into slavery, and the men of the caravan killed.

I will try my best to find her. If she is alive, I will try to bring her back to Don Miguel or take her on to her father's cousin, her betrothed, in California, depending on circumstances and her wishes in the matter.

I ask you to pray for my success in this and explain to Don Miguel that I will do my very best. I will not return as long as there is any hope that I might find her alive. I was told by the Apache Chief Two-Dogs, whom I have engaged to lead me there, that she has been taken north from here to a valley called the Yellow-Stone. She is being held by an Apache trapper there called Beaver-Catcher. I do not trust or respect Two-Dogs, so I do not know of the quality of the information. The cross he had around his neck is truth enough to make me attempt to do what I can.

Please treat Thomas Lyon, Juan Castro, and the woman Isabella, in that order, as my agents at Landers Station. They all have my confidence, and they will do the best they can in my absence. Should anything happen to me and I do not return, please see that these three people share in my estate equally, I have no relatives.

I have made a duplicate of this letter and am sending it to Thomas Lyon to be given to Don Miguel.

Two-Dogs named Slip Fields as the man who recruited these Apache Indians to raid Don Miguel's party with the band of sheep. I ask you to inform the alcalde in Santa Fé of this. Perhaps he can do something about it. Should I not be successful in my attempts to free María, perhaps someone else will take up the attempt to rescue her.

Please pray for the success of my endeavors.

Your obedient servant,

Caleb Landers

June 9, 1836, Green River Valley

The next afternoon, Chief Two-Dogs showed up ready to go. His eyes were still red and his hand shook from his drunk. "Where are your pack horses and the other person who is to go with us?" Two-Dogs asked.

"I have sent my packhorses up the Green River already so we will not have to wait for them. It is on our way, and we will catch up to them before nightfall," Caleb told him.

Just at dusk they caught up with Eagle-Man and Caleb's two packhorses.

"I thought we were going with the young Mexican boy," the Apache frowned, upset when he found that Eagle-Man had replaced Juan as Caleb's helper.

"No. He has gone away. This is Eagle-Man, and he is going to go with us to help me with the two packhorses that I am bringing. He is the man I always intended would go with us. He is my friend, and I need his help."

The Apache was unhappy that the Nez Percé was to be along. He had planned on killing both Caleb and the Mexican boy, and taking their goods right away. He did not share his plan with the warriors of his tribe before he left because he thought it would be easy for him to kill young Caleb and the even younger Juan, by himself. Now he was sorry that he had not laid out an ambush using the braves from his tribe. He would have to be careful dealing with this other Indian. He looked very capable, never setting his rifle down for even a moment, and he always stayed at a distance. He also had a pistol, something else to worry about.

Caleb was traveling with his flintlock rifle in his hands and two flintlock rifles in scabbards on his horse. In addition, he had his two pistols in holsters at his side. Caleb kept them covered from the Apache's view by their dust-flap, although he doubted whether this Indian had even seen a six-shot cap-and-ball revolver before. The revolvers would give him an advantage in case the chief tried to go after him and Eagle-Man.

Caleb had also loaded two additional shotguns for Eagle-Man and had them tied in scabbards on the lead packhorse along with extra powder and buckshot. Caleb had also given him a tomahawk hatchet to wear in his belt and a large butchering knife. If anyone attacked them, they would be well armed.

The Apache waited until late at night with the intention of sneaking off, but he could not find where Eagle-Man was. That meant he was away from the fire and would be watching. If Two-Dogs attempted to sneak off in the dark, he would be shot, of this he felt certain. In the morning, Two-Dogs informed Caleb, "My stomach now hurts, and I do not feel well enough to go on. I am sick. Now I must go back to my camp and rest for a few days. We can then complete this journey. It is too far for us to attempt to go when I do not feel well."

He looked about. Once again he could not see Eagle-Man. That meant, of course, he was watching Two-Dogs from some hidden place. Two-Dogs could almost feel the sights of the rifle aimed at him from someplace out of his sight.

"We can wait a few days until I feel better and then start out again." The Apache had become sullen and seemed to be afraid. Now his stomach really was upset with fear. He had set his trap, and he had caught himself in it.

While Two-Dogs was talking, the barrel of Caleb's rifle had shifted to the middle of Two-Dog's stomach. Caleb cocked it meaningfully, and then told him carefully and slowly, "Now, you listen to me! Put your guns and other weapons on the ground in front of you. I will keep them for you until we complete our journey. You have broken your word that you would guide me to the valley of Yellow-Stone, so I will now have to disarm you and tie you on your horse." Caleb held his hand up in the air and made a sign for Eagle-Man to come and hold his gun on the Apache.

Eagle-Man immediately stepped into view with his gun pointed at the Apache. He held it under his chin, cocked and ready to fire. Caleb took Two-Dog's weapons and tied his hands behind his back with a leather thong, as he told him, "Now, I will keep my part of this bargain if you keep yours. You move out right now, and I want to warn you: I am very nervous about going with you, so you be very careful, because my rifle will get you first if I have any trouble with you. If you lead me to Beaver-Catcher, I will pay you well. If you try any trickery I will gut-shoot you, make no mistake about it. I am only interested in the girl. And I mean the other man no harm, nor you either. I will give him fair trade for her. Now move out and be quick about it, or I'll gut-shoot you here and now, and leave you for the buzzards and wolves to eat while you are still alive. *Move!*"

CHAPTER 10
The Slave. The Valley of the Yellow Stone.

*D*on Miguel de Vargas and his cousin, *Don Alfonso de Vargas* of the Mexican Territory of *Alta California*, forged an agreement to trade some of Don Miguel's sheep for the Californian's horses and cattle. Since the sheep drive would be long and arduous, Don Miguel sent a large expedition, over fifty people, to deliver the sheep to his cousin and then bring the cattle and horses back to his rancho. The large party would traverse the old Spanish Trail on their way from Santa Fé to what was then known as the *Pueblo de Nuestra Señora La Reina de Los Angeles*, in Alta California.

There was a second, and perhaps more important, reason for sending such a large party: it was to escort Don Miguel's daughter, María, to *Don Alfonso de Vargas* for marriage, thus cementing the relationship and operations of both rancho families.

The caravan had so many guards that the travelers felt completely safe. The armed fighting force, however, was but twenty-five armed men. Ten of them were well-trained guards from the rancho of Don Miguel. The others, herdsmen and farmers, carried ancient weapons of various kinds that were vastly inferior to the weapons then used by the mountain men and even many of the Indians.

It was now late April, 1836. The caravan had been on the trail for over 350 miles when it camped on the banks of the Green River above where it empties into the Colorado River. The Green River was especially high, because the snow was melting in the mountains above. The caravan had left Santa Fé in early April, a full month earlier than was recommended by those familiar with the trail; and the leaders of the caravan had made the ill-advised plan to cross the river on May 1. Now they would have to wait until nature permitted them to ford the now wild, raging river.

Moving at the grazing speed of the sheep, it had been a leisurely and pleasant trip to the banks of the Green River. Now the sheep were spread out and feasting on the good early forage. Then, it had begun to rain, pouring down on the travelers and sheep, making the river rush even more, turning it brown in the torrent of mud. The tent that the servants put up at night for the daughter of Don Miguel and her aunt, her chaperon, protected them from the rain. But it was boring to sit inside the tent and wait for sunshine.

At three o'clock in the morning the guards heard a gunshot; but since they didn't hear anything else, they assumed that a herder had merely been chasing wolves away from the flocks. This happened nightly. Although not overly concerned, the leaders of the caravan sent out a patrol of three guards in the direction of the shot to make sure all was well. However, the men on patrol did not prime their rifles because the rain, though moderating, was making it too wet to prime their pans unless absolutely necessary. They would prime their rifles only if they actually had to take a shot. Wet prime would not fire the guns anyhow unless protected and kept dry.

The Apache raiding party moved like shadows, darker than the night. One hundred Apache warriors were suddenly in the camp. They knew their business. They immediately killed all of the guards, including the night guards, those sleeping, and the three-man patrol. The night guards did not get one shot off from their wet flintlocks. They were killed by arrows that, of course, were not much troubled with the wetness. The Indians also killed all of the Mexican fighting men. Only two of the Apaches were killed in the attack and they were killed by knives.

The herdsmen were spared after being disarmed, so they, with their dogs, could continue tending their flocks. The shepherds would continue to tend the sheep for their new masters, the Apache. The herds of sheep were to be scattered among the tribes, to be traded mostly for horses, but also some beaver pelts here and there, and used for food.

The Indians were elated with their great fortune in capturing such a huge flock of sheep and so many horses, to say nothing of the weapons they retrieved from the dead men. The Indians were to take all the sheep and all the women. The organizer of the party, Slip Fields, was to get all the horses and everything else in the camp. That was the agreement. Slip appropriated the tent in which María was captured for himself. The Indians not on guard duty or otherwise occupied gathered in front of the tent, where Slip was passing out tequila and wine from the stores he had captured. They were getting started on a victory party.

The women were brought forth to be presented to the organizers of the raiding party. They would eventually be presented to Two-Dogs, but in the meantime Slip and a young Warrior chief called "Marks-On-Face" would decide how to distribute them for the pleasure of the raiding party. It was now dawn. The sky was overcast, but the rain had stopped.

There were seven women captives, including María. They had all been stripped naked and their hands tied behind their backs with rawhide thongs around their wrists. The women had either been thrown or knocked down in front of the men, where they lay miserable and helpless with their feet tied together as well as their hands.

Their clothing was kept in a pack together with everything else they had been wearing, including jewelry, crosses, hair combs, and shoes. These personal items were to be delivered to Two-Dogs along with the women. María's black onyx cross with the fourteen tiny bands of gold was also to be delivered to Two-Dogs.

Slip, as leader of the raiding party, was giving orders. "I will take yonder young *rica*. I owe her fam'ly fer a ball they had put in my gut back in Santa Fé. Because o' her father I claims my rights to use 'er fer tonight, at least. It won't hurt her none fer me ter use her before she is turned over to Two-Dogs. Marks-On-Face can select from the ones he wants to use fust because he is the chief hyar. The t'other women are to be shared by the rest o' you warriors as wants 'em, one after the t'other. This be fair to all, an' no one will be left out o' the fun. Ye kin draw lots fer when yer turns come, iffen it matters to ye. But don't kill 'em! We promised Two-Dogs that we'uns would deliver the women to him fer granting us permission to make this hyar raid. But that don' mean we kain't make sport and have fun with these hyar womenfolk's an' mak'em happy in the meantime. Ha! Ha!" He laughed at his own joke.

"I think I gots me another o' Don Miguel's pups," Slip chuckled. "I had the male puppy-dog last time. This time, looks like I gots yonder bitch. I'll take her in the tent now an' see iffen I can get her pussy-cat warmed up ter my fire!" He untied María's feet and slipped a neck-rope over her head. He jerked the rope, signaling her to get up. But María did not get up, which made the Indians laugh at Slip. They could see she did not want to go with him and that she was defying him.

The Indians liked that. They didn't like the American much anyhow. They began to tease him. They said the woman did not like him because his color was too pale, and he was sexually inferior—and therefore he should leave the woman with them. They would be able to satisfy her. She would obviously prefer an Indian to the white man. They laughed and paraded, still taunting him. This was a great insult to the White Man, for if she didn't want to go with him then it meant she preferred the Indians.

By this time Slip was furious at the cat-calling Indians as well as María. He pretended to be laughing along with the braves but was extremely embarrassed over her refusal to obey him. He walked over to María and kicked her in the stomach, ordering her to get up. She still refused. He grabbed her ankles and dragged her on her back into the tent as she kicked and screamed, cursing him in Spanish. The Indians loved the spectacle and some of them knew what she was saying and translated for the others.

The Indians taunted Slip, "Let her come to us. We will be much better for her. See, she prefers us. She does not think you are man enough to satisfy her. Leave her with us, and we will take care of her for you. Maybe you could take her tomorrow night, after we tame her for you!" They laughed at Slip for being turned down by the woman.

Once inside the tent, out of sight from the jeering crowd, Slip untied María's hands and coiled up the rope at his feet. It was still attached to her neck,. He left her lying on the floor while he drank most of a bottle of wine. He studied her, liking what he saw. He knew her youthful, well-proportioned body could delight him once he mounted her. But it would be much better, he knew, if she would cooperate. That would be much more satisfying to both of them. But how could he get her to cooperate?

Smiling at her, trying to get a little cooperation to make the inevitable more pleasurable, he asked, "Is ye all ready yit? Is yer pussy-cat a-fire?" He put the bottle of wine with some still left in it, in front of her so she could get a drink for herself while he was taking his britches off, grinning in anticipation. His hard-on stood out in front of him. He grasped it between his fingers and shook it towards her invitingly. He laughed loudly. The potent wine had relaxed him. He was having fun with her.

"Come on, now. Be nice ter me ding-nab-it hyar. Look hyar! He's a standin' up fer ye like a gentl'man." He shook his penis toward her again as if introducing it. "Ye know's what's y'ur pussy-cat's fer. It will be good once't ye makes yer mind up, an' ye knows it. What say ye? We'll try th' fit once't to gets things started. I'll dip 'er in thar an' see iffen ye likes him. An' iffen ye don't, well then, I will let ye go on back out an' jine the t'other women in yonder partyin'." He knew she could hear the sounds of the singing, partying Indians, and cries of pain and terror from the captured women. Slip was positive she would rather be in here with him rather than outside with the cavorting savages. What woman wouldn't?

She studied the bottle. It had about four inches of wine in the bottom of it. Then she stood up and took a drink. "Gracias, *Señor!*" she smiled, and walked towards him. She tipped the bottle up, draining it, and stepped closer to him, smiling and acting friendly. She was near Slip when she lunged at him and hit him on top of the head with the bottle, with all her strength. The bottle broke, cutting a jagged hole in his scalp and down his cheek. Stunned, he fell backwards over his chair as she started chasing after him and cursing him.

"You *Gringo* American bastard! My father will have you skinned alive!" She was slashing madly at him with the broken bottle in her hand, inflicting more ugly cuts on his face and hands as he attempted to ward off the blows. Then she jabbed the bottle at his exposed genitals, but he jumped back out of the way, just in time. Then, because she was off balance, he was able to hit her in the face with a roundhouse blow that knocked her out the tent door. She held onto the broken bottle.

The Indians near the front of the tent were surprised to see her come tumbling out, with the broken bottle still clasped in her hand. She fell down and then got back on her feet. Her nose was bleeding from where he had hit her, and blood was gushing down her naked body.

Slip came cursing after her. He was still naked below the waist and blood was running down over his face and shirt. She brandished the broken bottle at him again. The Indians, who thought a white man in such a position was hilarious, were now laughing and encouraging her. "Kill Him! Cut him to pieces! You can do it. Go after him!" They laughed and gave her room to maneuver. Here was real drama: a young Mexican girl cutting up the American with a broken bottle. The Apaches were not happy to be following the orders of an American anyway. This was the best part of the raid as far as they were concerned.

"All rights, missy, iffen that's the way ye wants it! Ye thinks ye is so high an' mighty, do ye? Well, I have changed my mind 'bout wantin' ye." Infuriated, Slim shouted to the laughing crowd, "Ye kin all have her!" He waived his hands encompassing them all. "Throw her in the pot with the rest o' th' pussy-cats an' see how she takes to hit. Ye kin all takes turns on top o' her fer all I keer, and to hell with the lot o' ye!" Then he went back into the tent to nurse and bandage his head and look for another bottle of wine. His hard-on was gone. He did not want any woman now, particularly that one.

Ten of the Indian men circled María, smiling and laughing at her. The young men wanted to play with her. They would run in behind her to touch her; counting coup it is sometimes called. Daring to touch her and then jumping back before she could cut them with the bottle was a dangerous game. This was great sport.

After a while, one of the older men grew tired of the game and grabbed the end of the lead-rope that was still hanging around her neck. He jerked it hard, throwing her backward; then he jerked it again, making her drop the broken bottle and fall to the ground. Four of the laughing younger Indians rushed her, each one grabbing an arm or one of her kicking legs. They spread-eagled her on her back, opening her up so one of them could mount her. She couldn't defend herself any longer. She was not strong enough, though she tried to ward them off for a while. All she could do was twist and turn, and scream and curse at them.

One after the other they cast their sperm inside of her, laughing and enjoying themselves, having great sport with her. It was much less fun when she quit struggling and lay there dazed and unmoving, not responding in any way except an occasional moan. They tied her up with the other females when they got through with her. The next day, the Apaches tied her face down on top of a horse because she was unable or unwilling to walk.

While on the trail back to their village, the Apaches availed themselves of the women captives every night. And each morning they offered the women the opportunity to walk and carry their load on their backs or ride upside down tied on a horse, like María. Riding face down with their hands and arms tied under the belly of a horse was torture far worse than walking or carrying a load on their back, no matter how sore they were.

On the third day, they offered María the choice of walking and carrying her burden, or riding upside-down again on the horse. She chose to walk with the other women, though still in a daze. They fitted her out with a load, and a lead rope was secured around her neck. The rope was held by one of the braves on horseback. She was led just like any other pack animal. If she faltered or fell behind, the Indian leading her would jerk the rope around her neck and throw her down. She learned to keep up after a few lessons of being dragged behind his horse. Her soft feet began to bleed after an hour of walking barefoot on the rocky ground. The other women had walked barefoot all of their lives, but she had the benefit of shoes, until now.

María was duly delivered to the Apache Chief Two-Dogs in compliance with the deal he and Slip had made. During the next several days, the Indian women and children used her to carry their firewood. They poked her and beat her with sticks, and the little children of the tribe threw rocks at her and spat upon her.

One of Two-Dog's wives cut María's hair off in what resembled a crew cut. The woman could use the hair to make a rope halter for one of Two-Dog's horses. Human hair made the best and strongest of ropes. It could also be braided into small strings and used to decorate one of his shirts.

Two-Dogs used María at night in his blankets, but he found her very disappointing. She was not a willing blanket-partner. She had learned to submit and no longer had the strength or will to resist. But she would just lie there, dull-eyed and disinterested, making no attempt whatsoever to bring him any pleasure. He beat her until he grew tired of it. Soon, she was actually undercutting his authority. She was an embarrassment. She was dull-witted and unresponsive.

Then he loaned her out to members of the tribe who wanted a favor from him, hoping one might find her desirable and want to buy her. But none of them ever asked for her a second time. No adult wanted to use her under any circumstance. She was worthless. The teenage Apache boys got permission from Two-Dogs to use her behind the chief's brush-and-branch-limb shelter. Leading her there with the rope around her neck, several of the young bucks would whip her backside with switches to wake her up and put life into her. Then, amid much laughter, they drew lots to see who would be first to have her. They would make her lie down upon the ground and mount her one after the other. After all, they had to learn and practice to be men; and it cost Two-Dogs nothing to loan her to them.

Two-Dogs had been able to sell all of the other women and all of the sheep. But this one woman seemed to have no value to anyone. She had turned out to be worthless, just another mouth to feed, though in fact she was eating nothing. When he tried to sell her to other members of the tribe, everyone laughed at him because they knew she was worthless. She could not cook. She could not dress meat. She was no good under the blankets. She no longer had any hair that could be cut off and used. Even a dog had more value than this strange Mexican light-brown woman. Two-Dogs was so embarrassed that he would not let her sleep in his brush shelter. He tied her up outside with the dogs, instead.

María had quit eating. And instead of moving around during the day, she lay listlessly in the doorway of the chief's house. She was just sitting or lying there with the dogs, defiling the entrance to his house. She would not attempt to move unless they goaded her with a stick. And she had made no attempt to remove the spittle, dried blood, or filth that had dried on her after the Indian women and children attacked her during her first few days of captivity. She was filthy, and looked and smelled terrible.

Two-Dogs knew the signs. She would die soon. Or maybe he would have to walk her out of the camp and slit her throat. The wolves could eat her, and that would be the end of his problem.

CHAPTER 11
Beaver-Catcher.

Small-Bird, an Apache girl of thirteen had been captured by the Spanish with a group of Indian women and children and brought to the Mission of Our Lady of Spain, in the outlying territory of New Mexico. Along with several others, she had been converted to Catholicism and put to work tending the mission's fields of corn, wheat, and other crops. The mission was small and poor. The Indian population there was comprised of members of many tribes, some of whom had been captured and some of who had voluntarily joined the Mission in order to obtain food.

In 1800, at the age of fifteen, Small-Bird gave birth to her first child, a boy. The priests who baptized him named him José. When he was five, the priests took him away from his mother and put him in the dormitory with the other boys. The boys, from many tribes, were allowed to speak only Spanish so they could all communicate and learn their religious lessons from the Priests.

The priests theorized that if you taught children religion for several years when they were young, they would carry it with them for the rest of their lives. "Once a Catholic, always a Catholic," the priests would say knowingly. The children were given catechism lessons every day, Mass and Communion weekly, and were required to say their prayers at mealtime and when they went to bed at night. With the work in the fields and the religion they were taught, their days were full from dawn until dark. That was their life. They knew nothing else.

When José was 10 years old, the Apaches raided the mission and took him, Small-Bird, and her baby daughter to the Indian camp. Small-Bird was later married to one of the members of the tribe, who then adopted José and his younger sister.

Although José became an Apache, he was never a great warrior. As he grew into manhood, he did his share in raiding Spanish ranchos as well as the camps of other Indians of the region. However he found he did not enjoy raiding, fighting, and killing. He was not a coward. He simply did not like inflicting pain and suffering on other people, even enemies. He took no pleasure in it. He also knew enough to keep his ideas to himself.

José had one quality that earned him the appreciation and respect of all the tribe. He could break and train horses as well or better than anyone else. He even developed a special gentle method of breaking horses. It took longer, but in the end the horses were better trained and easier to handle.

When José was 25, Josiah Jebb, a trapper who was trading with the tribe, learned that this remarkable young man was very good with horses. He was mild-mannered and could speak fluent Spanish. Josiah hired him to tend his camp, and work for him skinning and drying out the beaver hides. José learned the beaver-catching trade quickly and worked for Josiah for two years. They became close friends.

When the trapper went back East, he gave José four beaver traps, a muzzle-loading rifle, and a horse for two years of work, together with all his skin-stretching frames and camp gear. José found himself in the beaver-catching business. The other Indians renamed him Beaver-Catcher when he began going into the hills to catch beaver on his own, and that was how he got his new name.

Beaver-Catcher stayed by himself in the high mountains much of the time. He was now an itinerant tribal member. He was only in the Apache camp occasionally, visiting his mother, sister, stepfather, and friends.

Before he went back into the mountains, Beaver-Catcher needed to replace one of his three horses, which had fallen and hurt its knees so badly it could not carry a load. Finding a beast of burden to help carry his equipment and supplies was taking him longer than he had expected. He was already late in leaving, and he was anxious to get back to the solitary life in the mountains that he enjoyed.

The Apaches used three beasts of burden to carry supplies: a horse, a woman, or a dog. A horse could, of course, carry a lot more than a woman, at least seven times as much. A woman could carry much more than a dog and also could be useful in other ways, of course. Beaver-Catcher's load was too much for a dog, so that was out of the question. He couldn't afford another horse in any event, but he had heard that Chief Two-Dogs had this Spanish girl no one else wanted.

Beaver-Catcher approached Two-Dogs in front of his brush hut and said, with respect, "Two-Dogs, I would trade you this lame horse for the Spanish girl, if you want to trade. I have heard that she is worthless, but perhaps I can make her carry my load. This packhorse is lame although it will recover. I want to go on my journey back up into the valley of the Yellow-Stone as soon as I can. Do you want to trade?"

"No! You try to cheat me!" Two-Dogs lost his temper for a moment. "You know a woman is worth at least two horses, and not lame ones either! This woman is not very old. You have no woman, and you sleep alone in your blankets? You can have her carry your load and sleep with you at night to warm your blankets, tend your camp, and do the work with the beaver hides, if you train her!"

"Does she warm your blankets, Two-Dogs?" Beaver-Catcher asked. "But I do not want you to take offense. Pardon me for asking if you wanted to trade her for my worthless lame horse. You are right. She is worth much more. But I do not have two horses to trade. I only have this one lame horse. You keep her, then. I will leave her for you to enjoy at night."

Beaver-Catcher then noticed María's pitiful form lying in the dirt with several of Two-Dog's dogs. "Is that your bed-warmer there lying by your house door?" he asked, pointing at her. He tried to keep the smile from his lips so Two-Dogs would not take offense again. But Beaver-Catcher could not help but smile, so he covered his lips with his hand so as not to insult Two-Dogs.

María, with the lead rope still around her neck, was lying naked on her side in the dirt in front of the chief's house. Listless and dull-eyed, she had curled up beside the dogs for warmth. She was breathing but not moving. Even the children had grown tired of throwing rocks at her or goading her with sticks because they could no longer make her react. She was black-and-blue from the many blows she had taken, and had sores all over where the children had gouged her to make her cry out so they could laugh at her. Dried blood and spittle were caked on her skin. She was filthy, and she had no hair.

Two-Dogs was frowning. He had already made up his mind to drag her out of the camp area and slit her throat. He scowled at her in disgust and said, "take her, then! I was going to kill her today anyhow. The horse may get well. This woman is worthless to me and a disgrace to my house. I'll accept your trade. Maybe you can beat some sense into her!"

Beaver-Catcher handed Two-Dogs the bridle to his lame mare. He patted the mare, talking to his horse, and saying good-bye. He loved this mare. He rubbed her on the neck, rubbed her nose with his knuckle, and put his arm around her, talking to her, saying how much he had appreciated her carrying his loads for so long. He hated to give up this horse. "Take good care of this horse, Two-Dogs. She has been faithful to me. When she gets well, I will buy her back from you for a good price when I return from the mountains with my beaver hides."

He picked up the end of the lead rope still tied about María's neck and ordered her, in Spanish, "Get up. You belong to me now." She did not rise or move. It was obvious that she was weak and sick. Beaver-Catcher did not kick or beat her as Two-Dogs would have done. Instead, he talked to her and helped her get to her feet, gently coaxing her. She was unsteady on her feet and ready to fall over. He got her moving slowly and led her to his fire outside the encampment.

Two of the children came after him, throwing rocks at María. But when they approached his campfire, he sternly told the children, "The next time you throw rocks at her, I will beat you with a stick. She is my beast of burden now, and I don't want you bothering my pack animals." He got a long stick and chased them away. He did not hit them, although he could have. But violence and meanness was not Beaver-Catcher's way. He just laughed at the children as they scampered off, their bare behinds showing as they ran away from him. He liked the children and enjoyed playing with them. The children knew this and were laughing as they ran away from him.

Beaver-Catcher sat down by his fire and studied his purchase. She had already lain down by the fire, seeking its warmth. He looked at her feet. He knew that no pack animal could carry a load if its feet were sore and bad, or if it were weak and sick. Her sore, swollen feet were still oozing blood and pus from walking barefoot.

He helped her stand up and gave her a drink of water from a gourd, even though at first she resisted taking it. Using the remaining water in the gourd, he began to wash her off. He started at the top of her head and washed her down as he would wash a muddy horse. When he thought she was clean enough, he sat her down and examined her feet. He gently washed the dirt and caked blood out of the wounds, and rubbed her feet and ankles gently, just as he would have done to his horse if it had hurt its ankle.

Then he offered her some leftover stew that had been warming on his fire. She didn't want to drink the broth, but he finally got her to do so. He did this not by beating her, as Two-Dogs would have done, but by gently coaxing her, and talking soothingly to her all the time, and gently pressing it to her mouth.

After Beaver-Catcher had fitted her with moccasins and a light empty pack, he packed his goods on his two beasts of burden and led her and the packhorse out of the camp and up the river. María was still naked except for the pack and the moccasins. He had not tied her hands. He knew it was difficult to walk and keep one's balance with tied hands (although he tied her hands at night for security). But after only two miles, María stumbled and fell. *This is far enough for today,* he reasoned. If she fell and hurt her knees, then she would be crippled like his other horse was. They were safely away from the influences of the Indian encampment now. It was enough to accomplish for the first day.

Beaver-Catcher built a small fire, and María lay beside it without moving. Building a fire was women's work, but he would do it for her today because she was obviously exhausted and in pain. He coaxed some water and broth into her, washed her feet, and rubbed her legs and ankles once again. He repeated the treatment of her feet the following morning.

The next day they started off north, paralleling the Green River. He had one packhorse overloaded with supplies and rode the other one, carrying part of the load on that horse also. Instead of pulling or jerking her lead rope, Beaver-Catcher simply allowed her to follow along. She seemed to be trying to keep up, so he set his speed to her pace. On the few times he talked to her, he spoke Spanish; but in general he left her alone to make her own way. He had decided if she could learn to carry the load that he had for her, that would be enough for her to accomplish. That second day they traveled over 5 miles before she stumbled.

One day followed the next. Every day they went a little further than the day before. Every morning and evening he made broth or stew and kept pouring it down her and talking soothingly to her. After she had eaten, he rubbed her sore muscles, patted her, and washed and massaged her feet.

Now that María was more alert, she noticed that Beaver-Catcher was not tall; he was barely as tall as she was. He was wiry, and his muscles were strong but sinewy. He had sharp features and a ready smile whenever she did anything that pleased him. He did not beat her or abuse her, even if she did something wrong.

By the third day, he had her eating pieces of meat and asking for more. He gave her all she wanted, feeding her out of his own hand, one piece at a time. Beaver-Catcher knew in his own mind, *it is good if a dog, horse, or any other animal knows where its food is coming from. It makes them grateful and happy to see you.* Beaver-Catcher, who liked animals and enjoyed training them, reasoned, *Could training a woman be so different from training a horse or a dog?*

He knew that a horse could not work without grass in its stomach. Therefore, he reasoned, neither could she work without food in her stomach. He knew that because of the food he had gotten her to eat, María was definitely regaining her strength. But they still covered only short distances each day. Every day, he added one small item to her pack, lightening the load on his horse.

On the fourth day out they made camp early. He was no longer tying her hands at night, and today he had taken the lead-rope off her neck. "*Señorita!* I have a long shirt. Would you like to wear it?" he asked. He held it out to her.

"*Gracias, Señor.* Thank you," she told him gratefully, as she slipped it on over her head. The shirt extended down to 6 inches above her knees. It would help keep her warm, cover her nakedness, and keep the brush limbs from scratching her. And, it was one more small item of weight off the horse's back.

Hesitatingly, she said, "*Señor,* if I had a thong of leather I could tie it around my waist." She was asking him for something, looking to him for her sustenance. That was a good sign. And it was something that he could easily give her. He searched in his pack and gave her a nice wide band of leather that she could use for a belt.

She tied the leather belt around her waist and then asked, "*Señor,* may I go to the river and wash? He smiled at her, nodding his permission, "Yes, you are free to go and wash any time you want to."

He taught her how to start a fire using flint and steel, and he showed her how to fix their food. He found her amusing. He was amazed that anyone could have gotten to be as old as she must be and still be ignorant about how to make a fire or cook food, or find berries, or dig for roots, or catch a fish. He soon realized that she knew absolutely nothing practical that would serve him. She knew how to sew, for she had learned it in school. But what good would that be unless she had modern threads and needles? She had never seen sewing done with sinew of animals and bone needles or even threading thin strands of leather with an awl. She was ignorant of the skills a woman needed to know in an Indian camp, but he could tell she was not stupid. Once he showed her something, she could do it. He shook his head in amazement and wondered if all Spanish women were as ignorant as she seemed to be.

As María regained her health and toughened up, Beaver-Catcher found they could make better time on the trail. He was also able to put more of a load on her so as to lighten the strain on his packhorse, and not have to burden his riding horse with packs. Soon she was carrying her full share, and they were traveling 15 to 20 miles a day.

Beaver-Catcher did not force her to sleep with him. He had only one bed roll. She had her choice of sleeping with him or lying without covers on the bare ground. So she started crawling under his covers at night to keep warm. After several weeks, they began to talk. She lost her fear of him. She found out about his youth and was surprised to learn he had been born on one of the mission farms.

"I learned to speak Spanish when a child," he told her. "We children pulled the plows in the gardens to grow vegetables for the priests, and of course to pull the weeds. When I was young, the Apaches raided the mission and took me and my mother and sister back to our tribe. The braves killed all the Spaniards. My mother was an Apache and had been made a slave by the mission priests. I do not know who my father was. One of the Spaniards, no doubt, perhaps one of the priests, I am not sure. My mother said it was one of the priests; but others slept with her, too, so who knows for sure?"

All of the many things two people can learn when sharing the same blankets is what Beaver-Catcher and María learned about each other. They talked like children. She told him about her life on the *Rancho de Vargas*; though much of it he did not even understand. It was so foreign to him. But it was conversation that she enjoyed, so he pretended to be interested.

During all of this time he did not scold her, punish her, or treat her badly. He asked her only to do what any Indian woman would do by way of work. He never beat her. He already knew it would not do any good. As far as she could tell, she could have run away from the security of his camp, had she chosen to do so.

Beaver-Catcher gave her a knife for her belt; and, using his hand ax, showed her how to chop and gather wood for the fire. He was amazed that he even had to show her how to skin and clean deer, tan leather, clean a fish and cure it for wintertime by smoking it. But she learned and did the things he wanted her to do after he showed her how to do them.

Finally, they reached his camp near the south end of Yellow-Stone Lake. He had a small cave, about 16 feet square. The entrance was a low crawl hole, which he had camouflaged with logs and brush. It was almost impossible for anyone to see it, even from a short distance. The only way to enter the cave was on hands and knees, not too convenient but good for protection. Someone inside the cave armed with knife or a club could easily prevent unwanted visitors from entering. For there was only room for one person at a time to enter and that was a tight squeeze. He had left his stretching equipment made of wood for the beaver pelts there, two extra traps, a spare knife the blade of which had broken and he had to reshape it, and some other equipment. It was all undisturbed when they entered the cave. There was a good supply of wood already there for fires left from his last year's stay.

The cave was warm in winter and cool in summer. A small hole high in the ceiling let light in and smoke out. The hole at the top was further camouflaged by a heavy covering of brush and a tree that dispersed the smoke from the small fire made inside. A leather skin could be draped over the crawl space entrance to keep the warmth in, and it camouflaged the entrance further. He also had a boulder almost as large as the opening that could be rolled in front of the crawl space for extra protection.

It was still cool enough in these mountains to catch a few beaver, but soon it would be too late in the season. Once the warm weather set in, the pelts would no longer be prime as the animals began to shed their fur. Beaver-Catcher set his traps and caught many beavers. He left María alone in the camp every day to clean the animals he caught, stretch the beaver skins, tan the deer hides, dry a winter supply of meat and work on her other chores.

After a couple of weeks, when he had stopped trapping and was ready to begin hunting more meat to store for the winter, she asked,

"Would you teach me how to catch the beaver so I can go with you? I get tired of sitting alone here in the camp."

He did not tell her that it was already too late in the season to catch beaver. That was not Beaver-Catcher's way. He would let her learn for herself. If she wanted to trap for beaver, what was the harm in letting her? For her to be interested in something, anything, was a good sign. He gave her a trap to carry and led her over to the river in the next canyon to the north. He knew there were some beaver still there, and they should be easy to catch.

"The first thing you must learn is how to read signs," Beaver-Catcher told her almost whispering. "We will go up this little creek, and you tell me when you think you have spotted where a beaver might be. Do not talk, and walk quietly. Just point things out to me." As they were walking up the creek, she spotted a newly felled tree with distinctive teeth marks on the pointed stump and pointed it out to him.

He smiled his approval and whispered in her ear, "Good! Look there. See where the beaver has been cutting the small trees and building his dam? He lives in the dam. That dam is his house. The door to his house is under the water. Look now along the edge of the banks until you find a slide where he goes in and out of the water. You can set your trap just below the water there so when the beaver comes down the slope he will step in the trap. When he gets his leg caught in the trap, he will pull the trap along the chain while he is swimming toward his house. But when he gets to the end of the chain, the weight of the trap and chain will drown him. It is very important that he drown quickly; otherwise, he will chew his foot off and get away."

With that, he handed her the trap and chain. She had never set a trap before. "Show me how to set it," she whispered in his ear. It was fun playing this game. She enjoyed trying to outwit the beaver, whispering with Beaver-Catcher, and trying to learn something new.

He took the trap and stood on its spring so his weight would hold the jaws loose and open. He bent over and moved slowly so she could watch him set the catch over the edge of the trap-jaw. He placed a metal holding pin over the top of one side of one of the jaws. He then inserted this piece of metal in a notch on the bait trigger or foot release in the center of the trap. The centerpiece, the trigger, when stepped on, would release the spring, and the trap would snap shut with incredible force on the leg of the beaver. When the beaver or anything else stepped on the center of the opening, the trap would spring shut, trapping the animal's leg in the jaws, usually breaking the bone.

When María started to reach for the trap, Beaver-Catcher held her hand back. Then he motioned for her to pick up a stick and push it down on the center-trigger of the trap. She did so and the force of the closing of the trap made her jumped back in shock at the force of the trap when it noisily snapped shut on the stick, breaking her stick in half.

Then he motioned for her to step on the spring as he had done and set the trigger to reset the trap. He held her and balanced her until she learned how to do it alone. She stood on it gingerly because she now knew the only thing holding its jaws open was her own balanced weight. He then instructed her to reach down into the jaws and set the catch over one side of the jaws under the trigger-catch as he had done. She followed his instructions slowly and cautiously, because both of her hands were inside the jaws while she was setting the trap.

María was acutely aware that if she lost her balance and stepped off the spring while her hands were inside the jaws, the jaws would snap shut, undoubtedly with sufficient force to break her fingers. She could feel her heart beating faster. "Be careful—it will catch you just as easily as it will the beaver," Beaver-Catcher whispered in her ear. He smiled at her with approval when she finished setting the trap. The trigger was set so she could slowly get off the spring she had held open with her weight. The trap's jaws would be held open until an animal, preferably a beaver, stepped on the trigger.

"Do not go near where the beaver slides to his house in the water," Beaver-Catcher warned her. "If you walk down the slide, the beaver will not use it because he will smell your presence. Wade out in the water and approach the bottom of the slide from the water side. Put your trap right in the center of the slide, under water, about two thicknesses of your flat hand, so he will step on the trap and not swim over it. Sometimes it is best to pound a stake out in the water to secure the trap by its chain, but here you can tie it securely on that tree limb hanging out over the water. It has to be securely fastened or you will never see your trap again, or the beaver."

Every day, she walked over the ridge to the north and up the river to check her trap. By the second day, she began to get discouraged about ever catching a beaver. But when she checked her trap on the third day, something was different. The chain that she had tied to the limb was hanging differently. It was now pointing out into the stream and away from the side of the river, not toward the slide as she had left it.

When she waded out in the river to retrieve the chain and pull in the trap, she was elated to see a dead beaver in her trap. It had drowned, just as Beaver-Catcher had said it would. She pulled the trap in, her heart pounding with the excitement every hunter feels. As she had been instructed, she pulled the trap in carefully so she would not pull the jaws of the trap off the beaver's foot, and lose the animal in the flowing river.

María proudly carried the 30-pound beaver back to camp, running most of the way in her desire to show it to Beaver-Catcher. "Look, Beaver-Catcher! I have caught one. Isn't he a beauty?" Despite the beaver's weight, she proudly held it up for Beaver-Catcher's inspection.

He beamed at her. "It is a very large one. You did very well! Come! I will help you clean it and skin it; and we will lay the hide upon the stretch-rack so it will not shrink. Tonight we will feast upon the tail. You will see it tastes better because you caught it yourself. I am proud of you, María!" And it did taste delicious that night, as they laughed and giggled through this special meal. The one she had provided.

Beaver-Catcher taught her all he knew about catching beaver. He explained to her that the trap could be baited or positioned in several ways. "Another way to set one," he told her, "is to use the castor, or castoreum as some call it. This is this strong-smelling, oily, substance obtained from the sex glands of beaver. You can take this material from the beaver you catch and put it around the traps, on a limb over the trap set under the water. It will attract beaver that are searching for an intruder or mate. See, I have cut these two sacs in the beaver open to show you this yellow stuff. It is strong bait for a beaver. Save this in this tiny bottle and try it the next time. You will see it works."

She caught several more beaver after that. She cleaned and stretched the skins, and made soup of the meat. Beaver-Catcher always had good things to say about the meals she cooked, especially when they had meat from the tails of the beavers she caught.

"Today I am going to go hunting for a buffalo or deer. You can go with me if you want to," he told her. "I want to begin storing our winter's meat. We will dry it slowly over a slow smoky fire to make jerky." Again, he rode his horse and she walked, as was the Indian custom. She carried two empty backpacks and some ropes. Although she walked rapidly behind him, there were times when she had to trot to catch up. He did not pay any attention to her. He had his responsibility, and she had hers.

He was the outsider in this Yellow-Stone country. The Indians here were definitely not friendly to the Spanish or Apache. This was the realm of the Nez Percé, Crow, Snake, and other tribes. If they found him, they would enjoy killing him and stealing his horses as well as making a slave of his woman. He carried his rifle for self-protection but would only use it if he had to. A rifle shot would pinpoint his position to anyone around who might want to find a solitary Apache. He would hunt the buffalo with his bow and arrows.

He found a small herd of buffalo, and dismounted. There was a fat cow in the group, and he would stalk it on foot with only his bow and arrow. María came trotting up, puffing a little from the exertion. "Here, María. Hold the reins of my horse. Here is my rifle, too. It is primed and ready to shoot. You hold them. I want to kill the buffalo cow with the bow and arrow so as to not make any noise."

He looked at her a moment. He knew he was giving her the power to get away from him. She could shoot him, or she could take his rifle and escape on his horse. Both of them knew what she could do. Both of them knew the other knew, also. He smiled at her. He was placing his trust in her. And in a way, he was releasing her.

Ever since she had been kidnapped, she dreamed of being home with her father and mother in the safety and comfort of the rancho. Was she tempted to escape? Of course she was, but now she had other things to consider beside her own freedom. *What of the trap I have set for the beaver? Who would tend it? Beaver-Catcher does not even know where it is.* For some reason, this troubled her.

If I killed him or just ran away, where would I run? I'm completely dependent upon him for food and protection, and everything else. Things had changed dramatically since Beaver-Catcher purchased her from Two-Dogs. On top of everything else, she liked Beaver-Catcher and the life they were living. Then too, she knew without him having to say it that he liked her. *Am I so much worse off here in this beautiful country than I would be married to an uncle who has eight children older than me?*

María looked at the herd of peaceful buffalo in the green meadow below them. She could see the grass move a little where Beaver-Catcher, nearly naked, except for his bow and arrows was crawling toward them. There was a small shallow lake just beyond the herd, and trees and mountains surrounded the meadow. Some of the mountains still had snow on them. She took a deep breath, savoring the sharp pine and other forest odors. *I am freer here, than anywhere else I could possibly be.* She was surprised by her own realization of that fact.

When Beaver-Catcher turned his back on her and began to stalk the buffalo cow, he knew that she would do whatever it was she wanted to do. She was now free. It was not his problem. It was now her problem. His problem was killing the buffalo so they could eat this winter.

It took Beaver-Catcher over an hour crawling on his stomach like a snake to get close enough to fire his arrow. He stood up in the tall grass on his knees just high enough to shoot it, ducking down again before the arrow struck the cow in the neck. The cow jumped from the pain but did not run away. She could not see or smell an enemy because Beaver-Catcher was down-wind, so she did not know which way to run. The rest of the animals looked up when the cow jumped, but they saw nothing because Beaver-Catcher was hiding in the tall grass again.

In a few moments he rose up and shot another arrow, this time hitting the cow just behind the right foreleg. It ran a few steps, snorting, but the rest of the herd still remained in place. He had to crawl around the herd to get in position for another shot. This time his arrow struck the front of the cow's neck. Blood spurted out, indicating he had hit an artery or vein. Then the cow buffalo spotted him and turned to face him, seeing him for the first time as her enemy.

He walked slowly toward the cow, shooting several more arrows into her throat until she lay down and died quietly. The smell of the cow's blood and Beaver-Catcher's appearance caused the other buffalo to run a short distance, where they began grazing quietly again.

María mounted Beaver-Catcher's horse and rode up to him. She handed him the rifle. "You hold it," he said, "while I slit the throat of this cow to make sure she does not come back to life." They smiled at each other. She had rewarded his trust in her.

They spent the rest of the afternoon butchering the cow and then loading the meat into the packs they had brought with them. There was so much meat on the horse both Beaver-Catcher and María had to walk, each carrying a backpack full of meat, while he led the horse. They would be tired when they reached camp, but were looking forward to having a feast that evening.

"I will show you how to cook the liver and maybe a piece of tongue," he said. "The tongue is very good, but it must be beaten with the blunt end of the ax, before cooking to make it tender. It will make us strong and happy. Tomorrow, we will begin drying the meat and scraping the hide. Once it is cured and dried, the hide will make a good blanket for our bed or better yet, a warm, soft cushion under us. We can take the sinew to sew with and make winter clothing. We will make you a warm coat and leggings for walking in the snow as well as a tall covering for your feet clear up to your knees for walking in the snow."

María knew that Beaver-Catcher wanted to make love to her. He had never forced her to have sex with him; he never even asked. He was waiting for her to want him, too. It was now almost two months after he had bought her from Two-Dogs. She had been thinking about it for days. She knew she should show her gratitude by making love to him under the covers at night, as that was the natural way of things. He shared his food, his supplies, his knowledge of how to survive, and his blankets with her. In his Indian way, he was kind to her. He respected her Spanish habits, leaving her alone as long as she shared their camp life and did her chores. He had seen the many scars on her back before when he had first purchased her from Two-Dogs. He could not understand why anyone would beat such a woman and mark her so.

She had but one thing to share with him. She resolved to remove her shirt-skirt this evening before getting under the covers with him, as she had seen the Indian women do in the Apache camp. Once she had made up her mind to do it, she began to anticipate it. She put an extra-thick layer of fresh grasses under the blankets for additional softness. Her cheeks were red, and she kept looking at him.

At dinner he noticed the change in her and asked her, "What has made you so happy today. Tell me; and if it is something I have done, I will try to do it again tomorrow." She laughed to herself, and her face got redder. She stood up and came over to his side of the fire. Putting her arm around him, she hugged him lightly and then kissed his lips, which surprised him. "Let us go to bed early tonight. We can talk under the covers," she told him.

He watched her take her long shirt off and get into bed. He knew what she meant and was glad of the change in her. He liked this strange Spanish woman, even if she was ignorant of so many things. Life would be better between them from now on, and he knew it.

As he got under the covers facing her, she reached over him with her leg and scooted toward him. He had waited a long time for this moment and was glad that the time had arrived. He placed his left hand on her breast, feeling its warmth. She moved closer, laughing now, making him smile with her eagerness. She put her hand on the back of his neck and reached forward with her lips to his. She kissed him hungrily. "You like that, Beaver-Catcher?" she asked, kissing him again. "Do you like to kiss?"

"Yes, of course I do. I have waited a long time for it, too!" They both laughed. They had become good friends. Now they were to become lovers. It was natural and right that they should. There was no one else around and no longer any restraint between them.

"I will try to make you glad you waited." She opened her legs to welcome the tip of his penis; reaching down with her hand she guided it inside of her. Since they were lying on their sides, she was able to move back and forth on him while kissing him, encouraging him, pulling him closer to her. She was slaking her own thirst while also quenching his.

His urges took complete hold of him. Being careful not to remove himself from inside of her, he rolled over on top of her and rested for a moment in this new position. He felt her rise up under him and squeeze her arms around his back, signaling him to move deeper into her. She kissed him and rocked on him, and encouraged him to continue. They slept well that evening, holding each other in their arms for much of the night.

The next day they worked on the animal skin and began the process of drying the buffalo meat. Like newlyweds, they found plenty of reasons to touch each other as they worked. They enjoyed their work much more now as they prepared the winter's food supply. They would dry and store enough to carry them through the winter months and the fall trapping season. Winter would be here in a few months in this high mountain country and they would be busy catching beaver, so it would be much better if they did not have to take time off to hunt for food. And when the snow got 15 feet deep they would not be able to travel and hunt, but with a supply of wood to burn, piled high on both the inside of the cave and near the opening, and dried meat, dried fruit, berries, and other stored vegetables, they would have plenty to eat. Water in the form of snow would be plentiful at the door of the cave.

It was early afternoon, and the cave was warm from the fire outside that was smoking the meat. She put her arms around his shoulders and kissed his cheek, resting her head against his forehead. They were both tired of cutting up the strips of meat. They had done enough work for one day.

"Would you like me to show you the Indian way?" Beaver-Catcher asked her, hesitating lest he frighten her. "Do you want to learn it? In the old days the Indians did not kiss, and still do not except where the white men have had influence over them. And there were other differences, too."

"All right. What should I do?" she asked, her interest aroused.

"Get down on your hands and knees on the blanket, with your backside up."

She did as he indicated. She remembered seeing one of the Indian men mount his woman this way in the Apache camp. It had looked strange to her. She did not understand exactly what they were doing, but she now began to understand it. It excited her to try something new and different.

He came around behind her. She was wearing nothing other than the long shirt and her moccasins. He lifted her long shirt up to bare her backside. Then he took his leather pants off and came up behind her on his hands and knees. She could see he was going to mount her Indian-fashion, from the rear.

She had an idea what he was going to do, and the outlandishness of it excited her more and more. The outer lips of her vagina were plump, fresh, plush, pink, with blood pumping faster and faster into her genitalia as he got into position behind her. Her entire genital area was already wet. She was ready to receive him. He pressed his already hardened and slightly wetted penis inside of her. She was surprised to feel it slide into her vagina so naturally. Then it was all the way in, and it felt good to her.

"Is it all right, or do you want me to stop?" Beaver-Catcher asked her. "Tell me if you don't like it." He was perfectly still then as he did not want to do anything she did not like.

"I like it! Don't stop! I like it!" she told him breathlessly. She was backing into him rhythmically, moving back and forth on him in a natural motion. "It is wonderful!" She moved her head back and forth, and tried to spread her legs further apart so as to get on the right level for him. Beaver-Catcher laughed at her obvious pleasure and approval. He was proud to be teaching her new and pleasurable things, and have her appreciate him.

She leaned her elbows down on the blanket and began to experiment with different positions. Her breasts were barely touching the blankets. This made it even easier for her to rock back and forth on him. For a while he knelt upright with his hands on her hips, working his penis in and out with the same rhythm she was using. His excitement was gaining strength. While he continued pumping into her, he bent over and encircled her body with his arms. Grasping her breasts firmly, he breathed heavily into her right ear.

"Oh! Oh! Beaver-Catcher, I like it! I love it!"

CHAPTER 12
Rescue.

Caleb trained his spyglass on the campsite he saw in the gulch below him from his vantage point on the ridge a quarter of a mile across the gulch. The smell of smoke had drawn his attention to the ridge, and a wisp of smoke from a campfire confirmed that someone was there. Caleb could clearly see the solitary Indian working and tanning hides, and two horses tethered below him in the gulch. This camp was so well hidden that Caleb could not tell exactly where the fire or the Indian's blankets were.

His heart skipped several beats. "There she is!" He recognized María immediately, even at this distance. She was wearing moccasins and a long shirt-like dress belted at the waist. He could see she was gathering firewood and carrying armfuls back into the cave, which he could now see through the bushes. He had seen all he needed for the moment. Soundlessly, he pushed himself back off the skyline and walked half a mile on foot to the two Indians who were waiting for him.

Taking Eagle-Man to one side, he said, "I feel that Two-Dogs has completed his contract with us. I am giving you this pistol. They are to be given to him with the skin full of whiskey that I promised him. I want you to escort him as far back along our trail as you can today and turn him loose. Don't let him know you are observing him, but watch him leave in the morning and make sure he is heading toward Green River. If he turns back in this direction toward us—shoot him!"

"I will wait here and watch until you return. I want to rescue the girl, and I will do so if the Indian leaves the camp and goes off somewhere. But if he stays close to the camp, I will wait until you return so we can figure out a way to rescue her without getting her hurt or killed if the Indian fights us."

Caleb moved his two packhorses another mile away and down the canyon to get completely away from the camp where María was being held. He did not want to accidentally do anything that might alert the

Indian. Then he hunkered down to wait. He was a mile-and-a-half south and across one gully from María. Being so close to her after all this time, Caleb found it difficult to wait for Eagle-Man instead of trying to rescue her immediately.

In the morning, he walked back up to observe the camp from the same place he had watched the evening before. Again he could clearly see the Indian scraping on some skins near the door of the cave, where they were obviously living. Caleb was too far away to hear what they were saying, or even see distinctly what they were doing.

María came out of the cave and said to Beaver-Catcher, "There are nice berries over there in the next canyon. I will go and pick some and bring them back to you for lunch. If I find a lot we will dry them for winter." She patted him affectionately on the back as she walked past him. "I will return by noon."

"Be careful today," Beaver-Catcher told her. "The horses are restless, and I am nervous. I saw a black bird looking down upon our camp this morning from up in the sky over us. That is not good. I think there may be a bear close by. Don't you want me to get my gun and go with you?"

"No, it's not necessary. I am not going very far. If I hear anything, I will holler for you to come and save me," she laughed.

Caleb saw María heading north, away from him. He saw the Indian watch her until she was out of sight and then go back to scraping his hides and mounting them on a rack to dry.

Caleb was in a quandary. *What should I do? If I circle around and if she goes far enough, I will be able to find her and help her escape. But if I do that, I will lose sight of the Indian. I will then become the hunted, and defending myself will be more difficult because I'll have María to watch out for as well as myself. I sure wish Eagle-Man would get back here so I would have someone to cover my backside!*

As far as he had been able to determine, there was only the one Indian in the camp, Caleb was still trying to formulate a plan. He could, of course, try to sneak in closer and shoot the Indian. That would of course solve the problem with the Indian. The more he thought about the idea, the better he liked it. *But what about the way she had touched the Indian when she walked past him? Was she being affectionate toward him? Is that possible? No, it couldn't be! It is unthinkable.*

Caleb was just about ready to creep forward for a better look when he heard a horse scream. The scream came from one of the Indian's horses that were tethered and hobbled in the gulch below the camp. It took a lot to make a horse scream like that. Few men who spent their lives around horses would be likely to hear such a rare sound of pain, anguish, and fright from a horse.

Caleb could see the horses stumbling and falling as they tried to escape from two attacking grizzly bears. One of the horses went down struggling, unable to kick and defend itself because of the tether rope and hobbles. The other horse had been backed into a growth of briars and thick bushes. It was cornered there at the end of its tether rope, shaking and trembling with fear of the somewhat smaller she-bear.

María also heard the horse scream. She was on her way back from picking berries. She came running back toward the horses and saw them being attacked by the two bears. But instead of running to the safety of the camp, she got on the steep cliff-like hill above the horses and the bears. The screams of the horse being eaten alive by one of the bears was unnerving as it devoured and tore pieces of flesh off its victim. The horse continued screaming and was trying to kick the bear as it was being eaten.

Beaver-Catcher grabbed his rifle and ran towards the horses, priming his gun as he ran. He was hollering in Spanish at María to stay back out of the way and get into the cave. Either she didn't hear him or she ignored him. When she got up the hill above the horse that was backed into the bushes, she began to throw large rocks down at the she-bear. She dislodged one rock over a foot in diameter, which fell right on top of the she-bear's head, knocking her down for a moment and opening up a large gash on her head. Then the she-bear turned to face the antagonist who was still bombarding her with rocks from above and backed away to get out of range of the rocks being thrown at her. María then began to throw smaller rocks so as to extend her range and keep the she-bear on the defensive.

The she-bear growled a challenge at María and ran around the steep face of the cliff. María had saved the horse from the bear, at least for the moment. Now she was horrified to see the she-bear scrambling up the steep slope toward her. María took off running up the gulch toward her camp.

From his post at the top of the hill, Caleb could see María running uphill toward the Indian, who was racing down toward her, with his rifle. Caleb now had to risk exposing himself to the Indian as well as the bears in order to get close enough to protect María. Had she run back to the Indian's camp, as she should have in the first place, and left the bears alone, Caleb could have merely sat on the hill and watched the Indian deal with the bears. But as it was, María was in danger and the she-bear was now heading rapidly toward her.

After Beaver-Catcher got himself between the charging she-bear and María, he aimed his rifle and shot the she-bear in the throat. When she growled in anger and screamed in pain, her mate came charging up the hill to see what was happening, blood from the horse he had been eating was still dripping from his jaws.

The she-bear was bleeding a lot, but she was still an intimidating animal. Standing on two hind legs, she would have stood at least two feet taller than Beaver-Catcher. She charged right at him. Beaver-Catcher was frantically trying to reload his rifle before she could get to him. He did not have time to tamp his shot down on top of the powder with his ramrod, though he had gotten the tamping rod in the barrel. Instead, he used the mountain man's trick of bouncing the butt of the muzzle-loader on the ground to set the shot, and immediately primed the pan. This short-cut loading gained him a few seconds in getting the gun ready to fire. The she-bear was only five feet away as he raised his rifle and fired once again with the tamping rod still in the gun barrel.

This time the ball and tamping rod went point-blank right beside the she-bear's heart, only partially disabling her. She was momentarily knocked backward by the force of the shot, but quickly recovered her bearings and lunged at Beaver-Catcher, knocking him to the ground. With a single downward swipe of her huge claw, she sliced long two-inch, deep gashes in his face and chest, exposing bone in his chest and ripping out huge pieces of muscle.

When Beaver-Catcher raised his right arm to protect himself, she snarled and then bit down on his arm. She severed the bone and muscle with a mere twist of her jaws. Now Beaver-Catcher's arm was almost severed at the elbow; it was only held together by a few fragments of skin and sinew. Blood was pouring out of the artery, and he collapsed on the ground. The she-bear lay down on top of Beaver-Catcher, still growling and pawing at him. She was playing with him like a cat might play with a mouse, roughing him up and punishing him for attacking her.

When María saw what the bear was doing to Beaver-Catcher, she began running back down the gulch again in an attempt to divert the bear's attention. But by now the she-bear was dying as she lay on top of Beaver-Catcher. The grizzly followed María with her eyes but would not leave the prize she held in her grasp.

Caleb was trying to get someplace where he could help María, but he was still 200 yards away. He knew she could have escaped easily enough; but for some reason he did not understand, she kept risking her life, first for the horses and now for the Indian.

Caleb saw the he-bear advancing on María. He came tentatively toward his dying mate, who was still not ready to let go of the quarry she still held. The she-bear, with her remaining strength, growled and mauled Beaver-Catcher again.

Caleb stopped running and began to suck gulps of air into his lungs in an effort to settle his breathing down as he got one hundred yards closer. He knew he would need a steady sight with his rifle if he was to kill the he-bear. Wounding it would be worse than missing it, but perhaps he could divert its attention away from María, and still have time to reload.

He was closing the distance between them. When he was 100 yards away from the he-bear, he laid the barrel of his rifle, the one he called Hair-Saver, against a small tree to steady himself. He got a rifle ball out of the bag and put it in his mouth so he could immediately spit it into the barrel to re-load. He also removed the cap on his powder horn in preparation for fast-reloading. Each second he could save in getting re-loaded might mean the difference between life and death, for him, or María. It took many shots from a rifle to kill a mature grizzly bear and he knew it.

The he-bear growled ferociously at María. She threw a stick at him, and he growled again. *"Haaaaaa!"* she screamed at the he-bear. *"Haaaaaa!"* She made noises at him as she circled both bears. It looked to Caleb as if she was still trying to lure the bears away from the downed Indian. Then the he-bear started toward her.

Caleb took aim very carefully, holding his breath at one hundred yards. *Bang!* And he immediately began to reload, without even looking at the results of his shot.

Bang! Another shot, this time from up the hill behind Caleb. Eagle-Man had returned and was backing him up. The huge grizzly had two bullets in him now. Caleb got his rifle reloaded as the he-bear came charging down the hill toward him.

Bang! He fired again.

Bang! Another shot came from above. The he-bear stopped and shook his head, Staggering sideways. But he was still roaring his defiance, now more slowly charging his enemies.

Bang! Caleb's third shot hit him just behind the right shoulder.

Bang! The final shot came from above as Eagle-Man hit his mark, the center of the heart. The bear sat down, looking confused.

The he-bear lay down, eyes beginning to glaze over, taking a few last breaths. He wheezed through his bloodstained jaws, with some of his own blood now mixing on his lips with that of the horse he had partly eaten. He seemed to look around as if wondering where the she-bear was as he gently lay his head down as if to go to sleep.

María had run over to the she-bear lying on top of Beaver-Catcher. She was crying as she tried to pull the dead bear off the Indian. The bear was too heavy for her, and she couldn't pull it off Beaver-Catcher to free him. Caleb reloaded, and then ran over to her.

By that time, María was so upset she didn't even look surprised to see Caleb, let alone thank him for saving her life. "Help me, Caleb! Please help me! I can't lift the bear off him. She's too heavy!" She was crying as she struggled to pull the bear off the Indian under it.

Without asking why she was trying to help the Apache. Caleb said, "When I get the bear rolled over, you pull the Indian out. This bear is too heavy for me to lift, but if we work together you can drag him backwards when I roll the bear up a little. Put your hands under his arms, and pull when I tell you to. I can only hold her weight over to the side for a few moments, so you will have to be quick about it. Now pull!"

She pulled Beaver-Catcher free. The lower part of his right arm was dangling, attached to his body by a piece of skin. Less blood was coming from the wound now, because he had already lost so much. María sat down upon the ground and cradled the Indian's head in her lap. She sobbed uncontrollably, and rolled her body forward and back as if trying to rock some comfort into him. He was bleeding all over her shirt and legs.

Beaver-Catcher's eyes opened, and María could tell he recognized her. She tried to brush the dirt off the side of his face. He tried to smile at her and say something, but nothing came from his lips at first. Then he managed to say to her in Spanish, "Put a cross on my grave so God will know me. Say a prayer for me . . . and ask the Father above to let me into Heaven. Tell Him I am a Catholic . . . I was baptized José by the priests at the mission of Our Lady of Spain. I did not leave the mission on my own but was taken away. Will you do that for me, María? God . . . . Will listen to you because you are good!"

María nodded her assent. She could not speak.

Had the priests been there, they would have smiled at their success. In the end, José was a Catholic. The catechism and lessons he had learned at the mission had not left him. "Once a Catholic, always a Catholic," the priests liked to say. And, here was proof of it on this dying man's lips.

Beaver-Catcher tried to say more, but nothing came from his lips. His eyes drifted to Caleb. Since Beaver-Catcher had heard the gunshots, he assumed Caleb must be a trapper. What else would he be doing here? Still looking at Caleb, he said, "My pack carrier is a good camp woman. She will carry your traps and be loyal to you. This Spanish woman is not worthless ... she can cook, clean beaver, and skin them for you. She will serve you well. She is a good beast of burden. And if you are kind to her and wait until she is ready, she will warm your blankets as a woman should!" Imperceptibly he nodded his head up and down for he was now talking to himself.

Caleb caught his meaning, or thought he did, and nodded his acceptance, thus giving peace of mind to the dying man. Beaver-Catcher's last thoughts had been for his beast of burden María. In a brief moment, Beaver-Catcher was dead. He had died thinking of what he loved most.

Caleb attempted to communicate gently to María that the Indian was dead and that she should let him go. But she did not want to let go of Beaver-Catcher, so Caleb gently pulled Beaver-Catcher from her lap.

"It's Caleb, María. Don't you remember me?"

"Of course I know you," she said, finally looking at him. "You are once again performing a miracle," she gasped between sobs. She let him hold her while she wept. Finally, he helped her stand and gently led her toward the cave.

She stopped walking, and almost screamed, "He is to be given a decent burial, you understand!" she was almost incoherent as she yelled at Caleb.

"Yes. Of course. It shall be, as you want it to be. We can dig a good grave and put a cross on it. I have my Bible with me. We will read scripture over him and pray for him." He tried to comfort her. "We will ask God to accept him into the house of heaven. The Lord has promised us that those who believe in him can find their way to heaven. The Lord has told us María, 'Verily, verily I say unto you, he that believeth in Me hath everlasting life.' If he was good to you, the Lord will treat him well."

Eagle-Man had come to the area in front of the cave, bringing Caleb's horses and his own. He was also leading Two-Dogs's horse. The pistol that Caleb had asked him to give to Two-Dogs was in Eagle-Man's belt. *I hope Two-Dogs was trying to come back to do mischief to us when you killed him. But whatever was done is done now, so I won't ask any questions*, mused Caleb.

Caleb led María into the cave and helped her sit down. He got a fire started from the circle of coals still burning in the center of it, which lighted and warmed the interior of the cave somewhat. He noted that the small cave was piled high with furs, a store of food, and one pallet of blankets on a mattress of freshly cut grass.

"His name was Beaver-Catcher," María told him, calmer now. "He was a kind and gentle person, and he saved my life. Please treat him with dignity." Then she began crying again.

Caleb tried to comfort her. "Lie down here and try to rest a little. I will go out and take care of Beaver-Catcher and get his grave ready. Then I will come and get you when we are ready to read scripture over him."

Caleb and Eagle-Man used sticks and their hands to dig a shallow grave near where Beaver-Catcher had died. They did not have a shovel. "I'll get María for the burial," Caleb told Eagle-Man. "The quicker we get him buried, the better. Let's lay him face-up in the hole and put one of those tanned deerskin he was working on over him. I'll get my Bible out of my saddle bag, and we will read over him to put him to rest."

Caleb brought María to the gravesite. He put his arm around her, holding her close as he read from the Bible. She rested her head on his shoulder for support. Caleb read for a long time, and ended with . . . "Then they came unto the Lord in their trouble, and He bringeth them out of their distresses. He maketh the storm a calm, so that the waves thereof are still. Then are they glad because they be quiet; so He bringeth them unto their desired haven."

Caleb hung the black onyx cross, trimmed with fourteen fine bands of gold, around María's neck. "This cross brought me to you," he told her.

"My angel," she said as she gave him a hug. Then she kissed the cross as she always used to, and took it from around her neck. She bent over Beaver-Catcher and pulled the animal skin away from his head. She placed the leather thong around his neck and centered the cross on his chest next to his heart. She kissed the tips of her fingers and pressed them against his now cold lips. Then she put the deerskin back over his head and began to cry again.

Caleb motioned to Eagle-Man that he should begin to cover Beaver-Catcher. But as soon as Eagle-Man started to fill the grave, María insisted on helping. The three of them scooped up soil with their hands and put it on the grave until Beaver-Catcher and the deerskin were completely covered. They put a stone layer on the very top of the grave to keep the wolves from digging up the grave. Caleb laid a small wooden cross, made of two branches lashed together with rawhide, among the rocks on top of the grave.

María looked up at him gratefully. Then she picked up the wooden cross, kissed it, and laid it back down on the grave. As a final good-bye to Beaver-Catcher, she placed rocks on top of the cross to hide the gravesite as best she could. "All right. It is done! Thank you both." She inhaled a great breath of air and let it out slowly, with a sigh. "Caleb, if you and your friend will come up to the cave, I will fix you some supper. It will be dark soon."

"We'll be up as soon as we clean and dress the two bears. If we don't dress them out and get the meat inside, the wolves will eat them during the night. We'll rest here a couple of days while we smoke and dry the meat, and then start back to the rendezvous on Green River. We can decide then whether you want to go back to Santa Fé or on to California," said Caleb.

CHAPTER 13
Heading West.

When Caleb, María, and Eagle-Man returned to the rendezvous on Green River, Caleb induced Eagle-Man to stay on with him while María made up her mind about what to do next. They put this time to good use.

Caleb and María were teaching Eagle-Man Spanish, while at the same time Caleb was attempting to refine his knowledge of both Nez-Percé and the sign-language of the plains Indians. He wrote the sounds of the Nez-Percé language in his journal as best he could and drew pictures of the sign-language. María helped teach Spanish to Eagle-Man. And she wanted to learn his language as well as sign-language.

Caleb would have set off immediately for Santa Fé, but María did not want to go there. "You have business to attend to here at rendezvous. Go ahead and do your trading for beaver pelts. I need to think things over and decide what I should do. Let me rest and relax here a little and be with you," she said. "I know that I am obligated to fulfill my father's orders, and I cannot decide if I should go back to Santa Fé or accept your offer to take me to my betrothed in California." She didn't mention that she had not been feeling well lately, and was sick at her stomach almost every morning.

Caleb continued his trading and soon had more than a thousand pelts in his inventory, again. And at the same time, the supply of goods he brought to trade was being rapidly depleted. He would need a large string of horses to carry the pelts he had accumulated.

Caleb had noticed that María was no longer the scatter-brained, rich Mexican teenager he had known at the rancho. She was capable of tending his camp, making his fire, cooking his food, taking care of the horses, and doing most of the other daily chores a woman should do in a camp. She could catch and clean fish, clean a deer, tan its hide to make shoes or leggings. Not only could she do these things, but also she seemed to want to do them. María was happy, smiling, and joking now, and she went out of her way to keep busy and do her share of the work.

Caleb decided to teach her to shoot. He gave her a rifle, two muzzle-loading pistols, and a muzzle-loading bird gun that was loaded with buckshot. The pistols also were loaded with buckshot for firing at relatively close targets. She would soon be able to protect herself when necessary. "If someone sneaks into our camp, you shoot first and ask questions afterwards," he told her. "No well-meaning friend or customer will ever sneak in here, so there is no harm in shooting those who do."

He put her to work sketching maps of the location of Landers Station, which she gave to each mountain man and even the Indians when they seemed interested. The maps were invitations to trade at Landers Station if they happened to come in that direction. She made copies on every piece of paper she could find. And when she ran out of paper, she sketched the maps on scraps of tanned animal-skin.

María had insisted on sleeping with Caleb in his blankets. He tried to dissuade her, but she would not hear of it. Even that first night in Beaver-Catcher's cave with Eagle-Man in his blankets on the other side of the fire, she had stripped off her shirt-dress when she got into the blankets next to Caleb. She just held him that first night. After the first night, she immediately began to tease him by reaching into his pants and feeling for his penis. It was as if they were still back on her father's rancho. Once she got hold of it and began to slowly work it forward and back, he relaxed and cooperated. It did not take her long to persuade him to get his britches and shirt off.

María had fallen in love with Caleb back on the rancho, and she still loved him, as he did her. She rolled over onto the top of him, as she had that first time, and slipped his penis up inside of her. Her breasts jutted out and up, rising and falling as she moved in the faint firelight. He grasped hungrily at them with both hands, as she had once taught him she liked it. The faint light shone on the side of her face, making her dark-brown eyes glimmer with passion as she sought her own response.

Eagle-Man smiled to himself from the other side of the fire as he heard them making love and moaning with passion. It was good to be with friends who were natural and affectionate with each other. He would be glad when they got back to his tribe so he could be with a woman too.

María did not want there to be any question that she wanted Caleb to make love to her frequently, and with all the variety they could muster. Fortunately, they both had voracious sexual appetites. They made love every night, with few exceptions.

The time soon came when they had to decide where to go next. Caleb reluctantly brought up the subject to María. "As near as I can figure it, María, it is about six-hundred miles back to Santa Fé from here and over a thousand miles to Los Angeles. The best way to go to Los Angeles, according to the trappers I have talked to, is to go west to Fort Hall and ask for directions from there to San Francisco. Then we might be able to book passage by ship to Los Angeles, or we can travel down the coast by horse."

"I don't want to go back to Santa Fé and my father's rancho," she responded immediately. "There is nothing for me there now. What I want to do, if you will put up with me, is to travel with you to San Francisco and then Los Angeles. I want to spend these months with you. This will be my last happy time. When you deliver me to my father's cousin in Los Angeles, I will be kept almost a prisoner with the other married women. But I gave my word to my father that I would obey him, so I must do as I promised."

"I am going to have a baby, and I want to be with you when I have it. I want it to be born before you deliver me into the hands of my family in Los Angeles. This child was fathered by the Indians who raped and abused me. It will be a mixed Indian child. I don't know how my betrothed will receive it. But unless I am well enough to protect it, they might even want to kill it because of the manner it came to be inside of me."

"A baby! Are you sure?" he asked incredulously.

"Oh, yes, I am sure," she laughed. "Why do you think I was sick every morning for so long? Thank God that is over." Her body was already developing and changing, but Caleb had not noticed. She was relieved that the period when her breasts hurt had passed. Her breasts had grown larger and the nipples more obtrusive, and they had turned a deep reddish-brown. She, of course, had noted these changes.

"María, if you want to go back to your father's rancho, I will ask his permission to marry you. I have a good business, and I even joined the Catholic Church. I am also a citizen of Mexico now, which was required of me before I could own land here. I think your father likes me, and I would hope he might give me permission to marry you."

"I doubt if he would," she said, pursing her lips negatively. "And in any event, he has already given his word to his cousin in Los Angeles that I will marry him. He could not break his word. It is very complicated for us Spanish, but he would be humiliated if I were the cause of his breaking his word. I also gave my word to my Father in Heaven when I was in The School Of The Nuns Of The Stations Of The Cross. I must go through with the marriage. That is, if my betrothed will have me at all with this Indian baby. That is the real question. He may reject me. In that case, I will go back to Santa Fé with you; and if you still want me, we will discuss it with my father. Come now, enough talk. I want you to make love to me. I need you and want you," she said, seeking out his lips with hers.

Caleb placed his hand on her stomach, which he thought felt the same as ever. The skin did not even feel tight. "How far along are you?" He asked, when he separated his lips from hers.

"Three-and-a-half months, more or less. Come on, we have a lot of time. I will tell you in a few months when I want you to stop making love to me, but I don't want you to stop until I tell you to. I want you to promise to make love to me every single night—and if the mood strikes you, in the daytime, too." She laughed at the audacity of what she was saying.

"Do you promise?" She was jacking him, fondling him, holding his penis in her hand and stroking him slowly, exciting him. "And when the time comes for me to stop, I will still stroke you every night. I want you to be happy and healthy. The Indians believe that to be healthy a man should cum every night, if possible. Now that is my responsibility with you."

"Tomorrow night I will show you the way the Indians do it," she said, giggling. "I am a different girl now from the one you took advantage of at the rancho under the grape arbor so long ago." She thoroughly enjoyed teasing him about making love and watching his face turn red. But most of all, she loved to have him inside her, kissing her and hugging her, fondling her breasts, stroking her clitoris, sucking her tongue, and her sucking his. Her appetite for sex was growing all the time.

He came over on top of her. She continued to hold him and placed his penis in her vagina. She was still touching him as she touched her clitoris with her right hand. He could feel her masturbating herself above his penis. She had done that previously; and it excited him, too. He enjoyed it when she did that, although probably not as much as she herself did. He could tell that she was making herself passionately happy.

"I like it when you do that, María," he said in a whisper, kissing her. Sitting upright, with his knees on either side of her, he grasped both of her breasts and gently pulled her nipples. Then he bent down to kiss her lips, holding himself slightly above her stomach so there was room for her to work her fingers on her clitoris.

"Not as much as I do, I would imagine," she laughed happily, "but it pleases me that you are so open with me and that you talk to me. And it especially pleases me that you make love to me." She circled one of her fingers around behind his penis as she masturbated, and pushed his back down with her left hand so he would go more deeply into her. Caleb could feel her getting more excited. He lay down on her, kissing her. She was sucking his tongue, pulsing on it. He pushed his tongue back and forth in her mouth in time to the rhythm coming from below.

She used her right hand now to hold him deep inside as she achieved her orgasm. "Ahhh! Caleb, I love you! I love you! Hold me close. You are so easy to talk to, so understanding. You are truly *simpático*! And now you have achieved another miracle, the miracle of satisfaction in lovemaking for me: Thank you! Thank you!" She laughed at his obvious confusion about what she was saying, or why. The key laid in a part of her life she never discussed with anyone: she often thought of Sister Seraphena when she made love to Caleb.

Caleb made an agreement with Eagle-Man to deliver his pelts to Landers Station. Eagle-Man would hire two young men of his tribe to help deliver the heavy load of peltry. Almost immediately, two young, enthusiastic Nez Percé Indian boys presented themselves to Caleb, ready to carry out their assignment on two ponies furnished by Eagle-Man. Caleb issued each of them a rifle, a pistol, a double-barreled shotgun, 4 pounds of powder, a supply of lead, a butchering knife, and a tomahawk hatchet, for the delivery. These guns and supplies would be part of their payment for safely delivering the hides.

The weapons were given to the Indian boys in advance, to make it easier for them to protect the goods and hunt for food on their journey. They were thrilled when he showed them how to melt the lead and pour it in the molds to make the balls for their rifles. The boys lost no time trying their hand at making their ammunition. Then he showed them how to shoot the rifles and keep them clean.

Caleb wrote the following letter to be delivered by Eagle-Man:

Thomas Lyon, Landers Station.

I am forwarding herewith 1,000 beaver pelts, 200 buffalo pelts, and 25 bear skins.

My good and trusted friend, a Nez Percé Indian named Eagle-Man, is doing me the honor and service of delivering these to you with two of his countrymen. These men are doing a lot for me in this matter and should be paid the following indicated additional amounts when they arrive there. Consider these men as honored guests. I hope they will begin to trade with us and bring us peltry down out of the hills on their own, so do what you can to encourage such trade with them.

Each man is to be paid another butchering knife, 3 feet of twist tobacco, 2 pounds of sugar, a hatchet, and two beaver traps, along with a packhorse and pack saddle when they make safe delivery of the furs to you. For acting as captain of the trip and using his horses for delivering the goods, Eagle-Man is to be paid two extra traps, two extra butcher knives, and two extra horses. If you do not have the horses, give him full value in trade for other goods.

I will appreciate it if you do not encourage the Indians to drink liquor. Eagle-Man abstains from it, but I do not know the habits of the other young men. I don't like the whole matter of getting Indians drunk in order to rob them. I will continue to sell it because that is what many of them want, but I am determined not to take advantage of any man that is senseless, whether Indian or white.

Pass my regards on to Juan and Isabella, and I hope your rheumatism is better. It might be possible for you to write to me care of the *Alfonso de Vargas* rancho, 40 miles south of Los

Angeles, although I am fairly sure I will be there and gone before your letter could arrive.

Your obedient servant,

Caleb Landers

August 16, 1836. Green River Valley.

Caleb also sent the following letter for delivery to Phillip Bartholomew:

Phillip Bartholomew, Santa Fé

Dear Phillip:

Enclosed is a sealed letter for delivery to *Don Miguel de Vargas* from his daughter, María. She has asked me to deliver her to California to her betrothed, which it is my intention to try to do. This will not be easy because she is not perfectly well. I will travel first to San Francisco, on the coast, thence to Los Angles, and spend the winter somewhere between here and those places when the weather gets too bad to travel.

Lest you think I am not paying attention to our mutual business, I still have further goods to trade and will continue trying to acquire peltry for my account with you. Please advise your brother in England that I may try to send something direct to him from ports along the coast of California, if that proves possible, rather than try the dangerous journey from Los Angeles back to Santa Fé overloaded with peltry. I will have to see what that leads to when I get there, but I will appreciate it if you advise him to expect it and ask him to receive it under my account with you.

In the meantime, please order from your brother in England books on the dispensing of medicines, the tools for repairing wounds, the setting of broken limbs, medicines for our sale, and what intelligence he can provide me on that subject. I would like to add medicines to my wares, especially pain medicines, and instructions how to properly dispense them. There is constant injury of the most awful kind around me, and no one with any knowledge of what to do ever seems to be present. I would like to try to inform myself on this subject at least to make emergency repairs to the human body, or eliminate pain, if that be possible. I would also like just a few business newspapers quoting prices and such. Even though long out of date, it would be better to be out of date than totally ignorant if I am to conduct my affairs properly. Place in my order two-dozen books, even school books would be appreciated.

As to the best route for traveling from here to California, these mountain men at rendezvous seem to know everything. One problem I am having is sometimes they contradict each other, and there is no way as yet discovered by me to tell for sure when they are jesting, lying, or totally ill-informed. They delight in fooling each other and every one else. It seems to be their very nature to see which one can lie the most. I am highly confused about the trip, but suppose if I can stay the course heading west I should eventually arrive at the coast. I am going first to Fort Hall, west of here and the last stop this side of California. I hope to get better directions there.

Please tell the *alcalde* in Santa Fé that María definitely names Slip Fields as the leader of the Apache Indians who attacked their party on its way to California. He was the principal leader of the Indians, with a young Chief named Marks-On-Face, under the main Chief, Two-Dogs. Two-Dogs is now dead, so you do not have to worry about him.
Please pray for the success of my endeavors.

Your obedient servant,
Caleb Landers
August 16, 1836.
Green River Valley.

The rendezvous was coming to an end. There were plenty of Indians left, and some of them would camp there until the next rendezvous. But other than woman-flesh and horses, they did not seem to have anything else to trade for. Almost all the mountain men had expended their peltry and had moved back up into the mountains or were heading for Taos where they would spend the winter. Only a few traders still hung around, trying to get rid of the last of their trading goods before making the long trek back home across the plains.

One trader, Tom McLaughlin, needed to sell his surplus trading stock because he did not have enough mules to carry his peltry and his leftover supplies. McLaughlin was an old trader, who was so sick with dysentery that he could hardly walk. He was anxious to get out of the mountains and back to civilization. He approached Caleb to try to induce him to take the surplus goods off his hands. And he was desperate enough to take whatever he could get.

"Sir, I understands ye might be interested in buyin' my outfit, except the portion I be carrying back to Missouri. I'll give ye the whole works fer half price iffen ye got any gold ner silver. I kain't take no more pelts. Got no room fer any more o'them. I'm already loaded down to the gunnels. What say ye?"

"What kind of merchandise are you talking about?" Caleb asked.

"All kinds. I got fifty pounds o' horseshoes with nails, ground flour two hundred pounds, two hammers, two saws, a small tent, an' I still got four square kegs o' whiskey left. It's not ordinary Injin trade whiskey, nither, but good sippin' whiskey from Kentucky. I still got nearly a hunert pounds o' tobacco too."

"I've got nearly a hundert pounds o'gun powder an' two hogshead o'lead. The firearms I gots are the ones I traded fer thet are all broken. They is not any good to me so's ye get 'em thrown in. Oh, an' one o' the trappers gave me two small cap and ball pistols. They be twenty-two caliber and not as big as the palm of yer hand. They is not much good out here; but you can have them, too. They is like a child's toy. I planned on takin' all the broken firearms back to Missouri. They must be twenty-five o' them. I was a-goin' to have 'em repaired an' then iffen I comes back hyar next year, I could bring them back an' trade them off ag'in. But all this goods is too heavy, an' my packs are already overloaded. The worst o' it is I is sick-er-un a houn' dog and kain't seem to shake it. I gots the shits so bad my brains is befuddled."

Caleb wrote down a list of the merchandise being offered so he could study McLaughlin's inventory before making a decision. "That's all heavy merchandise and equipment, and much of it cannot be sold to the Indians. They do not use horseshoes with their horses, and as far as I know they don't use flour. When you say half-price, I assume you are talking about half-price using purchase prices at Independence, Missouri. If that is what you mean, I will purchase all your surplus, the good and the bad, and pay you with silver coin of Mexico at half-price in Independence, Missouri. I can pay you in the morning if you want, when I inspect the goods and pick them up."

McLaughlin was scratching his head and frowning. "That's not what I meant, but I see what ye means. Iffen I don't sell it to ye, I'm a-goin' to have to give it away or destroy it, or maybe even try somehow to take the best back with me, which means I gots to buy more horses and get some help as I got mor'n I kin muckle by myself as it tis."

"I guess yer my onlyest market, so I'd best keep a stiff-upper-lip an' take yer offer an' I thanks ye fer being square with me. I guess yer offer be fair enough under the circumstances, though tight as a tick after lugging it all the way here. Make up your list o' prices an' give me a chance to look it over, an' we-uns'll conclude our deal in the mornin'. Make up a receipt, an' I'll sign it. I want to leave in the mornin' fer home. I've had it hyar! As far as I know, yer the only'st man left hyar with any silver. I'll shake your hand on it."

"I understand ye have a trading station north o' Santee Fé in a burg called Fernando or Taos. Is that true?"

"Yes, I do. It is called Landers Station. If you get over that way, and have goods for sale I might be able to buy, or if I have anything you need, I will give you honest prices and good merchandise. I am 20 miles north of Taos."

"I appreciate ye a-takin' these goods offen my hands. I heard tell ye were a honest trader. I'll pass the word along," said the old trader, "but I think this hyar might be my last trip. I'm feeling mighty poorly, and I wants to get to-headin' back home. At least I can be sick in comfort thar. I kaint take the fightin' with Injins, lack o' proper food, an' all the sleeping on the groun' no more. I gots a good load o' furs an' what I make offen them ought to last me to the end of my days on this hyar earth for me iffen I don't live too long an make a mess o' it."

Even though some of McLaughlin's goods were too heavy for packhorses and thus not very practical, most of it was good quality that Caleb would be able to use or sell. Once again, he had six packhorses weighted down with packs as heavily as they could be handled. The twenty-five broken rifles would give him something to do when he had long stops to make during the winter months. He would have a lot of time to repair them and get them ready for resale.

CHAPTER 14
To Fort Hall.

Caleb and María, leading the packhorses, set out for Fort Hall the day after McLaughlin headed back to Missouri. Caleb still had the map he and his father had made, and he had added details on it from time to time as he learned more about the area they were heading into. The map showed the California coastline and a few major rivers along the west coast. The Rocky Mountains, sometimes known as the Stony Mountains, and the Sierra Nevada Mountains were shown as little hash marks; but little else was shown west of the Rocky Mountains.

Caleb had tried to add details to the map from what the trappers told him, but none of them had actually been in the area. Most of the things they told him were simply hearsay, no doubt embellished each time one mountain man passed the story on to another. But he thought there had to be some truth in those tall tales. The problem was trying to figure out what it all meant.

They spoke of travelers who did not reach their destinations or return to Fort Hall. Others told horrifying tales of thirst, and the agony of crossing a hundred or so miles of desert. Some advised him to go to Fort Vancouver, which belonged to the Hudson Bay Company, and take a boat from there to San Francisco. Most men he talked with tried to discourage him from attempting the journey at all. But some hardy travelers had made the trip successfully. No one denied that. Caleb knew there was a good trail to Fort Hall because the settlement was on the main route to Oregon, so he could be sure of his way that far at least. But from Fort Hall to California, as far as he could find out, there was no regular trail. He would be completely dependent on his compass as he headed into unknown country.

Caleb had followed his compass all the way from Independence, Missouri, to Santa Fé in Mexico the year before. He was very comfortable in his knowledge that he could set a compass course and then follow it. Because of the maps his father and he had made, he had a general knowledge of the California coast and some of the principal mountain ranges. What he needed was detail to add to his maps. His knowledge of the general direction of where they were going should see them through if he continued west. Surely he would be able to find the Pacific Ocean, and once there he could find San Francisco. He hoped to learn more about the route from the settlers at the last stopping-off place—Fort Hall.

Caleb, thought he could travel through the worst deserts if only he carried enough water. After all, he had successfully crossed the parched prairies from Independence. He gathered up all the discarded twenty-gallon whiskey kegs he could find, ending up with two of the empty barrels for each packhorse. They looked ungainly sticking up above the horses, but they would hold a lot of water when he and María started across the desert country. He would carry them empty until he needed to fill them.

While they were on the trail, Caleb trained María, already a good horsewoman, to keep three of the packhorses in tow. He continued to teach her how to use his rifles and pistols. For additional practice, Caleb had her shoot most of the game they ate while on the trail. She had become a sort of armed fortress and could defend herself as well as any man was able to do. She was both willing and able to use her weapons. She was determined that she would rather die than ever be another slave to unfriendly Indians.

Caleb loaded her up with guns. Two extras were readily at hand on her lead packhorse. "At night always use the shotgun loaded with buckshot and bee-bees. It spreads out a wide pattern so when you're shooting in the dark you can hit your target better than with a rifle, at short range. Always keep your rifle fresh-primed, and carry it with you all the time we're traveling," he cautioned her. "And at the first sign of trouble, always, always, fresh prime all your weapons and stand by."

María had been eyeing his two small-caliber weapons for some time. "May I have those two small pistols? I think they would be easy to shoot, and I would like to keep them in my saddlebags. I could shoot rabbits and small game with them."

"Of course. They are not very powerful, but surprisingly accurate for such small guns and they don't cost much to shoot either. They use very little powder or lead. Keep them loaded but not primed. Here's a small powder horn to go with them, a sack of balls, a bullet mold, and patches."

Traveling to Fort Hall was not exactly easy; but the country was green, with plentiful water, with beautiful views every day, and plenty of grazing for the horses. The journey was thoroughly enjoyable. Although Caleb and María sometimes had to ride through rough terrain, there was generally plenty of good water, and comfortable campsites. But the terrain occasionally was so rocky that Caleb was glad he had not attempted to bring wagons over the trail.

This part of the Oregon Trail followed Ham's Fork of the Green River through a series of rolling hills. Clumps of poplar and cottonwood trees were everywhere near water and there were pines in the mountains. Caleb and María pressed hard the first day and camped that night in a beautiful setting. In just a few minutes, they caught enough trout for supper and breakfast the following morning. And they were in their blankets under the stars by dark.

This was a fine time for Caleb and María. Because of the ever-present dangers from savages, Caleb wanted to keep moving fast and not stop until it was almost dark. But although they were both exhausted at the end of the day. Every night was a sexual adventure.

One disagreeable morning a strong gale was blowing. It made traveling difficult so they made camp in the early afternoon in a clump of bushes and boulders for a wind break. Some of the bushes were loaded with currants and gooseberries. Starved for fresh fruits and vegetables by that time, they ate little else that evening.

Several days later, one of the heavily laden horses tripped and fell near the northernmost bend of the Bear River. Caleb decided to stop at a nearby camping place known as Soda Springs. Fort Hall was just 40 miles west on the Snake River.

María thought Soda Springs was an enchanting fairyland. The abundant warm soda-water gushing from the spring, the surrounding fir and cedar-covered mountains, and the scattered mineral deposits, deposited long eons ago by now-dormant springs, all contributed to the special atmosphere there. It would be a good place to stay for a couple of days so the horses could rest. Since they would be staying more than one night, Caleb set up the little tent he had purchased from McLaughlin. María was fascinated by the tent. It was a real luxury in this wild country not to be sleeping out under the stars, rain and wind.

"This will be our sanctuary," said María. "You can join me there, but only if you ask my permission. And I will never say no to you." She said to him. She was so serious Caleb did not know what to make of what she was saying. It seemed almost to be a ritual with her.

Caleb wasn't sure whether she was talking to him or to herself. He had heard her say these strange, meaningless words to him before. It was back on her father's rancho. It seemed like a long time ago.

She laughed again at his confusion. "Remember, Caleb, you may only enter sanctuary after I tell you that you may do so. Tonight when you come to me, I will try my best to delight you in sanctuary. Thank you for the tent for tonight. Now let us go to that warm pond over there and take a bath. I need a bath. And you certainly do too, or hadn't you noticed?" Holding her nose, making fun of him, she laughed and ran ahead of him to the pond, where she shamelessly stripped off her clothes in front of him, and got in the warm waters, motioning for him to follow.

After supper, he changed the staked areas for the hobbled horses to have better forage. The overloaded animals were bone-weary, almost too tired to eat. He had pushed too hard. He promised himself not to let his horses get into such a state again. If an emergency should occur, they would be too exhausted to travel very fast or very far to safety.

He realized now that he should have at least two extra horses in case one fell, got injured, or went lame. He was definitely short of horses. And he was ill prepared for a hard march into unknown rough country with over-worked horses. He went back to the tent. María was already inside. She loved to play games that always turned out to be fun for him. He could see a candle burning inside the tent. He was not very happy about wasting a perfectly good candle for no good reason, but he would soon feel better about it. Since there was no way to knock on a tent flap, he improvised. "Knock! Knock!" he said.

"You may enter. Put your nightgown on and come in," she called out sweetly. María was completely naked, sitting with her legs crossed under her, Indian-style. She was smiling at him, obviously waiting for him. She had some small wild flowers pinned in her hair. He could see the opening of her vagina in the shadow between her legs from the little light provided by the one candle. Surprised and a little embarrassed, he just stood there awkwardly, looking at her, as he stooped over to enter the tent.

Finally, she said, "You should ask me now if you can join me in sanctuary, that is, if you want to. You do not have to join me. It's up to you. You can go sleep outside with the horses if you wish." She was smiling as though they were sitting down for supper.

"All right . . .," he stammered. "May I join you in sanctuary?"

"Of course. Hang your clothes on the side of the tent and come to me here. I want to show you some things I like. And you will like them too, in time."

He took his clothes off, laying his guns and clothes as usual beside his bedroll. She had hers by her side of the bed as he had warned her to always be prepared. "Now sit there facing me," she directed him to the open space on their bedroll.

He sat as she motioned and moved a little so that he was facing her with his legs crossed under him. He could hardly take his eyes off her exposed vulva—all the parts he had explored under the covers at night, but never seen so exposed before. Now here he was, seeing for the first time what so delighted him night after night. He especially couldn't take his eyes off her vagina. Whatever she had planned, he was already in favor of it.

They sat there looking at each other for a time. His penis quickly grew hard in response to her nearness and his stares. He knew they were going to make love in time. He was anticipating it. Meanwhile, the odor from her vagina was wafting through the tent. And even his faint masculine smell was noticeable as he became slightly wetted at the tip of his manhood.

She lay down beside him. "Come lie down beside me. I want to take your hand, and I want you to watch it move over my body where I show you." She placed his right hand on her breast and showed him how she wanted him to knurl the nipple. She had him hold her breast for a while, and then gently she held his hand encouraging him to squeeze it as she indicated he should do it by touch. "Squeeze it! Look! Pay attention! See how my breasts are growing from your touch? You are making them do that. Isn't that wonderful?"

Then she pushed his hand down to her mons, the soft mound of hair, and tickled and scratched it, moving his fingers to arouse her pleasure. "Watch, Caleb. See my body open up for you? See my breasts grow? Your hands are doing that. You are causing this to happen." She was breathing harder and harder. You are truly a miracle worker. My miracle worker!"

She pushed his work-callused hand down to her clitoris. She showed him how to caress and rub it until her opening was engorged with blood and she was moaning in response to his touch. But she didn't have to tell him to work his finger in and out of her. And when he did that, she began to pant in ecstasy.

"Look! Look what is happening! Look how it is swelling up, opening up for you, my love," she whispered as she leaned toward him and kissed his lips tenderly. The cords in her neck were tensed and her lips pursed tightly. She started moving her head from side to side, tossing her hair in delight.

Caleb had had enough looking. He could hold back no longer. There would be no more looking and no more talking. He pinched the candle flame out between his fingers. He preferred the darkness. María was now lying on her back with her own hands kneading her breasts. In the darkness, he knelt near the top of her head and gently lay down over her until he could put his face between her legs. With his lips and tongue, Caleb sought out her place of sublime pleasure between her legs.

"Oh! Oh! Oh!" she sighed in pleasure. "I had no idea you had ever been to a cloistered school for girls." She made a giddy, silly laugh as she met her match in sexual stimulation.

Her hand found his erect penis where he lay on her, and she turned her head and brought it to her lips. She had wondered what oral sex would be like but had never tried it with a man. It had almost become an obsession with her. Her lips sought his penis, toying with it for a moment and caressing it with her tongue. She kissed it and tasted its lubricating fluid. Finding she liked the taste, she pressed his penis into her mouth and suckled it, knowing instinctively what to do. She held the base of his penis with two fingers, working it up and down slowly in her mouth and continuing to suckle on it. She was rewarded as a fresh rush of his secretions flowed into her mouth.

They would delight each other in this way many times over the next months, adding variety and spice to their sexual experiences. Caleb set up the tent each night and no longer resented her frivolously burning the single candle. The extra work in setting up the tent, and the expense of using their candles were worth it. The days were still hot, but the temperature was nearly freezing toward morning. The tent made them comfortable in the evenings with their clothes off.

It took them fourteen days to reach Fort Hall. Old Fort Hall was established in 1834 and sold to the Hudson's Bay Company two years later. It was a way station for travelers and trappers. The fort was near the confluence of the Snake River and a tributary known as the Portneuf River. (Pocatello, Idaho, would someday be built several miles southeast of this early fort.)

The manager was Captain James Grant. He was courteous and helpful to all who came looking for trade, or a place to sell their exhausted animals and buy fresh ones. Many friendly Indians were camped outside the fort. Caleb and María were glad to see the civilization the fort represented. Not only would they find a good welcome here; there would also be people to talk to. That would be a pleasure, after having been alone on the trail for so long. Caleb asked Captain Grant's permission to place his packs and goods inside the fort for the night, and to turn his horses out into the pole corral. The corral appeared to be the safest place to keep the horses. Permission was quickly granted.

Since there was no forage in the corral, Caleb and María led their horses to a nearby meadow to graze. While the horses were grazing they cut bundles of grass with their butchering knives while the horses were grazing, and gave the cut grass to the horses when they were back in the corral to further feed them.

Captain Grant invited Caleb and María to dine with him that evening. He and the other men were delighted with María. She was the only female there. They enjoyed visiting with a lady as much as she did them. They were able to communicate easily as some of the men spoke a little Spanish, and she spoke fair, if highly accented, English.

After Caleb described the kinds of goods he had for sale and where he planned to go, he used the opportunity to learn as much as he could about the route to San Francisco.

The men told him about the many dangers he and María would encounter if they tried to make such a journey alone. They warned about the vast areas controlled by many separate Indian tribes that they would have to traverse before reaching California. This area stretched from here to Pilot Peak on the western edge of the desert and then to the top of the Sierra Mountains in the west. Part of this land was home to three different tribes. They were strongly warned that they could expect trouble from all three tribes. The trappers urged them to avoid contact with the Indians, because of their hostility to white men.

The most difficult terrain they would have to cross was a desert area with little or no water, food, or fodder for their horses. Worse yet, this was the wrong time of the year to set out because of the approaching winter. Should they get caught by snowstorms, they would likely perish.

"The Sierra Nevada are a great stretch of steep, heavily forested mountains," said Captain Grant. "Snow gets 15 feet deep there in winter, and the temperatures are often below zero. In fact, there can be sub-zero temperatures even in the hottest desert from early December through the end of March. After it snows, all the passes will be closed until June or July. You really should wait here until next spring and then go if you must, but don't try it now. If you wait until next year, you might be able to organize a party of trappers to go with you. It is said there are good beaver there.

"I know that a man named Joseph Walker established a route through to California," he continued. "It is said he found a river that flowed west toward the Sierra where it emptied into a large inland lake. He called it the Unknown River (the Humboldt as later named). I am told that there is practically no water between it and the Snake River. It's over one hundred miles to the springs at the base of Pilot Peak from the Snake River. Once he got to the Unknown River, there was plenty of water the rest of the way and beaver, too. But Walker reported the savages were dangerous, and he had a large party of forty men with him. Still they had to fight as the Indians kept stealing from him."

"But did Walker get over the Sierra?" Caleb asked.

"Yes, he did. I know the Sierra can be crossed if there is not too much snow. Apparently the Unknown River runs west from near Pilot Peak. West of it you find another river flowing east and it too ends in a large lake. On the other side of the lake is a pass through the mountains along a river that runs east. Once you reach the Unknown River you could follow it to the lake and then follow the other river right to the base of the Sierras. Once you get to the river that runs east, it is only a few days' travel time to the Sierra. You will find plenty of water in those tall mountains I was told."

"The main problem occurs before that. Once you leave the Snake River, you have over sixty miles with little or no water until you reach

Pilot Peak and springs in that vicinity. Then it is 60 more miles to the Unknown River, but there is water in that stretch from the Peak to the Unknown River. In the desert there are constant mirages in the sky of forests and lakes that can lead you off in the wrong directions, because they look so real. Water hungry people tend to go crazy when they see the mirage of lakes in the distance."

"We have already committed to go, and we must go," Caleb said, more worried now with this negative report than he cared to admit. "We will be leaving as soon as I finish shoeing my horses, which I hope to do tomorrow." Looking at Captain Grant, he asked, "Sir, if you have a forge, I would like to use it to shoe my horses. Would you be kind enough to let me use it? I have everything I need to do the shoeing, including shoes, nails, hoof knife, and rasp file; but it would be better if I could heat up the shoes so I can fit them properly. Hot shoeing is much better than cold shoeing, as you no doubt know."

"You have horseshoes?" Captain Grant asked in surprise. "They're almost impossible to get out here. Not only can you use my forge, I would like to hire you to shoe my horse for me. I would be glad to pay the going rate, whatever it might be to get my horse shod."

"I will certainly shoe your horse for you, sir, but you cannot pay for it. That will partly repay your courtesy and kindness to us. It will be my very great pleasure to shoe your horse for you." Caleb spent the next day shoeing his own and the captain's horses. As he finished shoeing each one, María took their horses out to graze. She would hobble and stake the horses out in good grass, and then stand guard with her rifle and pistols ready. Occasionally, when she was convinced they were perfectly safe, she cut bunches of grass with her butchering knife for the horses to eat later in the corral.

The captain came out to talk to Caleb as he worked. "I have too many horses to feed through the winter. The horses I want to keep I would like to get shod. Would you be willing to shoe two more for me in trade for a couple of my extra horses?"

"Yes, I would be happy to. Since I need halters and packsaddles, I will give you four extra sets of shoes for them in trade, if you find the price satisfactory. Then you can shoe your horses yourself whenever you want." This exchange held Caleb over for an extra day while he shod his new pack animals and Captain Grant's extra horses.

Now that he had two more pack animals, Caleb was able to reduce the weight that each one would have to carry. Since one of the 20 gallon water barrels, when full, he estimated, would weigh about 160 pounds they would be carried empty except for one gallon of water to keep the wood wet sloshing around so they would not leak, when they got dried out, until they began to cross the desert. The barrels would be placed near the center of each pack when full.

When the barrels were full and they started across the desert, he would draw a ration for the horses from each barrel, the lightened loads would give the horses relief in weight as they progressed.

Caleb and María started off at noon. The first 60 miles of their route would be along the Snake River, so water was no problem.

The fourth day out, about 45 miles from Fort Hall, they came upon a camp of trappers who had been north, deep into the Oregon Territory. After trapping for many months, they were finished for the year, and were heading back for Independence, Missouri. It was a long way for them yet. They were tired and low on supplies of all kinds, and some of their horses were sore-footed and barely able to walk.

When they found out Caleb had various goods for sale, they immediately proposed that he and María stay with them and set up a trading blanket so they could purchase supplies, especially whiskey. Caleb traded them a one hundred pound sack of flour for two hundred beaver pelts. Then he made whiskey for them by adding six parts of water to each part of alcohol. He sold the whiskey by the pint. One twenty-gallon keg of alcohol made eight hundred pints, which bought him eight hundred pelts. The mountain men's appetite for alcohol seemed unquenchable.

Caleb also fixed several broken weapons for the trappers and sold them two reconditioned rifles, and some lead and powder. He spent three days shoeing their horses at a good profit. He charged them one pelt per shoe. It was cold shoeing, but he worked hard on it and the men were satisfied with the work he did.

Once again Caleb had almost more furs than he could pack, and this time he had no one to take them back to Taos. He would have to pack them all the way to California. To carry this heavier load over the long journey, Caleb bought two of the trappers' horses and shod them at the camp.

The trappers gave a dance the evening before Caleb and María were to leave. One man had a violin, and another a Jews-harp. María danced some with each man, and many of them danced with each other. They all showed her the greatest courtesy, thanking her profusely for the privilege of dancing with her.

She gave each man one of her hand-made maps of the location of Landers Station so they could sell their furs there if they ever got over into that part of the mountains. The captain of the group brought a young Indian boy of about 15 years old to Caleb. "This is 'Shoshone-Jim,' as we call him. He says he is a Shoshone Indian. We found him last spring starved nearly to death on our way out here. He has been working for us as a camp boy, and we have found him dependable. He is a good lad. He worked hard for us."

"He got lost in the great desert in the direction you're going. There was a big dust storm, and he got lost and disoriented because he could not see the stars or sun. The dust storm was followed by many days of cloudy skies, so he could not find his way home. He is sure now that he came from the west and wants to join up with you to cross the desert and look for his family. I will give him a horse for the work he did for us, if you will let him go with you. He can help you with your pack animals. He knows a little English now that he has learned while working for us, enough to be useful to you. He is good with the horses too."

"Yes," Caleb said, "we would be glad of his company. I can use the help with the horses and packs, and if he knows anything at all about this country we are heading into it will help us a great deal." Caleb, María, and Shoshone-Jim left the friendly group of trappers, who tried until the very end to dissuade them from trying to cross the desert without a guide, or larger body of men.

Caleb maintained a slow, deliberate pace along the descent down the Snake River to avoid tiring his horses unnecessarily. He successfully avoided contact with the Indians that seemed to be almost everywhere. When they were 60 miles below Fort Hall, it was time to turn away from the friendly waters of the Snake River. The real desert would begin now. Caleb decided to stay over one last day on the Snake River to let the horses graze and rest.

Then, before they set out, Caleb and Shoshone-Jim filled the water barrels for the first time. Jim also carried on his horse two twenty gallon canteens made of animal-skin canteens that Caleb had prepared, and Caleb and María each carried twenty gallons of water on their horses.

They had nine horses now. Caleb figured that if each horse was allowed a gallon of water a day, they would have enough water for about ten days, plus that which they each carried for their own use. They would make three water-stops per day, giving each horse a third of a gallon at each stop. One ration of water was to be given in the morning just before starting out; the second would be at noon and the last one in the evening. Caleb made a second leather nosebag so each horse could get its allotted share at each stop. He trained Shoshone-Jim and María how to distribute the water with as little spillage as possible.

Caleb's objective was to cover at least ten miles every day. If they could do so without overtiring their horses, it would be the ideal speed for them. And to make sure they were heading in the right direction, Caleb took a compass bearing every hour, or more frequently when he became uncertain or confused.

The desert proved to be much dryer and even more inhospitable than Caleb had expected. The heat was oppressive, even at night. They could often see nothing but the arid, grassless sand-and-rock desert. The heat waves made the view unsettled and constantly moving, which made them all dizzy.

Their supply of water made the trip less difficult than it could have been. This, and a bit of forage they were able to find, saved them from total disaster. Every time they found grass that the horses could eat, even dry brown grass, they stopped until the horses had their fill and a rest.

Caleb was once again following his compass, headed always west and occasionally south fifty to sixty degrees. The first leg of their journey was farther than they had been told. They would have to travel over 150 miles across the desert to the upper reaches of the Unknown River.

The desert heat was cooking the strength and sense out of Caleb, María, and Shoshone-Jim, as well as their horses. Fortunately, they twice were able to top off their water barrels and canteens when they came across water left in rocky basins by a thunderstorm. It was the lack of forage for their horses, and their own misery in the heat, that most affected them. The alkali-salty dust soaked into their clothing and onto their bodies, mixing with their sweat until they were coated all over with a whitish crust, as were their packs and the horses. They were continually fooled by the mirages that the men at Fort Hall had warned them about. Every time Caleb saw trees or lakes far off in the distance, he would take a fresh compass heading and press onward in the proper westerly direction.

María, tormented by the heat and almost crazy with a desire to be cool, finally rebelled. She saw cool waterfalls to the east, with trees and green grasses beside the pools of water. In a frenzy of discomfort, she screamed at Caleb, "You are crazy! You are killing us and the horses by your obstinate refusal to go where we can see there is water. We must go there and rest the horses as well as refresh ourselves! We can see these places with our own eyes. I am going to the water whether you go or not!" Then she started off in the direction of the mirage.

Caleb galloped after her and got in front of her horse to stop her. "No, María, there is no water there. That is just a vision, as they told us at Fort Hall would happen. We cannot go east; that is the wrong direction. We must keep going to the west!"

"Get out of my way she screamed!" María lifted and cocked her rifle, pointing it at him. She was swaying in her saddle, on the verge of heat exhaustion.

Caleb was looking down the barrel of the shotgun, fully cocked. "All right, María," he told her quietly. "We will go where you want us to. But now it is time to water the horses and take our mid-day drink." He dismounted from his horse and turned his back toward her.

María, in a daze, dismounted and was sick to her stomach. She vomited several times and had an agonizing headache, the pain pounded in time with her heartbeat behind her eyes and temples. Then María realized that she had almost shot the person in the world she loved the most. She stood there in the hot sun and began to cry. The sand and rocks under her feet were to hot for her to sit down, and the heat was burning her feet through the bottoms of her moccasin-shoes. They would get no relief from the heat where they were. There could not have been a worse place for them to stop, but they simply could not go on any longer.

Caleb put up a canvas to make shade and laid out their blankets beneath it so she could rest and have some protection against the sun. This camp was in the salt-encrusted desert with nothing for the horses to eat and with temperatures over 115 degrees. He laid her out on her blankets and used some of their precious water supply on a rag to bathe her temples, face and wrists, and attempt to cool her off, quietly talking to her. It was just as important to keep his sanity as it was for her. He rationed out half a cup, half a pint, of water for each of them to drink. The water was now warm, taking heat from the sun.

She kept saying over and over again, "I am sorry. I am sorry. I am so hot that I do not think I can bear it any more."

"It's all right, María. We are all worn out and half-crazy with the heat. Here, take a drink of this whiskey in your water. It might help your headache and make you feel better. We will rest here until late this evening. When it starts to get cooler, we will begin riding again. I think we will ride all night tonight when it is cooler. There is a moon we can see by, and we must get some grass for the horses soon, just as you said, or they will die and then we will too I think. Let me bath your face and wrists again with some water. It will cool you here in the shade of the canvas. He also bathed Shoshone-Jim's wrists and face as well as his own. It was only a temporary thing but it helped.

"But I don't want more water than is my share," she was crying again and now getting angry. "Please take us to water." He bathed his own face and that of Shoshone-Jim too. She soon fell into a troubled, exhausted sleep.

That night they kept moving on their journey by the light of the moon. In the moonlit darkness there were no mirages to distract them, and it was also a bit cooler.

On the twelfth hot, miserable, dusty day in the desert, Shoshone-Jim let out a holler. He pointed at the barely visible tip of a solitary mountain twenty miles away and yelled in good English, "water!" He was grinning and laughing. Caleb thought it might be just another mirage; but Shoshone-Jim had never before seemed so positive about anything, and he certainly seemed to know the area. The Indian did know where he was at now and told Caleb and María he was absolutely sure that water lay at the base of that mountain. They quickly changed their course a few degrees more southerly and headed for the mountain that rose up over 10,700 hundred feet. The mountain, named Pilot's Peak, would serve as a landmark for pioneers in their wagon trains in later years.

They were coming out of the worst of the desert now, and had only two days to go before they would be at the base of the mountain. Soon they would be resting in the springs and grass they would find, and savor fresh meat from the animals that were abundant there. They could tell this was not a mirage because instead of disappearing, this sharp peak got larger and larger during the two days it took them to reach it.

It was still hot, but there really was shade and grass and water for themselves as well as the horses in their new direction. It was hot, but tolerable when they reached their objective. Caleb, María, and Shoshone-Jim soaked themselves, and their horses, washing the alkali off themselves and the animals, in the water immediately after they arrived, and several times every subsequent day as they rested and cooled off in this oasis. They bathed their faces in the cool water and rubbed it over themselves and sat in it to cool off as much as they wanted. María and the Indian boy both went completely native and refused to wear any clothing despite Caleb's obvious disapproval. They laughed at him when he said they should keep their clothes on, and refused to obey him.

"This is Indian country! Do as the Indians do, and enjoy it!" she said laughing, as she ran off to splash and cool off in the water again. She would run back to him, soaking wet, and would kiss him and press her wet naked body against him shamelessly.

"Don't forget your promise! You have to make up for all the days across the great desert when you ignored me. Come on now. Do your duty. Make love to me." Then she would drag him back to their shaded blankets. Actually, he didn't put up much of a fight as she took his clothes off.

Caleb and María had abstained from making love when they were crossing the desert. It was too hot. They were too tired. And it was too dusty. But with three days' rest at the springs, bathing together in the nude and lying on blankets in the shade, they got back on schedule. It was like a new beginning that made their love-games all the more pleasurable. Her appetite was, as usual, inexhaustible, no matter how much he tried to keep up with her.

Caleb spent the days inspecting and tightening the shoes on the horses, working on the packs, making repairs on their equipment, resting, jerking meat from the plentiful game they killed, and just enjoying himself with María and Jim.

The time to head west again came all too soon for the weary travelers, but they could not risk staying any longer. This time Jim kept pointing and saying "water" as they traveled along. He had been right before, so Caleb had confidence in his knowledge. Jim was anxious to press forward, smiling and happy, as he kept pointing almost due west. Since west was exactly the direction Caleb wanted to go, they followed the Indian's lead. Their water casks were full in any event.

It was sixty miles across more desert to the Unknown (Humboldt) River. Within two hours after they reached the river. Jim led them to a camp of friendly Indians. He was home now with his own people. The Indians thought he had been lost forever, and so the tribe honored Caleb and María for returning him.

These Indians were unlike the ones they had camped with on the Green River. Some of the women wore short skirts made of grasses, sagebrush, or reeds tied around their waists; a few wore rabbit skins around their waists; or an occasional skirt woven of grass. That was all they wore, and most of the men wore no clothing at all.

Caleb and María were able to stay only a day with the cordial Indians before it was time to press onward. When it was time to set out the following morning, they gratefully accepted Jim's offer to ride with them for five more days, to ensure that none of the Indians bothered them as they made their way westerly down the Humboldt River.

María had become fond of their traveling companion, and she hugged him and cried when he was ready to turn back. Caleb gave him a generous supply of metal arrow-points, showy trifles, gaudy finery, and other gewgaws as the mountain men described the trade goods used with Indians. These were the items the Indians so much enjoyed. With these gewgaws and his horse, Jim was now the richest Indian in the whole tribe, perhaps in the whole world. He said good-bye and returned to his family. In parting, Jim warned them that the Paiute Indians to the west were not friendly, and should be avoided.

Once Jim left them, Caleb avoided all contact with Indians. They saw a lot of them along the river. At the first sight of them, he and María rode swiftly to the north away from the river. Then they would head westerly parallel to the river to avoid encountering them.

Now that Caleb and María were alone again, they moved steadily, but still slow enough to save the strength of their horses. The horses had lost weight coming across the desert, but they were now holding their own and even regaining a little weight. Slower was faster in the end, and Caleb had learned that it was essential for the horses to have reserve strength for emergencies. As long as the horses had forage and water, there was no reason to hurry.

Caleb breathed a sigh of relief. They had safely traveled through one Indian Territory. That left two or more Indian nations they knew absolutely nothing about between them and California. He worried about what dangers might lay ahead. Halfway along their route paralleling the Humboldt River, they entered the lands of the Paiutes.

CHAPTER 15
Paiute.

The term "Digger Indian" was used by Americans and Spaniards as a derogatory name to describe not only Jim's tribe, but a group of tribes who for one reason or another lived on the edge of poverty and obtained their living by digging for fodder or chasing it on foot. The Paiutes further to the west dug up much of their food with sticks, and lived on a diet that included lizards, rodents, other small animals, grasshopper, roots, including the larva of insects, and leaves of sagebrush. Digger Indians were among the most primitive Caleb had ever seen. Their tools, if they had any, were crude by comparison to those made by some of the tribes who lived in the mountains to the east.

Generally, the Digger Indians were malnourished, often physically inferior, and lived in primitive conditions. They were not skilled hunters, or they lived in areas where there was little or no game to hunt. They had retrogressed, compared to other tribes, and sometimes no longer even used fire. Their homes were caves and the crudest of huts and brush shelters. They had been pushed into these marginal subsistence areas by the more violent and better organized tribes of Indians. Here they lived a hand-to-mouth existence, and were barely able to survive.

The Digger Indians existed by digging and stealing whatever meager necessities they could find to keep from starving. They delighted in sneaking into the white men's camp to take food and supplies. The white men despised these Indians for their thievery so much that they shot or ran them off whenever they approached.

The Paiutes of this region moved constantly from one area to another, depending on what could be harvested at a particular season. They killed jackrabbits and occasionally a deer, snakes, and lizards. They also ate large amounts of grasshoppers, squirrels, gophers, and fly larva. Anything that could crawl or walk was food for the Paiutes. *Piñon* pine nuts were an important diet staple, because they could easily be stored and taken along on the Paiutes' travels. They also ate raspberries, chokeberries, and elderberries, as well as wild carrot, wild onion, bitterroot, and white sagebrush when in season.

In 1828, the fur trader, Peter Skene Ogden, came upon what he named the Unknown River. He and his party came from the north and found the river near what is now Winnemucca, Nevada. They trapped beaver there until the weather turned cold. Then they headed east without exploring the river toward the west. Joseph Walker and forty men, who were trapping beaver, explored the Unknown River in 1833, just three years before Caleb and María found it. Walker and his men had a lot of trouble with the Paiutes, who stole their traps and sneaked into their camp at night for whatever they could get their hands on.

After the trappers began to shoot the Paiutes, the Indians sent smoke signals to warn the other Paiutes who were further west to plan an attack of their own. When the Walker party reached the sink, or lake, at the end of the river, they were attacked by a war party of eight hundred Paiutes. They had several skirmishes with the Indians and killed many of them, more than forty in one encounter. These confrontations created the unshakable enmity of the Paiutes toward the white man, for which subsequent travelers through the area would pay the price.

Caleb and María did everything they could to avoid contact with the Indians as they continued westward, following their compass. They would only approach the river for water. And as soon as their water supply was replenished, they retreated to the desert north of the river, even though the grazing was less desirable there.

For several days now, Caleb had noticed the smoke signals. It was apparent they had been spotted by the Indians and were now being tracked. He knew no good could possibly come from it.

Several times groups of Indians on foot tried to approach them, but Caleb was always able to run off into the desert. The Paiutes did not have horses, but they knew the country and moved almost as fast on foot as he could on horseback. Caleb and María began to press their horses to outpace the Indians. They traveled longer distances each day, from daybreak to dark now. They moved on as long as they could see which direction to go in. When they pitched camp, they put their blankets down in the middle of their packs, as a sort of fort. Then they forced themselves to take turns and stay on guard.

Caleb awoke before dawn one morning. One of the horses had snorted loudly and was stamping his foot. Caleb had been priming one rifle and one shotgun for himself and for María every evening before they went to bed. "If an Indian comes into our camp, shoot him! Don't hesitate for one second!" he told her repeatedly. But he need not have worried, for María's resolve to avoid capture by Indians again was ten times stronger than his. She had no intention of being captured, raped, and tortured by savages a second time. She had already made up her mind that she preferred death.

He reached over and put his hand on her mouth. This was their pre-arranged signal for her to cock her gun and be fully alert. They could see Indians creeping stealthily toward their camp. It was still dark, but not so dark they could not shoot at the intruders, especially with shotguns. He gestured for her to shoot eastwardly on one side of the horses. He would select a target on the other side of the staked-out horses. He whispered in her ear that she should shoot, and he would shoot immediately afterward. Then they would both pick up the rifles loaded with buckshot and shoot at whatever moving enemy they could see, firing over and over as quickly as they could reload.

María searched the darkness until she spotted one of the Indians slowly coming forward toward the horses. His dark-skinned body was faintly visible because of its contrast to the lighter shade of his reed skirt. She carefully aimed at the top of the skirt that was moving slowly in the darkness.

Bang! She fired. And the scream was ample proof that she hit someone.

Bang! Caleb fired his flintlock rifle "Hair-Saver" and saw one of the Indians crumple. Then he picked up the shotgun and shot an Indian who was already running away. They could not see anything else to shoot at.

"Load up! Load up!" ordered Caleb, who was already loading his rifle and would then load his shotgun. "Stay here. I'll get the horses. It will be light by the time we get the horses loaded up. Get some jerky out of the pack, and we will put it in our waist bags and eat it as we move. Get the nosebag ready, too, and we will water the horses before we leave. We must get moving before they come back."

Caleb inspected the dead Indians. The Paiutes wore less clothing and looked quite different from Indians to the to the east. One had a rabbit-skin waistband. The one that María had shot wore a skirt of sagebrush twisted into a rough cloth-like material. The Indian he had shot with the shotgun was naked except for a sort of belt on which he kept his stone knife. Strung around his neck on a leather thong were half-a-dozen deer feet, apparently as decoration.

The Indians' faces and bodies were covered with drawings of half-moons, circles, triangles, dots, wedges, lines, chevron-shaped groupings, and wavy lines. The pictures on their limbs and bodies were mostly black with a few different colors here and there.

Their bows were shorter than usual but seemed to be adequate, and the arrows were tipped with pointed razor-sharp stone arrowheads. None of the arrows had metal points, which indicated that these Indians had not made contact with any traders. The Indians also had clubs, and sharpened stones that they used for knives. They kept the knives in bands or leather belts around their waists, although not every one of them had such a knife.

Caleb and María moved out at dawn. They rode up a small rise just as the sun was coming up. To the southwest was a good-sized lake with large marshy areas of tules. They could see Indians heading in their direction from the north and more behind them.

Caleb and María traveled as fast as they could to get away. They went around the north end of the sink into which the Humboldt River ended and then turned southwest. By late in the evening, when it appeared that they had outdistanced the Indians, they stopped and unloaded their horses so they could graze and rest. Although they were tired and jittery, they took turns standing guard all night, and were still tired when dawn came.

The practice of keeping the horses well fed and well rested was paying off now, when they were being pressed to exhaustion every day. They had traveled over 40 miles the day before, and Caleb was determined to put a lot of distance between them and the Paiutes today as well.

At daylight, they started off again and soon found a river that flowed north and then east. Happy as they were to reach this river, Caleb and María were frightened when they saw a long line of Indians to the north and behind them to the east. It was obvious that Caleb and María were being herded by the Indians. They both knew they were in trouble because the Indians knew the area well, while Caleb and María did not.

They realized they probably were being pushed into a trap of some kind. But what kind of a trap? How could they avoid it? They could not go back where they had come from.

"Why is it I have a feeling they are leaving the way open in front of us?" Caleb asked María. "I don't know if they are trying to get rid of us or are herding us some place for an ambush. This has to be the river we heard about that flows east and then north. But we are heading west, and that is the direction we want to go. Unless we want to attack the Indians, the best path seems to be to keep going as we are—but the hair is standing up on the back of my neck!"

A cut or pass through low, brown, rocky foothills loomed up in front of them. On both sides of the pass were rugged, rocky hills covered with brown grass and water starved sagebrush. The entrance into the pass through the hills was an area of green meadows, cottonwood trees, and tall grass, and many Indian camps along the river.

The dwellings were primitive. The lower walls were made of sticks, poles, reeds and sagebrush. The roofs and part of the walls consisted of grass, sagebrush, and twigs. The camps were abandoned although a little smoke was still coming from some of the their fires. Obviously, the camps had been left a short time ago. Caleb and María could see Indian men, women, and children hiding behind rocks in the foothills on either side of the pass, peering at them from protected hiding places.

Caleb stopped at a rise from which they could see in all directions, so the horses could graze and rest. They had been there half an hour when they noticed a large group of Indians moving in from the east.

"Let's shoot a couple of them to keep them back," he told María. "We can let them know it's going to cost them something if they attack us. You shoot first, and I will follow you. As soon as you hit one, reload and we will ride on. The horses have stopped breathing hard, so I think they are ready to travel again."

"If we have to stop, try to ride up beside me; we will use the horses on each side as a shield. I will tie the horses we are leading to the tails of the ones we are riding. This will free our hands for shooting and loading. We need to keep moving and not stop. If they stop us and we try to fort up, there are so many of them we won't have a chance. Once they get around us in a circle, we will be trapped."

María took careful aim as she leaned up against a cottonwood sapling to cradle the heavy rifle. *Bang!* She heard the surprised Indian scream.

Bang! Caleb shot another Indian, who crumpled on the ground, moaning and writhing. "There's a couple of shots that might hold them back some," shouted Caleb. "Now let's reload and mount up." The Indians following them had stopped in confusion at this display of marksmanship at such a great distance.

Caleb and María entered the cut into the rugged, arid mountains. With the Indians moving up behind them now, they had no choice but to go there. (They had reached the Truckee River near Fernley, where it turns abruptly and flows north to Pyramid Lake. The river would someday be named for an Indian scout.)

The narrow strip of lush green grass, cottonwood trees, and inviting country along the banks of the river would have been an ideal place to stop and rest the horses, but they didn't dare to stop because of the steadily increasing numbers of hostiles who had them almost surrounded. They had to press on. It was hot. Both Caleb and María were sweating, and the horses were lathered and breathing hard again from the fast pace.

There were signs of Indians everywhere. They could be seen running parallel to the river, just out of rifle-shot range. And there were more smoke signals. This time the signals were mostly to the east, behind them.

Caleb checked their weapons. They had the rifles they carried and the two shotguns, loaded with buckshot, in scabbards on his horse. There were two more shotguns on his first packhorse, and he loaded two more. He then had six loaded shotguns, his rifle, and his pistols. He hung extra powder horns and bags of buckshot on his horse and the two lead pack animals.

He had been told that the trail followed the river 30 miles through the steep, rugged hills that lay parallel to the Sierras, which they could not see yet. Once they came through this range of hills they would be in the valley that lay at the foot of the Sierras. With Indians on the hillsides on both sides of the river, this route would be extremely dangerous; but it was the only possible way for them now. Caleb considered going into the hills and trying to parallel the river from there; but he was afraid they would get into country so steep and rough that they would be easy targets. And in order to even reach the hills, they would have to fight their way through the line of Indians that was herding them.

They would clearly have to try to outdistance the Indians again. The best course seemed to be along the side of the river. They set off, Caleb leading four packhorses, and María leading three. The horses were getting tired but were still able to draw on the store of energy that they had built up for just such an emergency. With an occasional rest, they could still keep going. They had to!

Caleb and María proceeded rapidly for 8 miles, when the canyon narrowed and the river's steep banks and thick brush forced them down into the stream itself. Caleb was worried. "I don't like the looks of this, María, but we have to go forward. Keep your rifle pointed up and be ready to cock it. If you see an Indian, shoot him! Don't wait for me!"

Caleb led off into the river, trying to see the hills above the riverbank. The sides above him had huge boulders and rock, with dense undergrowth and cottonwood trees. This was a perfect place for an ambush. They were a 100 yards down the narrowing gulch when an Indian raised up twenty feet from the side of them him and let fly with an arrow. The arrow made a "twang" as it left the bowstring. It hit the hard leather below the saddle seat that held Caleb's stirrup and ricocheted downward into his leg. Although the sharp stone arrow-point penetrated his leg, much of its energy had been taken up when it hit the saddle first. Fortunately, the barbs were not buried. It stopped just short of that. The Indian let out a whoop of joy, pointing and yelling that he had made a hit. He stood up grinning his joy and telling his comrades that he had made a hit.

Caleb raised his rifle and shot the Indian just before a dozen large rocks rained down on top of him. The Indian caught his bullet and tumbled down over the top of the rocks, screaming in pain and kicking his legs wildly. He was silenced when he hit the rocks along the riverbank.

The rocks from above rained down onto Caleb. One hit him on the back of the neck and knocked him off his horse as several others landed on top of him. Dropping his rifle into the water, he fell into the river. He was stunned into unconsciousness. The fast current of the river sent him, floating face down, back toward María. She dismounted and jumped in front of him, lifting his head out of the water to keep him from drowning. All the while, the Indians were shooting arrows and throwing rocks down on them.

María stood in the stream with the horses on either side of her, which temporarily protected her. She placed Caleb's chest and head between her legs, making a vice to keep his head up out of the shallow water while she handled the packhorses. Her horse was hit twice by arrows that were driven deep into its shoulder. Still holding Caleb's head out of the water in the vise between her legs, she leaned her rifle against her horse's saddle and took careful aim at the nearest Indian.

Bang! She shot him in the stomach, and he screamed with pain. He fell to the ground twisting and writhing in agony, forcing the other Indians to pull back. She pulled one of the shotguns out of the scabbard. *Bang!* She shot an Indian who was peering over the edge of the bank and shooting arrows. She calmly shot him in the head with several buckshot pellets. The Indian came tumbling down into the river, splashing and screaming. Still cradling Caleb's head and trying to lead the horses, she pulled the shotgun out of the scabbard on the other side of the horse, replacing it with the spent shotgun.

Now the Indians were attacking from the rear. *Bang!* She shot at a group of four Indians who were 50 yards from her, running upstream from behind her. The shotgun spread out its load and hit the lead Indian, knocking him down into the water. His blood turned some of the water a deep red. One of the buckshot pellets went beyond him and hit one of the other Indians in the knee after ricocheting off a rock in the water. He screamed and limped as fast as he could back down the river, and the other two followed him. María suddenly realized that it had grown perfectly quiet. They were no longer being pelted with arrows and rocks. She had beaten back the attack, at least temporarily.

Blood was bleeding out the back of Caleb's neck into the rushing water as he tried to get up. She put his hand on her stirrup so he could steady himself and stand up out of the water. Using her knife, she cut the edge of her saddle blanket and put it under his shirt, tying a leather strap around him over the top of the blanket piece to hold it in place as a temporary bandage. It was wrapped across his chest, and over his shoulder to press on the bandage. She tied it in front of him. "Can you stand up?" She asked him worriedly. Her hands were shaking, and her face was gray.

"I guess so." He was groggy but trying to get himself upright. She helped him get to his feet. "I'm all right, I think," Caleb said as he assessed their predicament. "We have to load up your rifle and shotguns and get moving. We have to get out of this gulch so they can't pitch rocks down on us again." His rifle lay in the water where he had fallen off his horse. It would need to be dried out before he could reload it. He helped María reload her weapons.

"You did good, María! You fought the whole bunch off all by yourself. You kept your head and did everything you should have done, not to mention that I owe you my life! I'm really proud of you."

"I'm kind of proud of myself," she responded. "But these Indians do not fight as well as the Apaches and Comanches back in New Mexico. Of course, it is easy for me to say that. You're the one who got shot with the arrow and had the rocks dropped on his head. How is your head now? And what are we going to do about that arrow in your leg?"

Although the barbs had not gotten embedded into the muscle of his leg, the wound still hurt. He took a deep breath, and carefully so as not to pull the arrowhead off the shank of the arrow, pulled it out. Then he tied a leather band, tightly, around the wound to keep pressure on it.

"We've got to pull the arrows out of your horse's shoulder, María. They are buried in there deep, I'm sure that when we pull on the arrow shafts of the arrows, the stone arrowheads will come out inside the horse. Put your coat over the horse's head and try to hold him still. I've got to pull them out. I don't know what that will do, but we've got to try it. I'll just jerk them out and leave the heads in. That will have to do for now."

He pulled the arrows straight back, and the heads did remain embedded in the horse's shoulder. Caleb was glad to see that the horse did not bleed a great deal. The wounds would heal over, he knew, unless they got infected. He decided that María should continue to ride the horse until it became too lame.

"Let's move out," he said. They pushed their horses west, upriver, as fast as they dared, until the gulch widened out again. There they found a small tree-covered grassy area where they could let the horses blow and rest. After 15 minutes, they resumed their dash up the side of the river.

They passed several groups of Indians warily and rapidly. None made any hostile moves towards them. It was mid-afternoon when they broke out into a large meadow. Looking back, they could not see any smoke signals. They had passed through the gauntlet of the Paiutes.

CHAPTER 16
The Sierras at Last.

Caleb and María were in what is now called the Truckee Meadows, which was home to the Washoe Tribe. The Washoe Indian territory extended from Lake Tahoe and the crest of the Sierra to the vicinity of what is now Reno.

These Indians differed from the Paiutes in that their area included the green forests of the Sierra to the top of the crest of the mountains that now lay before them. As a result, the Washoe's had more deer, antelope, and even bear to harvest, plus a variety of fish in the many rivers and lakes. After having traveled over the arid, high-desert country since they left Fort Hall, this lush green land was incredibly inviting. Tempted as they were, they did not tarry, because they wanted to get as far away from the attacking Indians as possible.

They hurried on through the meadow, staying away from the river itself but paralleling it. They could see huge mountains rising up in front of them. Caleb was sure these mountains were the Sierras, because they fit the descriptions given him by the trappers at Fort Hall. Crossing these mountains had become their objective, and they hoped they would be safe once they got started into the mountains. In their minds, the Sierras would be the last obstacle before they reached California. It looked easy on Caleb's maps. But, looking ahead to the high mountains and the dense forests, he was not so sure now. These mountains looked like the Rocky Stony mountains, and he knew how steep and difficult passage through them could be.

It was getting dark as they penetrated the first pine forest upriver at the foot of the mountains. They found a clearing with good grass, where they stopped and unloaded the exhausted horses so they could eat and rest from their long, tiring run for safety. The wounded horse was not even limping. The two arrow-points inside the horse's shoulder would be little more than an irritation after a while.

Caleb and María hoped the Indians would leave them alone. They had seen numerous Indian encampments close to the river as they dashed across the valley. Although the Washoe Indians stared at the pack train, they did not chase them. Both Caleb and María were relieved that no Indians were near their camp.

It had taken them forty-five days to cover the 450 miles down the Humboldt River, through the Truckee River canyon, and then over a large meadow to the base of the Sierra Mountains. They had a new objective now. Caleb was anxious to get over these mountains before the full blast of winter hit them. It was already October 25, and the temperature was freezing every night now at this altitude. María was now six months pregnant. She was feeling the effects of her pregnancy. She tired more easily, but she was strong and determined and she did not complain.

"We have to decide if we should make a permanent camp here or try to get over the mountains before winter," said Caleb. "I think it would be better if we could get over the mountains first. What do you think is best? How are you feeling? Do you want to stop here and wait for your baby or keep going? We can wait here for spring and then go over the mountains. Once the snow gets deep we might have to stay here six months, until it melts. Or do you want to push on and try to get over the top before winter catches us? I think we might get across in ten to fifteen days. And from what I have been told, that country on the other side is better to winter in although I don't know for sure. It might be worse. We can do it whichever way you think would be best for you. We're still close to those Indians who attacked us, and I feel uneasy here so close to them. Of course, the Indians on the other side might be just as bad, if not worse."

María answered him without hesitation. "I want to try to get over the mountains if we can. We should try it. The horses are in good shape, and if we get to California I will feel much better. I feel good. I get a little tired, but I see no reason to stop now. Let's get going. You lead, and I will follow!"

Caleb and María headed westerly along the banks of the river. They stayed as far away as they could from the Indian camps along the river and traveled as fast as they could. The Indians watched them curiously but did not make any aggressive moves. When Caleb and María reached a relatively flat area with grassy meadows, they thought they had reached the top of the mountains. But they were shocked at what they saw. Here were incredibly rugged granite mountains rising to the west and equally forbidding mountains to the south and north.

The river they had been following suddenly changed course here, turning south through a gap in the hills. There was no reason to follow it any longer if it did not appear to be going west. Since Caleb could see no reason to go in a direction other than their main heading, he took a compass direction due west and followed that heading. He put enough water in the casks to ensure they had an adequate supply for a few days in case they needed it. But it didn't look like they would run short of water in these mountains because of the many small streams and seeps they passed every day. The timber was thick, and game was plentiful.

At nightfall, they were looking for a spot to camp. "There's a deer, María," directed Caleb. "Shoot her, and we will stop and dry the meat so we don't run short. We can let the horses rest one day tomorrow. And we can rest ourselves while we dry the meat. This is a good grassy meadow, and I don't see any Indians about. If you hit the deer with your first shot, I will set up the tent for you tonight." Grinning, he knew how much she enjoyed having the tent to sleep in, as he did too, aside from the work in setting it up.

"You're just trying to upset me so I'll get nervous and miss my shot at the deer!" she laughed. "But I'll show you that I can shoot as straight as you can. Just you watch!" She loosed the priming powder in the pan of her muzzleloader, and walked toward a tree about a hundred yards from the deer. The deer seemed to be more curious than afraid of her.

Then she noticed half a dozen other deer sitting in the tall grass. Some stood up when she walked toward them. The fat doe she had selected as her target continued to stare at her inquisitively. Caleb quietly held the horses, watching María approach the tree. María slowly glanced around the tree, and eased her rifle against it to steady her aim.

Bang! The doe jumped up in the air and fell to the ground, pawing the air. The well-placed bullet had hit her heart right behind the foreleg. The other deer ran, as the one she had shot lay upon the ground squirming and shaking in its death throes.

"Now be sure you knock before coming in tonight," she laughed, looking at Caleb.

"Load up. Load up. Always load your rifle immediately. What if an Indian was behind one of these trees and came running at you? But don't worry. I'll knock just as you asked me to."

She was already reloading her rifle. María had become an expert markswoman, and perfectly capable of handling her weapons as well as anyone could. She certainly had demonstrated her prowess by holding off the attacking Paiutes when Caleb was unconscious from his head wound. They cleaned the deer and began cutting it up, working rapidly. Again, they were enjoying working together to secure the next week's food supply. They would eat some of the meat tonight, and dry some over the fire, tonight and tomorrow.

"Let's eat the liver tonight," she said. "I will look for some roots to mix in with it, and I still have some wild onions. We will have a feast tonight." She put her arms around him and kissed him. "In more ways than one, too!" she said, smiling at him and holding him close to her despite her now-protruding belly.

One day followed the other but they kept slowly making their way up the mountain seeking a route over it. As they steadily worked their way westward higher up into the mountains, they took their time, but still managed to ride westerly almost ten miles a day. Occasionally however, they had to backtrack when they encountered impassable steep mountains. They once spent a whole day backtracking to their previous night's campsite because of a steep granite cliff they were unable to get over, or around. But once they knew where the cliffs were, they were able to work their way around them from further back away from them.

Throughout one night the wind blew loudly, rocking their tiny tent and chilling them inside their bedroll, making them cuddle closer than usual. There was an inch of snow on the ground and on the tent when Caleb and María got up in the morning. The sky was gray, and they were cold and miserable. After several hours, the howling wind blew in gray storm clouds, which soon enveloped them. Still, they kept moving slowly and carefully, always westward. Without the compass, they would not have known which direction to travel in this rugged cloud covered country. The rocks were slippery with several inches of snow.

The next day they had been riding all morning through wet clouds and snow. They were cold and dripping wet. Suddenly Caleb held his hand up to stop and looked around. For some time they had been heading downhill westerly. They had been using an animal or Indian path that followed a small river—suddenly he realized the creek was flowing west. He took out his compass to verify which way they were going.

"Look, María, this little creek is running due west! We have been following it for an hour. We must have come over the top of the mountains. Let us stop and read scripture for a few minutes. I know it is cold, but we should stop and say thanks to the Lord for our deliverance over the mountains. I think we must now truly be in California, and barely in time from the looks of this weather."

"Give me your hand, Caleb. Let us pray on our knees and thank God. You read from the book. After we say some prayers, I will walk for a while to warm up and lead the horses so my feet can touch this land and get used to it."

Caleb read from his Bible, ending with the following passage "Thou wilt shew me the path of life: in thy presence is fullness of joy; at thy right hand there are pleasures for evermore."

On November 10, 1836, Caleb and María arrived in the foothills along the west side of the Sierras. The streams were teaming with fish, the slopes of the hills were covered with winter grass, and beaver dams could be seen in the rivers everywhere. Birds and game animals were plentiful. Caleb and María would not starve, and though overcast, it was decidedly warmer.

Sitting their horses by a river, they watched beaver swimming and cavorting, and diving for the door to their homes inside the dams they had made. Caleb liked the warm plentiful feeling of the place. "I think we could spend the winter trapping along the foothills. I have never trapped for beaver before, but everyone else seems able to do it. It shouldn't be too hard to figure it out."

"Hah! That's what you think! First, you have to be smarter than the beaver! Come let us set up our camp, and I will show you how to catch beaver. I will teach you how to clean them and then build and put the hides on stretchers so they don't shrink. We will scrape the meat off them so they are clean and in proper condition to sell. Then I will cook beaver tails for you and make soup. I may not be an expert trapper, but I have caught several of them. Beaver-Catcher showed me how, and I will show you."

Caleb had all the traps in his store of goods that they could use, and he proved to be an apt pupil for María. Together they worked their way along the lower stretches of the rivers, amid the foothills of the Sierra, adding more and more skins to their inventory as they slowly headed south.

"I think the time is coming soon for the baby to be born," María finally told Caleb. "I think we should try and find a shelter or make a place to have the baby. You can trap from here up this river, and we can prepare for the baby to come. Let us make camp for good until the baby is born."

"We can go down to the coast and seek the aid of other women, if you want to. I would be more than happy to find someone to help you," Caleb suggested.

"NO! I don't want anyone but you. I want you to help me. I don't want anyone else to touch me. Put your hand on my stomach. Can you feel him kick? That means it will be a boy, I think!"

María was getting larger and larger, and it was getting very difficult for her to wade out into the icy water and service the beaver traps. Riding the horse was also becoming uncomfortable for her, although she did not complain. She had finally given up having sex with Caleb because it made her uncomfortable, and she no longer enjoyed it. Since her breasts had begun to leak fluid, she had made herself a halter in which she could place pads of cloth to absorb the moisture. She was certain this indicated her time was short.

They worked together making a cradleboard like the ones they had seen the Indian women using at the Green River rendezvous. Caleb made the back out of reeds from the river, which he held together with leather thongs. For the baby's comfort, they lined the cradleboard with deerskins they had softened by scraping and soaking, and scraping again. It was then further filled with some old clothing that Caleb had to make padding. They both marveled at how rough and amateurish the cradleboard looked by comparison to the ones the Indian women had made. But it was the best they could do.

Caleb also built an addition to the tent, a small room made of upright limbs and poles like a Mexican *jacal*. It resembled the brush huts of the Indians and *peóns*. The idea was that the room would be supplemental to the tent. But the room proved to be so comfortable that they moved their blankets into it and abandoned their tent entirely to store their supplies and beaver pelts in.

The small shelter had a fire circle near the door, and the smoke would rise up through the ceiling like in the Mexican *jacals*, or huts. Caleb piled dirt up along the outside of the wall to make the room as windproof as possible, to hold it steady when the wind blew, and to hold in warmth. He cut the side out of one of the water barrels and placed it close to the fire. They would fill it with water and drop hot rocks in to make hot water. After the hot rocks had heated the water, they could be fished out with two sticks and put back close to the fire to heat up again. They could even make the water boil if they kept rotating the rocks quickly enough. Everything was ready for the baby. All they had to do was wait. They both wanted the baby to hurry up and come, but they knew it would come when it was ready, and not before.

Caleb built a workbench at the front of the *jacal* and began to keep himself busy repairing his store of broken and out-of-date rifles. He tended the horses daily. They were growing fat again after their cross-county ordeal. He trapped for beaver, and hunted deer, elk, and antelope whenever they needed meat. But when he tended the traps or went hunting, he did not go more than a few hours' distance from their camp.

CHAPTER 17
Time for Baby.

Neither Caleb nor María had actually assisted in the birth of a child. María had been around women on the ranch who were pregnant, and she had talked to them up until the time of the birth. But she had never been present when the birthing took place. This work was for the midwives.

Caleb had never been around any woman who had a baby. He had, however, a great deal of experience with the birthing process of horses, cows, dogs and pigs. He had midwifed the horses and other livestock on his father's farm. But the childbirth experience intimidated both of them. The closer it got to the birthing time, the more apprehensive they became. María was trusting that nature and Caleb would see her through the labor and delivery.

After they had been in the camp for nearly six weeks, María noticed a pinkish-reddish discharge from her vagina. "Is that normal?" she asked Caleb worriedly. "Do you think the baby is all right? What is happening there? Would you take a look at me, please? I am worried. Is the baby all right?" María had grown impatient and irritable lately. She was uncomfortable almost all the time now from her pregnancy. Her back ached all the time.

"I'll do anything you want me to do," said Caleb. "I'll do anything that I can to help you. But I will not know what it is that I am looking at. I have no way of knowing whether or not everything is normal. But perhaps if I take notes we can at least have a written record to follow." He prepared to write his observations of her condition and the almost daily changes in her body in his diary.

María lay down, and Caleb gently pulled up the deerskin shirt-dress that Beaver-Catcher had given her. He had offered several times to make her a longer one or even make her a new outfit out of leather or cloth, but she refused. She had him make her pants because the weather was now cold, but she did not replace the shirt. She loved this long leather shirt, which reminded her of Beaver-Catcher. She thought about him often. Frequently he was in her prayers too, along with Sister Seraphena; her brother Don Pedro; her mother and father; and the old priest, Father *de Silva* at her father's rancho, and of course Caleb and Eagle-Man. The list of people María was trying to remember in her prayers was ever growing.

Caleb saw the discharge from her vagina, but it did not look like profuse bleeding of any kind. "I don't think it is serious," he said, laying his hands gently on her stomach. "I suspect it may be just part of the process. Everything looks normal and healthy to me. Let me get some warm water, and I will bathe you and see if that gives you any relief. Is there any pain?" he asked as he gently massaged her stomach, legs, and vulva.

"No, there is no pain. I have occasionally a sort of twinge, a little pain, but nothing sharp. Nothing major. My back hurts, but that is all. It is good of you to take so much time with me. I am so much trouble to you." She was feeling better already. The tension went out of her, and she was able to relax for the first time in several days because his gentle touches relaxed her. His laying hands on her in themselves indicated his love and care for her which seemed almost healing in their gentleness.

Caleb continued talking to her. "From all I can observe, even though your body has grown much larger than I would have thought possible, everything looks healthy and normal. I will not attempt to wash anything inside, but I will wash and rinse the outer skin and gently massage it for you. Tell me immediately if I do anything that brings any sort of pain, and I will stop." He gently washed her with warm water and a piece of cloth rag.

"María, do you have any idea how long it should take or how long it has been since you became pregnant?" he asked her.

"No. I have no idea." She shook her head sadly. "I have completely lost track of time. I have read somewhere that it takes nine months to have a baby normally, but I do not even know how long I was with Two-Dogs as his slave. That whole period of time is foggy in my memory. Nor do I know how long I was with Beaver-Catcher. It seems that it has been a very long time, but I don't think I am much larger than the pregnant women that I have seen on my father's rancho. In the last few days I have felt out of breath, and it is getting harder for me to move about. But I don't feel sick. I am not ill, I don't think."

"My diary suggests we are only now approaching nine months since you were taken captive," said Caleb as he rubbed her legs, especially her thighs. "I can't tell the exact date, but I am sure that I can tell within a few weeks, a month at the most. If we assume you became pregnant around May 1, when you were captured in the raid on your caravan on your way to California, your time is just now approaching nine months. So your baby might be born on the last day of January. You see, everything we know about this suggests you are progressing naturally."

"I will read from the Bible. We will assume the Lord is taking care of us and will guide us so that we do as he intended. We are resting well here. We have plenty to eat. I am catching beaver, and our horses are getting fat. Everything is progressing as he wishes for us. We will do our best. And if he will but help us a little, we will suffer for him. You once told me that pain is not so bad on one's knees if the pain is offered for our Lord. Can you apply this same principle in this case?"

"Yes, that is a good idea. I will try to do as you suggest," she answered thoughtfully. "Please read to me. I will dedicate my discomfort to Christ and the Mother of Christ. After all, she went through this same thing for our sins. She bore Christ into the world much as I am doing, in a manger not too different than we are doing here. Could you make me a small wooden cross and put it over on the wall there so I can look at it?"

"Of course, I can. I will make it this afternoon. I don't know why I didn't think of that sooner myself. It should bring us both comfort."

Caleb now not only washed and massaged her genitals twice a day but he also washed and massaged her whole body, even her feet, using water warmed in the wooden barrel he dropped hot rocks into. He even washed her hair as he talked soothingly to her.

On several occasions María became slightly excited sexually by this ministration. She insisted that she kiss and hug him, and undress him and jack him off to relieve any pressure that might be building up in him. She did it because she wanted to please him and because she loved him. "I will always love you, Caleb. Remember that! I will always love you!"

Something new was happening to María. She noticed when she got up this morning that her stomach seemed smaller and less distended. "But where could it have gone to?" she asked Caleb, looking down at her stomach in wonderment. "Do you think perhaps it has moved downward and is on its journey to come out?"

They finally decided that the baby was lower down now, getting ready to come out. What other explanation could there be? The baby in her womb had in fact settled downward. They did no know this was the normal birthing process that would precede the birth of the baby.

On Feb. 1, 1837, she awoke Caleb at dawn. "Caleb! Wake up! I'm having pains. Something is going to happen soon, I think." The contractions had begun at midnight. At first she thought they were cramps that she had been having lately, because they did not hurt much at first. But when they became more frequent and more intense, it was obvious that this was the time for the baby to be born. Soon the pains were coming every 15 minutes, and she developed a more painful backache.

She described her pains to Caleb, and he did his best to talk her through the pains. She held his hands and squeezed them during the contractions. He wiped her face and brow with cool water and tried to comfort her, reassuring her as much as he could. He had always been strong and self-sufficient, and he was amazed at how helpless he felt now. There wasn't a thing he could do to ease her suffering, except talk to her and try to comfort her by just being there. Several times he feared that she was going to die from the pain, but he could not let her know what he was thinking. He wanted to mount his horse and go look for some Indian women who might come to her aid, but he was now afraid to leave her even for a moment.

She kept trying to talk to him. She seemed compelled to tell him her most innermost thoughts. It was as if he were her confessor. He did not encourage her to do so, but he listened as sympathetically as he could. It seemed to help keep her mind occupied so she could rest between the agonizing contractions. She told him the complete story of her love affair with Sister Seraphena. She described how the priest, Father Ignacio, had raped her and Sister Seraphena, and how it actually enhanced their love for each other. This astounded him, but he kept his surprise to himself.

"Are you disappointed that you were not my first love, Caleb? I do love you with all my heart, but I loved, and still love, Sister Seraphena. Can you forgive me? Is it all right? Is it that I have sinned so much to be thus punished?" A bead of sweat lay across her upper lip, and her forehead was creased with pain and worry.

"We all have loves that change over the years," he said soothingly. "I had a great love for another woman before I met you. I mentioned her to you once or perhaps more than once. Her name was Polly. She died at the hands of foul mountain men. In fact, they were part of the gang that Slip Fields was with that raided your caravan and turned you over to the Apaches. They are terrible, cruel men, as bad or worse than any Indian."

"But the fact that I loved her did not diminish my love for you, María. She liked me and was good to me. But she had loved another, her man Jeremy, and she never really came to love me, at least not as you do." He tried to explain to her what he could not understand himself. Still in trying to keep her mind busy, he comforted her and encouraged her through each spasm of pain.

Caleb noticed that her vagina was beginning to discharge a thick, slippery, colorless mucus that was obviously provided by nature as a lubricant to assist the passage of the baby through the birth canal. Then, much to their surprise, water suddenly swished out of her vagina and soaked the blanket on which she was lying. They did not know it was the water that surrounded and cushioned the baby in the placenta where the baby had been nurtured since conception. This "breaking of the bag of waters" signaled the beginning of the second phase of the labor.

Her pains, which had been about five minutes apart, now were coming every two minutes and growing in intensity. Not only had the contractions increased in severity, duration, and frequency; the whole character of the pain was different. This pain was associated with the expulsion of the baby within her. All of her muscles were directed now toward that end. María sensed that these bearing-down pains, although much more severe, seemed directed toward a specific outcome; and thus they were more tolerable. This is a strange contradiction; but it is what María experienced, and every mother experiences.

She began to puff and pant, and sweat and cry out with pain and the exertion of expelling the baby, much as a person does when trying to go to expel excrement while constipated, only much more so. She innately knew it was time for her to push as hard as she could. She was no longer squeezing Caleb's hands with each contraction. Now she was pulling them. She tugged on them as if to pull her to him and expel the baby.

As the baby's head entered the lower part of the vagina, María screamed from the excruciating pain. The pains were now centered in the lower end of the rectum, and by this time María had little control over her body functions. She was greatly embarrassed when she involuntarily urinated and passed a bowel movement. These were forced out of her body by the downward passage of the baby and the natural contraction of the same muscles used in expelling the baby. "I am ashamed. But I could not help it. It just came," she cried.

"My goodness, don't be silly!" Caleb said reassuringly as he wetted her brow with cool water. Here, I will merely clean it up just like we will do for the baby when it is born. Don't fight anything. Do what your body tells you to do."

For about a week now, Caleb had been attributing everything that was happening to María as being a normal part of a process, to reassure both himself and her, although he had no idea what would be considered normal. Now he was sweating and nervous, and almost as miserable as she was, but certainly not in her pain. He wanted to help, but what more could he do?

Suddenly María remembered, "At the Indian encampment, when I was lying in front of Two-Dog's tent, I saw an Indian woman having a baby. She was by herself and was leaning forward. I feel like maybe I should lean forward. That it might help push the baby down. Do you think I should lean forward or lie back?"

He thought a minute and then answered, "In the Bible, the first chapter of Exodus talks about the midwives. I didn't understand it before, but I remember now what it said. 'When ye do the office of midwife to the Hebrew women, and see them upon the stools...'" "This probably means that the Hebrew women sat upon a stool when they had their children. So what you are telling me fits with the Bible."

"If the Indian woman did that, and your body says that, then by all means I think you should do it too. I will lay some things behind your back to prop you up and help you into a sitting position. It makes sense to me that this will bring pressure and help the baby pass out of you. I think you should try to lean forward as the Indian woman did." Caleb tried to sound confident, but this was nothing like a cow's or a horse's birth or a dog or a pig. Calves and foals just seemed to plop out without any trouble or struggle. But this birth was terribly painful, and it was taking a long time. Caleb would help all he could, but in the end she had to do all of it, and take all of the pain unto herself, as every new mother had done before her. He was already exhausted.

Suddenly, Caleb saw the baby's head begin to come out of María's vagina as she yelled with pain and panted, almost like a dog. His hands were shaking at the drama of it and sweat was pouring off his brow. It was dark again, and the light from two candles and the fire was all he had to work by. The baby's face was pointed downward. Caleb supported its head and watched the body rotate to the left as the shoulders and then the rest of the body came out of the vagina with another gush of liquid. The baby began to cry before it was all the way out. It was a boy. It was alive.

"It is a boy, just as you said it would be, María. He looks healthy, as far as I can tell."

Upon hearing the baby's cry, María cried out, *"Ah, mi corazón! Mi cariño, querido corazón!"* Oh, my heart! My son! My dear heart! Caleb laid the baby upon the soft deerskins that they had prepared. He cut and tied the umbilical cord just as he and his father had done back in Missouri for their horses, only more gently. Then he wiped the baby off with warm water, cleaning away the liquids, including some blood that was expelled during the birth and the substances that still covered his body.

He dressed the baby in a diaper they had made from one of the precious cotton blankets they had cut up for him. "You are all right and the baby is all right." He then wrapped him in the cotton cloth of the blanket and softened deerskins. At the least, he could help with this part of it. Now that he was busy doing something, he no longer felt so inadequate.

Then he washed María's sweaty, tear-stained face with cool water. He wiped off her sore and abused vagina as well as her legs and stomach. About ten minutes later, she wanted to sit up because she instinctively knew something else was going to be expelled from her body. As he helped her sit up, she expelled the afterbirth, or placenta and other membranes that had surrounded and sustained the baby during pregnancy. He soothed her during the pains of afterbirth, which was the third phase of labor. Then he buried the afterbirth outside.

"You did good, María. Your baby boy looks healthy and fine to me! Here, hold him to you. I think he wants you to hold him!" María was still gasping, somewhat confused, and certainly exhausted, as he lay the baby on her chest. She cradled the baby in her arms and began to talk to it in a soft motherly voice. She named him Pedro, after her brother, who was with her when the Apaches and Slip captured her at the Green River crossing.

It was snowing when they awoke from a brief rest after the baby was born. Caleb got the fire going and began to prepare a meal. He would bake sourdough bread this morning in celebration of the baby, fashioning an oven from their frying pan and a lid. He also began to warm a stew María previously had made out of fresh roots, fatty meat from a beaver's tail, and venison from a deer Caleb had killed several days ago. The stew was rich and nourishing. He repeatedly encouraged María to drink the broth from the stew to give her strength. Within a few hours, she was able to eat some of the bread soaked in the juices of the stew and some of the stew itself.

The baby started nursing when it was two hours old. He seemed already to know how to suckle at María's breast. Caleb made her a backrest out of a large stack of beaver skins so she could sit up and nurse the baby in comfort. He continually fussed about her, helping her, and talking to her about the baby. He seemed to be as excited as she was.

At least for now, Caleb, María, and Pedrito, were a healthy, happy family.

CHAPTER 18
Mission Nuestra Señora de la Soledad.

When Pedro was six weeks old, María announced that she was ready to travel. "We should continue our journey. But to tell you the truth, I would like to stay right here for the rest of my life. We have plenty of food, we could harvest beaver to trade somewhere and be happy. I could plant a garden. Unfortunately, we both have obligations. I have to keep my promise to my father, and you have to get back to your station in New Mexico. The people there are depending on you."

In seven days they began traveling once again. Before the baby was born they had moved southerly along the foothills, trapping beaver as they went. They continued south now because a number of large rivers and areas of heavy timber prevented them from going due west, though Caleb kept trying to work his way more westerly.

They encountered more Indian villages along the way than they had seen during their earlier travels. And with a new child to protect, they were even more cautious about keeping themselves hidden and detouring carefully around the villages. They still had no way of knowing whether the Indians were friendly, and Caleb had decided there was no reason to find out.

He and María were perplexed when they passed over several fairly well traveled trails going north and south. Should they turn and follow the trails or should they continue westerly and build a crude raft to cross the river? They decided to turn west when they reached a large river (the San Joaquin River). They did not know what river it was because it was not marked on Caleb's crude map. The village of San Francisco was their objective, but they had to reach the coast in order to orient themselves and find it.

After trudging for days across a large, lush valley they went over some low hills and below them, they suddenly saw buildings in the distance. One of them they were sure was a church. They could hardly contain themselves. It had been a long time since they had seen a friendly face. As they drew closer they could see a small, dilapidated church, its adobe bricks decomposing in the hot sun and rain, and some ramshackle outbuildings. This was obviously the site of an abandoned mission, or at least one that was in disrepair. The cross on the front of the church marked it as a Spanish mission. It was similar to the missions they had in New Mexico.

"I don't see how this can be San Francisco. It is too small. And there is no ocean that I can see," said a puzzled Caleb.

Caleb was correct. It was not San Francisco. It was the remains of *Mission Nuestra Señora de la Soledad* in the Salinas Valley. The *Soledad Mission* was the thirteenth California mission constructed by the Mission Padres for the Catholic Church. It was built to act as an intermediate way station for travelers making the long hundred-mile journey, between the Carmel Mission, near Monterey, to the north. It was also to be a Mission to treat the heathen Indians in that area and Christianize them. It was a way station after the San Antonio Mission to the south. *Soledad*, which means solitude in English, properly and adequately described the site and life of this mission.

The Spanish built twenty-one missions eventually in a chain from south to north, beginning with the first one, *San Diego de Alcalá* established in San Diego in 1769. The last one in the chain from south to north was *San Francisco Solano (Sonoma)*. The missions were planned to be a long day's journey, or about 40 miles, apart. However they did not end up that way. *Soledad* was built because it was a hundred miles between *Mission San Antonio de Padua* to the south and *Mission Carmel* to the North. *Mission Soledad* was built to break up that long journey. It became the thirteenth in the chain.

Mission Soledad seemed fated to live up to its name. One disaster after the other visited it including floods and earthquakes. The Indians were organized in primitive shelters, but it took six years to even get an adobe chapel built, after it was first populated. The first priests who were appointed there could not get leave from there fast enough, and none wanted to stay longer than a year. Thirty Priests came and went during its forty-four year life as an active mission. Its hot dry summers and miserable cold winters made life there uncomfortable for the priests. Finally in 1803 Father Florencio Ibanez arrived there to stay fifteen years and the mission bloomed with success. Good crops and many Indian converts were obtained, and it reached its hay-day with over seven hundred Indians living there.

In 1824 the church was flooded out and it was never rebuilt to its former self. Flood waters again destroyed what was left a few years later. Father Sarria finally came there. No more dedicated man could be imagined. He was so dedicated to the care of the Indians that he finally starved himself to death so the Indians could eat.

A road, actually a trail, called *El Camino Real*, or royal road, linked the missions from south to north for 650 miles, some located at bays on the ocean and some inland from the coast. The highest number of Franciscan priests assigned to the Alta California missions at that time numbered only thirty-eight. Yet, so skilled were they at organization and management of the mission system, that they were successful in subjugating huge numbers of Indians and controlling vast quantities of land, cattle, and agricultural production.

In 1834, in the aftermath of the Mexican revolt from Spain, the Mexican government, who could not afford to keep financing them, ordered the Catholic Church to return the mission lands to the Indians, which they had taken from them several decades earlier, or if the Indians did not want them, to sell them to the highest bidder. As a result of reorganization, the former *Mission Nuestra Señora de la Soledad* had been absorbed into the *San Antonio Mission* and was no longer operated separately.

Despite the fact it had over seven hundred Indians in its care at one time; by 1836, when Caleb and María arrived, it was almost totally abandoned and lay in partial ruins. Most of the Indians had gone back to their Indian ways, though a few continued to occupy the site. Occasionally a priest would stop on his way to somewhere else to look after the property or harvest the cattle. The fertile fields had been extensively tilled at one time and orchards had been planted. Only a few trees were still growing and now there were some small gardens serviced by the few remaining Indians. The intricate system of canals that watered the fields had fallen in disrepair and grown up with weeds, and water no longer flowed in them. The Indians lived in crude but practical teepee-like structures made of poles, reeds, and grass.

Vincente Francisco Sarría, one of the last Spanish priests at *Soledad*, was widely regarded as one of the best priests ever to work for the mission system. He was a truly great man, who always worked for what he conceived to be the best interests of the missions and Indians under his care. His reputation for honor and integrity was known throughout California, Spain and Mexico.

Accordingly, rather than punish him because he refused to bear allegiance to the Mexican government after the revolution, the government and Church, sent him to *Soledad* to live out his life serving his Indians, as he wanted to do, and bring them to the Catholic faith.

Father Vincente Francisco Sarría, who was a Franciscan, practiced asceticism. He believed that a higher spiritual state in life could be achieved by means of rigorous self-discipline and self-denial. His personal habits of self-castigation were characteristic of some of the most devout Franciscans. When he preached to the parishioners, for example, he would beat himself on the chest with a stone until his flesh was raw, or lash his shoulders with a sharp piece of metal. Finally he died by starving himself so the Indians in his care could be fed.

The Indian policies practiced by the government of the United States at that time were ostensibly to do what was best for the Indians. Congress passed legislation stating that their policy toward Indians was to educate them, teach them to farm, to accommodate them, and always to pay money for their land. Politicians like to say that this was all for the good of the Indians. In reality, however, the Indians were always moved out of the way of the European and Eastern American settlers who took the Indian lands, and killed their game animals, which was their only food supply, while the politicians stole the money allotted to feeding them and ultimately stole their land.

While the Indians were still strong and free, they successfully fought to preserve their place on the land. One of the main reasons why they eventually lost that fight was due to the United States government's policy permitting the sale of alcohol to Indians, if not exactly legal under the law. This led to high rates of alcoholism among the Indians, and Indians themselves were pitted one tribe against another. The white settlers took advantage of the fragmentation of the tribes and simply took whatever they wanted, even where it was illegal. The white man's diseases further decimated the tribes, ousting the Indians from their native lands and sometimes obliterating entire tribes.

In contrast, Spain's policy toward Indians was to absorb them into the Spanish culture. The Catholic Church established the missions to transform the Indians from savages to hybrid Spanish-Indian-Catholics. This was the stated policy, but the practical results, unfortunately, were different. The largest number of Indian converts living under the church in California was 21,000 in 1824. The process of building missions in California lasted 65 years. That was long enough to kill half the Indians, and ruin most of the rest by taking away their freedom and will to fight. The Spanish also brought diseases that contributed to the loss of many Indian tribes who had no immunity against the diseases brought by the Europeans.

When construction was begun on a mission, the resident priest and the Spanish soldiers would make friends with the Indians by giving them blankets, food, beads, or other trinkets. Once the Indians agreed to convert to Christianity and be baptized, they were thereafter prohibited from leaving the mission grounds without permission. Indians, who did not embrace Catholicism, were simply murdered.

The converted Indians spent their days planting and harvesting in the fields, or working on the mission buildings. A contingent of soldiers enforced the rules of the mission padres during the early period and punished those Indians who broke the rules. The Indians were treated as slaves or wards, not as citizens. The church taught that the Indians belonged to God and the priests managed them for God's benefit. The priests were like overseers. They not only held the lands of the Indians, but held the Indians as well.

As soon as the Spanish were able to induce the placid Indians to give up their freedom, the yoke of Christianity became just as debilitating as the armies of the United States and the American settlers to eastern American Indians. Under the Catholic Church, the Indians became children of the Spanish God as they got down on their knees to get a blanket or a free meal. When they lost the freedom to worship their own gods, on their own property, they also lost much of the will to fight for their way of life.

When the Mexican government found they did not have money enough, or will enough, to sustain the missions it ordered the Church to return the land by a law called secularization. The lands, cattle, and other worldly goods were to be offered to the Indians, who were unprepared to manage it, nor did they understand it. They had not been taught how to live as free men, and had little education. They no longer knew how to live as the Indians once had. Once the Indians were no longer under the protection of the padres at the mission, they were easy prey for opportunists. The *mestizos*, Spanish-Indian half-breeds, immediately fleeced the Indians of their worldly goods. It happened so rapidly that the Indians were barely aware that they had let so many things slip through their fingers. The Indians simply had neither the will nor ability to fight off the human predators.

It is hard to say whether the results achieved by Spain's "enlightened" policy toward the Indians was any better than the U. S. government's attitude toward the eastern American Indians. Whole tribes and some entire nations disappeared under both policies. It is also true, that no Indian had land anywhere that he did not take from someone who previously resided there. Could it be that what happened to the Indians was merely the natural order of the progression of things, the land passing always to the most ferocious who drove off the previous occupants? Was this only God's justice taking away from those what they had taken from others?

Caleb and María sat their horses for a long time, looking in wonder at some civilization after their long stay in the wilderness. They could see fields of grapevines and orchards of fruit trees, many of which were dead or dying. They were surprised when they realized that they had never seen or heard of some of the fruits and vegetables they saw growing there. As the travelers learned later, the small population of Indians still at *Soledad* cared for sheep, cattle, horses, and the gardens under the management of the priests at *The San Antonio Mission*. *Our Lady of Solitude* was surely an apt name for this run-down place, but Caleb and María were glad to see it. They had finally arrived somewhere, and it appeared peaceable.

"Well, I don't know exactly where we are, but someone here should be able to tell us. Let's go down to the church and see if we can get directions," Caleb said.

"Yes, and I want to have Pedrito baptized if we can find a priest" she said enthusiastically.

An old priest was standing on the church steps watching them lead the pack train toward him. "Welcome travelers," he smiled speaking in

Spanish, "Welcome to *Mission Nuestra Señora de la Soledad*, or at least what is left of it. The Salinas Valley welcomes you. Do my eyes behold a child that you wish baptized, by any chance, *Señora?*" His twinkling, smiling eyes saw the cradleboard bundle tied behind María's saddle. This was not the first cradleboard he had seen with a pair of dark eyes peering out of it. "There is no regular priest here. I am here helping for a few days. I have been ordered to pull the red tiles off the roof and sell them, and to send the money to the Mexican Government to which a lot of money is owed, it seems. Once that is done, the wet weather will melt the walls and that will be the end here. I come from *The San Antonio Mission* to the south. But if you are looking for a baptism, I can take care of that matter for you."

"Yes, Padre. How did you guess?" María asked him, wondering how he knew what was on her mind.

He laughed pleasantly, "Well, just let us say you are not the first young mother I have ever seen looking to baptize her baby. Come get off your horses. I will have a bite to eat prepared for you. You look like you might have come a long way, and might need a good glass of wine and some food. Come inside with me, young lady. And you, sir, go with this Indian lad and unload your goods in the storage room next to your bedroom. You will find a comfortable room there that opens into the courtyard. You can lock the door and not worry about your goods. They will be safe here. Then put your horses in the corral."

"You will stay with us as our guests, of course." The priest led María into the small, whitewashed room. The only piece of furniture in the middle of the room was a bedstead covered with a tightly stretched rawhide. A pitcher of water was on the dirt floor as was a night-vase. The window overlooked the courtyard. It was just an opening and had no glass in it.

"Make yourself at home, my dear. I will leave you alone with your baby for a while. He looks like he might be hungry. I will see to your husband and make sure he feels comfortable. I will tell your husband to bring in your blankets for the bed." She did not tell him that they were not married, and he would not ask, assuming they were.

Any traveler was welcome at the missions or ranchos in California and would be given free room and board. It was the custom. Visitors to a Church were expected to pay only for the baptismal or other religious services that the priest might administer. Caleb agreed to pay one peso for the baptism of the baby Pedro. The ceremony was short, held the following morning. The room of the main part of the chapel was bereft of furniture now. The *reredos*, the ornamental partition behind the altar, was all that was left in the main room.

The priest was disappointed when Caleb said he and María could only stay overnight. "We want to leave right after the baptism for San Francisco. We have these pelts to deliver to a ship bound for England, if we can find one that will carry them for us. We are anxious to get them loaded and on their way. They are a lot of work to pack around, and they might get lost or damaged if we keep carrying them with us."

"But, of course," replied the priest, sorry to see the young family leaving so soon. "San Francisco will be easy to find. You can follow this fine road, which is the *El Camino Real*. It begins in San Diego south of here and ends at San Francisco to the north. It connects to all the Alta California missions."

"But you may not have to go that far if your objective is to find a ship. Monterey Bay is much closer, and the same ships usually stop over there to deliver cargo and pick up hides and tallow. You should try Monterey first. It has a good harbor, and the *alcalde* is a good and honorable man. He will not cause you any grief. There is an American trader there also, who has a store. He too is a good and honorable man. His name is Thomas O. Larkin. You will be able to get directions for disposing of your cargo from him."

Caleb and María thanked the priest for his hospitality and for the baptism. They promised him that they would stop by on their way south to Los Angeles, or if he had already left here for his own church, the San Antonio Mission, to the south.

They had ridden about two miles when they came upon *vaqueros* and mission Indians slaughtering a large herd of cattle. This slaughter, which was called the *matanza*, was usually done only in the fall. But since the *Mission of San Antonio* was short of money and had a surplus of cattle, they were having a springtime *matanza* this year.

Over a thousand cattle would be slaughtered. Most had already been killed by the time Caleb and María rode by. The hides were stacked into huge piles that would be carried to the ships. The *vaqueros* and Indians were cutting fat off the carcasses to be sold or rendered into a salable product known as *sebo* (fat). After it was rendered and poured into bags made of hides, it was worth about 6 *centavos*, or 6 cents, per pound. From 75 to a 100 pounds of fat could be procured from one cow. *Sebo* was used to make candles as well as soap in England and the eastern United States.

Except for the small amount of fresh meat that would be used for food, all of the rest of the animal's meat and entrails were left spoiling upon the ground. The meat could not be saved and transported, so it had no value beyond what could be consumed locally. Vultures, coyotes, bears, and other carrion were already feasting on the surplus meat, but they could not consume the great quantity of rotting, valueless meat. The stench from the rotting meat was almost unbearable. Caleb and María covered their noses with a cloth, and hurried by without stopping.

CHAPTER 19
Monterey Bay.

They wound their way up the sometimes steep but well-marked trail until they reached the crest of the hills and saw gray clouds hanging along the coastline. Riding into the gray, moisture-laden clouds, they were soon looking down upon the great Bay of Monterey. It was a magnificent sight. They wound their way downward through groves of pine and wild walnut trees toward the bay and the heavy fog bank. Moss hanging from the oak and cypress trees dripped moisture. Although Caleb had encountered fog in his travels across the prairie, María, who had grown up in the arid high-desert country had never seen fog before. It was eerie, and they both felt uncomfortable in its wetness and silence.

When they descended beneath the fog they could see again white sandy beaches stretching up the coast to the horizon as well as crashing waves where there were rocks that reached out into the ocean. Forests of giant redwood trees, and smaller wind swept trees, came down near to the water's edge. The amazingly fertile soil over which they traveled produced lush foliage and flowers of incredible varieties. Wide marshes and quiet, peaceful lagoons were home to many birds, including red-winged blackbirds, meadow larks, ducks, sea gulls, pelicans, and many others they could not identify.

Caleb and María, neither of whom had seen an ocean before, thought the restless sea beating constantly against the shore was beautiful and majestic. It also struck them as being somewhat mysterious and frightening. They were fascinated by the ever-changing colors of the water, foamy where it crashed into the rocks, and the shapes of the waves as the restless ocean thrashed itself into white foam and then back again into dark colors, always moving. The smell of salt, seaweed, and other odors of the ocean were completely new to them. Now that they were closer to the ocean and its crashing waves, they sat staring, spellbound, just looking.

"What makes it so restless and forever trying to beat the shores?" María asked incredulously about the incessant motion.

"I simply do not know," Caleb admitted. "There must be some logical explanation for it, but what it is I cannot guess. Perhaps someone here can explain it to us."

When they were a little higher in the hills overlooking the water, they noticed that two sailing ships were in the port of Monterey. The ships were riding at anchor, and several small boats could be seen rowing people and commercial goods between the shore and the ships. Caleb and María admired the beauty of the two immense, graceful ships. Caleb had seen smaller versions of such ships on the river at Independence, Missouri but María had only seen pictures of them in books.

Finally after staring a long time they moved down the trail. Monterey itself was a small village spread out along the shores of a great bay. It was a jumble of log houses with a sprinkling of cut wooden structures, gardens, and haphazardly laid-out pastures in which various farm animals were grazing peacefully. The tranquil scene seemed to welcome them. Not far away from Monterey was the *Mission San Carlos de Borromeo de Carmelo* (Carmel). It had previously been *The Monterey Mission*, but the padres had moved it to Carmel to keep the Indians, especially the females, away from the soldiers.

The Presidio of Monterey was a walled enclosure more adapted to withstand an invasion from the sea than an inland attack by Indians. The Spaniards had quickly discovered that the central California Indians were generally placid and not at all warlike. The primary danger to the coastal cities was from marauding English and French ships at times of political unrest in Europe.

For the most part, these Indians were easily manipulated. But their non-warlike ways also had disadvantages: Since they were simple and primitive people, they simply would not work very hard. Before they were Christianized, they took their sustenance from the abundant fruits, vegetables, and animals that were native to the region. Their staple diet had been acorns gathered by the female Indians and ground into meal, together with the animals, birds, and fishes they harvested. They were self sufficient with only a little effort.

Even in their earliest forays in this area, the Spaniards seldom had to defend themselves against Indian attacks, beyond petty thievery. Later, some of the tribes learned, from the Spanish, and as they physically mixed with the Spanish and learned their ways they become more savage in order to defend themselves against being forced to give up their freedom for a life tilling in the fields at the direction of the Spaniards. In addition, there had been occasional revolts by tribes who had learned how to fight from the Spaniards themselves. But the Spanish rulers were always able to suppress any serious threats to their safety. Had all the natives gotten together at the beginning, it would have been easy for them to throw the Spaniards out. But instead, they succumbed to the offers of petty gifts and food, and the entreaties of the priests. As had happened elsewhere, they became wards and servants of The Priests, and of course the Catholic Church.

María and Caleb found the store of Thomas O. Larkin with no difficulty. Caleb got off his horse and went inside. "My name is Caleb Landers," he announced. "The priest at *Soledad* told me to say hello to Thomas Larkin and introduce myself. Are you he by any chance?"

"I am he all right. And welcome you are." Larkin smiled and offered his hand. Looking out the front door he could see María holding the baby. "Come in and bring the missus and the baby with you. I will make you a cup of coffee. Looks like you've got quite a pack train there. Where do you hail from?"

"I have a trading station in New Mexico," Caleb responded. "I've brought some pelts down from the Rocky Mountains to get them transported to England on an English ship, if I can find one that will carry my pelts to my factor there. This is María, and the baby is Pedro. We are going to Los Angeles as soon as I can make arrangements for transportation of my peltry from here."

Larkin said he was an American from Boston. "You'll be needing a place to stay and a place to keep your horses. I would like to have you be my guest while you are here in Monterey. That's the Spanish custom and a good one, too. I have plenty of room for you and María, and we will have a chance to get acquainted. I have heard of the New Mexico territory but have never been there, of course. How far have you traveled?"

"I don't know exactly. We have been traveling since last summer. I went first to the rendezvous at Green River from my station, which is at *San Fernando de Taos*. Then we came here. I figured it must be at least a thousand miles from Green River to Los Angeles. We spent the winter mostly along the foothills east of here, trapping. And then María wanted to stay there in the foothills while she had the baby."

"I can let you use my small-boat and point out which ship you should go to," Larkin said with a smile as he showed them into the kitchen for coffee. "I have a strong lad here who can row you out to the ship. You can ask for Captain Beeman. He's a good captain and completely reliable. There are two ships in port now, one American and one English. So if you want your goods to be shipped to England, you should deal with Captain Beeman. His ship is named the *Dover*."

After having coffee, Caleb stored his packs and trading goods in a shed behind the store and was given a room in the living quarters of the large house that was adjacent to and behind the store. The next morning, while María was resting with the baby, Caleb went out to the English ship. He was surprised to see so many Monterey residents on board the ship, until he realized that the crew had laid out a display of goods for sale, and the local residents were going on board to pick out what they wanted.

One of the crew members pointed out the captain to Caleb and he went to him, "Captain Beeman, my name is Caleb Landers, from New Mexico. I have some peltry furs I want to transport to England with you, if you have room for my goods on board your ship." He and Captain Beeman shook hands.

"Ha! Ha! Room I got aplenty. The only trade goods being shipped out from California are wool, hides, furs, and tallow. So far I haven't been able to get a full enough load to get started back. I have been sailing up and down this coast for nearly three months. What kind of furs do you have? Are they otter? I have received some local otter furs here in the past but none lately."

"No, these are beaver pelts and a few bear. I have never heard of otter. Where do they come from?" asked Caleb.

"They come out of the ocean along the coast. They have a good market, but the supply has been depleted. It's hard to find them any more, so I am told." Captain Beeman shook his head sadly.

"Well, my load won't fill up your ship," Caleb said, "but I have fifteen hundred beaver and about twenty-five bear skins. I want to ship them to Bartholomew's on Threadneedle Street in London, England. They have stores in London; Independence, Missouri; and Santa Fé in New Mexico. I do business with them and have accounts with them. Do you know of the Bartholomew's in London?"

"No, I don't know them, but don't worry about that. I can find out about them and make your delivery all right." The captain shook his head and stroked his chin in thought. "How big is a beaver pelt? I've never carried any before, and I need to know how much they are worth. I need to know their value so I can insure them for you."

"They're about the same size as a forty-pound dog, I guess. And I think they are worth about eight pesos each."

"So much? All right. I'll charge you a peso each and deliver them for you at the other end, if that's satisfactory. I'll use our skiff to pick up the pelts on the beach and deliver whatever else you might want to buy from me at the same time. That price, by the way, might seem a bit high to you; but it includes insurance for guaranteed delivery. That is worth a lot to you if my ship sinks or they get ruined by sea water if I should spring a leak, or sink in a storm. If I don't deliver your goods, you will still get your eight pesos apiece, less the one peso for each that I get for hauling them. If those terms are satisfactory to you, we'll call it a done deal, subject to my approval and inspection of the goods on the beach. I will collect my bounty on delivery at the other end. I assume you're like everyone else around here—without any hard money." The Captain was grinning now with the prospect of a good load to come aboard.

"That's close to the truth, all right. When I deliver them to the beach I would like to send a letter with them to the Bartholomews in London."

"Sure. We can take care of your letter all right. Take a look at these other goods I got displayed on the deck. I got plenty of goods to sell yet. Some of it is from China even. I can take your note against your goods and let you have what you want against delivery of your pelts. Take a look. If you see anything you want, I'll give you good prices. What sort of trading station do you have in New Mexico? What kind of goods do you sell over there?"

"Most of the usual, I guess, guns, powder, lead, bolts of cloth, flour. Do you have any medicines? I've wanted to get some medicines that I could handle through my station. I especially want some painkillers. People get hurt, and I can't do anything for them. No one else I know of sells those kinds of things over that way."

"Well, let's see." The Captain scratched his head. "I got some opium from China. Lots of doctors use those opium pills for painkillers."

"Oh? What is it? Do you know how it is made? I have never heard of it."

"I don't know much about it myself, although I've taken a few pills on occasion. It works wonders for a headache, I know that. But we have a doctor on board. He knows about such things. I'll get Doc Simms to tell you about it."

"Doc Simms! Doctor Simms! Will you come over here?" A middle-aged man leaning against the ship railing, smoking a pipe, turned when his name was called. "I want you to meet Caleb Landers, here. He has a store in New Mexico, and he is interested in medicines. I was just telling him we have a lot of opium on board and that you use it as a painkiller. Tell him about it."

"Glad to meet you, young fellow!" Simms had a warm smile and a firm handshake. "So you're interested in medicines, are you? Well, you have to be careful using opium. If you use it over too long a period of time, it loses its strength. And you can get addicted to it. Lots of people smoke it, too. Gives you quite a high. I use it myself sometimes, but in moderation."

"The English have government-protected companies that grow it in India in large quantities. They have huge plantations. They sell a lot of it to the Chinese. The Chinese even outlawed its sale in China a few years ago because so many people were using it to get high. It was costing the Chinese government foreign-currency reserves, so they outlawed its sale. The British have been selling it in China anyhow. They are threatening to send a fleet to blast the Chinese into submission if they don't legalize the sale again. The British government and its citizens have a huge investment in the opium plantations, which is very profitable for the government as well as some of its influential citizens. Whether they really will go to war about it or not I don't know, of course; but I think they might just do it. Can you believe that, sending a fleet to start a war to force the sale of opium? You're lucky. Because it has been outlawed in China, it is dirt-cheap now. We sell it here on this boat for less than half what it used to bring us in China."

"How's it made? What's it made of?" Caleb asked. His curiosity was aroused to try and understand how it works.

"Believe it or not, it's made out of a white, milky juice extracted from the immature flower of the poppy. The plants develop a little round head like a hen's egg, only smaller. It's an unripe flower, actually. You cut it and get the milky juice out of it, draining overnight. Then you dry it in a small bowl, and it becomes a rubbery substance. At this point you cook it in vats and make it into little balls or pills. You take one of those, and it kills pain very well. The pills come in a little box like this one here."

Doctor Simms produced a small box full of the little pills from his pocket. "Each box carries ten pills in it, and a case has a thousand boxes in it. The active ingredient in it is morphine, so I was told in medical school."

"What effects does it have if you take one?" Caleb wanted to know as he examined the box, sliding the small drawer in and out, exposing the pills.

"Here. Take a couple home with you. It won't hurt you." Dr. Simms laughed. "You'll enjoy it. Take it when you go to bed this evening. Shortly after you take it, it will make your mental activity increase. Then you will get dreamy, sort of, and then you'll go to sleep. That's all there is to it. But you'd be surprised how much some people enjoy opium, especially if they have pain."

Caleb again examined the small box and the small pea-sized pills inside it. "There don't seem to be any doctors in this country," he told Simms. "People get hurt and are in terrible pain, or they get a toothache or a broken bone; and it is almost impossible to help them. I plan on putting some medicines into my trading station in New Mexico if I can get hold of any. I have sent for some medicines and painkillers and doctor's tools and books on the subject. I hope to learn enough about it to help someone, a little bit at least, if they get hurt. Just recently my friend, María, whom I am escorting to Los Angeles, had a baby. I've never seen such pain in my life. To tell you the truth, I was sure she was going to die. Is there always so much pain in childbirth?"

"So you acted as midwife, did you? I wish I could have been there. That should have been very interesting. My practice here on this ship is pretty much limited to the treating of men with injuries or illness of one kind or another. I've never done much treatment concerning women. Oh, a little when I did some time in a hospital while I was studying but nothing much since."

"You have an interest in medicine, do you? I'm surprised to find a person as young as you interested in medicine out here in this country. I'm getting ready to amputate an injured hand on a seaman who had his hand crushed yesterday, and I have one patient who has gangrene in his thigh. Would you like to see them? I'll show you how I am treating the gangrenous patient. Then you could help me amputate the seaman's hand and wrist if you want. I'm going to do it in a few minutes in our infirmary here.

"He's resting now. I'm waiting for the effect of the opium and whiskey to overtake him. I have given him two of these pills plus what I gave him earlier this morning. I will give him another pill just before I begin working on him. And I've also been feeding him all the whiskey he wants in order to get him as drunk as I can. It's going to hurt him like the devil anyhow, but the opium and whisky will help a lot. It won't stop all the pain, but it will help him. Why don't you come on into the infirmary room with me, and I will let you help me. Would you like to do that? There's going to be a lot of screaming and cursing, and I could use someone to hold him down. Are you up to it?"

"I think maybe I am, if you think I could help and it wouldn't be too much trouble for you." Caleb looked serious at the prospect of helping to amputate someone's hand.

"It's no trouble. I'll enjoy the company. Most people don't want to know anything about doctoring until they get hurt. Well, come on, then. Let's go and do it." The obviously happy doctor headed off towards the infirmary with Caleb following him. Caleb couldn't understand why the doctor acted so happy at the prospect of cutting off a man's hand.

As Dr. Simms prepared for surgery, Caleb told him about his recent experience at midwifery and how he felt so ignorant about the whole experience. "In a case like that, would you want to give the woman opium? She seemed in such great pain."

"No!" Dr. Simms said emphatically. "No! You wouldn't want to interfere with labor and the natural process of childbirth. You would only use painkilling medication if you were experiencing serious trouble with the birthing process. Your case sounds to me like everything was normal. When that happens, you don't have to do much of anything other than stand by, clean up, and do just what you did by assisting the mother, talking her through it. If you had trouble, that is an entirely different matter. My professors in medical school advised us that the worst thing you can do is give a woman pain medicine in childbirth. If it's a normal birth, that is. Some doctors do it, mind you, but my professors always told us not to be a 'meddling midwife' unless there were serious medical complications."

"From your description, the only thing you might have done that you did not do was to give her an enema, before the birthin'."

"A what? I don't know what that is." Caleb looked mystified.

"An enema. It cleans out a woman's bowels so she doesn't have a bowel movement right in the middle of the birthing. You see the same muscles that are used in childbirth are used in urinating and defecating. If there is anything in the bladder or in the bowels, it will come out in the birthing process. The best thing to do is to give them an enema, or even two or three of them, during or just before early labor. It keeps the mess down during the birth itself. You take a bag of tepid water and wash it up in the rectum with a tube. It causes a bowel movement and cleans the bowels out. I have a regular setup I can put in with the goods you buy for yourself if you want me to. It's simple to use."

"Getting back to the opium, if the mother cannot give birth and becomes too weak to labor, that is an instance that you might use opium. But be prepared to pluck the child out yourself in that case. It is only under extraordinary circumstances, when the woman is diseased or where something is wrong in the presentation of the child that the accoucheur, or birthing doctor is called in to interfere with a process so natural as childbirth. The chief part of the surgeon's duty is to give directions and inspire confidence, which the woman might lose under the terrible pains of it. If the birth be abnormal, then is the time to know what to do. Other than that, do nothing. I have not attended many childbirth's myself, being mostly on a ship full of men. It is out of my line of specialty, that's for sure. But I do know that a woman's mind goes into a sort of tumult during the birth of a child, and it is helpful for her to get encouragement from someone in whose integrity she has great confidence. Usually that is another woman, a midwife, with experience in helping her."

"Seeing as how you're interested in the subject, I will let you have this book. It tells all about it." He handed Caleb a leather-bound volume titled, *Obstetrics: the Science and the Art.* "Obstetrics, you see, is the science of woman's nature, reproductive organs, diseases, and accidents. This book also gets into several related subjects. It includes the baby, the differing kinds and qualities of a birth, the problems you run into, surgery, and the care of the newborn child. Midwifery is the art of assisting women in labor and of guiding their conduct during the following confinement. As long as things are perfectly normal, I have always thought that midwifery is all a woman needs. It is only when a serious problem ensues and some complication develops that you need to get into obstetrics."

"Once you have read all of this book, you can hang out your own shingle and become a midwife or doctor as far as this primitive country is concerned. But since there are no rules concerning being a doctor, here, you can go into that business if you want to. Doctors certainly are scarce. I have been traveling up and down this coast for nearly three months, and I have yet to find one person who could claim to be any kind of doctor. Having read medical books and using the proper tools and techniques, you will be the only person within 500 miles who knows anything technical about the subject, it seems like."

"I also have a medical dictionary I can let you buy. My tools and such belong to the ship. But I will ask the captain if he will let me put together a few medical instruments and medicines for you if you want me to. He'll charge you an arm and a leg for them, but they will probably be the only ones on dry land here in this country."

"I even have an old set of forceps, which are used to force the birth of babies that won't come down out of the woman's womb on their own. I'll never use them on this ship, what with only men aboard. It is very tricky to use them, and you would only use them as a last resort. But when necessary, nothing else will do but for you to reach up in there and grab the baby and pull it down and out. If you don't do that, both the baby and the mother will die."

"Yes, I'd like that," Caleb told him, "and I'd like to learn what I can about medicines and such."

"Now look here at this man," said Dr. Simms as he folded back bandages that covered an appalling wound on a pale, thin seaman lying in a wooden-framed bed. "He has gangrene in his leg. It all started with a rusty fishhook he got stuck in his thigh. See here how this hip is swollen and discolored? Portions of it are black and putrefied. You can smell the putrefied rotting flesh."

"I wanted to cut his leg off at the hip, but he wouldn't consent to it. Now look at it. It's infected terrible with gangrene. I'm treating it with what we call maggot therapy. You can grow your own maggots. All you need is piece of rotten meat, liver works best, and some flies. You let the flies lay their eggs on the meat, and they will form maggots. I started out by putting twenty maggots on this wound. See how these little critters have eaten up only the rotted flesh? They eat rotted flesh but leave the healthy tissue alone, the smart little buggers."

"I've been treating him with this for two weeks, and almost all of the gangrene is gone now. If he's real lucky, I won't have to cut his leg off. Sometimes these maggots work, and of course sometimes they don't. But if that gangrene isn't stopped before it gets above the hip, this man will die. There won't be anything I can do about it once it gets above the limb. I think maybe this is going to work this time. At least we hope so, don't we, Mack?" The doctor covered up the seaman's wound again and laid his hand on the man's shoulder.

The man smiled weakly up at him and said, "Aye, aye, Doc. We'll beat this for sure. And I keeps me leg, too."

"My other patient over here is not so lucky." They walked over to the second bunk as the doctor picked up a pitcher of water. "This man's hand and wrist were caught under the anchor chain. The rocking of the boat squashed his hand and wrist. The only treatment that makes any sense in this case is to amputate his hand above the wrist. He's asleep now with the opium and whiskey I've been giving him. I'm going to give him another opium pill now."

"Here, sailor, open your mouth. I want you to swallow another opium pill, and have another slug of this whiskey and water to wash it down. That's a good fellow. Now get yourself ready. We're going to take this squashed hand off now. Are you ready?"

"Not really, Doc, but go ahead. Do what has to be done. Got any more whiskey?" His speech was slurred, and he was pale.

"No more for now! I don't want you getting sick on me. Tell you what though; I'll promise you a whole bottle all of your own after this is over with. This young fellow here is going to assist me. His name is Caleb. Here, now, I'm strapping you down so you don't move during the operation. I've given you opium and as much whisky as I dare, so that's about all I can do for you as far as killing the pain. This is going to hurt, and I'm sorry for it; but we are trying to save your life. You scream or holler all you want, but I don't want you moving. Lay back, and I'll put this bite of leather in your mouth. When we begin, bite down on it as hard as you can. Do your best not to move. Moving will make it hurt more."

"Now look here, Caleb. I have his hand set on this hard pillow with what is left of his fist pointed up. This line I have drawn is to guide my knife. This is called an elliptical incision. See on this page in this book I have been studying? It lays out the procedure I am going to follow step by step. These books are a Godsend, especially for a general practitioner like me. I don't do these procedures every day. If you have time you can study this book and study what they have written in it. That's why they call it 'practicing medicine.' Ha! Ha! Practicing. That's a joke, don't you know!"

"See here on this page of the book? It shows the two bones in the forearm and the skin, the nerves, and the muscle. Don't worry about those fancy names written on the various parts; just pay attention to which parts they are showing in the drawings. That fancy language is just for the doctors so they can charge a lot. Ha! Ha! Common language works just as good or maybe better, because people can understand it." Dr. Simms was enjoying himself as he explained the operation to Caleb.

"I have now placed a tourniquet above the place where we will be working so as to keep him from bleeding to death. We have to cut all the skin, muscle, arteries, veins, nerves, then the bones. Then we will push up the muscle, meat, and skin above the bones so the bones can protrude and be in the clear for the saw."

As Dr. Simms talked, he began swiftly cutting on the skin. The man on the couch let out a groan and then screamed around the leather mouthpiece. His eyes bulged out as he looked at the cut the doctor made. It was so swiftly done it was almost completed before the man realized the operation had started. He involuntarily tried to pull his hand back, but the restraints that tied his hand in place prevented him from moving much. Moving just increased his pain, as the doctor had warned him. Dr. Simms withdrew his knife for a moment until the patient stopped writhing.

The upper portion of the cut through the skin was parallel with the place where he intended on cutting the bone. The lower portion extended downward so the skin itself would form a flap over the end of the amputated portion.

The seaman fainted. "Good, that will make our job easier," said the doctor. "Let's hurry now. Watch as I roll that flap of skin back up in order to get it up out of the way until we need it to cover the end of his stump."

"The next thing we must do is cut the muscles, veins, nerves, all the meaty portions. Just like in that picture in the book. I have studied this over carefully. I memorized every single thing I am going to do. Here are the two bones. Now we must make our cut of the meat square, so we must first cut the meat between the bones. There, now that looks good. Keep it clean and don't let a lot of waste and blood get inside the skin flap."

"See this device I have made? It looks like a little metal dinner plate with two small holes in it. The holes should fit right over the two bones, like this. Good. They fit just right. Here, you hold it!"

Caleb gently put his hands on the small plate that encircled the two bones.

"Push, man! Push it up!" Simms told him sternly. "What I want you to do is push all the skin, meat, and such out of the way so I can get a clear shot at the bones with the saw."

Caleb's face was now pasty white. Between the odor coming from the gangrenous leg wound of the other seaman and that from this open cut, he was afraid he was going to be sick to his stomach. But he was into it now and could not back out.

"That's right," Doc Simms told Caleb. "Now hold it up hard. I want to get a three-inch section of the bone exposed for the saw. Notice how I make this cut. It's just like sawing a limb off a tree. You can cut just one bone now or both at the same time. I'm cutting both so's they will be square. See that bone dust? It's important to keep it out of the raw wound. There now. It's cut, and no splinters either. It's a nice smooth cut, if I do say so myself."

"Note how I take this file and gently round off the sharp edges of the bone until they are smooth. By the way, always keep your knives and saw blades sharp. And keep dried tissue out of your files, too. Be sure to wash your files when you are done with them. Then soak them in boiling water. I'll clean these bones off with a rag and alcohol to get rid of the tiny particles of flesh and bone dust. Then I'll wash the ends of the bones with alcohol."

"Do you see in the book how it says that if the ends of the bones in the stump become united, supination and pronation are lost? That just means movement will be lost if the bones grow together. So what we are going to do is suture, or sew, the muscles together between the two bones so the bones can't grow together." While he was talking he was concentrating doing the things he was talking about. "There, now that is done. See how the sutured muscle between the bones will hold the bones apart? Neat job, wouldn't you say?"

The patient was once again partly conscious and moaning.

"Now then, you can pull that device off the ends of the bones and let the skin and veins and nerves extend back over them, naturally. See there? The whole mass of muscle now just extends a little further than the bones. First, I am untying the tourniquet for just a second to clean the veins and wound of any foreign matter. Now then, I am using catgut to suture the veins and to avoid excessive bleeding."

"I am now taking just a tiny bit of the muscle and tying it over the end of the bones. This will keep the muscle from retracting upward and leaving the sharp ends of the bones protruding against the skin. That would make it hurt and be sore all the time. That's important because it would be painful after the surgery, and he couldn't put any pressure on the stump. Now I am pulling down and cutting off as much of the nerve endings as I can reach." Simms's hands were moving with such speed that it amazed Caleb.

"Now all that is left is to flip this skin up over the wound and suture it in place. There is just a little too much skin here, so the flap will not be nice and tight and smooth. I'm trimming this excess off with these scissors to make it fit just right. Now there, that looks good, just right, wouldn't you say?"

"What do you think? Will the patient live? Sure he will! That's a nice neat job if I do say so myself. I will leave an opening at each side so any excess fluid can drain out. Notice I used silk string to sew up these outside stitches. I can pull them off after the skin grows together. The ones I left on the inside are catgut and will be absorbed by the body eventually as the veins and other pieces I sewed grow back together. If this outside flap will grow together and if we don't get any infection, we have saved this man's life. He is young and vigorous, and can be fitted with a wooden stump-end and a tool on the end of his arm. There is no reason why he can't live a productive, healthy, and happy life, even have children and be a family man, if he wants."

"Now then, I am all finished! Boy, does that make me hungry! Let's go and have something to eat! That's a good day's work. How about a drink?" The happy surgeon poured a whole pint of whiskey into a tankard, sloshed some it over his hands, washed the wound with it, and drank the rest.

He grinned when he looked at Caleb's pale and drawn face. "It's a mess, I know, but there is a lot of satisfaction in saving a man's life, or even in trying to do it. You did good for your first time. Don't worry about those butterflies in your stomach. We all get them at first. You know how to cut a man's arm off now; and with these books you could do almost as good a job as I can. Common sense, man! Always remember, common sense! Leave your patients their dignity and act assured of what you are doing!"

"The name of this book is *Surgery of Modern Warfare*. It shows and explains all kinds of surgery and repairs a man can do. I'll ask the captain if I can include it in your kit. He'll charge you too much, but there's a lot of information in it. Your patients will pay as much as you want when you're operating. No one ever argues with a surgeon holding a knife in his hand when a patient is on the table in front of him. Ha! Ha! An old doctor's saying is that 'the more you charge, the better the cure.' Remember that and believe it!"

After the spectacle of the amputation of the man's smashed hand and wrist, plus the maggot therapy, Caleb asked to be excused from lunch. He had begun to feel lightheaded during the surgery, so he leaned against the ship's railing until he began to feel better. The fresh salt air smelled especially good to him right then.

When he felt stronger, Caleb continued his inspection of the goods the captain was offering for sale. There were many kinds of small mirrors, beads, and trinkets that the Indians enjoyed, and metal tips to be applied to wooden plows. There were also many varieties of cloth and hardware items. There were metal arrow-points and hatchets and knives. Caleb ordered a small quantity of almost every item, including some long-bladed knives that could be attached to a pole for cutting grass or hay.

He also bought six iron pick heads for digging, six shovelheads, and some plow points.

In the back of the array of goods were two boxes of revolving pistols and two boxes of rifles fitted with revolving chambers. There were twelve guns in each box. The rifles were identical to the pistols except they had long barrels and stocks. There were two boxes of single-shot rifles that were ignited with caps. They had shorter barrels than the long Kentucky-style rifles Caleb was used to. He knew they were meant for use when on horseback. The revolving-type weapons were similar to the experimental revolving pistols that Caleb had. They used the new percussion caps. All of the revolvers, single-shot pistols, and rifles were rusty. They looked terrible. "Captain! Oh, Captain! What is the story on these damaged goods here?" Caleb asked.

"Those are some kind of special guns that were put on the ship at the last minute by the company's purchasing agent. They're some kind of new invention," the captain said. "I have not found anyone who knows anything about them. They got wet with sea water on the journey over, which is why they are damaged and rusty. I plan on taking them back and returning them to the manufacturer, if he will take them back. They are too expensive, and no one will buy them."

"Those with the revolving chambers I carry on my inventory at sixty-five pesos each, my cost. But as I said, no one can figure out how they work or what they are for. The single-shot ones are fifteen pesos each. If you'd take them off my hands, it would save me from having to take them all the way back to England. I will give you a real bargain on them. You're buying a lot of other items, so if you wanted these you could have them for half my cost because they are in such bad shape, if you think that's fair. But you have to take them all, or it's no deal."

"Yes, I'll take them with my other goods." Caleb tried to hide his pleasure at acquiring the weapons at such a good price. He could clean the rust off, and they would be as good as new. "Do you have any caps for them?"

"I don't know what a cap even is. You look through the boxes. And if you find them, there will be a number on the box that I can use to price them out off my manifest list. See that boatswain, warrant officer, over there? He is in charge of my inventory. Maybe he can help you find what you are looking for."

"Say, if you're interested in firearms why don't you look at those two small brass skiff cannons over there. Ha! Ha!" he joked. "They would really be a novelty back in your country, I bet. Ha! Ha!" He laughed again and pointed at two small cannons that could be mounted on a small boat. "They take 2 inch balls. Or you can load them up with grapeshot or birdshot and kill a lot of birds with them. If you want them, the price includes the ramrods, swabbing sticks, lighter sticks, and several barrels of about a hundred cast-iron balls to shoot out of them. You can have them for forty-five pesos each, including what goes with them."

Caleb already knew he would take them, but he didn't say so yet. His mind had already pictured those small cannons mounted one on each corner of his fort-like store, back in New Mexico, with Thomas Lyon sitting at one of them and him at the other blasting away at marauding Indians or renegades. But now he was still thinking about the caps for the pistols and rifles.

The bo's'on knew about the caps that Caleb was looking for. They had to go down in the hold into a special dry-room magazine where the explosive powder was kept to find the two metal boxes that held the caps. The boxes were sealed with beeswax. They held the precious caps for the percussion rifles and pistols. Without those caps, the weapons could not be fired at all. Caleb and the boson carried them up to the growing pile of goods that Caleb intended to purchase. To make sure they were the correct size and fit for the rifles, he opened up one of the boxes. There they were, dry and safe. They were inside of small metal boxes holding twenty caps each. If he could get some of the trappers to use these kinds of rifles and begin to sell them caps, he could build a steady trade. He knew that the trappers would purchase these guns if they were available. They were much faster to shoot, dependable, and produced greater firepower.

Caleb looked closely at the caps. They were made of thin copper, with a closed dome at the top of the cap and a round, flaring open end. There were four tiny slits halfway up from the opening toward the dome. The slits made a tight fit when pressed into a rifle or a pistol gun-barrel chamber where the powder would be. The explosive that charged the caps was made of half grain of fulminate of mercury, mixed with half its weight in saltpeter. They were identical to the caps Caleb had for his twin revolvers.

These caps held the explosive charge that was set off when struck with the hammer of the gun. It, in turn, ignited the powder in the gun barrel by traveling down the hollowed-out pin that rested upon the back of the barrel. Two large fourteen-pound metal tins each held several thousand of the tiny caps. Inside the tins, the caps were packed in small metal boxes containing 250 caps each, and further packaged into the small tins holding 20 caps each. Both the outside metal boxes and each inner box were marked by the manufacturer as being from Eley Brothers, London.

Caleb had never in his life seen such a smorgasbord of goods and merchandise. "Books. Do you have any books?" he asked the boson who was helping with the goods and displaying the merchandise.

"Not many. There are a few in this trunk, mostly just Bibles. The Spanish won't buy them. Their priests don't want ordinary people to have them anyhow and most of the people over here can't read anyhow. Worse yet, these are written in English, so why they would be sent to a Spanish-speaking country, I don't know. The cost of them is one peso each. I realize that's a lot, but they are leather-bound and written on very good linen paper." Caleb took six Bibles and several other books he found buried under them.

Captain Beeman had been kidding when he offered the skiff guns to Caleb, but he was glad to sell them when the serious-faced young man accepted his offer. Captain Beeman would have sold anything on the boat. He would have been glad to sell the boat, too, if he could find a way to get back to England. He had been gone too long from his home, and was anxious to leave. Caleb was one of the best customers he had found, other than a couple of store owners. This sale was by far the largest the captain had made for more than a month.

Caleb's new cannons were a matched pair of brass swivel guns. The small cannon only weighed 60-pounds each. Thus, they could easily be lifted up to the second floor of his trading station, and put into various holes in the wall to be pointed in any direction. The cannon also could be mounted at the front door for firing through the door opening.

The captain assured him the cannon could propel a ball half a mile or more. The balls that Caleb received were iron; but lead balls could be shot, or scrap metal could also be used. He would put the boxes inside of a roll of leather so no one would know what was in them while he was on the trail.

Planning this trip south, Caleb intended to load the goods on the horses that had carried the furs to Monterey. He would now have a full load of merchandise to carry back to New Mexico, and his station at Taos. He would use the supplies for trading on his way to Los Angeles. He wondered what they had in this country to trade for if they did not go after beaver. There were beaver in the Sierra Mountains to the east. He had seen them and trapped them himself. But no one here seemed to be catching them. It was puzzling, that the Spanish had not ventured far inland from the coast.

CHAPTER 20
Renegades.

Caleb and María stayed in Monterey two weeks, resting themselves and their horses, and getting their packs repaired, while Caleb traded. Now it was time for them to move on down El Camino Real toward Los Angeles. They were sad to be leaving their new friends. They had enjoyed meeting new people, trading goods, and resting up from their long journey. The hospitable Californians had invited them to all sorts of dances, picnics and dinner parties during their stay. They would deeply miss the friendliness of the people of Monterey.

Shortly before their departure, Caleb surprised María with the gift of a small gold crucifix and gold chain to replace the cross she had left with Beaver-Catcher. He also bought her a rosary, and gave her one of the English Bibles. After Caleb hung the crucifix around her neck, she burst into tears and rewarded him with many kisses and hugs. He had purchased the cross, gold chain, and rosary from their host, Thomas Larkin.

Numerous people in Monterey, and travelers who had just come north, warned Caleb and María again and again to be careful on the road, El Camino Real. A gang of horse and cattle thieves, mostly renegade Indians and a few *mestizos*, Mexicans mixed with Indian blood, were plundering ranchos, and even missions along the coast road and attacking travelers. Twenty of them were operating out of Tulare Lake and the area east of there. Half the marauders had armed themselves with stolen weapons, such as old flintlocks, blunderbusses, and even ancient matchlock rifles. Two of the leaders were known to have cumbersome flintlock pistols in addition to their flintlock rifles. A pack train consisting of a man, a woman, and a child would be easy prey, so every one of Caleb's new friends thought.

Caleb and María planned to cover 10 miles a day, sometimes a little more, a reasonable goal that would not overtax them or the horses. They would still be moving at a good pace, but one that would permit them to savor the spectacular beauty of the area. And most mornings they would be able to see that evening's campsite ahead of them.

Several times a day they rested in scenic places and always selected a campsite that had good grazing for the horses. Contrary to the warnings they had received in Monterey, they planned to stay overnight at their own campsites along El Camino Real rather than any of the missions, except to make a stop for one night at the Soledad mission to visit the kindly priest who was their first acquaintance in California, to keep their promise to visit him on their way south.

Although Caleb and María didn't talk much about it, they both dreaded the inevitable separation from each other that was coming sooner with every passing mile.

At noon one day when they had been on the trail for two weeks, Caleb held up his hand indicating that María should stop. He could see where the road ahead of them narrowed and wound into a group of hills with huge boulders on each side. The trail followed a wash and was surrounded by hills. He took his glass out and studied the rocks. Then he rode his horse onto a high spot of ground and studied the trail where he could see it winding ahead. He could not see anyone but it was an ideal place for an ambush. He realized the birds that were usually singing were quiet. Did that mean someone was up ahead?

During their stay in Monterey, Caleb had completed cleaning and repairing six of the revolving-cylinder rifles and four of the pistols. He and María each adopted two of the revolving rifles for their own weapons, replacing their old-fashioned flintlocks. These new rifles each had six revolving cylinders. He had put this firepower to good use, arming the pack train against marauders.

Because María had to take care of the baby, Caleb made the weapons as convenient for her use as he could. He placed a pistol on either side of her saddle and two rifle scabbards under the stirrups. The cradleboard rested on her back much of the time, but was also sometimes hung behind her saddle. He also gave her a pistol to put in a holster on her thigh so it could be used quickly.

For the first time since María was captured by the Apache, she was wearing Spanish clothes. She was dressed in a mannish riding outfit that she had acquired in Monterey. Highwaymen would not be likely to expect such a beautiful and stylish young woman to be well armed and such a good shot. Caleb had two revolving rifles in scabbards under his stirrups, one on each side, and carried a revolving rifle in his hands as he had always carried his flintlock. Their old flintlock rifles had been stored away, but the two shotguns were still on the leading packhorses.

"María, get out your rifle and make sure your caps are properly in place. Loosen the dust covers on your pistols, too, and make sure you are ready to shoot. This narrow gulch ahead looks too much like that place the Indians attacked us back on the other side of the Sierra Mountains. I don't like the looks of this. It is a perfect place to get on both sides of the road and shoot down on us. You be ready to shoot anybody you see that looks hostile. Are you ready?"

They had practiced with their new weapons before they left Monterey. And María, as usual, caught on fast. She had her rifle out and looked it over carefully. "I'm set. Don't you worry about me. I won't hesitate to shoot if anyone tries to bother us!" Her expression was grim.

"All right. Let's move out, María. Cock your rifle, and I'll do the same." Caleb tied the two lead horses' tails to the horses they were riding so their hands would be free in case of attack. As they began to move, he carefully looked around one last time.

As they got well into the gulch, the sides of the hills rose steeply up on either side of them. Around a bend in the trail half way through the hills, they came upon two men, a Mexican and an Indian on horses in the middle of the road. In English, Caleb told María quietly, "Ride right up to them. Then get off the left side of your horse and point your rifle at the stomach of the man on your side. I will get off the right side of my horse and cover the other man. We will have the protection of the horses standing on both sides of us. We will face only those two men." He forced a smile on his face and waved to the men as if he wanted to see them.

The men, who looked partly Spanish, were smiling and still sitting their horses. One had a flintlock rifle in his hand, and the other had an ancient blunderbuss. They both looked confident and seemed pleased with the bounty they thought they were about to collect. They were so confident in fact; they had left their weapons lying carelessly across their saddles in front of them. They did not want to frighten them into turning and running away.

The Mexican and Indian had clearly robbed travelers using this plan before. They obviously expected any travelers to stop as soon as they saw them in the middle of the trail. The would-be robbers blocking the road were backed up by eighteen more renegades hidden behind boulders on each side of the road, ready to shoot the travelers when they tried to retreat. This superiority of numbers made the two men in the road extremely confident as they faced the two young people, one of whom, it was now apparent, was only a woman with a child on her back. Never before had anyone been so stupid as to ride right up to deliver their goods to them.

Instead of stopping and trying to run away going back down the trail, where the other men were ready to shoot them down as they came back down the trail. Caleb and María kept going and even increased their speed until they were only 10 feet from the two men.

"Welcome to our road! We like it that you use our road! My name is Palo," said the Mexican man on Caleb's side. He then said insolently to Caleb and María: "I am the *patrón* who owns this section of the highway. We will now discuss the payment that you must make for using my road." He was smiling broadly, almost laughing. His flintlock rifle was not cocked. Caleb guessed the man with the blunderbuss would have it loaded with buckshot or birdshot. At such close range, it would be devastating if he could cock it and shoot before María shot him.

Caleb thought the Indian was drunk. This was a bad condition for him because if his judgment was impaired and he tried to bring his gun up, María would immediately shoot him. The men in the rocks around them would then fire, and they were too close to miss. He could tell she was unhappy with the very thought of it. He glanced at her out of the corners of his eyes and saw a flash from her teeth, part of her tense smile. The man she was facing had no idea that he was within a fraction of a second of death. This gave Caleb his idea.

Caleb and María simultaneously swung down off their horses and pointed their rifles directly at the two men' stomachs. The robbers' guns were still across their saddles.

This young man and mere child of a woman with a babe on her back should be easy to separate from their goods. We'll get all the horses too. Palo was thinking to himself as he inspected the large quantity of merchandise on the six packhorses. *I can take the woman too and keep her for a while before selling her. We will kill the young man so there will be no witnesses.*

Then Caleb told them, in a whisper, "If you make even the slightest move with your hands or any other part of your bodies, we will immediately gut-shoot you both here and now. Get off your horses on the inside so you are facing us. Hold only the barrels of your rifles with your left hands. Move rapidly now. It is your only chance to live a few moments longer."

The two surprised men blanched as they looked down the barrels of the two steadily held guns only 10 feet away. *"Señor,* do not be frightened," Palo said, sobering up fast as he looked down the barrel of the weapon held by Caleb. "We mean you no harm. We only expect to collect the toll for the use of our road. We are starving and entitled to take what we need to live. We only want your guns and two horses. Me and my men are hungry for horsemeat. We will take your guns and the last two packhorses, and let you proceed."

"You cannot pass here without paying the toll. There are twenty of us. You can look around you, and I will call my men out so you can see them. They are well armed. Think what you do! You endanger yourself, this woman, and the baby by your actions."

But the men did as they were told. They dismounted on the inside so that they were between their horses. The horses screened the two *mestizos* so the men on each side of the road could not see their leaders. And because the men in the rocks could not see exactly what was going on, they hesitated to act.

"No, there are not twenty of you any longer," said Caleb. "There are only eighteen. You two are dead men. You're still speaking only because I have permitted it. Blow the priming out of your pans and tie your guns on the thongs of straps of your saddles. Now! Then turn around and face the other direction. I have decided to let you live a few moments longer."

"If you believe in prayers, say them quickly because if any of your men up in the rocks shoots so much as one shot or one arrow you will be dead before you could hear the echo. If you have any signal or way to communicate with your men, hurry up and tell them not to shoot because it is you who will die first! They must not make any move toward us, or your few moments of life on this earth will end before ours do."

The spokesman, Palo, was sweating profusely. His confident smile turned into a frown of fear as he nervously tied his rifle on the thongs of his saddle after emptying the priming powder out of the pan. He cautioned the man with him not to make any overt act. The man with the ancient blunderbuss flintlock, who was about to try to bring his gun toward María, was stopped by the words of the man who seemed to be in charge. Palo ordered the other man again not to make any sudden moves and to tie his rifle on the thongs of his saddle as he had just done. Then they turned around, facing up the road.

"Well, *caballeros*, gentlemen, what is it to be?" asked Caleb. "Have you completed your prayers? Are you prepared for your death? As soon as we have killed you, we will kill these other eighteen so that we may continue our journey. This is our lucky day. We now have your two horses to add to our string and your guns, too. We thank you for this delivery to us. You see we collect all horses from men we meet such as you. We thank you for the gift of your weapons, too, and any other valuables you may have on your dead bodies. You will no longer need them because you are dead men. This is as it should be for thieves and robbers."

Palo's eyes bugged out in terror. "No, *Señor*! No! You see, I was only jesting. You can pass down this road. You owe us nothing. I will guarantee you that my men will do nothing toward you. They have orders to do nothing as long as my hat stays on my head. It is only if I remove my hat that they will begin shooting. You are completely safe. Please do not shoot us. It is entirely unnecessary. You can pass in peace."

"For that we thank you!" Caleb said matter-of-factly. "We also thank you for the two bullets you have saved us. We do not want to waste our lead shooting you in the back. If you think it is safe for you, then you lead off up the road and escort us through this canyon. Perhaps God will create a miracle and allow you to live a few moments longer." Walking slowly, the two men headed up the road. They were less confident that their men would hold their fire than they pretended to be. But there was little else they could do. They began to move rapidly.

"Not fast! Slow and steady. Do not get out ahead of us any farther. Do not hurry, dead men!" Caleb cautioned them so quietly that only these two men could hear what he was saying.

They walked over a mile until they broke out of the hills into open country. The confused men who had been up in the rocks followed along staying 200 yards behind them. They walked their horses across the open country until they crossed a small arroyo and Caleb called a halt. Caleb liked this small gulch where they could get the horses out of the line of fire, as well as give him and María a wash-bank of boulders to hide behind when they mounted their defense. He looked back through his spyglass at the group of gunmen who were following. Half of them had various types of rifles and half had bows and arrows. They were poorly armed. These two men here were the best armed of the group. He looked at them.

"Palo, you and your friend take your belts, powder horns, and ball bags off. Hang them on the saddles of the two horses that are now mine. Take all your clothes off too, and hang them on the saddle. Your shoes, too."

"But *Señor*, you cannot mean to rob us of everything."

"Take them off and be quick about it!" Ordered Caleb as he pointed his rifle at Palo. "If you do not move immediately, I will take them off the corpse. It is up to you. I prefer not to have them with holes in them and blood stains. "

He told María, in English, "Take your cradle-board off and put Pedrito down by the rocks in the gulch so he is safe. I am going to let these men go a few yards toward their friends and then order the other men to come forward. When I give the signal, shoot all the mounted horsemen or horses, whatever you can hit starting on the right side. I will do the same starting on the left. We can let these two call their friends in closer. We should be able to cut the size of the group down to something we can handle. Get your other rifle out of your scabbard too, and get ready."

The two naked men were standing miserably, and with great embarrassment, waiting to see what was to happen next. They were being humiliated, and in front of their own men. They had been bested by a young man and a woman. It was almost more than they could tolerate.

Caleb got his second rifle out. "You two men walk back down the road thirty paces and then stop. If you go one step farther, we will shoot you in the back. Then call your companions to come and get you. You can ride off with them if they come to save you. But mind you, don't go one step closer to them! They must come to you."

In the meantime, María rode into the arroyo and began to put all of her weapons out, laying them on top of the large rock she had selected to get behind. She was a one-person fortress. She had her two revolving rifles, two revolving pistols, two shotguns, two powder horns, her bullet pouches, and buckshot for the two flintlock shotguns. Peering over a big boulder, she was ready. The adrenaline rushing through her veins was making her hands shake a little, which made her worry how accurately she could shoot when the fighting began. She took a deep breath and let it out slowly as she decided that she would put her elbows down on the smooth boulder rock to steady her aim. She had set Pedrito down in the shade out of sight. He was asleep for the moment, but she knew with the first firing of a gun he would start crying as he usually did.

Palo and the other man walked the prescribed thirty paces down the road toward the rest of the men. At thirty paces, they began to wave and call to their comrades to come forward and get them. They had their hats on but were otherwise stark naked. The group started forward, but only four of them continued up to within 50 yards of the two naked men. They could see Caleb standing in plain sight. He had leaned his rifle against the large boulder he was standing beside. All he had to do was reach down and grab it. He was standing with his arms folded in front of him, looking at the men.

María was behind a rock, out of sight, and resting her rifle on top of the rock. She whispered to Caleb, "I will try to shoot the men with rifles first. Say when you want me to start shooting."

"I will tell you when, but if one of them fires begin shooting. We will start firing as soon as I think they will not come any closer."

Four horsemen had stopped 50 yards in front of their naked companions. "We are afraid to come closer because the stranger has weapons, and we cannot now see the second one. What has happened? Why have you given them your horses, guns and clothes? If we come too close, they may take ours, too. You come here to us, and we will take you back to the others."

"Shoot the two on the right, now!" Caleb said.

Caleb knelt to give himself a good shooting posture. María started to fire slowly but steadily. She hit the man on the right who had been doing the talking and then shot the horse out from under the second man, as he wheeled his horse to go in the other direction. Caleb shot the other two as they retreated.

The group of fourteen riders, now about 150 yards away, began to scatter. Caleb and María kept shooting until they were out of sight. They killed or wounded five more renegades and hit several of the horses. The two naked men were nowhere to be seen, apparently crouched down in the bushes hiding or crawling back to where they had come from. Several wild shots had come toward Caleb and María, but nothing was hit by the wildly fleeing group.

"Let's clean and reload our weapons. That was pretty good shooting, María. I don't think I will give you any more lessons. I think you know too much already. You act like you enjoy shooting thieves."

"I am not sure those men are Indians. They are mixed breeds and speak Spanish. But I must confess, it's nice to win. I have also been where I lost; and believe me, winning is better." She was grinning happily.

Pedrito was crying loudly, upset and scared by the loud gunfire. María got him out of his cradleboard and sat down on a rock. She encouraged him to nurse at her breast, which he did enthusiastically. At the same time she was feeding him, she was trying to load her weapons. It was a quite a sight to see the baby lying on his back in her lap, with her bending over him so he could suckle while at the same time she was trying to load her weapons.

Caleb, shaking his head at the way she could change from trained killer to nursing mother, said, "I'll load the weapons. You take care of feeding the baby. When he is finished, get some dried meat out of our food sack. We can eat it on the trail as we move. I would like to go as far today as we can to get away from here. I hope those fellows will have had enough of us. But if they have a large group of friends, we might have more trouble from them."

CHAPTER 21
Los Angeles.

María was growing more irritable every day as they were approaching the end of their journey. She unconsciously began a campaign of delaying tactics to postpone what appeared to be the inevitable. She would suddenly break into tears, especially in their bed at night, for no discernible reason. She would ask Caleb to stop early. She would get up late. She would find a reason for not mounting her horse. The closer to Los Angeles they got, the more she worried about the pending meeting with her betrothed. She was also greatly troubled by a foreboding as to how he might treat her baby, Pedrito. Part of the problem, of course, was that she had fallen ever more in love with Caleb and could not bear the thought of having to marry another.

Los Angeles was founded in 1781 when King Charles II of Spain sent settlers to form a pueblo at the Los Angeles River and keep the Russians, who were moving south from Alaska, from taking over all of Alta California. The English were active also, moving toward California from Canada. Los Angeles was founded by forty-four settlers of eleven families that traveled over a thousand miles from Spanish-Mexico, or New Spain, as it was known then.

The Russians, already actively settled in Alaska, had set up a fort and trading post in California 100 miles north of San Francisco in 1812 at what was called Fort Ross. John Augustus Sutter bought the land held by the Russians in 1841. Sutter had previously bought land from the Indians for three blankets, three pair of pants, two axes, grubbing hoes, and a few trinkets. The Russians had declared their intention to extend their influence down the California coast. That is why Spain had to populate Alta California. If the Spanish did not establish a presence in California, they would soon lose their claim to it to the advancing Russians, or so they thought.

The Mission at San Gabriel, near Los Angeles, had been established earlier to Christianize and save the souls of the Indians. The Mission was four leagues, or 20 miles, from Los Angeles. It has been estimated that at one time, the Spaniards, had the souls of forty million natives on the two continents, North and South America, under the Spanish flag and under the King of Spain's rule of law and the Catholic Church.

The *Alfonso de Vargas Rancho* was one of forty large ranchos in the area around Los Angeles. Many hundreds of natives and mixed-Spanish people lived and worked on the ranchos, but no one kept an exact count. Each rancho was a self-sufficient community growing its own food and cattle, with its own harness makers, *vaqueros*, superintendents, and servants.

These early settlers were great Spanish soldiers and had fought Indians all over North, South, and Central America. They were the best men the King of Spain had to offer. They were anxious to serve the King and their religion, and they were not afraid of anything. They had sworn to keep California under the rule of Spain, and they did so as long as they lived.

Don Alfonso, María's betrothed, was the son of *Don Francisco Alvarez de Vargas*, one of the first settlers in this area. He had been ordered by the King of Spain to come to California to help Spain overcome the threat of Russian colonization. He was one of the soldiers who had originally subdued the savages in this area, and had settled near Los Angeles. He was a direct descendent of the Catalan Spaniards who had come from Spain 200 years earlier. A strong, imposing, famous fighting man from central Mexico, he was known throughout California and Mexico as "The Great One."

The Great One had a rather bloodthirsty streak. When he rode forth, he would be disappointed if he could not find some sly, treacherous Indian intent on doing mischief so he could slay the heathen with sword or musket. When he found a likely prospect, he would grin in delight and his firm white teeth would shine in his black beard as he spurred his horse with sword swinging to chop off a head, arm, or leg.

The King of Spain, who owned everything, always had a reason if he gave away some of his holdings. In return for the estates he gave to his dedicated followers, the landed gentry were expected to be loyal to the King while at the same time subduing the savages, repelling the Russian invasion, and spreading the word of God. The King had granted Don Francisco an immense rancho in recognition of his services to the crown over the years. Don Francisco passed it on to his son, Don Alfonso.

One of Don Alfonso's favorite memories was of his father dressing in his original leather-fighting suit. The leather was made to resist the arrows of the Indians. It was hard, stiff, and thick. His leather-armored suit also included heavy leather hip-high boots and a great black cape. A leather doublet too thick for arrows to penetrate extended down to his knees. He carried a heavy leather shield, a huge sword, musket, and lance. On his head, he wore a metal helmet, and on his feet were huge roweled spurs made of iron, inlaid with silver decoration.

His large Andalusian Spanish saddle was the same shape as those that Cortéz brought with the Spanish invaders. Inlaid with silver and semi-precious stones, the saddle was a work of art. Fine pictures and designs hand-crafted by expert silversmiths had been worked into the leather. The pommel, on the front of the saddle, was shaped like a horse's head and jutted boldly up into the air. The horse's eyes on the pommel were small but genuine rubies. The cantle, or hind part of the seat, was high and curved backward slightly.

The shape and construction of this saddle originated in the days when knights on horseback jousted each other with long, pointed lances. The back of the saddle, which pushed against their behinds, provided the stability to better resist the thrust of an opposing knight's lance. Don Alfonso kept his fathers saddle in his office, on a stand, under the painting of his father. Don Francisco's armor, black cape, sword, spurs, horse pistol, and metal helmet were hung upon the wall over the saddle and beside the picture. These mementos constituted a shrine so that Don Alfonso could pay daily homage to his father, and remember the honor that was so important to his family name.

Don Alfonso had grown up in the shadow of his famous father. Those who knew Don Francisco had trouble visualizing Don Alfonso as his successor. Don Alfonso decided when he was very young that although he loved and admired his dashing father, he would not attempt to emulate him, for he had neither the good health, he was an asthmatic, or have the temperament to do so. Instead, he would devote his managerial and business talents to overseeing the family rancho so well that his father would have been proud of him.

At last Caleb and María reached *El Pueblo de la Reina de Los Angeles*, the Town of the Queen of Angels, Los Angeles. María shuddered as it came into view, realizing that her time with Caleb was about to come to an end.

They were both disappointed when they saw Los Angeles. They had expected a larger settlement, but Los Angeles was but a village of fewer than six hundred people. It was spread out over a large area so Los Angeles itself was only a small central village. At this time in 1837, there were only four thousand Mexicans of Spanish decent in the entire territory of Alta California.

Caleb and María soon realized that there was no hotel. Where could they stay? Caleb had always thought they would go directly to the home of *Don Alfonso de Vargas*. After all, he was the one they had come so far to see, and he had a large ranch and could no doubt accommodate them.

María, however, had decided differently. "I don't want to go to the *de Vargas Rancho*, yet. I want to stay here in Los Angeles. I must talk to Don Alfonso in some neutral setting first. Once I go onto his rancho, he will be in charge of everything, even the life of my child and me."

It came to Caleb's attention that there was a former American living here who had taken out Mexican citizenship and had married a Mexican woman and fathered several children. The Pinkerton's situation was very modest by comparison within those who had huge ranchos. He had gardens and raised horses on his 800 acres of land.

Caleb contacted him and explained the situation. He explained to his host why María needed to meet her intended on a neutral ground. "We need a place to stay for a few days. I am delivering María to *Alfonso de Vargas*, her betrothed. She has been sent here by her father in an arranged marriage. *Señor* de Vargas owns one of the ranchos south of here. Do you know him, by any chance?"

"I know of him, but I have never met him personally," Pinkerton answered. "He has a very large rancho known as the *de Vargas Rancho*. He has a good reputation as an honorable person. His father was a great man and one of the original dons who settled in this country. He was rewarded when the King of Spain granted him the huge rancho now owned by his son. But to tell you the truth, as an American I am not very much welcomed into the social fabric of the old families, except my wife's family, of course. I don't know what they might do in a case like this.

You will just have to ask him, I guess. But in any event you are welcome to stay here with me. And if María wants to talk to *Alfonso de Vargas* in a home here, you are welcome to use mine as if it were your own."

"Will you go to my betrothed, *Alfonso de Vargas*, and ask him to come here and talk to me?" María asked Caleb. "I've got to talk to him about the baby. I'm not going to let anyone hurt Pedrito. If Don Alfonso doesn't want both of us, then I will go with you to my father to New Mexico. There is nothing else I can do. I love Pedrito more than my own life. I want to negotiate with *Don Alfonso de Vargas* about the welfare of this baby. I want him to come here and talk to me face to face. I have to know where we stand. Will you do this for me? Will you go and ask him to come here and talk to me? I beg you, please!"

"Yes, of course I will." Caleb told her. "I will start for his rancho tomorrow morning. It will take me several days to go over there and return. I will bring him back here with me, if I can. What do you want me to tell him?"

"Tell him nothing! I will tell him everything once he gets here. I am going to tell him everything about the raid on the rancho caravan and my enslavement. I want him to understand exactly what happened to me so he will understand about the baby. I will tell him the truth about the Indians and what they did to me. He can then decide whether or not he wants Pedrito and me. I will leave it up to him, but he has to take both of us or neither of us."

Caleb nodded. "I agree to your plan, but I think I should tell him about the baby in a general way. He needs some time to think about that. You must give him a chance to do that. Then if he agrees to come, you will know that he will at least listen to you. I have to give him some reason why you did not go to him in the first place."

"All right, do as you think best and thank you for going to so much trouble for me." María was very disturbed. She worried about the outcome of the interview, but this was the best plan she could think of.

Caleb rode out of the small village of Los Angeles south on a well-traveled if a rough road, worn deep and dusty from heavy cart and horse traffic. It took him two days to reach the rancho. He got there at noon on the second day. He knocked on the door of the hacienda, and a servant greeted him.

"My name is Caleb Landers," he explained. "I would like to see *Señor Alfonso de Vargas.*" Caleb certainly did not look like the kind of visitor Don Alfonso would welcome. He was wearing his pistols but was young looking. He was roughly clad in his dirty, trail-worn deerskin clothes, had an unkempt overall appearance, and he did not even have spurs on his hand-made moccasins on his feet.

"What is your business?" the haughty servant asked.

"It is a private message that I bring," Caleb answered politely.

"Wait here!" The servant went into the house to inform the secretary to Don Alfonso, who came with the servant to the front door.

"I am Don Alfonso's private secretary. You will have to explain your business to me if you want to see him," the private secretary said imperiously.

"I am sorry, but the message I have for him is private and confidential. I cannot give it to anyone else," Caleb explained.

"Then you may wait on this bench here by the front door. He may be a long time." The secretary closed the door, leaving Caleb to wait.

Caleb found a place to water his horse. He loosened the cinch on his saddle and prepared to wait. It was getting dark when Don Alfonso himself came walking out of the house. He was discussing ranch business with several other men, who appeared to be managers of the rancho.

Don Alfonso would have walked right past Caleb had Caleb not spoken to him. "*Señor,* if you are *Don Alfonso de Vargas,* I have a message for you. I have been waiting here since noon."

"Oh?" the elderly man spoke haughtily and somewhat peevishly, "I knew nothing about it. What is your message? Who are you?" Don Alfonso was annoyed at the interruption, and he didn't like *Gringos* anyhow. Don Alfonso was balding; half his head was devoid of hair at the front, and the balance was thinning and gray. He wore it in a straggly ponytail hanging down the nape of his neck. He was thin and slightly stoop-shouldered. Although he was now 57 years old, he looked and acted 70. Unfortunately, he had been plagued with poor health since childhood. His asthma bothered him constantly and he could not sleep very well at night when he coughed and wheezed.

"My name is Caleb Landers. I am from the New Mexico Territory. I have brought you information about your betrothed, *María de Vargas,* the daughter of *Don Miguel de Vargas* of New Mexico, near Santa Fé. I need to talk to you about this matter."

"Yes, I know of it already." Don Alfonso was on the verge of dismissing Caleb because of his rough appearance. "She was killed by Indians while on her way here to be my wife. I received a letter from my cousin about the matter. It was a terrible tragedy." Don Alfonso was anxious to continue on his walk with his managers and was not paying much attention to Caleb.

"But, Sir. She is not dead. She is alive! That is what I have come to tell you."

"What! What are you saying! Alive? How do you know this? Are you sure?" He turned to the men he had been talking to, "You men go away from us. I will talk to this gentleman alone."

"Come with me back into the house, *Señor*. I will offer you some refreshment. I cannot understand why you have been sitting out here all day like this with such an important message for me. Something is very wrong. I humbly apologize to you." His whole manner had changed when he learned the importance of the message. Don Alfonso showed Caleb to a seat in his office and then walked over to the private secretary's desk. "Emanuel! What is the meaning of this? Why did you not tell me this *caballero* was waiting for me? What is wrong with you?"

Emanuel jumped from his chair at the sharp tone of his *patrón's* voice. "But, Sir, I did not think you would want to be bothered with this *Gringo*."

"You stupid, stupid man! Get out of my sight! Get out of this office! Have some food brought to us here this minute, and wine. I will punish you later." Don Alfonso was red-faced with rage at the cavalier manner with which his secretary had treated this guest with so important a message. Don Alfonso believed that such shoddy treatment reflected on his own manners or good sense, if not both.

"Please forgive the bad manners and the stupidity of that man. It is of course my fault. He is my servant. Now tell me what it is you have to tell me. Here, have some wine. I feel as though I have insulted you, *Señor*; and I humbly beg your forgiveness."

Caleb sized Don Alfonso up as he poured the wine. Although Don Alfonso was reputed to be intelligent, and a good and reasonable man, Caleb thought that a woman such as María would hardly find him appealing. He certainly didn't.

"*Señor*, your betrothed, María, is waiting for you in Los Angeles. She will tell you all the details of the story as to how she got here. She wants to see you to explain everything to you in person. It is a very difficult story, and only she knows all the details of it. I am a friend of Don Miguel in New Mexico, and I knew María on their rancho there. While on a trading expedition in the Stony Mountains, I found out she had been captured by the Apaches. I helped her come here, at her request, in order to fulfill her father's command to marry you. She has suffered a great deal."

"Do you mean you rescued her from the Apaches?" Don Alfonso was incredulous. He stood up again, staring at the unkempt young man.

"Yes, with the assistance of a Nez Percé Indian friend of mine. She had been sold as a slave and then carried off into the Oregon Territory to an area called The Yellow-Stone, in the Stony Rocky Mountains. If you want to see her, we could leave tonight for Los Angles. She is waiting to meet you in the house of Mr. Pinkerton, near Los Angeles."

"I don't know what to think of this. I must reflect on this matter." Don Alfonso was frowning. "I should not have to go to her in some strange man's house. She was to come here. I do not like this! This is very disturbing!"

"But Don Alfonso, this is not an ordinary situation. She is very disturbed. You need to hear from her how she has suffered trying to do her father's will and keep his agreement with you. After all, she did travel over a thousand miles to keep her father's word to you. Surely you might reconsider and travel to her in Los Angeles? Could you bend a little and listen to what she has to say?"

"Yes." Don Alfonso studied the serious young man in front of him, measuring him, and feeling the urgency and sincerity of his entreaty. "Yes, I will go to her. I must do that for the dignity of my pledge to my cousin if for no other reason. I must extend her every courtesy. I am sure her journey and troubles were difficult for her to bear. I suppose you are right. I suppose I can humor her. We can go there in the morning. I am simply amazed at this news. But why didn't she come here? This is where she belongs. I am the *patrón* here, and I could give her every comfort."

"She has her reasons, *Señor*. She will explain them to you herself. I am authorized by her to explain to you that the Indians abused her, and she has had a child by them. She wants to discuss this child with you to see if you still want her. She is uncertain how you will receive her. She is very worried for the baby's welfare. I have made arrangements for her to stay with Warren Pinkerton until you can come to her. The Pinkerton's are a gracious and courteous family. They are taking good care of her. They offer her and you the use of their home to discuss these matters."

Don Alfonso became agitated when Caleb said María herself wanted to tell him about the circumstances surrounding the baby and her other experiences over the last 18 months. Caleb decided it would be best to assure the don that although María had lived with Indians and had a child by an Indian, at heart she was still the beautiful, educated, dutiful daughter of his cousin.

"Don Alfonso, I will tell you this. It would be impossible for you to find a better person than María. She has traveled almost a year by horseback and even sometimes on foot to come to you, to honor the will of her father. It was a very difficult journey across lands that few, if any, white men and probably no white woman has ever traveled. She wanted to keep her father's promise to you. Please let her explain. Then whatever you decide, she is willing to abide by your decision. She is prepared for you to reject her if that is your decision. It is your decision entirely."

Don Alfonso met with María in the dining area of the Pinkerton rancho. He was very uncertain about meeting in this tiny *Gringo* house that he had never been in before. They were sitting at either end of the large rough hand-hewn dining table, just looking at each other. She had borrowed a dress from *Señora* Pinkerton for the interview. She looked thin, young, and very pretty although she had dark circles under her eyes. She had worried a great deal about this meeting.

Don Alfonso greeted her coldly but courteously. The conversation had not gone very far. Things seemed to be stalled. Neither was talking. They were just sitting there, in discomfort. The baby, who was still in his rough cradleboard, began to cry. María got up, took the baby out of the cradleboard, and sat down beside *Don Alfonso* at his end of the table.

"*Señor*, Sir, this is Pedrito." She showed him the baby, dressed in his crude handmade animal skin clothing. María wanted to hold the baby, to keep him from fussing and irritating Don Alfonso. But on the spur of the moment, she thought this would be a good time to introduce him formally to Don Alfonso.

She nervously blurted out, "I love this baby, *Señor*. I must know that if you want me you will accept Pedrito as well. It may be that you want neither of us. I can understand that, and I am prepared to return to my father if that is your will. My friend Caleb Landers has offered to escort me and the baby to Santa Fé should you decide that you do not want me here. I could not help what has happened to me. I am what you see before you."

"But María, it would be improper for a young lady to be escorted by a man alone like that back to Santa Fé." He frowned in frustration at what she was saying. He did not like either the implication that she would travel alone with a young man or her lack of modesty in suggesting it, and he told her so.

"I am sorry, but it is too late for such modesty for me, *Señor*. Caleb rescued me from an Apache Indian named Beaver-Catcher to whom I had been sold as a slave. I was traded for a crippled horse. I lived with Beaver-Catcher alone in a cave in the mountains for many months. That was after I had been abused by many Indians and was near death. This baby is the result of that. Many, many savage Apache Indian men had their way with me before I was rescued. I have been on the trail here with Caleb many months since then. He was the only person who helped when I gave birth to this baby."

"You must understand, Sir, that I am not a virgin. I lost my innocence a long time ago. I did not want to lie to you about these experiences. If we are to be together, you must know the truth about me and be willing to accept me the way I am. And if you take me, then you must take both of us, Pedrito and me. I cannot let any harm come to my baby." Pedrito had been crying and fussing while she talked. Automatically, she tried to quiet him, rocking him in her arms. She was, herself, on the verge of tears.

He could tell she was on the verge of tears, which disturbed him, for here was a woman to whom he had been betrothed in the Spanish way, a young woman who he had thought dead. Just then, the baby's hand reached out toward Don Alfonso. Pedrito looked at him and stopped crying, holding his hand out.

Don Alfonso looked down at the brown child in his rough clothing. He could not help but smile at the two brown eyes looking up so inquisitively at him, a single tear was still on his cheek. "Well, look here at the diplomat," Don Alfonso laughed. "So you would like to enter into this strange conversation, would you?" He reached out to the baby and held his tiny fingers in his hand. "What kind of baby are you, boy or girl?"

"He is a boy. His name is Pedro, after my brother who was killed when our caravan was raided by the Apache. All the men were killed. That is when we women were made slaves to the Indians."

"A boy, is it?" He responded, "Amongst so many female cousins. I never yet had a son. They would be your sisters if we wed. How would you manage it, I wonder?" He smiled again at the peculiarity of it, and what the gossips were bound to say. All her sisters would be older than her, some old enough to be her mother, some perhaps even her grandmother.

Then Don Alfonso had some astounding news for María. "María, your brother was not killed. I received a letter from your father advising me that you had been killed. He said that your brother threw himself in the river and somehow got away. He spent two months alone and on foot in the desert getting back to your father. He almost starved to death, but he is alive. They thought you were dead. Your family will overjoyed to find out you are alive."

"You need not tell me anything further about your unhappy adventures," said Don Alfonso, caressing the baby's tiny hand. "I do not want to know any more details of your ordeal. It was bad enough that you had to experience it once, and I will not be the means by which you have to suffer it again. You have been honest with me in these trying circumstances. I thank you and respect you for that. You are as honorable as your father is. I thank God you are alive!"

"Take this baby's clothes off. I want to examine him," he said suddenly.

Without questioning him, María did as she was told. She thought he was instructing her to change Pedrito's diaper because it was wet, and she started to put a dry one on him. "Wait!" Don Alfonso ordered her. "Turn him over. I want to examine the back of his legs." He watched intently as she turned the baby over onto his stomach.

He gasped when she turned him over. "Look! Look there!" He pointed at a tiny brown-red birthmark on the baby's leg. It was the shape of a flying butterfly. "It is the mark of *de Vargas*! This is more than an accident. The Lord's hand is somehow in this." He went down on his knees to examine the tiny oblong red mark on the inside of the baby's thigh. "Did you know that was there? Do you know what that is?" He looked at María expectantly.

"I have seen this tiny mark, but I merely thought it was a small birthmark. It is no larger than my smallest fingernail."

"Of course you would not know the significance of that," he affirmed. "Only the men in our family might know of its significance. That mark my grandfather had, and my father, too. I have that mark. Your blood is *de Vargas*, too, because your father is my cousin. God has delivered this baby to me because I have no son! There is the proof of it right there. This is more than a mere accident. Surely this is a miracle! That is the mark I have myself."

"If you will let me hold this fine *de Vargas* boy a minute, I will tell you that I have always wanted a son. Perhaps God will grant that you and I can have one between us. But just in case that does not come to pass, Pedrito will be my son, and with *de Vargas* blood in his veins. I will adopt him legally and keep him as my own. Your young emissary, Caleb Landers, gave me all the other details that I need to know."

"Do you have any other demands to make of me, young lady?" he growled. He looked sternly at her, frowning, as he reached out and took the naked baby carefully into his arms, making sure he had the diaper underneath him just in case.

"None, Lord!" María dropped to her knees in front of Don Alfonso and clasped her hands in a prayer of thanksgiving. "None, Lord!" she repeated, lowering her head in subjugation to Don Alfonso. "I shall never ask you for anything else as long as I live, except to serve you and bear you sons if God is willing, and you will it." She averted her head in supplication, and meant it too.

CHAPTER 22
Priest from the Past.

Once Don Alfonso decided to marry María, he wanted it to be done as quickly and quietly as possible because of the nature of the circumstances and the fact that she was already a mother, and an unwed mother at that. He wanted to keep the ceremony simple, with only a few close friends present.

He sat down and began to draw up a guest list, beginning with his eight daughters. Six of them had husbands and children already. Then there were their families, who would be insulted if they were not also invited. And he couldn't leave out his closest friends, their wives, their children, and their families. Finally, he realized that he could not leave anyone out if he did not want to insult them.

The only way out of his dilemma was to invite everyone that he even remotely knew. That seemed to be the only possible solution. The simple, somewhat tarnished marriage evolved in his mind from one of timid modesty and some embarrassment about his new wife and her bastard son, to one of pride and defiance. *To hell with what people would think about it. I am the Patrón here! They can come or stay away, whatever they wish. My son will be my heir, and they will have to come to grips with that.*

"Leave no one out, Emanuel," he instructed his secretary. "We are going to have a regal wedding that will last five days in the best Mexican tradition. This must be the finest, biggest, and best wedding this area has ever seen. It will honor the *de Vargas* name!"

"We will introduce the entire countryside to my extraordinary wife and my son. My son, Don Pedro, will be present at the wedding and will meet everyone. We will start right out by honoring him. If some people do not like it, they can stay away! This is still the frontier country, and we all run risks living among the savages. Any one of the wives or daughters of any of us living here on the frontier might be stolen at any time by the savages and made a slave. That is a risk we all live with daily."

"María!" he called out. "Come here! I want you to have the finest wedding dress that you can possibly imagine. I do not want anyone present to have ever seen a finer one. Make it of silk and lace, and I will give you my mother's jewels to wear. These jewels are now yours to keep! Make special clothes for our son to. I want the church to make provision for him to be right at the altar with us when we take our vows. I will want to hold him in my arms as soon as the priest pronounces us man and wife! He will be my recognized first son in the eyes of the Church no matter what it costs me. It will be the main event of the wedding!"

Now that María's problems seemed to have been resolved, Caleb was anxious to get started back to New Mexico. But both María and Don Alfonso insisted that he stay for the wedding. He was to be godfather to Pedrito, which was a very heavy responsibility because a godfather was responsible for the child if anything happened to the parents."

Caleb stayed in Los Angeles most of the time with the Pinkertons, before the wedding and visited the *de Vargas Rancho* only occasionally. He was trying to get his mixed emotions about María straightened out in his mind, and he felt it was best for her if he stayed away as much as possible. He kept himself busy making a few trades with some of the local ranchers and townspeople. He sold many of his reconditioned flintlock rifles, lead, powder, and molds, and was surprised to be paid in gold and silver coin.

María was also having trouble adjusting to her new circumstances. Although she was so busy preparing for the wedding that her mind was preoccupied during the day, she frequently cried for Caleb at night. Sometimes she could hardly stand to be separated from him. But she was determined to keep her promise to her father. Furthermore, she had also to consider Pedrito, who was being accepted, as she had demanded. He would be heir to this great rancho when her husband died, and that was important to her son's future, a heavy burden for her consideration now.

"I will have the priest from the Mission San Gabriel officiate at our wedding," Don Alfonso told her. "I hope this pleases you." He expected praise from her because it would cost him a great deal of money to have so high a religious person officiate at the wedding.

She smiled demurely at him. "Of course, Don Alfonso, if you think that is best. However, for my sake I would prefer to give this honor to your own parish priest, Fra Pacheco. He has served you and your father before you, and he would be greatly honored if you should allow him the privilege, don't you think? Fra Pacheco has lived on this rancho for over 60 years, I am told. He officiated at your own baptism, and he is old and will soon be gone from us. Don't you think he should do it? It would honor him, I think."

María was going to Mass every day again. Don Alfonso was irritated that she attended Mass in the chapel used by the *peóns* instead of his own personal chapel attached to his house. But he was hard pressed to say too much about it when María offered: "Lord, I will be most pleased to attend Mass with you anytime you are there. But in your absence I would be there alone, which is a great imposition on the old priest. He can hardly walk because of his age. And I would like to worship with the other women of the rancho. It gives me an opportunity to meet them. God does not care, and the Church does not care, so why would you care so?"

María's desire to ask the old priest to officiate surprised Don Alfonso. Of course he would have preferred the Bishop of San Gabriel do the honors, but the more he thought about the idea the better he liked it. Unfortunately, Don Alfonso had already invited the Bishop of San Gabriel to conduct the Mass.

After agonizing about what would be the best action for him to take to get out of the dilemma, he decided that he should write a letter to the bishop explaining that the reason for having Fra Pacheco officiate was to honor him for his many years of service, which would reflect honor on the Church as well. Don Alfonso would ask the Bishop himself to make such an announcement before the wedding ceremony began, and introduce Fra Pacheco as one his charges who had so exemplified the honor of those under him. This should smooth the matter out, and let him claim credit for Fra Pacheco too. In this way, Don Alfonso could honor both men, and it would increase the prestige of the wedding if the bishop himself gave honors to the priest on the rancho. This should not insult the Bishop, Don Alfonso thought, provided the proper payment, even a larger-than-required payment, were made to the Bishop.

"All of these things have to be done delicately and with due deliberation," Don Alfonso told his secretary Emanuel. "Be sure to add *Señor* Pinkerton's name to the list. He accommodated me in my meeting with María and let them stay at his home. It would be impolite not to ask him to attend the wedding."

The wedding itself was a grand event. Never had anyone seen a more beautiful and gracious lady than María. She was by far the most beautiful woman in the room, dressed in white silks and lace, bejeweled, and radiant with excitement. Her dress had a huge, gracefully flowing train that required two young girls to follow her everywhere, holding the train off the dirt, though covered by rugs, floor. Don Alfonso could not have been more proud of her. After all, he was the one to whom it mattered most.

At first, a few of the women made snide remarks behind María's back. They giggled and gestured at the baby. They laughed as they pointed out Caleb as the man with whom she had traveled alone for so long. But most of the women at the wedding were used to frontier life. The frontier women knew that any one of them could have fallen into the hands of the Indians at any time, and suffered as María had done. Thus, the cruel remarks were limited to a few women who were newcomers to the area. Without an audience to savor the cruel gossip, it quickly faded away at the frowns they received. The frontier women were more jealous of María's beauty and grace. They envied her ability to marry such a fine catch as Don Alfonso, and accepted her baby and her circumstances. Her charm and graciousness put them at ease also. Don Alfonso was proud of her ability to win over the other wives. Before the end of the fifth day of the celebration, he showed Pedrito to everyone. He announced to the world that this was his baby, his adopted son, and that Pedrito would inherit the entire estate when he died. It was also documented in the church records.

After drinking much wine, he disrobed the baby, ignoring María's protests. "See here! Look at this mark on the inside of his leg. This is the mark of a *de Vargas*! My grandfather had this mark. My father had this mark. I have this mark. And now this baby, Don Pedro, who has *de Vargas* blood, my blood, has the mark! This baby has been delivered to me by the hand and grace of God! He is a miracle baby!" He said it over and over again.

At the end of the celebration, everyone was exhausted. And Caleb, who was staying at the rancho, would be leaving in three days. María was looking out the window when a party of priests came into the yard. She almost fainted in disbelief when she recognized one of them. It was Father Ignacio, the priest who had raped and beaten her, and raped Sister Seraphena at The School Of The Nuns Of The Stations Of The Cross.

María tried to tell herself it was not possible that Father Ignacio could be at this rancho, at this crucial time. She studied him intently. He was smiling and waving his arms in animated conversation with Don Alfonso. There was no mistake about it. It was Father Ignacio. Even now, he was carrying a long wooden staff that looked to be the same one he had whipped her with so long ago.

All her anger and indignation of that night when Sister Seraphena took the beating meant for her, crowded back inside her head. The thoughts of the torn and mutilated body of Sister Seraphena focused once again in her mind's eye, as well as her own pain and degradation. It was as if she were there again, trying to help the tortured nun back to her quarters. It seemed as though the beating had happened just five minutes before. María began crying tears of rage.

She looked around the room, and her eyes fell upon one of her revolving pistols that Caleb had given her. This time Father Ignacio would not get away. María was no longer an innocent fourteen year-old schoolgirl. She would shoot Father Ignacio. Since she had last seen him, she had survived torture and beatings. She was now perfectly capable of killing him, and carefully checked the pistol to make sure its caps and powder was fresh.

She rushed down the hallway in tears and came bursting out the door near where her husband was standing. He was welcoming the three priests, who had come by to pay a visit after they heard that Don Alfonso had married. The priests were from the Church on the seacoast at Laguna, to the west.

"That priest is a rapist and torturer of women and children!" she screamed, cocking and pointing the pistol at Father Ignacio.

María did not notice that Caleb was standing by the door when she came rushing through it. He alone knew what she was capable of. He saw her finger tightening on the trigger. Just as she pulled the trigger, he pushed her arm up just enough to deflect the bullet. It missed Father Ignacio's head by several inches, clipping the side of the staff he held in his hand. She could hardly believe what happened. Her face was a mass of tears and rage.

Now she directed her wrath at Caleb, who had spoiled her aim. He had robbed her of the opportunity to kill the evil man. "How dare you protect that rapist and defiler of children and nuns? What kind of man are you? Let go of my arm. I will kill him! Let me go! I will kill that son-of-a dog! I have told you who he is. That is Father Ignacio, the man who raped Sister Seraphena and me!"

She turned on Caleb and tried to wrest her pistol out of his grasp while he was trying to hold her hands so she could not shoot him. He was amazed at the strength that rage had given her. With a scream, she forced him backward until he fell over a chair.

"Stop it, María! Stop it! You must not do this!" he yelled as he tried to get to his feet.

Don Alfonso came running up behind her and pinned her arms to her sides. "Stop it! Stop it! Have you lost your senses? This is Father Ignacio. He is the priest in charge of the Church near Laguna. You must be mistaken in your accusation. I order you to stop immediately!"

But no one could reason with María at that point. She did not even hear Don Alfonso's orders. She kept trying to get at Father Ignacio, and the actions of Caleb and Don Alfonso only increased her frenzy. She continued to fight them off. Finally, with Don Alfonso carrying the upper part of her body and pinning her arms, and Caleb holding her legs, she was carried unceremoniously inside the house. She was sobbing and crying hysterically, cursing them for stopping her.

Two of Don Alfonso's daughters and several female servants helped get her into her bedroom. "All of you stay here with her, and keep her here," Don Alfonso ordered the women. Sweat was pouring off his forehead from the physical exertion he had expended. His wheezing breath was loud from his exertions in stopping her. "Do not let her out of this room, even if you have to use force. She has broken down emotionally."

Caleb went out to his packs and got a small box of the opium pills he had purchased in Monterey. He gave them to the women who were trying to quiet María. "Here, these are opium pills. They will calm her and put her to sleep. Do not give her more than one pill every 4 hours."

Father Ignacio and the two priests accompanying him were ushered into the offices of Don Alfonso. They were seated at the conference table and given a glass of wine. Father Pacheco, the resident priest on the rancho, had been sent for and was also there.

Father Ignacio was ashen-faced and still trembling. He had barely missed, by only a few inches, his opportunity to meet the God he served face to face. "Thank you, *Señor* Caleb, for saving my life. Had you not spoiled that poor, distraught, crazy woman's aim, I fear that I would now be dead. That was a very close call, and I must admit it frightened me."

"I am most disturbed, Your Excellency," Don Alfonso apologized. "I humbly beg your pardon. I do not know what happened to set her off like that. I fear she may have gone temporarily insane. She must have mistaken you for someone else. Without the intervention of my friend Caleb here, I fear the worst could have happened."

"Yes, I was just thanking your friend here for my life. It is obvious to me that the poor woman is in the employ of the devil to want to kill an innocent priest. That she is possessed by the devil is the only possible explanation. Do I understand it correctly, this is the woman you just married? Is she truly your wife? Is this poor woman the one who has been living in a sinful state among the savage Indians? Perhaps that explains her deranged behavior. If she has been with the heathens in a sinful state, it can certainly be at the root of the problem."

"We were just married five days ago," Don Alfonso responded grimly. "With the celebration and so many guests, I must confess the marriage has not even been consummated yet. We have been celebrating since the marriage ceremony. Now I do not know what to do or think. I have adopted her son as my own, but I had no idea that anything was wrong with her mentally. I have never seen a woman so possessed. I can't imagine what overcame her to cause such behavior."

Father Ignacio stroked his bearded chin until he decided what to do next. "If the marriage has not been consummated, that makes the matter much easier. Under these circumstances, you can have the marriage annulled if it has not yet been consummated in the marriage bed. With my recommendation, and that of the two priests with me who witnessed it, it could be easily accomplished. I may even have the power to grant it myself. But we must consider what to do with the poor deranged devil-plagued woman. She should be taken back to the Church near Laguna and examined by me there. We have to try to rescue her soul. She should be tied up and gagged. We can put her in a cart and haul her to the church, so we can try to help her."

"There I can minister to her and see if we can cure her soul. I will try to root the devil out of her. I am an expert at such matters. I was trained in Spain, you know, in just such cases as this. It might take a considerable amount of time; but we will get the devil out of her, I can assure you of that. Once I have her chained, she will be calm! They always are more receptive when they are tightly chained."

The implication of what the priest was saying was clear to Don Alfonso. He was well aware of the history of the Dominicans in the Inquisition and their means of removing the devil from one's soul. He knew that all too frequently, the soul was only cleansed when the person being interrogated gave up his or her life. He, like all Catholics, put great store in the Catholic Church, but he was also a pragmatic businessman and knew a lot about life.

"What of the baby then, my adopted son?" He told the priests about the mark on Pedrito's leg that was emblematic of the males in his family's bloodline. He said it had been passed on by his cousin, María's father.

Father Ignacio nodded. "That, too, could either be genuine or a trick of the devil. Send the child with her, and I will examine him at the same time. It is highly unlikely that God would have sent a bastard child through intercourse with heathen Indians to gain this great fortune." He opened his arms to include the whole rancho in his description.

"When you pass on to heaven, this whole place and all the souls in it will belong to your heir. It is my view that this bastard child is almost certain to be the work of the devil. Think of what mischief the devil could do if it gained this great rancho and all the souls of the people on it? If we find this to be true, when we make inquiry into the child, we could have the adoption nullified also. The whole procedure could be done together in one inquiry. In a month or two we will know the truth."

Father Ignacio was ready to go. He was smiling now, and nodding his head up and down accepting his plan for the confused Don Alfonso. "We are in agreement then? I will hurry back to the Church grounds on the coast and prepare for the arrival of these two poor wretched creatures of the devil." He kept making motions as if he were washing his hands or wringing them. It was clear that he could hardly wait. "You will send them to me immediately?" he said, pointing his finger at Don Alfonso. It was an order from the high priest.

"I will leave Father Benedito here to accompany them and deliver them to me. He will pray for the rescue of their souls every step of the way. We can begin their examination in a few days. I always like to begin an examination of so complicated a nature by having the penitents fast for several days first. This is the best way."

Turning to Father Benedito, Father Ignacio continued, "Father, you will not give them food or drink until they are delivered to me. We can begin our examination sooner that way, and they will be the more receptive. Then when they are at the Church facilities, I will give them my personal attention. I will conduct the examination myself. This I promise you!" He held up the wooden cross that was hanging around his neck and made the sign of the cross with it for emphasis. He was smiling and nodding his head up and down in assent with his own words. With his eyes closed, he put his hands together in front of him as if in prayer, still holding the cross.

Don Alfonso was greatly disturbed. He wondered what he should do next. This man of the Church commanded deep respect. His orders carried great weight. "Things are moving so fast," Don Alfonso stammered. "I do not know what is the right thing to do. What is your counsel, Caleb? You know María better than anyone here. Can she be possessed of the devil? Should I have my marriage annulled? Could this child with the mark of de Vargas be a plot by the devil?"

Caleb did not answer the question directly. Instead, he asked Father Ignacio, "Were you a priest at The School Of The Nuns Of The Stations Of The Cross near Mexico City three years ago, as María has said?"

The question elicited an unexpected expression of interest on the part of the old priest who had come with Father Ignacio. He was known as Father Alvaria. He had been in charge of the church at Laguna for many years. He would retire shortly, and Father Ignacio would replace him. Father Alvaria, who had remained quiet up to that point, looked up sharply at Caleb's question to Father Ignacio. He was an honest religious man, and he had seen the list of Father Ignacio's previous assignments.

When Father Ignacio did not answer, but only looked irritated at the question Fra Alvaria said in surprise, "In Father Ignacio's records it is written so. I have read it there!" Don Alfonso and the other priests turned to look at Father Ignacio, realizing for the first time that there could be some truth to María's story. These were not stupid men. They all knew that some priests were not good men. If he and María had been at the same place at the same time, it meant that María could be telling the truth, even if it was unlikely.

Caleb took the floor again. "Then everything has been considered here except the possibility that María may be telling the truth about what happened back near Mexico City in the School. If what she has said is true, then it is Father Ignacio who represents the devil and not María. Such a course of action as being discussed here would dishonor Don Alfonso and his word to his cousin, María's father, in New Mexico."

"Just five days ago I heard Don Alfonso say in front of Father Pacheco here," Caleb gestured toward Father Pacheco, who was silently watching, "that he would love and honor and cherish María, and adopt this baby as his own. Is this how these vows should be kept? Would Don Alfonso's vows not be broken in such a course of action? It would be dishonorable for him to do so!"

A furious Father Ignacio jumped to his feet. "Sir! You insult me! I am a priest of the Dominican Order and the new prefect of the Church of the Coast at Laguna. I am not subject to your insults. I am the highest ecclesiastical authority here! I can have you excommunicated and arrested for such statements against the authority of the Church. I am not on trial here! It is this evil woman who is being considered, and that bastard child."

"No! Your word is not supreme on this rancho. It is not so! On this rancho *my* word is supreme!" Don Alfonso growled, even though he coughed. He walked over and put his hand on Father Pacheco's shoulder. "This was the priest who was brought onto this rancho the same year that I was born. Father Pacheco has been working for the religious welfare of the people on this rancho further back in time than I can remember."

Father Pacheco was an imperfect priest, and everyone on the rancho knew it, including him. He was very human. In his youth, he had lived with a woman of the rancho. He did not hide it. And he always drank too much wine at Mass. At times, his behavior even brought humor into the endless Latin repetitions of the Mass. The children of the rancho, watching Father Pacheco drinking goblets of wine during the Mass on an empty stomach and swaying, hoped he would actually fall down. That certainly made the Mass more interesting, if less pious. In addition, he was known to use profanity on occasion. But he had lived here most of his life, laboring for the welfare of those on the rancho, and its *patrón*, Don Alfonso's father, and now Don Alfonso. He had heard confessions from everyone on the rancho, including María and Don Alfonso.

Don Alfonso would know if there was a devil in María through the counsel of his own priest, whom he trusted absolutely because of his years of service. "What say you, Father Pacheco? What is your opinion on this matter? Should I turn María over to the Church authorities here to be interrogated and have my marriage dissolved? You just married us a few days ago. Should I now undo it and have the marriage annulled?"

Father Pacheco had listened quietly to all that had been said. Looking directly at Don Alfonso, he responded, "I know very little of the world outside of this rancho. I do know that not all priests are perfect, myself included, nor are any of the rest of us. That is true of the highest and the lowest of us. Only Christ was perfect. María has been here for about two weeks now. In that time she has gone to confession frequently, every day in fact, and taken Communion every day, more frequently I might add, than most others on this rancho."

Don Alfonso, who for months at a time missed confession and Mass, knew that Father Pacheco was speaking to him, if indirectly, reminding him of his own imperfection. Father Pacheco continued, "She has conscientiously been preparing herself for the wedding and fit to be the wife of our *patrón*, Don Alfonso. She has also been helping me in the infirmary. I have come to know a kind, gentle, religious, beautiful child of God who prays as much, or maybe more, than I do."

Then he looked directly into the eyes of Father Ignacio so there could be no mistaking what he was saying. "If you want to take someone to the *Church of the Ocean Lagoon at Laguna* and examine them in the ways of the Dominicans, take me instead. I believe in my heart and with my head that I deserve it more than María does."

Father Ignacio's chair fell over backward as the furious priest jumped to his feet again. Father Pacheco was looking at him with an old man's distrust and loathing. "You go too far, old priest!" screamed Father Ignacio. "You are questioning my authority! You are questioning my integrity! I will have you punished and removed as the priest on this rancho! You shall be excommunicated!" Father Ignacio was in a rage as he shrieked at the old man.

Don Alfonso was looking at the enraged priest in amazement. This was not the reaction of an innocent, religious man. Don Alfonso knew at that moment that what María had shouted out was the truth. She and Father Ignacio had both been at The School Of The Nuns Of The Stations Of The Cross at the same time. That was the proof of it. It all fit together now.

He looked up at the picture of his father hanging on the wall. The thought struck him that if his father were here, he would have taken his sword and chopped off the head of the false priest. But times were different now, and the weight of the huge sword was too much for him anyhow. People were more civilized now in these modern times. He was not his father, but he drew strength from looking at the painting of The Great One. Still, Don Alfonso had his honor. And he was the *patrón* here.

"Silence! Silence! This is my rancho, and I am the master here on these premises!" Don Alfonso spoke quietly but firmly. "There will be no inquiry and no annulment of this marriage. I will deal with my wife in proper fashion, as a husband should. You Sir, Priest, Father Ignacio, I ask you now to leave this house and this rancho and never return. These other priests who have accompanied you have witnessed what has happened here. I leave it up to you and them to determine what the church wants to do about these matters."

"*Señora de Vargas*, my wife, will remain here on this rancho under my protection. I understand that my wife may not be perfect, but as Father Pacheco has reminded me as he has done so often in the past, none of us are. On this rancho, Father Pacheco shall be in charge of our souls for as long as God gives him breath and he wants to remain here. No one will question his religious authority here, nor will I on religious matters."

"This interview is at an end! I, *Alfonso de Vargas*, master of this place, declare this matter to be ended!" He left the room then, passing by the picture of his father on his way out. He steadied himself laying his hand on the cantle of the back of the saddle on his way out as he often did. The others would have to find their way out on their own.

Caleb had been asked by *Alfonso de Vargas* to have a glass of wine with him in his office. They had not spoken much since Caleb had brought his first message. Polite but distant conversation only had passed between them. Caleb felt his coldness toward him. Caleb was surprised when he had been sent for, for he felt the owner of the ranch here tolerated him here but did not particularly like him. He apparently felt intimidated by Caleb and was resentful of his close association with his wife. He was to leave tomorrow.

De Vargas looked up at him and spoke, "You would never have permitted me to let that false priest have my wife would you? You would have taken your pistols and shot all of us, am I right?" *De Vargas* was very calm. The matter of fact statement caught Caleb off guard and he had not even considered the answer to the question himself. He did not answer for several minutes. Finally he said, "I would not have permitted you to give her or Pedrito to the priest. No."

"Good. You will be a good Godfather for my son to have. Have no fear for María. I will protect her with my own life, I promise you." He held out his hand and smiled at Caleb, as they shook hands.

Caleb had delayed his departure a few more days to make sure that the matter of the attempted shooting of the priest was in fact laid to rest, but it was now time for him to leave. His horses were packed and waiting. He was saying good-bye to Don Alfonso and his family. They all felt awkward that the unpredictable María was not there to say good-bye. No one ever seemed to know what she might do next.

Just as Caleb was about to mount his horse, she came running out of the front door. Great sobs of anguish were coming from her throat, and tears were streaming down her face. She threw herself into his arms, laying her head on his chest. "My heart is breaking," she sobbed. "I cannot stand it that you are leaving me like this. Please do not go!"

"I must go, María. You know that." Caleb motioned for Don Alfonso to come forward and take her. He lay her gently into her husband's arms. "I am not leaving you, María. Remember, I am Godfather to Pedrito. I will always be your friend. The memories of you and our times together will always remain with me. You can write to me, and I will write to you and Don Alfonso. We will always be together in that way."

Then Caleb turned away from her. He set his left foot into the stirrup of his horse and swung up into the saddle. Resolutely, he rode swiftly away, pulling his pack train into a trot. María was sobbing and clinging to the arms of Don Alfonso, crying, but also waving as long as he could be seen riding off into the distance.

Caleb's heart was heavy, too, and his throat was raw and sore. He began to travel at greater speed. He wanted to get away from the unpleasant emotion and hurt in his chest. Distance might ease the pain of leaving someone he loved so deeply. A tear rolled down his cheek. He wiped it away in disgust with the back of his hand. His inability to keep from giving way to so much emotion irritated him. It was not manly. It was a sign of weakness for a man to cry. Or was it?

He considered racing back and sweeping María into his arms, and then running full-tilt back into the North Country and the Stony Mountains. She wanted to go with him. He knew that. But what of the baby? She would not be able to leave Pedrito. No! Her place was here. Her father's honor was here. Caleb's honor was for him to have delivered her to the rancho safe and sound. Her marriage vows were here.

He set his lips firmly and tightly as he told himself, *this love affair is over. This is the end of this chapter of my life.*

But it hurt. It hurt!

His blankets would be very cold, and he would be lonesome without her laughter and her passion. He would have no need to set up the tent or give her candles to play at her games, which so delighted him. Would Don Alfonso ever think to have her get on her knees Indian-style and throw her head in passion as she backed toward him? It was hard to visualize such a thing. Her full round lips would no longer grasp him in sanctuary. Perhaps, most of all, he would miss her passion flower, with its nectar of sweetness and joy to drive him crazy with the scent and want of her.

He was an empty, lonely person now, alone and on the trail again. Alone. All *alone!*

CHAPTER 23
Two of a Kind.

María quickly found that having to be on hand for the baby's frequent demands to be nursed, changed, and bathed were very confining. She was unable to ride her horses, or work on the other projects in which she was interested. Many women, she knew, would nurse their children for two years and sometimes longer. But to María, nursing had become a boring chore she wanted to hand off to someone else.

To free herself from Pedrito's feeding schedule, she enlisted the aid of a wet-nurse, one of the women on the rancho, who would also take care of the baby. The woman was glad to be able to earn something while she also nursed her own baby. It was only a little more trouble for her to nurse two than one. The nursing duty was quietly transferred to the wet-nurse as María dried up her own milk production. This left her time to do as she wished. María spent time with the baby in the morning and evening, giving him love and teaching him what she could and playing with him. Sometimes she would even take him about the rancho, showing him the animals, and talking and laughing at him as she got up close to them and let him put his little hands upon them.

Six months had gone by since the wedding, and María was still trying to adjust to the light demands of her new husband. He was a good and honorable person, and María liked him. She didn't feel love or passion for him like the intense feelings she had for previous lovers. She felt toward Don Alfonso almost the same feelings she had toward her father. In fact, Don Alfonso was more like her father than a lover in every respect.

At first, running the household had been interesting and fun for María. She had taken over the duties of overseeing household operations. She directed the household activities through the head housekeepers, who had previously done it themselves. They resented her youthfulness and sometimes peculiar demands, but they adjusted. They had no choice.

She would confront them and not give in until her will was obeyed and her instructions followed to the letter. The household staff soon learned that María could be firm, even ruthless, when it suited her.

María had matured into a tough, independent, woman since the Apache ambush at Green River. A house full of Mexican servant women was no match for her. It didn't take them long to learn to do things for her exactly as she wanted. After they accepted the fact that she was the final authority, she handed back to them the authority they would need to follow her instructions. But before long, she was bored with the endless repetitive tasks of running the household too. She missed the intellectual and physical stimulation of being on the trail, and the challenges that life on the trail had presented to her. She now realized she had enjoyed the danger, and the challenges. To sum up, she now knew she was bored stiff. Her only relief, and the one thing she never tired of, was the time she spent with her son. That did interest her and she made sure he was well cared for in every way.

It had not been too difficult for her to establish her authority over the household staff, but she had some difficulty with the two daughters of Don Alfonso who still lived on the rancho. María had helped broker the marriage of one, and she was now working on the remaining old-maid daughter. Everyone on the ranch seemed to have given up hope that this daughter, an overweight woman of 27, would ever find a suitable husband, despite the large dowry a suitor might expect.

Although the woman seemed to be totally unaware of her problem, she was cursed with a foul odor that could be smelled from 10 feet away. This strange odor was a mystery to María, who tried to do something about it. She personally scrubbed the woman with lye soap. The odor would be gone for one day, but then there it was back again as bad, if not worse, than before. María ordered her to take a bath every day and enforced it by screaming at the poor woman if she failed to do so. María said if she could smell her, then she was obviously not clean enough and could never get a husband in such condition.

The poor woman was relieved when Don Alfonso announced he had found a respectable widower with six children on a remote rancho near Anza, ninety miles farther south, for her to marry. She was now on her way to wedded bliss with her sixty-four year-old *patrón*. It would have been impossible to marry off a 27-year old had things been different.

But because she was Don Alfonso's daughter, a large dowry could be expected.

María dealt with her boredom by trying to enter into the operations of the rancho. She wanted to ride, round up cattle, chase Indians, and fight bears with the men. But that was where Don Alfonso drew the line. "No! You are not to go out and work with the men. You are to stay here and run this household, as a woman should. These activities of which you speak are not proper for a lady of your station. It would dishonor me. You can ride your horses any time, but stay away from the men and their work. Your place is here in the home. Under no circumstances are you to follow the men or interfere in the operation of the *Rancho de Vargas*."

"You will stay at the *hacienda* here and run it as you wish. I realize you have lived an extraordinary life up to now, but you must maintain the dignity of our name. The time has come for you to settle down and hide your differences. I command it of you!" Don Alfonso was red in the face and he was coughing by the time he finished his commands.

María knew that he would not change his mind on this subject. Her own face was red and her temper was ready to burst forth, but she held it in. She would have to bend on this subject and find another outlet for her restlessness. At least she had her own horses, as many as she wanted. Every day she could be seen dashing off across the rancho, but she did not ride like a lady of her station. In the first place, she refused to ride sidesaddle on slow, gentle horses. She rode astride, like a man, and on spirited horses. And as if that wasn't enough, she carried a large multiple shot revolving pistol on her side and the six-shot rifle that Caleb had given her in a boot under her stirrup. Unknown to anyone, she also secretly carried the two tiny pistols that Caleb had given her secreted under her clothing. Any Indian or renegade who attempted to bother her would be in for a very great and sorrowful surprise.

But María still managed to get herself caught up in some of the activities she dearly missed. One time, the men were target practicing with their old single-shot flintlocks and blunderbusses. They had set up rocks for targets on top of the corral's top railing and were shooting at them from a hundred yards away. Don Alfonso was watching and encouraging the men to practice, although he was not shooting himself.

María, hearing the shooting, came riding up in a swirl of dust, sliding her horse to a stop. She asked her husband, "May I try shooting at the targets?" He did not smile a welcome. He was irritated that she would approach the men and bother them. He was training them to defend the rancho. This was not woman's work at all.

An ancient old man was standing nearby, watching the young men shoot. He had been a great warrior in the early days, but now he was too old. They had long ago taken his weapons away from him. He was still a loyalist to Spain, and hated the new Mexican government that had revolted from the King of Spain. His mind was no longer clear, and he spent a great deal of time mumbling to himself about the old days, when he had been one of the old Don's fiercest, if youngest, warriors.

María asked, "Antonio, will you hold my horse's reins for me?" as she jumped off her hard-breathing, foam-lathered mare. The old man took hold of the reins of her horse. She was smiling at him. She knew who he was. He had been pointed out to her by Father Pacheco as one of the last of Don Francisco's men from the old days of the early conquest of the territory. Nobody knew how old he was. He didn't know himself.

Antonio had come to California as a baby, in 1775 with *Don Francisco Alvarez de Vargas*, The Great One. Antonio was the remaining man who had participated in that fifteen hundred mile journey by foot, horse, and mule from central Mexico. Together, he and Don Francisco had fought Indians, starvation, the wilderness, bears, and had worked with the others who came with them to build this great rancho. He was too old to work as a vaquero any longer, and had been relegated to cleaning the chicken coops and gathering eggs. The managers and younger men considered him senile now. He could remember everything from fifty years ago, but frequently forgot what had happened yesterday or even earlier today.

Don Alfonso would not have told María that she could not shoot with the men, had she asked him in private; but here in front of them, he was unable to do that. This was too public for him to rebuke her. He still wanted to say no to her and would have done so had the men not said, laughingly, "Let her try, *Señor.* If she destroys your fence, we will repair it." This brought laughter from the men.

"Let her load bird-shot into the gun, *Señor!* Then maybe she can hit the targets," joked another. All the vaqueros in the group laughed and laughed. But the challenge had been made. They had no idea what they were asking for. None of the men, not even Don Alfonso, had ever seen a revolving multi-shot weapon in action before. No one expected that María would be such an expert shot.

Don Alfonso knew or thought he knew what was coming, but there was no way he could avoid it now. "All right. Go ahead, María, if you must." But he was not happy. María laughed as she pulled her rifle out of its boot and walked up to the firing line. Her flashing smile was deceiving the men.

Old Antonio, who had been a confidant of the old Don, The Great One, was watching her intently. His rheumy eyes were squinted in concentration. He saw something in her smile that none of the others could see. He made the sign of the cross and took his hat off which he had not done for years for anybody, and knelt down on his knees for the first time in many years.

When she reached the firing line, she lifted the rifle rapidly and fired six fast shots, hitting the easy targets with all six of them. Then she moved to within twenty five feet of the remaining targets and walked along them, shooting six more times with her pistol and knocking five more of the large rock targets to the ground. This was good shooting with a pistol, although the rifle shots had been easy. The men with their ancient muzzle-loaders could not even come close to her exhibition. Laughing again, her teeth flashing behind her smile, she blew the smoke away from the barrel of her pistol in an exhibition of bravado. The she spun the bullet cylinder in a circle and holstered her gun. She looked disdainfully at the frowning men.

The men were no longer laughing. She had shown them up. They did not appreciate it. None of them could do what she had just done. None of them wanted to shoot any more. No one was smiling now except Antonio. She had ruined their day. All were upset with her now.

All, that is, except one.

Old Antonio laughed delightedly. He was contemptuous of the quality of men the rancho was producing. He referred to them disdainfully as "these traitors against the King!" But the men, who regarded him as a confused old man, no longer respected him.

He had already taken his hat off and now knelt down again in front of María as she walked back toward her horse. He had seen the miracle of the guns that never needed to be loaded. This was, of course, a miracle of the first order. It could only have been achieved by a person like The Great One, the original *Don Francisco Alvarez de Vargas.*

Antonio whispered to María, "Sir, it is good to have you back. But I wonder why you have chosen to come back in this woman's body. Of course I recognized you immediately!"

"*Señor* Antonio, you honor me. But please stand up." She looked down at the old man and helped him get to his feet, lifting him up and leading him, holding his bewhiskered cheek in her hand. "Thank you. But I am only María, *Señora* to Don Alfonso!"

Antonio looked at her with a crafty conspiratorial expression and then glanced at the others, who were still scowling at her. He hid his lips with his hand and winked at her, whispering, "Do not worry, *Señora*, I will henceforth call you *Señora*, just as you command. I knew you would come back some day. We will punish these traitors for swearing allegiance to the upstart Mexican revolutionary government."

"We will re-establish the rightful Spanish Government to Spain for his Catholic Majesty. We will start the movement together, you and I. They took my guns, but I still have my original knife! It is worn thin but is all the sharper for that. We will return Mexico to the King of Spain and our God. It will be once again as it was in the old days. I will join you when the time is ripe. I have never sworn allegiance to this new upstart traitorous government, so I am free to fight with honor and dignity. I told them to give me death because it would be more honorable than living this way." He laughed quietly. "With guns that never need loading, we will not need many others to help us."

"I have noticed you with the chickens," María said. "Did you know that on my father's rancho in New Mexico we have honored the chicken? We have a hen-chicken on top of our chapel there as a wind vane. I have been meaning to tell you that. I hope to see a new chapel built here on this rancho. Perhaps we can have a chicken on top of it here, too." They walked away together to look at his chickens, chatting and talking like old friends.

"I have fighting cocks as well as ordinary chickens," Antonio told her. "Would you like to see them?" He took her horse's bridle as they walked slowly towards the chicken coops at his pace. She set her pace to his.

"But, of course! Let us look at them together. And tomorrow morning with the sunrise, I will be going to Mass and Confession. Would you come with me? These young men need leadership and guidance, I think."

"Ha! Ha! Yes, of course I will come because you asked it of me. But it will frighten Father Pacheco to see me there. I haven't set foot in the place since I heard Mexico had declared its independence from Spain. But yes, I will see you at first light. It is good to go to Confession and Mass before a great battle!"

Don Alfonso tried to discourage María's wild riding about the rancho several times, but he did not push it too hard. She just laughed at him, and invited him to come with her to give her his protection. He tried that a time or two, but he got plenty of riding just taking care of the rancho. Pleasure for him was quietly sitting in a chair with a glass of wine in his hand, in a cool place out of the sun on the veranda.

Don Alfonso liked to sit back in his chair on the porch, sipping his glass of wine, and watch the expert horsewoman, as her white-lathered mount would slide to a stop in front of him. She was doing just what Alfonso had watched his father, Don Francisco, do when Alfonso was a young boy. These were the times he thought she seemed the happiest. She actually reminded him of his father. At times, he thought the resemblance was uncanny, not in looks but in mannerisms, actions, and temperament.

When Don Alfonso was young and his father, the Great One, *Don Francisco Alvarez de Vargas*, still had his youth, he would ride with abandon just like María. Her body, like that of his father's, was as if it were one with the horse. Don Francisco almost never walked his horse on the rancho, or anywhere else for that matter. He rode his horses at a run, or at least a gallop, laughing and twisting and turning in his saddle, always in the lead of his men. He kept track of everything that was going on around him. Don Francisco was one of the most daring of Alta California's caballeros. He would frequently use up three horses in a day.

Don Alfonso enjoyed remembering one particular time when he was only a small boy, when frequent *bailes,* (dances), were held at the rancho. During these celebrations, Don Francisco would put silver coin and sometimes even a small gold coin, on the ground for his vaqueros. Riding their horses at full speed, they would bend over in their saddles and try to pick up the coin as they rode by. On one particular occasion, the vaqueros had tried to pick up a large silver coin, and had failed. Don

Francisco laughed, jumped off the porch, and threw himself onto the nearest horse and ran full speed toward the coin. He then bent down, hooking his leg behind the saddle, and reached down to the ground for the silver *peso*—coming up with it in his hand, to the admiration and applause of all the people in attendance. Gallantly, holding the coin up for everyone to see, he rode his horse up the front steps of their porch and presented the coin to his *Señora*, Don Alfonso's mother.

Don Alfonso had this silver coin mounted into the wood frame surrounding the painted picture of his father in his office. He thought this addition to the shrine would help him remember the event, and call attention to the story as one of his father's many exploits.

Don Alfonso admired, honored, and even feared his father. He loved him very much too and like everyone else in the family, was extremely proud of him. But because of his lifelong poor health, all he could do was sit with his mother and watch his father's exploits; and listen cough and sneeze. When his father died, Don Alfonso inherited all of the lands. He did not achieve fame as a brave, strong, savage fighter like The Great One. Still he became a talented administrator, who held the rancho lands together and made them prosper.

María enjoyed helping Father Pacheco in the infirmary. She had even served as a midwife for one woman. But there was not enough activity in the infirmary to keep her occupied. She needed another project to engage her interest. She and Father Pacheco petitioned Don Alfonso to let them develop a plan for a new chapel for the rancho. Don Alfonso was against it at first. It would cost a great deal of money to build a new chapel, he feared. He was against spending money on a new chapel.

"But, Don Alfonso, we are not suggesting that this chapel be built," said María, smiling demurely. "We only want to make plans for one, one like my father built on his rancho in New Mexico. I worked with him and helped develop its theme. Here we will only put it down on paper and make drawings. Then you can study it and think about it. All we are asking is to be permitted to do is design it for your future consideration."

"All right! All right! But only on paper. I am not making any promises about building a new chapel," he sternly admonished them.

"Of course, of course." María smiled innocently at him. She was already planning the next phase of her campaign to build a grand new chapel, one bigger and better than the one her father had built in New Mexico. The chapel was to be twice as large as the one she had helped plan in New Mexico, because the rancho here was twice as large. There would be an infirmary in the complex. There would also be a special room, the purpose of which María would not divulge. She just laughed off Father Pacheco's questions about it. In María's mind, this was to be a schoolroom so the children of the *rancho* could be taught to read and write.

"This is a secret right now, Father," she told him. "I am praying about it. When the Lord lets me, I promise to tell you first what its purpose is. But I will tell you this; it will benefit the people of this rancho. It will honor Don Alfonso's son, our Pedrito, as well as the other children on the rancho. That is all I am going to tell you right now. Have faith, Father, have faith!" She would laugh and laugh, and he would laugh, too. He was happy just being with and knowing that she was planning mischief that would test them all, he knew.

She secretly had a large frame made with a huge piece of canvas stretched on it. She put it in the rear of the *peón's* chapel and circulated a sketch of the picture she wanted painted on the canvas. She offered a reward for the best sketches submitted by an artist on the rancho. The artist would then be allowed to paint the picture. When the picture was finished, it could be shown to Don Alfonso in the setting of the dirt-floored, tumbled-down chapel the *peóns* used. It would be a picture of the Madonna like the one that haunted her visions, with a wooden black painted cross beside it with fourteen tiny gold bands, that suggested the fourteen stations of the agony of Christ.

María thought the contrast of the painting and its surroundings would certainly prompt Don Alfonso to agree to have the new chapel built. If that did not work, she planned to invite the head of the Church in San Gabriel to come and look at the picture. Don Alfonso would then be so ashamed to have the priest look upon the picture in the decrepit chapel; he would probably show the priest the plans for the new chapel. In time everything would take place in accordance to her plans. She had become a schemer in addition to everything else she was.

María had her own suite of rooms in the hacienda. Her rooms were between her husband's suite and the nursery. They were two of the nicest rooms and had belonged to Don Alfonso's daughters before they married.

To guarantee that she could have her privacy, she had the carpenter fit all the doors with inside locks.

María had decorated the rooms with mementos of her trip from the valley of the Yellow-Stone. This had become her shrine of memories. Hanging prominently on the wall was the deerskin shirt that Beaver-Catcher had given her, together with the knife he had let her have. Next to it were two pistols. One was the muzzle-loading pistol that Caleb had first given her, which he had made himself with his gunsmith father's guidance. She also had places for the two smaller .22-caliber pistols when she did not have them on her person. Next to them was the shotgun muzzle-loader that had been at her right hand across the desert and over the Sierra. Next to it was the wooden cross Caleb had made her in their tiny brush shelter where she had given birth to Pedrito.

She still had her revolving pistols and revolving rifle, which she loaded and used regularly. She killed deer and other wild game and cleaned them herself, bringing the game she had killed and cleaned to the kitchen, or giving them to the needy on the rancho. The household staff had trouble believing that the *Señora* did such unladylike things, but they were happy to have the meat that she brought home.

On her wall, too, was the beaver trap that Beaver-Catcher had let her use. The paraphernalia of her pistol belt, butchering knife, tomahawk, powder horns, extra lead balls, ball-bag, buckshot-bag, and molds for her bullets, were all ready for her to see and use. She also displayed the Bible that Caleb had purchased from the ship at Monterey and given to her for a "wedding" present. A carpenter had made her a special stand for it with places to put burning candles beside it. She had a special candle for religious purposes.

She had another candleholder, too, which she revered greatly. It was one of her favorite items, and was the small one-candle-holder that had given her so much pleasure on the floor of Caleb's tent. She would frequently lock the doors to her apartment, take her clothes off, light the candle, and masturbate herself to sleep. Sometimes she fantasized she was with Caleb; sometimes her passion was with Sister Seraphena, and sometimes she was with Beaver-Catcher. Occasionally, María would cry her lonely heart out until sleep brought her escape. María was lonely and unhappy, dissatisfied, especially at night when she was so alone.

Sexually, Don Alfonso left a deep hunger in María. He seemed to only want to lay with her about twice a month. At her age of 19, she would have preferred coitus at least once and preferably twice a night. Their sexual differences were great. Don Alfonso's previous wife had slept in a room next to him, leaving him alone at night so he could treat his breathing difficulties. When his asthma made breathing difficult, he drank wine before going to bed to relax him. He frequently slept sitting up so he could breathe more easily. Because he slept so poorly, he preferred to be alone at night most of the time.

María was completely baffled by it. She could hardly believe he was serious, at first. But he indicated that this was what he preferred. She dutifully but reluctantly followed his direction that she would be more comfortable in her own quarters, away from him at night. He would tell her when to attend to him.

The days were not so difficult to get through. She would select a horse, always a mare, and always the wildest one in the corral, which she would rope and saddle herself. She would then take her pistols and rifle for protection, and ride off into the hills alone, exploring or hunting. Don Alfonso told her he did not think she should ride like she did; it was not ladylike. She should not go off by herself. She should stay home and tend the baby and work in the house. Perhaps she could make cloth from the excellent wool from the rancho.

"What! What are you saying?" she exploded. "You must understand, my husband, that I mean no disrespect; but I am more than a normal child of a Mexican-Spanish family, pampered, worthless, and spoiled. I have been a slave to the Indian Two-Dogs. I was the beast of burden to Beaver-Catcher as well his trapping partner. I cleaned the entrails out of wild animals. I am a trained Indian fighter who killed half a dozen Indians on my own, not to mention several men on the way here from Monterey who tried to rob and capture me."

"If it is my safety you worry about, I will challenge you to a target-shoot. Then we will see who is the better shot. I take my pistol and rifle along, and I am perfectly capable of taking care of myself. If your complaint is that I take pleasure in riding my horses, you must get used to that. I must have the freedom to go riding and feel the wind in my face. I will die without that bit of freedom!

"I stay away from your men and their work, as you ordered me to. But I must have some personal freedom. I will try not to embarrass you, but you must get used to some of my peculiarities." She was red in the face from shouting at him by the time she finished her tirade.

"All right. All right," Don Alfonso retreated a little, "but be discreet. Consider, for my sake, taking a servant with you."

"I will consider that, part of the time at least," she told him. She did not want to fight with him. All in all, he was good to her and allowed her more freedom than would almost any other man in his position. She tried to keep herself busy and helped the priest with the sick, the old, and the infirm, as well as managing the household. He appreciated that which she was doing, and in fact enjoyed watching her youthful vigor.

"My husband, you are very good to me. I hesitate to ask for anything else, but I would like to select from among your subjects here on the rancho a personal servant. I would like to have someone to help me with my bath and take care of me in my quarters. I may also take her riding with me as you requested, at least some of the time. Do you object? Do I have your permission to look for someone?"

"But, of course!" He was surprised but pleased that she asked him, "You may take as many personal servants as you want. You can have a dozen if you want them. I am surprised that you would even ask. You do not need my permission for such trivial matters. You are the *Señora* here on this rancho. I want you to be satisfied and happy. I must say, my dear, you have made me very happy. If you want to know it, I have written my cousin Don Miguel, your father, what a wonderful wife you have made for me. Does it please you that I have written him so? Come, give me a kiss."

"Yes, My Lord. It pleases me very much that you feel I have served you well. I will continue to try to do my best for you." She kissed him on top of his head and then his cheek. She kissed him as she had come to learn he liked for her to kiss him, warmly but not overly enthusiastically on the cheek, putting her arm around his shoulder. Not passionately, but in a friendly and respectful way. She did it exactly as he had instructed her to do.

One day Don Alfonso announced to María, "I will be gone down south for a few days checking on our roundup of cattle for the *matanza,* cattle slaughter. We will be gathering up a thousand cows and then dressing the skins for sale, and of course collecting the *sebo*, fat."

María used the free time to ride off to the east exploring an area near the foothills where she had never been before. When she came upon a well-worn path that led up into the hills, she turned her horse up the canyon trail. This was a new and nervous mare that she had only ridden once before. The canopy of trees was heavy, and she rode much of the way in shadows. She came out of the cover of the trees into a clearing on a small knoll that looked down into the bottom of the gulch. She looked down upon the hidden small valley a short distance below her.

There was a small house made of logs, a barn, a garden, corrals, and an unusually large number of pigs in a pen. Pigs were not much favored for eating, but the fat was used to make candles and soap. On occasion some pig-meat was salted away in wooden barrels and sold to the ships in the harbor at San Pedro.

She saw three men standing next to the pigpen, laughing and drinking *aguardiente*, brandy, from a gourd-vessel. Inside the pigpen was a vertical fifteen-foot pole with a cross-member at the top. It looked just like a Christian cross. A naked young girl was tied to it. Only her arms were bound onto the cross member; her feet and body were hanging loose except for a single loose rope around her waist that tied her back to the upright member. She tried to keep her legs up away from the pigs, which were surrounding the pole and trying to bite and eat her. The men were throwing handfuls of mash and foodstuffs onto her twisting, protesting legs to attract the pigs. She was bleeding from a bite on the calf of one leg, and the smell of her blood was further exciting the pigs. She was obviously tiring from twisting and turning and holding her legs up out of reach of the voracious animals swarming and jumping up toward her from below. Even from this distance, María could see the bleeding lash-marks where the girl had been whipped.

María was astounded at the spectacle. Never in her life had she witnessed such an atrocity. Quietly, in a practiced easy motion, she pulled her rifle out of its scabbard. She then loosened the tie-down dust cover straps on her pistol, folding the cover back behind the holster so she could get her revolver out in a hurry if need be. Slowly and silently, she rode down behind the men whose attention was riveted on the game they were playing with the girl and the pigs.

"What is going on here?" she demanded to know. "Who are you men, and what is the meaning of this?" Her rifle was cocked and ready. It was laying across her saddle, pointing generally in their direction.

The men had been drinking. Surprised they turned toward her, at her unexpected presence. "We are the sons of Frederico Gonzales. My name is Felipe and this is Eduardo. This is my youngest brother here, his name is Manuel. Who may I ask, is this great pompous lady on the horse?" Felipe laughed disrespectfully and did not remove his hat.

His brother Eduardo spoke up. "This is the *Señora* de Vargas, Felipe. Be careful what you say!" Eduardo took his hat off and greeted her respectfully although his speech was slurred by his drinking. *"Buenos días, Señora,* Good day Madam. Please forgive my brother's bad manners. He has drunk too much *aguardiente* and did not recognize you. How may we serve you, Mistress?" He took two steps forward. His lips were smiling, but his eyes were not.

María had stumbled onto one of the most outlying parcels of land on the *Vargas Rancho*. Although it was a part of *Don Alfonso de Vargas's Rancho*, this canyon had been granted by The Great One to one of his most trusted and loyal lieutenants in the early days. He was now dead, and his sons had succeeded him. These brothers were probably much worse than the Indians for stealing and looting; but out of memory for the service of their father, Don Alfonso had left them alone.

Their duty was to keep the Indians who populated the mountains from looting his herds of cattle, and this they did well. Don Alfonso did not know how cruel they were, nor did he care. They enjoyed hunting the Indians down and killing them, whether they were good or bad. They had almost exterminated the Indians in this region. These men thought of themselves as owners of this small rancho, but in fact it was still legally owned by Don Alfonso.

It was no secret in the area that the father, and now the sons, often fed Indians alive to their pigs as a lesson to the other Indians. The sons had made a sport of it. They enjoyed it as much as cockfights or a bull-and-bear fight. Sometimes they would cut the hamstrings at the back of Indians' ankles to prevent them from escaping. At other times, they would put the Indians in leg irons, cut them so their blood flowed freely, and then turn the pigs into the area with the victims a few at a time. They enjoyed betting on how many pigs it would take to run them down and eat the chained victims. Sometimes, as in this case, they would tie the victims' arms to the cross member and let them kick and swing, trying to avoid the pigs, until they became so exhausted they could no longer hold their legs up. When the victims were too exhausted to keep their legs above the pigs, they would eventually be devoured, eaten and bled until dead.

The third brother, Manuel, said nothing. He was edging his way along the fence toward the three flintlock rifles leaning against the woodpile. They were an effective good team, working together as they had since children.

María pointed the rifle at the closest brother, Felipe. Her horse was dancing, moving nervously, excited by the squealing pigs and the smell of the blood and pigpen. She was trying to control the horse with one hand and point the rifle with the other. "Get the pigs out of that pen and untie that girl immediately," she ordered the trio.

Felipe said, "Now, Mistress, this girl belongs to us. We purchased her from one of the other families on the rancho. We do not think you should interfere. We are only disciplining her. She refused my brother and tried to run away. She must be punished. We are only having a little fun with her to show her the error of her ways." He laughed.

A faint grim smile played upon María's lips. "I will count to three. If you have not started to get those pigs out of there and free that girl and bring her here to me, I am going to shoot you. You should believe this because it is the truth," she said to Felipe, almost in a whisper but certainly loud enough for them all to hear her demands.

Felipe lunged at her. He was drunk and clumsy, and it was a stupid thing for him to do. María pulled the trigger on her rifle, and the ball caught him low in his groin, knocking him to the ground, screaming and writhing in pain. The horse she was riding, who had never been near gunfire before, reared back and whirled away from the blast of the muzzle of the rifle beside it's ear. María was thrown off balance but was still able to stay partly in the saddle. While reaching for the saddle horn to steady herself, she dropped her rifle.

Manuel, who had reached the woodpile, threw a piece of wood at María. It hit her on the head and then glanced off, hitting her horse. The terrified animal reared again and threw her to the ground as it spooked out from under her. As she fell, she grabbed her pistol out of the holster and cocked it in a smooth practiced motion. She hit the earth knocking her wind out, but she sent a bullet into Eduardo as he was running toward her.

Manuel grabbed his rifle, but he took off running with it when he realized it was not primed. María came up onto one knee, gasping for the wind that had been knocked out of her. Fighting for breath, she took careful aim with her pistol and shot Manuel in the back. He staggered for a while then fell to the ground 20 yards up the canyon.

María had turned her ankle as she fell and was still slightly dazed from the piece of firewood that had skinned her forehead. Shaking her head to clear it, she got to her feet. Eduardo had stopped screaming and was now only moaning. He was holding his stomach, bleeding internally, and glowering at her. She reloaded her rifle and pistols. Then she moved around him, and limped over to the pigpen and opened the gate, chousing the thirty-five pigs to set them free. They spilled out, running up the canyon.

The young girl, who was still suspended on the cross, had watched the strange woman trying to help her. She realized that for the first time since the brothers tied her up, she could relax and let her body hang loosely down. Her feet were a few inches from touching the ground, but she no longer had to worry about the pigs. *"Gracious, Señora. Muchas gracias!* Thank you Madam. I was getting so tired I could barely hold myself up out of the reach of the pigs any longer. They had trained them this way."

"What is your name?" asked María as she cut the tightly tied leather thongs suspending the girl's arms along the horizontal cross member, using the butchering knife from the sheath on her belt.

"Felicia, *Señora*. Thank you for the gift of my life! They truly would have fed me to the pigs. They told me that they did it to the Indians they caught all the time. They are cruel, bad men."

"Well, I don't think any of them will be bothering anybody, for a time at least. Can you walk?" María was helping the girl to her feet. They were both limping. "We must try to catch my horse." María picked up her rifle and the men's. Not only were the three wounded, they would also be without their rifles to protect themselves for the first time since they were children. *The trained pigs would smell their blood and take final care of them,* she thought. *That will be a fitting end to this fiendish cruelty.*

Two pair of Indian eyes high on the mountain had witnessed the whole battle below. The men's cabin would burn down that night, and the three wounded men would disappear from the face of the earth. María would swear Felicia to secrecy about the incident, but the Indians in the mountains and those who worked on the ranch would know of it in a few days.

María would never have to fear Indians in this part of the world again. She had hundreds of new friends who loved her and respected her because of this act. Nothing she could have done would have made her any more popular with the Indian population than attacking this cruel trio. Many of the Indians extended families worked on the rancho. Henceforth, as she rode her horses, the Indians in the hills, the Indian vaqueros, and eventually even the other vaqueros would take off their hats and wave to her, smiling at this young women who fought for one of their own against these cruel men. No man would ever tell the *patrón* because they knew she did not want him to be told.

"I think I can walk," Felicia said. "To get away from this evil place, I will crawl on my hands and knees if I have to." Felicia was still completely naked.

The horse had run down the canyon a short distance before it stepped on its own reins and come to a halt. It was grazing calmly when they reached it. María put the *serape* from behind her saddle on the girl, and they rode double back to the rancho.

María warned Felicia, "We will say nothing about this to anyone, do you understand? I don't want anyone to know of this because it would upset my husband, and I have trouble enough with him not wanting me to ride my horses. Can you keep this secret between us?"

"*Sí, Señora*, yes madam, I will tell no one. I thank you again for troubling yourself over me. I will always be grateful!"

CHAPTER 24
Sex With The Master.

S exually, María was in deep trouble. Don Alfonso was totally inadequate for her wants and needs. María knew it on the first night they were in bed together. Don Alfonso had given her several nightgowns of coarse homespun wool material that had belonged to his previous wife, and a robe. They were made of heavy homespun woolen cloth woven on the rancho.

"Here are these nightgowns," he said as he handed her the folded pieces of clothing. "I know you probably do not have much in the way of clothing for nighttime wear, so I thought you would like to have these. Please wear one of these and come to my apartment tonight at dusk. It is time now that we consummate our marriage. We can hope that the Lord will bless us with a son, and we must meet our obligation to the Church to allow that to happen. It is our duty."

Duty, obligation, and an appointment later tonight? María's thoughts were in turmoil. She was truly confused and upset. *Can he possibly be talking about making love to me?* Dutifully, as she had been told to do, she put on the nightgown. Because María was far more petite than Don Alfonso's previous wife, the sleeves of the nightgowns hung down across the palm of her hand. The gowns were so long they dragged on the floor and she had to hold up the hem so she could walk. The necks of the gowns were only just large enough to slip over her head. The heavy homespun wool made her skin scratch and itch.

It was too early for her to go to his room yet, so she sat down on her bed and waited for the appointed time. She had no clock to tell her the time. The longer she waited the more agitated, she became. Finally, she just sat on the edge of her bed with a long face, staring at the floor in front of her. She was confused.

Someone knocked on her door.

"Yes, who is it?" María asked.

"Mistress," one of the servants said through the closed and locked door. "The master has sent me to tell you that it is time for you to come."

"All right, I will do so," María answered. Reluctantly, and with trepidation, María went out the door and down the dimly lit hallway. She went into Don Alfonso's bedroom and found him sitting in a chair by his bed, dressed in a nightgown similar to the one that she had on, only with a pointed hat upon his head.

His bed was wooden-framed, with tightly drawn cowhide for a bed. There was a thin mattress filled with straw on top of the cowhide. Several blankets were on top of that. There was a feather filled pillow at the head. It was just wide enough for one person with a foot of extra room on either side.

"Lie down on the bed, please," he asked her in a kindly fashion. He too was obviously embarrassed and uncertain. She did as she was told. Then he came to her and sat down on the edge of the bed.

María was not only confused, she was actually frightened. She had no idea what to expect. She lay there not saying anything, with her eyes closed tightly and her hands tightly crossed in front of her.

"This should not hurt," he told her. "Remember, this is for the glory of God and is our duty!" He lifted the bottom of her gown up just high enough for her vulva to be exposed. He then began to very gently work his finger into the opening of her vagina, until it was lubricated to his satisfaction. The natural juices began to flow. As soon as she was wetted, he spread her legs, lifted the bottom of his gown just high enough, and mounted her in the missionary position. He pressed his penis inside of her.

There was no kissing, or fondling beyond the wetting. He merely got on top of her and pressed his penis into her, and pumped a few times. That was it, after he came. It took less than five minutes before he withdrew himself. She had not even become aware that he had cum. *Or had he?* She wondered, her mind was in a turmoil.

He stood up then and said formally, "Thank you, *Señora*. You may now go back to your room. We have completed our obligation to our marriage." This, then, with slight modifications would be their ritual consummation of their marriage. It would occur every two or three weeks with regularity, by appointment.

Still confused, María went back to her room. She closed and locked her door, and immediately threw off the itching heavy woolen nightgown. She grabbed up one of her pistols and held it in front of her.

She was angry and disappointed, and red-faced because somehow she felt ashamed of this manner of being with her husband. It was so mechanical. It was so without love or affection or warmth, or any passion or spontaneity. She sat on the edge of her bed, then got up and went across the room and got a bottle of red wine. She did not get a glass she just sat down and began to drink from the bottle. She took several deep draughts, and thought about what had happened, as the wine relaxed her.

She looked down at her vagina. There was the mons. There was the top opening, which she felt with her index finger to make sure it was still sensory. It was, and it felt good as she petted herself a little just to make sure she was alive. She knew the pain a vagina could feel. She also knew the delights it could offer. Here was total confusion. She knew the wonder of bearing children out of it. But this sexual appointment to become impregnated for the glory of God was a new and confusing experience.

Then the humor of it came upon her. She started to laugh. She laughed out loud, not to let it out of the privacy of her room, but just for her own relaxation and relief. She drank the entire bottle of wine, which put her to sleep. She would not like having sex with her husband. She knew that. It was nothing she would look forward to. But on the other hand, she knew she could endure it. It was hardly worth the bother to get drunk over when you got right down to it. She laughed again.

Then she cried!

On most Sunday afternoon's, Don Alfonso had the habit of riding a short while about the rancho. He liked to ride slowly and look at the men and women doing their Sunday tasks. He usually invited María go with him.

But what was this new respect the men and women were paying toward him. Wherever they went he could see the vaqueros, even in the distance, taking off their hats and smiling and waving them toward him. What was this unusually large smile the women had as they greeted them and curtsied and so happily made the sign of the cross. Something was different now, but why? It seemed almost to center on María. Even one of the men who had been shamed when María had shown him up with the rifle practice stopped in the street and took his hat off and greeted them with unaccustomed enthusiasm. Suddenly Don Alfonso realized that for some inexplicable reason the people were all greeting them both, with enthusiasm. She seemed to know the names of every man, woman and child on the rancho, more so than he did. She even knew the names of the new babies. She spoke to the people as they rode along as if they were all her friends.

Here was Father Pacheco on the steps to the *peóns'* chapel. Respectfully he bowed more deeply than usual, it seemed. *But why?*

Father Pacheco spoke: "Ah, *Patrón!* Did you know that we are having a viewing of the painting of the Madonna holding the Christ Child? It is now displayed at the back of the *peóns'* chapel. Some day I would like you to look at it and see if it pleases you. It was painted by those on our own rancho."

"María says it is so similar to the one your cousin in New Mexico has in their new chapel that it would be hard to tell the difference, except this one is actually much larger and more beautiful, which honors you. It was painted by our own people here, and the frame was made by our carpenter, under the direction of *Señora* María, of course. Believe it or not, more of our people than ever before are attending Mass and going to Confession because of its beauty, and your goodness Master. Thank you *Señor.* I would like to have you see it and advise me if you feel it is worthy of our keeping it in the *peóns'* chapel to inspire our people. We would be grateful if you felt it worthy of your blessing."

"That is very good, Father." Don Alfonso tried to hide his confusion. He had not previously heard of the painting, but he would of course be expected to look at a religious painting created by and for the *peón's* chapel. He turned around in his saddle and looked intently at María for a moment. She had obviously been busy with church work, which pleased him.

"Perhaps next Sunday María and I can come and look at it when we go for our Sunday ride." Don Alfonso's thoughts were perplexed. *Could this painting be the reason for the strange friendliness and attention the peóns seemed to be directing toward my wife. It seems so genuine and respectful, yet personal and enthusiastic, and directed towards the Señora. There is nothing really wrong with it, still it is unsettling occurring so suddenly, and so universal amongst all the peasants.* He was sure that last Sunday, only a week ago, there had been no such display of affection.

Until now, María had been unable to find a young woman on the rancho she liked for a companion and maid. Then María remembered Felicia. María had delivered Felicia to the rancho infirmary after she returned with her to the *rancho* from the mountains. She had wounds that needed tending. There, Father Pacheco could take care of her until her pig-bitten leg healed. When Felicia was on her feet again, he turned her over to the head housekeepers of the hacienda. She still limped a little from the pig bites.

Felicia was already 16 years old. She was disobedient and insolent. In disgust, the house manager advised María not to have anything to do with her. "She is a terrible girl," reported the head housekeeper. "She is insolent, resentful and impolite. She is already fighting with the other girls. She even went so far as to ask that she be assigned duties taking care of the cows, which is work exclusively for men."

In exasperation, the head housekeeper had put Felicia in charge of cleaning out the night-vases every day for the *ricos*, or rich family members. The other servants in the house were expected to travel out to the outhouse when they needed to go to the toilet. It was the only task Felicia had been found suitable for. This was now her permanent assignment.

"Have nothing to do with that strange acting girl, *Señora*, she is too different!" cautioned the head housekeeper.

But there was something about Felicia that intrigued María, so much so that María asked her to come to her quarters. María looked at her carefully, noticing particularly her short haircut. Of course, María's hair had once been cut short, too. The first time it had been cut by one of the nuns at The School Of The Nuns Of The Stations Of The Cross. She would never forget the humiliation and sorrow she had felt about losing her long black hair. The nuns said it was done so the many girls living so close together would not get lice in their hair. They also thought that short hair was much easier to manage. What the nuns did not say to the girls was that short haircuts were a good way to make the girls less prideful and more likely to conform to the nuns' teachings.

María's hair had started to grow long again when the Apache wife of Two-Dogs had cut almost all of it off to use for making rope and things such as the bridle for Two-Dogs' horse, together with decorations for his shirt.

On the long journey with Caleb, she had him cut it short because it was easier to manage on the trail. It was now much shorter, and she continued to cut it even shorter. It was so much less trouble when short. She knew it did not particularly please her husband. He had even complained to her about it once. She put him off explaining that the back of her neck sometimes broke out if her hair was too long.

María mused that her hair, which had once been so all-important to her, had been shunted aside over time until now. The less time and trouble it caused her, the better she liked it. But her desire for some of the other things that had been so important to her was still undiminished. There was something about Felicia that reminded María of Sister Seraphena. Her shoulders were square. She was thin, very thin, but her arms were sinuous, muscular and strong. "I notice you have short hair, Felicia. Why is it cut so?"

"I don't know, Mistress. I like it so. Long hair is a burden and gets in the way, and much time is spent in brushing and tending it. I lived with my aunt, and we always kept our hair short. I notice yours is cut short also. May I touch it?"

María's heart skipped a beat at the girl's peculiar request. It was an impudent thing for her to say. It was out of character for what a maid should say, but she did not ask it in a disrespectful way. She did not know why this conversation was even being held. *Why am I even talking to this girl? Felicia is pretty in a boyish kind of way.* Strange thoughts seemed to be going through María's mind.

María was sitting on the edge of her bed. "Step closer here and let me see how clean your hands are before I let you touch my hair."

The girl laughed. "Yes, Mistress, they are clean. I am very clean all over. Not like the first time you saw me, hanging on the cross in the pigpen." She came forward and presented her hands to María, who grasped them. The girl's fingers were hardened by work, callused and rough; but they were also long and supple, and warmth was emanating from them. She let María hold her hands, and her fingers curled naturally over María's fingers as if they belonged there. She gently squeezed "hello."

On an impulse, María brought Felicia's palm up to her lips and kissed it. She did not know why she did that. She could feel her heart pounding. "Go and lock the doors to these quarters. Then come back here, and you may touch my hair. I am soon going to take my bath, and I do not want to be disturbed while I am bathing. I am looking for a private maid to help me with my bath every day and to take care of me. Would you be interested in the job?"

"Of course, I would like to serve you, Mistress. It is more than I ever could have hoped for. Would I still do night-vases?" Felicia asked as she closed and barred the doors.

"Only mine and yours," responded María, "You will do nothing for anyone else, and answer to no one else. You would stay here in my quarters with me."

Felicia returned to the side of the bed. She walked up close, very close, to María and put her hands upon her hair. She began to slowly rub María's head, combing the short hair through her fingers. "My aunt used to rub my head like this. Do you like it, my Lady?"

María's eyes were closed, and she did not answer. Relaxation and happiness seemed to have overcome her. The girl knew she liked it from the way she was responding.

Felicia continued to rub her head, then the temples, and then the back of the neck. "Does this please you, My Lady? Do you want me to stop?" she whispered. Then she stepped in front of María, close in, so María could rest her head against Felicia's chest as she moved her hands down behind María's shoulders and back, rubbing her and pulling her taught, tense muscles towards her, using her own chest and body as a sort of pillow. "My aunt loved to rub my back like this. I miss her so. Do you want me to stop now, My Lady?"

"Don't stop. It feels wonderful. You have such good hands. The water is ready there in my buckets. Would you like to undress me and give me my bath now?"

"Of course. But I have not done this before. I feel so excited. So full of pleasure. You will have to instruct me what it is you want me to do so that I do not do it incorrectly. Is that the way it always is when you take your bath?" She had pulled María's unresisting head against her tiny breasts. She had large nipples but almost nothing in the way of breasts. The breasts themselves were tiny by comparison to María's, which were small enough. The girl pulled María's blouse up over her head and got her skirt off so she would be ready for the bath. Then she began rubbing her Mistress again. "I think rubbing is good for one. It is very relaxing. Do you want to get into the water now?"

María walked forward and stood in the water filled tub. "Pour the warm water over me. Use only a little soap on your hands to wash me, then rinse me off quickly with more water. The soap is strong and will make a rash if left on for any length of time."

The girl did as she was told, continuing to rub and caress María. She washed her breasts three times, very slowly, making sure all places were done. She pulled the nipples through her wetted soap slippery fingers. They were getting harder now. She cupped the breasts in her hand as if in an embrace. Laughing now, she asked María, "Should I do your private places or should I leave them alone?"

María kissed her. "By all means, do them. And take your dress off so you do not get it wet. I will wash you next. You must be clean. Very clean, if you are to attend to me."

"This is what my aunt used to do to me, My Lady, before she died last year. I have been very lonely for my aunt. She had raised me since I was a baby. We were very close. I have had no one to sleep with since then." The girl was suddenly weeping quietly.

"Here, my child. Don't cry. You can sleep with me sometimes, when my husband does not want me with him. And you can sleep here in this room if you want to. Lie down beside me here on the bed. We will rest a while here. We are both clean now.

"Here, put your head on my chest, and go ahead and cry. I know how difficult it can be when one loses someone who was loved very much." The girl had stopped crying. She laid her head onto María's chest. María moved so Felicia's head was in a comfortable position, with a nipple close to her lips.

Felicia's lips found the breast. It felt good to María to have her breast suckled once again. Her own hand found Felicia's breast. "Is this as your aunt did?"

"Yes, but her hand also was between my legs," Felicia giggled. "And she was not really my aunt. She was just my friend, but we told everyone she was my aunt so we would not be separated."

"Show me what she did," María directed, her voice breaking.

"Everything, My Lady. She did many things. And I enjoyed them so. That is why I have missed her so much. I truly loved her."

It was getting dark. María got up and lighted the single candle and put it on the stand by the bed. It was the special candle-holder that Caleb had given her, which had come to mean so much to her when the two of them had their special times in the tent while coming here.

María held her arms around Felicia's head and shoulders in a warm comforting embrace. "Yes, my dear, you must show me everything you and your aunt did. But do not hurry, and do not do anything that you do not want to do. But do not stop doing anything that you want to do. Here in this bed will be our sanctuary. It is not just for you, and it is not just for me. It is for both of us, and nothing will be held back. You can come and go from this sanctuary where we can be alone, and it will be our secret."

María felt Felicia touch her mons with some hesitation, so she reached down and lay her hand on Felicia's, directing the girl's fingers down into her vagina, encouraging her to experiment and move around the edge of the vagina. She felt wonderful. And wasn't that Felicia's scent in the air?

They had a road to travel, and the journey had finally begun.

THE END.

MORE BOOKS BY FRANK W. LEWIS

RUMPAH. ISBN 0-9653923-0-9

An adventure story situated in a small Nevada town during the 1990's. The story is about a struggle between Bill Aaron and an old prospector, Whiterock, with a large mining corporation over mineral rights. Intrigue, murder, love.

FRONTIER JUSTICE – 1835. ISBN 0-9653923-1-7. Book 1 of the series.

Santa Fé Trail – 1835. William's father, a frontier muzzleloader rifle smith, is killed by a frontier low life. After taking personal retribution against the killer of his father, William is on-the-run and sets off across the frontier prairie on an 800-mile journey to Santa Fé in what was then Mexico.

His adventures in crossing the plains and eventually arriving at Santa Fé, Mexico, is the main plot of this story.

Polly, a young woman was left with a farmer's family since she was 7 years old. After being abused by the farmer's son for years she was kicked off the farm.

She takes up with Jeremy, an Irishman who works as a freight wagon driver. Polly accompanies him toward Santa Fé. They begin across the plains together in party with a small wagon train. They are much in love despite the fact Jeremy is much older. Their lovemaking adds spice to the story.

The wagon train is attacked and all perish except Polly, who is rescued by William. They then go on together to Santa Fé.

An action filled historical novel in an authentic setting; full of humor, drama, tragedy, and action.

The description of day-to-day living, butchering their own food, fighting with Indians, and renegade mountain men are descriptive and exciting.

The 3 Sisters - 1837. ISBN 0-9653923-3-3. Watch for book 3.

Three teen-age Spanish sisters are disgraced in their father's eyes, and are outcast by him and his family.

They are affianced to men they have never seen, remote relatives, across the Atlantic Ocean in far off Mexico's frontier to get rid of them. On the way a shipwreck sends them to a tiny village called Los Angeles, in the Mexican Territory of Alta California.

It was there they were captured by Mexican slavers and their worst troubles begin.

Available in 2006. Order from amazon.com.

www.ingramcontent.com/pod-product-compliance
Lightning Source LLC
Chambersburg PA
CBHW051230260626
47162CB00002B/359